The Art of Murder

JOSÉ CARLOS SOMOZA

Translated from the Spanish by
NICK CAISTOR

An *Abacus* Original

First published in Spain as *Clara y la Penumbra* by
Editorial Planeta S.A. in 2001

This edition has been translated with the help of a grant from
the Dirección General del Libro, Archivos y Bibliotecas de
Ministerio de Educación, Cultura y Deporte de España.

A CIP catalogue record for this book is available from
the British Library.

ISBN 0 349 11706 3

Typeset in Palatino by M Rules

Printed and bound in Great Britain by Clays Ltd, St Ives plc

Abacus
An imprint of
Time Warner Book Group UK
Brettenham House
Lancaster Place
London WC2E 7EN

www.twbg.co.uk

For Lazaro Somoza

*For Beauty's nothing
but beginning of Terror we're still just able to bear*

RILKE

INTRODUCTION

Clara and Shade

The teenage girl stands naked on the plinth. Her smooth stomach and the dark curve of her navel are at eye level. She is looking down with her head tilted to one side, one hand shielding her pubis, the other on her hip. Her knees are together and slightly bent. She is painted in natural sienna and ochre. Shading in burnt sienna emphasises her breasts and moulds her inner thighs and her little slit. We should not say 'slit' because this is a work of art we are talking about, but when we see her, that is what we think. A tiny vertical slit, stripped of all hair. We walk round the plinth and observe the figure from the back. The tanned buttocks reflect patches of light. If we step away, her anatomy acquires a more innocent look. Her hair is strewn with small white flowers. More flowers surround her feet – a pool of milk. Even at this distance we can still pick up the strange scent she gives off, like the smell of wood after rain. Next to the security rope is a little stand with the title in three languages: *Deflowering*.

A two-note loudspeaker chime breaks the spell: the museum is about to close. A young woman's voice says so in German, then in English and French. Everyone seems to understand, or at least gets the intended message. The teacher of a select Viennese secondary school gathers her uniformed flock and counts them to make sure no one is missing. Even though the exhibition is of nudes, she has taken the children to see it. It is of no importance, they are works of art. What matters to the Japanese is that they have not been allowed to take photos: that is why none of them is smiling as they file out. They console themselves at the exit, where they can buy catalogues for fifty euros with full-colour photographs. A nice souvenir of Vienna.

Ten minutes later, after the room has emptied of visitors, something unexpected happens. Several men arrive, wearing ID tags in their suit lapels. One of them goes up to the plinth where the young girl is standing and says out loud:

'Annek.'

Nothing happens.

'Annek,' he says again.

The eyes blink, the neck straightens, the mouth opens, the body shudders, and the budding breasts heave as she takes a deep breath.

'Can you get down on your own?'

She nods, but hesitates. The man holds out his hand.

Eventually the girl manages to descend from the plinth, trailing a cloud of petals in her wake.

Annek Hollech opened the first bottle from the rack by the chrome metal shower, and the water turned green. She opened the second and rubbed herself with red water. After that, she soaked herself in blue, then purple. Each of the liquids in the bottles took off only one of the four products which had been applied to her skin: paints, oils, hairspray, artificial aromas. The bottles were numbered and each showed their purpose by turning the water a different colour. The paints and sprays were the first to come off, in a shower of drops. As always, the hardest thing to get rid of was the smell of wet earth. The cubicle filled with steam, and Annek's body disappeared behind a rainbow-coloured curtain. Each of the other twenty cubicles in the room was occupied by a shadowy silhouette. The only sound was the hiss of the showers.

Ten minutes later, enveloped in towels and mist, Annek walked barefoot to the dressing room. She dried herself off, combed her hair, rubbed first a moisturising and then a protective cream all over her body – using a long-handled sponge to

2

reach her back – and protected her face with two layers of cosmetics. Then she opened her locker and took out her clothes. They were all new, purchased in shops on the Judengasse, Kohlmarkt, the Haas Haus and the elegant Kärntner street. She liked to buy clothes and accessories in the cities where she was on show. During the seven weeks she had been in Vienna she had also bought porcelain and glassware and sweets from Demel's, as well as a few trinkets for her friend Emma van Snell, who was also a work of art but was being exhibited in Amsterdam.

On that Wednesday 21 June, 2006, Annek had gone to the museum wearing a pink blouse, military jacket and a pair of baggy trousers full of pockets. Now she took these clothes out of the locker and put them on. She did not wear anything underneath – it wasn't recommended if one was on show completely naked (underwear leaves marks). She put on a pair of felt slippers in the shape of two little bears, fastened her black slimline watch on to her wrist and picked up her bag.

Sitting next to her in the labelling room was Sally, the work of art on plinth number eight. She was wearing a sleeveless mauve blouse and a pair of jeans. They said hello and Sally commented:

'Hoffmann says my purple's fading like Van Gogh's yellows. He wants to try a more intense colour, but in Conservation they're worried it might damage my skin. Wouldn't you know it? The same old contradiction: some people want to create you, others want to conserve you.'

'That's true,' Annek said.

An assistant came over carrying two boxes of labels. Sally opened hers and picked out one of them.

'I can't wait to get to bed,' she said. 'I don't think I'll go to sleep straightaway, I'll just lie there on my back, stare at the ceiling and enjoy being horizontal again. What about you?'

'I have to call my mother first. I phone her every week.'

'Where is she now? She travels a lot, doesn't she?'

'Yes. She's in Borneo, taking pictures of monkeys.' Annek put one of the labels round her neck and fastened it. 'Sometimes she emails photos of monkey couples.'

'Really?'

'Yes, really. I'm not sure whether she's trying to tell me I should get married or what.'

Sally laughed quietly behind two rows of perfect white teeth.

'At least she sends you something. My father in New York can't even be bothered to scan in a couple of hotdogs for me. He never liked the idea of his daughter becoming a valuable work of art.'

Silence. Annek did up the last label round her ankle. Her neck, wrist and ankle now boasted three 8×4cm labels, painted bright yellow and tied with black strings. Sally had also finished doing up hers. They watched as the first works of art left the room: Laura, Cathy, David, Estefania, Celia. A parade of athletic, labelled figures.

'I haven't had my period again this month,' Annek said expressionlessly. 'It's been irregular since Hamburg.'

Sally looked at her for a moment.

'It's not important, it happens to all of us. Lena reckons it's like an umbrella: first she has one, then she loses it, then she has one again, but then she loses it yet again. It's all part of being a work of art, you know.'

'Yes, I know,' Annek was still staring into the mirror. 'And anyway, I feel better when I don't have one.'

'Hey, have you got anything planned for next Monday?'

The question puzzled Annek. She never planned anything for the day the museum was closed, apart from her frenetic shopping sprees with her inexhaustible credit card. Everything else – the solitary walks in the Hofburg, Schönbrunn, or Belvedere – which were not in fact so solitary because she was always accompanied by bodyguards – or visits to the Art History Museum or Saint Stephen's cathedral, even the ballets and performances put on for Vienna's June festival left her feeling bored and slightly nauseous. She wondered what a work of art like her was doing in this kind of city, where everything was art. She was looking forward to the time when the tour left Europe. The next year, 2007, the Foundation had promised them they would be travelling to America and Australia. Perhaps she could find something there she would really enjoy doing.

'Nothing,' she replied. 'Why?'

'Laura, Lena and I thought we might spend the whole day at the Prater fun fair. Want to come along?'

'OK.'

A warm surge of gratitude swept over her. At fourteen, Annek Hollech was the youngest work of art in the exhibition (Sally, for example, was ten years older). On their day off, the others all did their own thing. Nobody worried about her. To anyone but Annek – who was used to the solitude and silence of museums, galleries, and private houses – the situation would have been intolerable. That was why she was so moved at Sally's offer. But her face betrayed nothing of this: it only ever showed the emotions a painter put there.

'Thanks,' was all Annek said, gazing at her companion with her greeny-blue eyes.

'Don't thank me,' Sally replied. 'I'm doing it because I enjoy being with you.'

Her friendly reply made Annek feel doubly grateful.

They took the lift down together. Two tall and slender Anneks, with straight blonde hair and two yellow labels tied round her neck, were reflected in Díaz's dark glasses. Oscar Díaz was the guard on duty with orders to accompany her back to the hotel. He always had a friendly smile and a polite word for her. That Wednesday, however, he was unusually laconic. Annek felt very relaxed after her talk with Sally and would have liked to start up a conversation, but remembered that works of art were not supposed to talk to their guards, so she decided to ignore his silence. She had other things on her mind.

She had been *Deflowering* – a Bruno van Tysch masterpiece – for two years now. She had no idea how much longer it would be before the painter decided to substitute her. A month? Four? Twelve? Twenty? It all depended on how quickly her body matured. At night, lying naked in the ample hotel beds she slept in, she would run her finger round the edge of the labels attached to her neck or wrist, or feel for the tattoo on her right ankle (an indigo BvT) and mouth a silent prayer to the distant God of Art for her body to stay calm, for it please not to start changing in secret, for her breasts not to grow, her legs not to rise like clay on

5

a wheel, pray that her hands stroking her thighs would not have to travel a longer, more curvaceous route.

She did not want to have to give up being *Deflowering*.

It had taken her six years to become a masterpiece. She owed everything to her mother, who had discovered her talents as an artwork and taken her to the Foundation when she was only eight years old. Her father would have forbidden it, of course, but as he no longer lived with them, he did not count. Her parents had split up when she was four years old, so Annek's memories of him were vague. What she did know was that he was a brutal, unstable alcoholic, an old-fashioned painter who still worked on canvas, insisted on making a living by painting, and refused to admit that non-human works of art had gone out of style. Ever since Annek's mother had gained custody of her, and especially since Annek had begun her studies in Amsterdam with a view to becoming a work of art, this irascible stranger had done nothing but pester them, except of course during the frequent periods he was in hospital or jail.

In 2001, when Annek was being shown as *Intimacy* at the Stedelijk Museum in Amsterdam – the first work that Van Tysch had painted using her – her father had suddenly burst into the room. Annek recognised the ghastly wild look and bulging red eyes staring at her from the other side of the security rope, and realised what was going to happen moments before it did. 'She's my daughter!' he shouted, beside himself. 'She is being shown naked in a museum, and she is only nine years old!' A whole team of security guards had to be summoned. The incident caused a scandal, then a brief trial, and her father was locked up again. Annek preferred not to recall that dreadful episode.

Apart from *Intimacy*, the Maestro had painted two more works using her: *Confessions* and *Deflowering*. The latter work was considered one of Bruno van Tysch's greatest creations; some of the specialist critics even went so far as to call it one of the most important paintings of all time. Annek had become part of art history overnight, and her mother was very proud of her. She kept telling her: 'This is nothing. You have your whole life before you, Annek.' But she loathed the idea of 'a whole life before her': she did not want to grow, she hated the idea of having to leave *Deflowering*, of being substituted by another adolescent.

Menstruation had burst upon her like a red stain on an empty canvas. It was a warning sign. 'Be careful, Annek, you're growing up, Annek, you'll soon be too old for the work', was the message it brought. She was so happy it had stopped, at least for a while! She prayed to the God of Art (she detested the God of Life) – but the God of Art was the Maestro, who would not lift a finger except to announce one day: 'For the work to last, we have to replace you.'

The car park was dark and haunted by the sound of engines. That evening a Turkish immigrant by the name of Ismail was on duty. He waved to Díaz. As he smiled, the tips of his black moustache lifted. Díaz waved in return and opened the back door of the SUV. Ismail could see Annek's body bend over to get in, and the ochre shadows of its interior gradually swallowing her up: first her shoulders, then the outline of her hips, her behind, her long legs, one felt slipper and then the other. The car door slammed, the vehicle moved off, swung towards the exit, then disappeared down the street. The Vienna Marriott was in the Ringstrasse, only a few blocks from the MuseumsQuartier complex, the city's cultural centre: it was a short, safe journey, there was no reason for Ismail to suspect that anything bad or even out of the ordinary might happen.

He could never have imagined that would be the last time he would see Annek Hollech alive.

First Step

The Colours of the Palette

White, red, blue, violet, flesh tint, green, yellow and black are the basic colours of the palette for painting human bodies.

BRUNO VAN TYSCH *Treatise on Hyperdramatic Art*

How nice it would be if we could only get through into Looking Glass House.

LEWIS CARROLL *Through the Looking Glass*

1

Clara had been painted titanium white for more than two hours when a woman came down to see her. Gertrude was with her. Out of the corner of her eye Clara could see a pair of sunglasses, a small flowery hat, a pearl-grey suit. She looked like an important client. While she was assessing Clara, she went on talking to Gertrude.

'Did you know Roni and I bought a Bassan a couple of years ago?' She spoke with a strong Argentine accent. 'It was called *Girl Holding up the Sun*. Roni liked the way her shoulders and stomach shone. But I told him: 'Good heavens Roni, we have so many paintings, where are we going to put it?' And he said: 'We don't have that many. And besides, the house is full of your little knick-knacks, and I don't complain.' Laughter. 'Well, guess what we did with the painting in the end? We gave it to Anne.'

'Good idea.'

The woman took her glasses off and bent over Clara.

'Where's the signature? . . . Ah yes, on the thigh . . . it's beautiful . . . What was I saying?'

'That you gave the painting to Anne.'

'Oh, yes. They loved it – Anne and Louis, you've met them. Anne wanted to know if the rental was expensive. So I told her: "Don't worry, we'll pay. It's a gift from us to you." Then I asked the painting if she had any problem about going to Paris with my daughter. She said she didn't have.'

'A painting that's been bought should have no problem following the purchaser wherever it may be,' Gertrude asserted.

'But I like to show them I care . . . This is a wonderful painting, of course.' The 'w' boomed out like a distant foghorn. 'What did you say it was called?'

'*Girl in Front of a Looking Glass*'.

11

'Wonderful, wonderful ... If you don't mind, Gertrude, I'll take a catalogue.'

'Take as many as you like.'

Clara was still immobile when they left. Wonderful, wonderful, but you won't buy me. That's obvious from a mile off. She knew it was not good to let her mind wander while she was in the trance-like state of quiescence, but could not help it. She was worried no one would buy her.

What was wrong with *Girl in Front of a Looking Glass*? The canvas was nothing extraordinary, but she had been bought as worse things. She was standing completely naked, her right hand covering her pubis and the left one out to the side, legs slightly apart, painted from head to toe in different shades of white. Her hair was a dense mass of deep whites, her body gleamed with brilliant glossy tones. In front of her stood a looking glass almost two metres tall, inserted directly into the floor without a frame. That was all. She cost two thousand five hundred euros, with a monthly rent of another three hundred euros – not exactly expensive even for a second-rate collector. Alex Bassan had assured her she would be sold at once, but she had been on show for almost a month now at Gertrude Stein's gallery in Madrid's Calle Velázquez, and as yet no one had made any firm offer. It was Wednesday 21 June, 2006, and the agreement between the painters and GS expired in a week. If nothing had happened by then, Bassan would withdraw her, and Clara would have to wait until another artist wanted to use her to paint an original. And in the meantime, what would she live off?

Without the paint, Clara Reyes had slightly wavy, platinum blonde hair that reached down to her shoulders, blue eyes, high cheek bones, a look that lay somewhere between innocent and mischievous, and a slender frame that gave her a delicate appearance which was belied by her surprising strength. And to keep it that way, she needed money. She had bought a white-walled attic in Augusto Figueroa, and in the living room had set up a small gym with a Japanese tatami mat surrounded by mirrors and apparatus.

Whenever the galleries were closed and she had no chores to

do, she went swimming. Once a month she went to a beauty clinic. She used three kinds of cream each day to keep her skin as firm and gentle as canvases should be. She had got rid of two small moles from her body, and had had a scar removed from her left knee. Her menstruation had stopped as if by magic thanks to a special treatment, and she used pills to control her bodily needs. She had removed all her body hair completely and permanently, including her eyebrows; all that was left was her hair. Eyebrows and pubic hair are easy to paint if the artist so wishes, but they take a long time to grow. None of this was a whim – it was her job. Being a canvas cost a lot of money, and she could only make a lot of money by being a canvas. A strange paradox that made her think that Van Tysch, the greatest of them all, was right when he said that art was nothing more than money.

Yet this had not been a bad year for her. A Catalan businesswoman had bought her for Christmas as *The Strawberry* by Vicky Lledó – but then Vicky had a very faithful following, and sold all her works at a good price. In that painting, she had been with Yoli Ribó. The two of them were seated on a pedestal painted in skin tones, arms and legs intertwined, a plastic strawberry painted in quinacridone red held in their mouths. It was an easy position to hold, although they had to use an aerosol every day to reduce the saliva they produced ('Just imagine a painting that dribbles,' Vicky had said. 'Can you think of anything less aesthetic?') When you got used to it, having to put up with a plastic strawberry in your mouth for six hours a day seemed like the simplest thing in the world. And thanks to hyperdramatism, the exchange with Yoli had been ideal: they shared the strawberry, their breath, looks and touch like real lovers. Vicky had signed them on their deltoids with a horizontal V and L in red. They spent a month in the businesswoman's house before they were replaced. And then Clara had to find more work. In March she had taken over from a French model in an open-air piece in Marbella by the Portuguese artist Gamaio, and in April had replaced Queti Cabildos in *Liquid Element II* by Jaume Oreste, another open-air work, this time in La Moraleja, but she did not earn as much as when she was the original.

Then in May, good news. She got a call from Alex Bassan. He

wanted to paint an original with her. 'Alex, you're an angel,' she thought. He was someone who didn't apply himself to his work, but sold well. He had already painted Clara in two originals a few years back, and she was used to his way of working. Quick as a flash she accepted.

She came to Barcelona at the start of May and installed herself in the split-level apartment on the avenida Diagonal where Bassan lived and worked. Bassan and his wife lived on the upper floor of the apartment, while Clara slept on one of the three fold-up beds kept in the atelier. The other two beds were inhabited by a young Bulgarian (or was she Romanian?) girl who must have been about eleven or twelve, and who Bassan used as a sketch from time to time, and another sketch called Gabriel, nicknamed *Misfortune* by the painter because the first time he had used him had been for a work with that title. *Misfortune* was skinny and submissive.

While Clara was at work, the young girl wandered round the atelier like a ghost, clutching one of those Japanese toys that you have to push buttons to feed, raise and educate. During the fortnight Clara spent at Bassan's, this was the only thing she ever saw her with: it was as if the girl had come without any possessions or clothes. And all *Misfortune* did was come and go all the time. Clara guessed he must be working with several artists in Barcelona at the same time.

Bassan had made several studies before Clara arrived. He had used a North American sketch called Carrie. He showed her the photos: Carrie standing, Carrie on tiptoe, Carrie kneeling – always in front of a looking glass placed at varying distances from her. But the results had not satisfied the artist. For the first few days, he used Clara without a glass. He painted her black and white with trial aerosols, and tested her against strong lights on a dark background. He sprayed her hair and had her stand on one leg for several hours.

'What is it you're trying to achieve, Alex?' she asked him.

Bassan was a huge, strong man built like a woodcutter. The hairs of his chest protruded above his artist's overall. He painted the same way he talked: in great bursts. His thick fingers sometimes grazed Clara's skin when he was outlining a delicate area.

'What am I trying to achieve? That's some question, Clara my love. How the fuck should I know. I have a looking glass. I have you. I want to do something simple, with simple colours, perhaps a range of brilliant whites. And I want you to express . . . I'm not sure . . . I want you to be sincere, open, with no barriers . . . Sincerity, that's the word. To discover what we are, to pass through the looking glass, see what it's like to live in a looking-glass world . . .'

Clara did not understand a word of this, but then she never understood any of the painters. That didn't worry her: she was the painting, not an art critic; her job was to allow the painter to use her to express what was in his head, not to understand what that was. Besides, she had a blind faith in Bassan. With him, everything was unexpected: he found what he was looking for by chance, all at once, and when that happened it touched your soul.

One day midway through the second week, Bassan put a looking glass on the studio floor and told her to crouch on it naked and look at herself. Several hours went by. Hunched up on the mirror, Clara could only see rings of condensation from her breath.

'Do you enjoy looking at yourself?' the painter asked her all of a sudden.

'Yes.'

'Why?'

'I think I'm attractive.'

'Tell me the first thing that comes into your head. Come on, don't think about it, just tell me.'

'Navel,' said Clara.

'Someone's navel?'

'Not someone's. *My* navel.'

'You were thinking about your navel?'

'Aha. Right at this moment, yes. Because that's what I'm looking at.'

'And what were you thinking about your navel? That it was pretty? Ugly?'

'I was thinking how extraordinary it is. The idea of having a hole in your belly. Isn't that strange?'

Bassan stood still (his way of thinking) and almost immediately slapped his thigh (his way of announcing he had discovered something).

'Navel, navel . . . hole . . . the beginning of the world and of life . . . I've got it! Stand up. You're to cover your sex with your right hand, but raise your thumb a bit. Let's see . . . like that . . . No, a little higher . . . That's right, pointing up towards your navel . . .'

In the end, the work was very simple. Bassan had placed her standing up, arms and legs slightly apart, right hand on her sex and thumb raised rather less than he had at first thought. He mixed a lot of zinc white and covered her completely, including the 'natural stains' (facial features, aureolas and nipples, navel, her genitals and the crack between her buttocks). He used white lead to cover the brightest parts, then painted over them with titanium white. He sprayed and moulded her hair in a compact white mass that stuck close to her scalp. He used a small sable brush to paint some simple traits on her face: eyebrows, lashes and lips in a Naples brown diluted with white. He stuck a full-length mirror into the floor a short distance from her and put three halogen spots on two parallel strips to highlight her body. The powerful lights made the oil paint gleam. On 22 May he tattooed his signature on her left thigh: a capital B and two small esses. 'Bss'. It sounded like a soft whistle, she thought, or the buzz of a wasp.

'I think it'd be best to try Madrid,' Bassan said. 'I've had an interesting offer from the GS gallery.'

Bassan himself prepared the catalogue. He claimed exhibition catalogues were more important than the works themselves. 'Nowadays, we painters don't create paintings, we create catalogues,' he said mockingly. As soon as he received the first proofs from the printer, he sent Clara a copy. It was beautiful: a large white satin card with a photo of Clara's painted face on the front. Opening the card, the text in gold letters read: 'The painter Alex Bassan and the GS gallery have the pleasure of . . .' Bassan described it perfectly with one of his impulsive phrases: 'It looks like the invitation to an elf's first communion.' The opening was at eight on the evening of Thursday 1 June at the GS gallery in

Madrid, an event like many others. Gertrude Stein shared the cost of the drinks. People got drunk in the foyer, then went down into the basement to look at Clara, who was positioned in the centre of a tiny room. Opposite her stood the looking glass, with no frame or base, as if it had appeared by magic. Behind her on the white wall was an inscription: 'Alex Bassan. *Girl in Front of a Looking Glass*. Oils on a twenty-four-year-old girl with full-length mirror and lights. 195×35×88cm.' Under the title was a shelf with a pile of catalogues. There was no podium or any kind of security rope: she was simply standing on the bare white floor that shone as brightly as the looking glass and her body did. The room was really cramped, and as it filled up, Clara was worried someone might step on her foot. A white fire extinguisher hung from the wall in a corner. 'At least I won't go up in flames if there's a fire,' she thought.

She could hear the art critics praising the work. A few criticisms as well. Not of her, of course, but of the work. Yet it was her they were staring at: her thighs, her buttocks, her breasts, her unmoving face. And the looking glass as well. There was one exception. At a certain point out of the corner of her eye she caught sight of a silhouette coming close to her, and mouthing an obscenity into her left ear. She was used to this, and did not even blink. Often in hyperdramatic exhibitions some crazy person got in who was not in the least bit interested in the work, but in the naked woman on show. To judge by his breath, this guy was drunk. He stood right next to her for quite a while, staring at her. Clara was concerned he might try to touch her, because there were no security guards anywhere. But a few moments later he moved off. If he had tried anything, she would have been forced to abandon her state of quiescence and give him a verbal warning. If he had continued to pester her despite this, she would have had no problem kneeing him in the balls. It wouldn't have been the first time she had stopped being a work of art to defend herself from a troublesome spectator. HD art aroused a mixture of passions, and the female paintings who had no protection soon learned the lesson.

Girl in Front of a Looking Glass would fit easily into any reasonably spacious living room. Her percentage from the sale and rental, together with the money she had already received for her work with the painter, would have lasted her the whole summer.

But nobody wanted to buy her.

'Clara.'

She breathed in sharply when she heard Gertrude's voice on the stairs.

'Clara, it's half past one. I'm going to close the gallery.'

It was always an effort to emerge from her state of quiescence and step back into the world of real objects. She twisted her head from side to side, swallowed several times, blinked (two cameos of her face were imprinted by light and time on her retinas), stretched her arms and stamped her feet on the floor. One of her legs had gone to sleep. She massaged her neck. The oil paint tugged uncomfortably at her skin.

'And there are two gentlemen to see you,' Gertrude added. 'They're in my office.'

Clara stopped sketching and looked at the gallery owner. Gertrude was at the foot of the stairs. As usual, her green eyes and scarlet lips gave nothing away. She was no longer young, and was as tall and white as Mont Blanc; so white she almost glistened. If she had fallen into snow, all you would have seen of her would have been a pair of almond-shaped emeralds and a stain of red lipstick. She liked wearing white tunics, and talked as if she were interrogating a prisoner of war under torture.

'I'm German, but I've lived in Madrid for several years,' she told Clara when they met. She pronounced 'Madrid' like a robot from a B-movie. 'GS are my initials.' She went on to tell her her surname, but Clara couldn't remember it. 'Pleased to meet you,' Clara had replied, and was rewarded with a smile. Bassan said she was a successful gallery owner and had a select clientele of hyperdramatic art collectors, but Clara hadn't been able to discover if this was true or not. What she had found was that Gertrude was rude and disdainful towards the paintings. Perhaps she was a little more pleasant with the painters. On top of that, she was a cleanliness freak. She did not allow Clara to use the bathroom to wash or make up after work. She said she had no wish to see paint anywhere else apart from on the skin of her paintings. On Clara's first day she showed her a small space at the back of the upstairs office and said that all the works got on just fine in there. Each day before work Clara had to go into this wretched cubicle and put on the porous swimsuit and the hair-dyeing cap, soaked in the colours Bassan had prepared, and wait for almost an hour until they had dried on her skin. Then she took off the swimsuit and cap and emerged naked and gleaming white, walked down to the basement and took up the pose and expression the painter had chosen for her. When the gallery closed, she was forced to make her way home with her body still painted under her tracksuit and wearing a ridiculous beret to hide her white hair; all she could scrape off was the paint on her face. It was no fun driving with her skin stiffened with oil paint.

'Two gentlemen?' Clara had to clear her throat to get the words out. 'What do they want?'

'How should I know? They're waiting in my office.'

'But did they come down to see the work?' Often she was unaware of how many visitors there had been.

'Not today, that's for sure. They asked for Clara Reyes. They didn't mention any work of art.'

As Clara mulled this over, Gertrude went on:

'I suppose you're not going to want to see them like that. You can put on one of the robes from the loft. But don't touch anything. I don't want any paint marks in my office.'

The two men were standing waiting for her, looking at glossy catalogues of other works she had been. She recognised *Tenderness* by Vicky, *Horizontal III* by Gutíerrez Reguero, and *The Wolf, in the Meantime, Is Dying of Hunger* by Georges Chalboux. The illustrations showed her naked or half-naked body painted in a variety of colours. There were also a few *Girl in Front of a Looking Glass* catalogues. One of the men was throwing the catalogues on to the table after showing them to his companion, as if he were counting them. They were dressed in expensive suits and looked foreign. When she realised this, Clara's heart skipped a beat: if they had come a long way, perhaps that meant they were really interested in her. Hey, slow down a bit, you've no idea what they're going to propose, she told herself.

19

They offered her a chair. As she sat down, her robe opened over her knees like a petal, and one leg painted titanium white and white lead was revealed halfway up to her thigh. She crossed her hands under her chest and sat there like a patient child.

'Well?' she said.

The men did not sit down. Only one of them spoke. His Spanish was full of errors, but was easily understandable. Clara could not place his accent.

'Are you Clara Reyes?'

'Aha.'

The man took something out of a briefcase: it was the résumé Clara usually sent out to the most important artists in Europe and America. Her heart beat faster still.

'Twenty-four years old,' the man read out loud, 'one hundred and sixty-five centimetres tall, bust eighty-five, waist fifty-five, hips eighty-eight, blonde hair; light blue eyes tinged with green, depilated, no skin blemishes, firm and well-toned, primed four times . . . is that correct?'

'Correct.'

The man went on reading.

'Studied HD art and canvas techniques with Cuinet in Barcelona, and adolescent art in Frankfurt with Wedekind. Also in Florence with Ferrucioli. Is that correct?'

'Well, I was only with Ferrucioli for one week.'

She didn't want to hide anything, because that always led to difficult questions later on.

'You've been painted by both Spanish and foreign artists. Do you speak English?'

'Aha. Perfectly.'

'You've done interior works and open-air ones. Which are you better at?'

'Both. I can be an interior work or a seasonal outdoor one, or even be outside permanently, depending on the clothes and the time of year, of course. Although I can pose permanently outside with adequate protec—'

'We've seen other works you've done,' the man interrupted. 'We like you.'

'Thanks. But haven't you been downstairs to see *Girl in Front of a Looking Glass?* It's a really impressive Bassan, and I'm not just saying that because I'm the work, but—'

'You have also done mobile works of both sorts: *performances* and *reunions*,' the man cut in again. 'Were they interactive?'

'Aha. They were sometimes, yes.'

'Were you ever bought?'

'Almost always.'

'Good.' The man smiled and peered down at the sheets of paper as if there was something there that amused him. 'This résumé is for promotional purposes. I'd like to hear your private one.'

'What do you mean by that?'

'I mean your whole professional career, and what you can't put in a promotion leaflet. For example: have you ever been an ornament, a mobile, a utensil?'

'I've never been a human artefact,' Clara replied.

It was true, although she had no idea whether the man believed her or not. But her own words sounded rather haughty to her, so she quickly added:

'Human ornaments have not really caught on yet in Spain.'

'Art-shocks?'

She hesitated before replying. She straightened up in her chair – her painted buttocks making a swishing sound – and told herself to stay on her guard.

'I'm sorry, but where are these questions leading?'

'We want to know what demands we can make of you,' the man responded calmly.

'I should warn you, I won't do anything illegal.'

She waited for a reaction that did not come. She hastened to add:

'Well, it would depend on the circumstances. But first of all I want you to tell me what you're going to do, where you're going to do it, and which artist is thinking of contracting me.'

'Your answer first, please.'

She decided there was nothing to lose by telling the truth. She was not a minor; the two art-shocks she had been bought in that year were not the hardest of their kind, and had been put on only in private for an adult audience. But it was also true that on

21

both occasions elements had crept in that perhaps went beyond the limits of what was permitted. For example, in *625 + 50 lines* by Adolfo Bermejo, one of the human canvases chopped the head off a live cat and squirted its blood on Clara's back. Was that illegal? She wasn't sure, but the question had been a general one, so she could respond in general terms, too.

'Yes, I've done art-shocks.'

'Porno ones?'

'Never,' she said firmly.

'But you've worked with Gilberto Brentano, I believe.'

'I did two or three art-shocks with Brentano last year, but none of them was porno.'

'Have you ever belonged to any group providing underage material for works of art?'

'I worked with *The Circle* for a few months.'

'How old were you?'

'Sixteen.'

'What did you do there?'

'The usual. They painted my hair red, I had to wear lots of rings, and I took part in a few murals like *Redhair Road*.'

'Was that your first artistic experience?'

'Aha.'

'As far as I can see,' the man said, 'you like tough, risky art. But you don't seem the tough, risk-taking type. You look quite soft to me.'

For some unknown reason, Clara liked the man's cold disdain. A smile stretched the oil paint on her face.

'I am soft. It's when I'm painted that I toughen up.'

The man showed no sign of taking this as a joke. He said:

'We've come to propose something tough and risky. The toughest and most risky thing you've ever done in your life as a canvas, the most important and the most difficult. We want to be sure you're up to it.'

All of a sudden she realised her mouth was as dry as her paint-covered skin beneath the gown. Her heart was pounding. The man's words excited her. Clara loved extremes, the dark zone the other side of the frontier. If she was told: 'Don't go,' her body stirred and went, just for the simple pleasure of disobeying.

If something frightened her, she might try to keep it at a distance, but she never lost sight of it. She detested the instructions vulgar artists gave her, but if a painter she admired asked her to do something crazy, whatever it might be, she liked to obey without question. And that 'whatever it might be' recognised few limits. She was obsessed with discovering how far she would allow herself to go if the ideal situation occurred. She felt she was still a long way from her ceiling – or her floor, for that matter.

'That sounds good,' she said.

After a few moments, the man went on:

'Naturally, you'll have to drop everything else for a considerable length of time.'

'I can drop everything if the offer is worth it.'

'The offer *is* worth it.'

'And I'm simply supposed to believe that?'

'Neither of us wants to rush into this, do we?' The man put his hand in his inside pocket. A black leather wallet. A turquoise-coloured card. 'Call this number. You have until tomorrow evening, Thursday.'

Before she put the card into her robe pocket, she glanced at it: the only thing on it was a phone number. It might be a mobile.

Gertrude's office was small, with white walls and no windows. Despite this, to Clara it seemed as if it had started to rain outside. There was, at least, a muffled impression of rain. The two men were staring at her, as if waiting for her to say something. So she replied:

'I don't like accepting offers I know nothing about.'

'You don't need to know anything. You are the work of art. The only one who needs to know is the artist.'

'Well then, at least tell me the name of the artist who wants to paint me.'

'That's something we can't reveal.'

She accepted this refusal without protest. She knew the man was telling the truth. The great painters never revealed their identity to the canvas until their work had started: it was their way of maintaining an element of secrecy about the painting they were going to do.

The door opened and Gertrude appeared.

'I'm sorry, but I'm going out to lunch and I need to shut the gallery.'

'Don't worry, we've just finished.' The two men picked up the catalogues and walked out without another word.

While she was on show that afternoon, Clara's breasts moved up and down with her breathing. She was so nervous that a state of quiescence was much more difficult to achieve than usual. But daydreaming helped her to stay still, because when dreaming one can move without moving. The time went by and nobody came down to see her, but she wasn't concerned, because she had her fantasies to keep her company.

The toughest and most risky. The most important and difficult.

Her greatest desire was to be painted by a genius. Various names sprang to mind, but she hardly dared speculate that it might be one of them. She didn't want to raise her hopes up too high, so as not to be disappointed. She kept in her pose in the silent whiteness of the room until Gertrude told her it was time to close.

Outside it really was raining: a violent summer shower that had been forecast on TV. On other occasions she would have run to the car park entrance, but today she preferred to walk slowly in the downpour, with her make-up bag slung over her shoulder. She realised her tracksuit was clinging to her like a wet sheet, and the beret was dripping on to her face, but it wasn't an unpleasant sensation. In fact, she welcomed it. Cold diamonds of water showering down upon her.

The toughest and most risky. The most important and difficult.

What if it was a trap? It had been known. You were contracted – supposedly on behalf of a great maestro – taken out of the country and forced to take part in porno art. But she didn't think this was anything like that. And even if it were, she would take the risk. Being a work of art meant accepting all the risks, all the sacrifices. She was more scared of being disappointed than of facing danger. She could accept falling into any trap except that of mediocrity.

The toughest and most risky. The most important and . . .

All at once she felt as though her body was melting. She felt fluid, at one with the rain. She looked down at her feet and saw what was happening. She had forgotten she was still painted, and the raindrops were washing off all the white paint. As she walked along, she was leaving a trail behind her, a curving milky stream that flowed from her tracksuit on to the pavement of the Calle Velázquez, only to be quickly blotted out by the rain, as sharp and precise as a Pointillist painter. White, white, white.

Little by little, as the water cleansed her, Clara grew darker.

2

Red. Red was the overwhelming colour. Red like a huge mass of crushed poppies. Miss Wood took off her glasses to examine the photos.

'We found her early this morning in a wooded part of the Wienerwald,' the policeman said, 'about an hour's drive from Vienna. Two birdwatchers who had been studying the cries of owls raised the alarm. Well, in fact they told the uniformed police, and lieutenant-colonel Huddle called us in. That's what usually happens.'

As the policeman spoke, Bosch passed the photos to Miss Wood one by one. They showed a grassy clearing, with beech trees and flowers, and the surprising presence of a flycatcher on the grass next to the pink blouse that had been torn to shreds. But everything was covered in red, including the slipper shaped like a teddy bear lying behind a tree trunk. There was a broad smile on the bear's face.

'All these things scattered around . . .' said Miss Wood.

It was an enormous table and the policeman sitting opposite Miss Wood could not see what she was pointing at, but he knew exactly what she meant.

'Her clothing.'

'Why is it so torn and bloodstained?'

'You're right, it is strange. It was the first thing that we noticed. Then we found bits of material stuck in her wounds, so we concluded that he cut her up with her clothes on, and tore them off later.'

'Why would he do that?'

The policeman wafted his hand in the air.

'Sexual abuse, perhaps. So far we haven't found any evidence, but we're waiting for the forensic expert's final report. And anyway, people like that don't always behave logically.'

'It's as if . . . it were on show, isn't it? All draped around for photos to be taken of it.'

'Is this how she was found?' Bosch asked the policeman.

'Yes, on her back with her arms and legs spread out.'

'He left her labels on,' Bosch pointed out to Miss Wood.

'So I see,' said Miss Wood. 'The labels are hard to get off, but whatever he used to make this kind of wound would have cut through them like paper. Has the tool been identified?'

'It was electronic, whatever it was,' the policeman replied. 'We think it might have been a scalpel or some kind of electric saw. Each wound is a deep single cut.' He stretched his hand out across the table and tapped one of the photos closest to him with a pencil. 'There are ten of them altogether: two in the face, two in the chest, two in the stomach, one in each thigh, and two in her back. Eight of them forming crosses, so four crosses altogether. The two in the thighs are vertical. And don't ask me the reason for that either.'

'Did she die from the wounds?'

'Probably. I've already told you, we're waiting for the report from—'

'Do we have an estimated time of death?

'Taking into account the state of the body, we think it must have happened on Wednesday night, a few hours after she was driven away in the van.'

Miss Wood was holding her glasses between the fingers of her left hand. She used them to gently tap Bosch's arm:

'I'd say there isn't that much blood in the photos. Do you agree?'

'I was thinking the same.'

'It's true,' the policeman said. 'He didn't kill her in the wood. Perhaps he cut her up in the van. Maybe he used some sort of sedative, because the body showed no signs of a struggle or of having been bound. Afterwards, he dragged her to the clearing and left her on the grass.'

'Then spent his time tearing off her clothes in the open air,' Miss Wood chimed in, 'ignoring the risk that those amateur bird-watchers might have decided to study their owls a night earlier.'

'Yes, that's odd, isn't it? But as I already said, these people behave—'

'I understand,' said the woman, interrupting him as she put her glasses back on. They were dark Ray-Bans with gold frames. The policeman thought it must be impossible for Miss Wood to see anything in the red-tinged gloom of this office. Reflected in the glasses, the red curve of the desk formed two pools of blood. 'Could we hear the recording now?'

'Of course.'

The detective bent over to reach into a leather briefcase. When he straightened up, he was holding a portable cassette recorder. He placed it on the desk next to the photos, as if it were just another souvenir of a tourist trip.

'We found it at the feet of the corpse. A two-hour chrome-coloured cassette with no writing or marks on it. It seems to have been recorded on a good machine.'

He jabbed at the start button. The sudden roar led Bosch to raise his eyebrows. The policeman quickly lowered the volume.

'Sorry, it's very loud,' he said.

A pause. A whirring sound. Then it started.

At first there was heavy breathing. Then the crackling sound of a fire. Like a bird enveloped in flames. Then a hesitant breath, and the first word. It sounded like a complaint, or a moan. Then it came again, and this time it was audible: *Art*. More anxious breathing, then the first tentative phrase. The voice was nasal, interrupted by panting, the sound of paper, microphone hiss. It was an adolescent's voice, speaking in English:

'*Art is also destruc . . . destruction . . . in the past that's all it . . . was. In the caves they painted what . . . what they wanted to sa . . . sacri . . . sacri . . .*'

Whirring sounds. A brief silence. The policeman pressed the pause button.

'He stopped recording here, probably to make her repeat the phrase.'

The next part was clearer. Each word was pronounced slowly and clearly. What came over from this new declaration was a desperate attempt by the speaker not to get it wrong. But something else, that could well have been terror, broke through the icy pauses:

In the caves they painted only what they wanted to sacrifice . . .
Egyptian art was funerary art . . . Everything was dedicated to
death . . . The artist is saying: I have created you to hunt and
destroy you, and the meaning of your creation is your final
sacrifice . . . The artist is saying: I have created you to honour
death . . . Because the art that survives is the art that has
died . . . where beings die, works endure. . .

The policeman switched off the recorder.

'That's all there is. We're analysing it in the laboratory, of course. We think he did it in the van with the windows closed, because there's not much background noise. It was probably a written text they forced her to read.'

An intense silence followed these words. It's as if by hearing her, hearing her voice, we've finally understood the horror of it all, thought Bosch. He was not surprised at this reaction. The photos had impressed him, of course, but to some extent it was easy to keep your distance from a photo. In his days as a member of the Dutch police, Lothar Bosch had developed an unexpected coldness when confronted with the ghastly red phantoms that appeared in the darkroom. But hearing a voice is very different. Behind the words lay a human being who had died a horrible death. The figure of the violin player appears more clearly when we hear the violin.

To Bosch's eyes, accustomed to seeing her posing in the open air or inside rooms and museums, naked or semi-naked and painted in many different colours, she had never been a 'little girl' as the policeman had called her. Except once, two years earlier. A Colombian collector called Cárdenas with a somewhat obscure past had bought her in *The Garland* by Jacob Stein. Bosch had been concerned what might happen to her in that hacienda on the outskirts of Bogotá while she was posing eight hours a day for her owner wearing only the tiniest of velvet ribbons round her waist. He had decided to give her extra protection, and summoned her to his offices in the New Studio in Amsterdam to tell her this. He still had a clear memory of it: the work of art came into his office dressed in T-shirt and jeans, her skin primed and eyebrows shaved off. She was wearing the customary three yellow labels, but apart from that had not been painted at all. She held out her hand: 'Mr Bosch,' she said.

It was the same voice as the girl in the recording. The same Dutch accent, the same smooth quality.

Mr Bosch.

With a simple gesture and these few words, the canvas had been transformed into a twelve-year-old girl right before his eyes. It happened in a flash. Bosch's mind was flooded with images of his own niece, Danielle, who was four years younger than Annek. All of a sudden he realised he was allowing a 'little girl' to go and work more or less naked in the house of an adult male with a criminal record. But the giddiness soon subsided, and he became neutral and level-headed once more. She's not a girl, she's a canvas, of course, he told himself. As it turned out, nothing had happened to the work of art in the Bogotá hacienda. Now though, someone had cut her to pieces in a Viennese wood.

Listening to the recording, Bosch had been recalling the gentle pressure of her right hand, and the words 'Mr Bosch' pronounced with such unconscious delicacy. Two different sources for his impressions, but they gave the same reply: softness, warmth, innocence, softness . . .

The policeman was leaning forward, as if expecting him to say something.

'Why would he leave a recording?' Bosch asked.

'This kind of madman wants the whole world to hear how he sees things,' the policeman said.

'Has the van been found yet?' Miss Wood wanted to know.

'No, but it soon will be, if he hasn't got rid of it somehow. We know the make and the licence number, so . . .'

'He was very clever,' Bosch said.

'Why do you say that?'

29

'All our vans have a tracking device. A GPS satellite system which transmits the position of the vehicle at all times. We installed it a year ago to guard against the theft of valuable works of art. On Wednesday night we lost the signal from this van soon after it left the museum. He must have found the device and de-activated it.'

'Why did you take so long to get in touch with us? You only contacted us on Thursday morning.'

'We didn't realise we had lost the signal. The tracking device sets off an alarm if the van leaves the pre-established route, if there's an accident, or if it's stationary for a long while before reaching the hotel. But in this case, the alarm did not go off, and we did not realise we could not pick up the signal.'

'Which means the guy knew about the device,' the policeman observed.

'That's why we thought Oscar Díaz must have been in on it, or have murdered her himself.'

'Let's see if I've got this straight. Oscar Díaz was the person responsible for taking her to the hotel. He was some kind of security guard employed by you, is that right?'

'Yes, one of our security agents,' Bosch agreed.

'But why would one of your own security agents do something like that?'

Bosch looked first at the policeman, then at Miss Wood, who still sat without saying a word.

'We have no idea. Díaz has an impeccable record. If he was crazy, he managed to hide it very well for years.'

'What do you know about him? Does he have family? Friends? . . .'

Bosch reeled off the details he had learned by heart from looking at the file a hundred times over the previous few days.

'He's single, twenty-six years old, born in Mexico. Father died of lung cancer, mother lives with his sister in Mexico City. Oscar emigrated to the States when he was eighteen. He's athletic, enjoys sport. He worked as a bodyguard for Hispanic business-men living in Miami or New York. One of them had a hyperdramatic work of art in his house. Oscar asked for infor-mation about it, then started as a guard in small New York galleries. Then he came to work for us. We helped him get on, because he was intelligent and a hard worker. The first important Foundation work that he was security for was a Buncher shown at the Leo Castelli gallery.'

'A what?'

Miss Wood explained drily.

'Evard Buncher was one of the founders of orthodox hyper-dramatism, together with Max Kalima and Bruno van Tysch. He was Norwegian. During the Second World War he was arrested by the Nazis and sent to Mauthausen. He managed to survive. He travelled to London, where he met Kalima and Tanagorsky and began to paint his pictures on human beings instead of can-vases. But he enclosed them in boxes. Some people say he was influenced in this by his experiences in the concentration camp.'

This woman is like a computer, the policeman thought to him-self.

'They're small boxes, open on one side,' Miss Wood went on. 'The work is put inside and stays there for several hours.' She turned her head towards the wall behind her and pointed to the large photo on it. 'That's a Buncher, for example.'

The policeman had noticed it as soon as he'd arrived, and had wondered what on earth it meant. Two naked bodies painted red were crammed into a glass box, which was so small they had to cling together in a complicated knot. Their genitals were visi-ble, but not their faces. To judge by the former, they were a man and a woman. The enormous photo filled almost the entire wall in this room in the MuseumsQuartier. So *that* is meant to be a work of art, the policeman thought. And anyone could buy it and take it home. He wondered if his wife would want something like that decorating their dining room. How on earth did they manage to stay in those impossibly contorted positions for such lengths of time?

He recalled the exhibition he had seen that same afternoon.

As a detective in the homicide squad of the Austrian police force's Criminal Investigation Department, art had never partic-ularly interested Felix Braun. Like all good Viennese, his predilection for art started and ended with nineteenth-century music. Of course, he had seen various hyperdramatic works of art exhibited in public in Vienna, but before that afternoon he had never been to a full exhibition.

He had arrived at the MuseumsQuartier – the artistic and cultural centre containing most of Vienna's modern art museums – forty minutes before his appointment with Miss Wood and Bosch. Having nothing better to do, and given the special circumstances of the case, he decided to visit the exhibition in which the murdered girl had been taking part.

It was being shown at the Kunsthalle. An enormous poster of one of the figures (he learnt soon after that it was *Marigold Desiderata*) filled the entire façade of the museum. The title of the exhibition was written in German in huge red letters: 'Blumen' by Bruno van Tysch. A simple enough title, thought Bosch. 'Flowers'. Before gaining access to the exhibition, every visitor had to pass through a metal detector, an X-ray machine, and an image analysis cabin. Of course, his police revolver set off the alarm at the first stage of the screening process, but Braun had already explained who he was. He pushed open double doors, and found himself in the inhuman darkness of art. At first he thought the exhibits were painted statues placed on pedestals. When he came closer to the first work, he could hardly believe it was a real flesh and blood person, a living human being. Waists bent like hinges, legs raised vertically, backs arched like bridges over rivers . . . None of them moved, or blinked, or took breaths. Their arms imitated petals, from a distance their ankles looked like stalks. He had to approach the security rope and peer very closely before he could distinguish muscles, breasts crowned with the red bud of nipples, genitals that had lost all their hair and their obscenity, genitals as free of sexual associations as the corollas of flowers. Then Braun's nose took over, telling him that each of them was giving off a distinctive, penetrating perfume that could be perceived even above the different smells (not all of them pleasant) produced by the general public crowding into the room, just as one hears a solo instrument above the orchestral accompaniment.

'*Blumen* – Flowers.' Bruno van Tysch's collection of twenty flowers. *Marigold Desiderata, Iris Versicolor, Rosa Fabrica, Hedera Helix, Orchis Fabulata*. The titles were almost as fantastic as the works themselves. He remembered having seen photos of some of these *flowers* in a magazine, a newspaper or on television. They had already become cultural icons of the twenty-first century. But never until now had he contemplated them *au naturel*, all together, on show in that vast room of the Kunsthalle. And of course, he had never *smelt* them. For half an hour Braun wandered from one podium to the next, slack-jawed with shock. It was an overwhelming experience.

It was the one painted in scarlet that attracted him most. The colour was so intense it produced a kind of optical illusion: an aura, a stain on the retina, the shimmering effect an extremely hot object produces. Braun drew closer to the podium as if in a trance. He believed he could detect something familiar in the perfume, as penetrating and fantastic as a marketstall of Arab essences. The work was crouching down on tiptoe. Both her hands were covering her sex, and her head was tilted down to her right (Braun's left). She was completely shaven and depilated. At first he thought the work had no features at all, but beneath the intense vermilion mask he could discern the prickle of eyebrows, the swelling of the nose and the bas-relief of a pair of lips. Two tiny breasts indicated it was a young woman. Braun walked right round the podium without spotting any kind of support that would allow the woman to stay on tiptoe for so long. The work was a naked, shaven girl balancing on the tips of her toes.

It was then he thought he recognised the fragrance.

The figure in front of him reminded him of the perfume his wife used.

When he got out into the street, still bemused, he tried in vain to remember the title of the *flower* that smelt like his wife. Purple Tulip? Magic Marigold?

Even now, he was still trying to identify it.

'Buncher created a collection called "Claustrophilia",' Bosch was explaining. 'Oscar spent a long period of time at the house where *Claustrophilia 5,* the model Sandy Ryan, was being exhibited. She was the seventh substitute. He was polite with the works: occasionally he talked too much, but he was always respectful. In 2003 he bought an apartment in New York and made that his base, but since January this year he has been in Europe, looking after the paintings in the "Flowers" exhibition. Here in Vienna he was staying in the same Kirchberggasse hotel as the rest of the team. The hotel is very close to the cultural centre. We've questioned his colleagues and immediate superiors: none of them noticed anything strange about him in the past few days. And that's all we know.'

Braun had begun taking notes in a small notebook.

'I know where Kirchberggasse is,' he said. His tone seemed to emphasise that he was the only person from Vienna in the room. 'We'll have to search his room.'

'Of course,' agreed Bosch.

They had already searched the place, and his apartment in New York, but he was not going to tell the policeman that.

'There's also the possibility that Díaz is not to blame for this,' Bosch added, as though wanting to play the devil's advocate against his own theory. 'And if that's the case, we have to ask ourselves why he's disappeared.'

Braun waved his hand dismissively as if that kind of question was not Bosch's concern.

'That's as may be,' he said, 'but as long as we have no proof to the contrary, we'll have to consider Díaz as our prime suspect.'

'What does the press know?' Miss Wood asked.

'As you requested, we have not given out the identity of the young girl.'

'What about Díaz?'

'We have not made his identity public, but we've set up controls at Schwechat airport, the train stations and at our frontiers. We have to take into account though that today is Friday, and we only received the information yesterday. The guy had more than a day to slip abroad.'

Miss Wood and Bosch nodded their agreement. They had been thinking along the same lines. In fact, they had swung into action much quicker than the Austrian police: Bosch was aware that ten different security teams were already scouring Europe for Díaz. Still, they needed the national police's help: this was no time to spare any effort.

'As far as the victim's family goes . . .' Braun said, casting a nervous glance at Bosch.

'She only had a mother, but she's away on a trip. We've asked permission to inform her personally. By the way, we can keep the photos and the tape, can't we?'

'Of course. They're copies for you.'

'Thanks. More coffee?'

Braun paused before replying. He had been gazing at the maid who had just crept silently into the room. It was the dark-haired girl with the long red dress and the silver coffee pot who had served him earlier. While there was nothing particularly unusual or beautiful about her features, there was something about her that Braun could not define. The way she moved, what seemed like a rhythm she had learned, the subtle gestures of a secret dancer. Braun knew about human utensils and ornaments. He also knew they were banned, but this girl stayed within the limits of the strictly legal. There was nothing criminal about her appearance or movements, and everything Braun imagined while looking at her could well have been simply in his own mind. He said yes to more coffee, and watched as the girl poured the dense, steaming jet of Viennese *mokka* into his cup. As before, he was convinced she was barefoot, but the length of her dress and the darkness of the room meant he could not be sure. She too gave off waves of perfume.

Neither Bosch nor Miss Wood wanted more coffee. The maid turned to leave, her long skirt making a swooshing sound as she did so. The door opened and closed. Braun sat for a moment staring after her. Then he blinked and came back to reality.

'We are very pleased to be able to count on the cooperation of the Austrian police, Detective Braun,' Bosch was saying. He had gathered together all the photos on the table (a red lacquer swirl in the shape of a painter's palette) and was taking the tape out of the recorder.

'I am simply doing my duty,' Braun said. 'My superiors told me to come to the museum to keep you informed, and that is what I've done.'

'We can perfectly understand you must think the situation is somewhat anomalous.'

35

'"Anomalous" is putting it mildly,' Braun said with a smile, trying to make his words sound as cynical as possible. 'First of all, our department does not normally keep information from the press about the activities of a possible psychopath. Tomorrow another young girl could turn up dead in the wood, and we would have a serious problem on our hands.'

'I understand,' Bosch agreed.

'Secondly, the fact that we have revealed details of our investigation to individuals such as yourselves is also uncommon for the police, in this country at least. We are not used to collaborating with private security companies, especially to this extent.'

Further agreement.

'But . . .' Braun spread his hands as if to say: But I've been ordered to come and keep you informed, and that is what I am doing. 'Well, I'm at your service.'

He had no wish to show his disgust, but could not help it. That morning he had received no less than five phone calls from different departments, each successive one from higher up in the political hierarchy. The last had been from a top-ranking official in the Ministry of the Interior whose name never appeared in the newspapers. Braun had been told on no account to miss his appointment in the MuseumsQuartier, and had been urged to give Miss Wood and Bosch all available information. It was obvious the Van Tysch Foundation had wide-ranging and powerful political influence.

'Your coffee,' Bosch said, gesturing towards the cup. 'It'll go cold.'

'Thanks.'

Braun did not really want any more, but out of politeness lifted the cup and pretended to take a sip. While the two people opposite him exchanged routine remarks, he took a good look at them. He found the man called Bosch more agreeable than his female companion, but that wasn't saying much. He thought he must be around fifty. He looked serious enough, with a shining bald pate ringed with white hair, and distinguished-looking features. When they first met he had confessed to Braun that as a young man he had worked for the Dutch police, so in a way they

36

were almost colleagues. But Miss Wood was something else again. She looked young, somewhere between twenty-five and thirty. Her straight black hair was cut short *au garçon*, and showed a perfect parting on the right-hand side. Her skinny frame was moulded into a sleeveless dress, and at the neckline was the red pass of the Van Tysch Foundation Security Department. Apart from that he could only see tons of make-up and those absurd dark glasses. Unlike her companion, Miss Wood never smiled, and spoke as though everyone around her was there to serve her. Braun felt sorry for Bosch for having to put up with the woman.

All at once, Felix Braun felt very odd. It was almost as if he had a split personality. He could see himself sitting in a room lit by red bulbs and decorated by a huge photo of two people squashed into a glass box, at a red table in the shape of a painter's palette, opposite two outlandish figures and waited on by a maid like an odalisk. He had just come out of an exhibition of naked, painted youngsters who all gave off different perfumes, and he was finding it hard to work out what a murder detective like him was doing in the middle of all this. He also found it hard to see what all this had to do with the events that had taken place. The ravaged body they had discovered that morning in the Wienerwald was of a poor fourteen-year-old adolescent, brutally murdered in one of the worst acts of sadism Braun had ever encountered. What link was there between that murder and this red room, an odalisk, two ridiculous characters, and a museum?

'In fact,' he said, and the change in his voice led the other two to break off their conversation and stare at him, 'I still can't quite grasp what role you two have to play in this case, apart from being the directors of a security firm that the main suspect belongs to. A brutal crime has been committed, and that is the sole responsibility of the police.'

'Do you know what hyperdramatic art is, Detective Braun?' Miss Wood suddenly asked.

'Who doesn't?' Braun replied. 'I've just seen the "Flowers" exhibition. And I've got a cousin who's bought a book of art for beginners. He wants to practise on all of us: every time I see him he wants to use me as his model . . .'

Bosch laughed together with Braun, but Miss Wood was as solemn as ever.

'Give me a definition,' she said.

'A definition?'

'Yes. What do you think HD art is?'

'What's she after now?' Braun thought to himself. She made him nervous. He straightened the knot on his tie and cleared his throat, looking around as if he might find the right words in some corner of this red room.

'I'd say that it is people who stay stock-still and which others call paintings,' he replied.

His irony bounced off the woman's stern face.

'It's exactly the opposite,' she retorted. She smiled for the first time. It was the most unpleasant smile Braun had ever seen. 'They are paintings which sometimes move and look like human beings. It's not a question of terminology, but of points of view, and that is the point of view we have at the Foundation.' Miss Wood's voice stung icily, as if each of her words was a veiled threat. 'The Foundation is responsible for protecting and promoting Bruno van Tysch's art throughout the world, and I personally am responsible for the Security Department. My task, and that of my companion here, Mr Lothar Bosch, is to make sure that none of Van Tysch's works suffers the slightest damage. And Annek Hollech was a painting worth much more than all our wages and pension plans put together, Detective Braun. She was called *Deflowering*, was a Van Tysch original, was considered one of the key works of contemporary painting, and now she has been destroyed.'

Braun was impressed by the cold fury of her staccato, almost whispering voice. Miss Wood paused before she went on. Her dark glasses stared at Braun, the twin reflection of the table gleaming from them.

'What you see as a murder is for us a serious attack on one of our works. As you will understand, we therefore feel ourselves intimately involved in the investigation, which is why we have asked to collaborate. Is that clear?'

'Perfectly.'

'Don't for a moment imagine we are going to get in your way

at all,' Miss Wood went on. 'The police must do as they see fit, and the Foundation will do likewise. But I would ask you to inform us of any developments that may arise in the course of your investigation. Thank you.'

That was the end of the meeting. Led by the public relations woman who had received him when he arrived, Braun walked back along the labyrinthine corridors of the oval wing of the MuseumsQuartier. It was only when he was out in the street again, in the bright sunlight, that he regained his calm.

As he drove home, the exact name of the exhibit flashed into his head without warning. Magic Purple.

That was the name of the bright-red work of art who had the same fragrance as his wife. Scarlet, carmine, blood red.

3

The card was a turquoise-blue colour, the colour of magic spells, bluebirds over the rainbow, the azure sea. It glinted in the dining-room light. The phone number was written in the centre in fine black lines. All that was on the card was the number, probably a mobile, although the code was strange. While she was dialling it, Clara noticed that her fingernail was still shining with traces of paint from *Girl in Front of a Looking Glass*. At the second ring, a young woman's voice answered. 'Yes?'

'Hello, this is Clara Reyes.'

She was still thinking of what to say next when she realised the other person had hung up. She thought it must have been by accident, as sometimes happened with mobiles. They were such ghastly inventions which could be used for anything, even to talk, as Jorge used to joke. She pressed the redial button. The same voice replied, in exactly the same tone.

'I think we got cut off,' Clara said. 'I . . .'

Someone hung up again.

Intrigued, Clara tried a third time. Was hung up on again.

She thought about it for a moment. She had just got in from

the GS gallery, and the first thing she had done after taking a shower and washing the paint from her hair and body had been to look for the card and make the call. She was sitting in the dining room on the navy-blue tatami, with her legs crossed and a towel wrapped round her body. She had opened the windows, and a cool evening breeze was fanning her back. A gentle blues number was playing on the stereo. It can't be a problem with the phone. This time they hung up at once. They're doing it on purpose, she thought to herself.

She decided to try another strategy. She used the remote control to switch off the stereo, checked the time on the bookcase clock, and called again.

This time when the woman answered, Clara said nothing.

The silence at both ends of the telephone line grew, deepened and became ridiculous. There was no sound, not even of breathing, although it was obvious that this time they had not hung up. But they were not speaking either. How long will I have to wait for them to make up their minds? thought Clara.

All of a sudden she was disconnected. The clock showed it had taken a minute.

So the silence was the message. This time it had taken longer, which probably meant they did not want her to speak. But they had hung up anyway.

Angrily, she swept back the strands of wet blonde hair covering her eyes. It was clear she was facing some kind of stretching test.

All the great painters stretched their canvases before they began a work. This stretching was the doorway to the hyperdramatic world, a way of preparing the model for what was to come, of warning them that from this point on nothing of what was going to happen would follow a logical pattern or society's accepted norms. Clara was used to being stretched in many different ways. The method usually employed by the artists in *The Circle* and Gilberto Brentano was the full gamut of sado-masochistic techniques. Georges Chalboux, on the other hand, used more subtle means of stretching. He created emotional upheaval by bringing in specially trained people who pretended to love or hate the models used in his works; these people could by turns be threatening, elusive or affectionate, all of which created a great sense of anxiety. Exceptional painters such as Vicky Lledó used themselves to stretch their canvases. Vicky was particularly cruel, because she used genuine emotions – it was as if she could split her personality, as if there was a Vicky-human being and a Vicky-artist in one and the same person, working completely independently of each other.

In order to get through the stretching phase, the canvas had to be aware of two things: the only rule was that there were no rules, and the only possible reaction was to go on.

So it was no use Clara ringing up again and staying silent: she had to take the next step. But in which direction?

Alex Bassan's signature on her thigh was itching. She scratched herself, taking care not to use her nails, while she considered what to do.

She had an idea. It was absurd, which made her think it might be correct (that was nearly always how it was in the world of art). She left the receiver on the mat, stood up and went over to the window. Naked beneath the towel, her damp body did not feel cold or uncomfortable as she felt the cool rush of air.

The rain had washed the night clean. There was no smell of garbage, traffic, or excrement . . . of the centre of Madrid; instead the smell of the sea in the city, the kind of evening breeze that occasionally makes Madrid seem like a seaside resort. Yet there was traffic. The cars went by sniffing each other's backsides and winking at one another with their big luminous eyes. She looked at the building opposite: three windows on the top floor were still lit, and in one of them, which had cobalt-blue curtains, there were some flowerpots. They looked as though they contained blue hyacinths. Clara leant over her balcony ledge and looked down at the street from the top of her four-storey block. The breeze ruffled her hair like a tired puppeteer.

There was no sign of anyone watching her. It was absurd to imagine anyone was spying on her.

Absurd, and therefore correct.

She picked up the cordless phone, again looked over at the clock, then walked back to the window and called the number on the card another time.

41

'Yes?' asked the woman's voice.

Clara waited in silence, as close as she could get to the window, without moving a muscle. The breeze rippled through the fringe of her blue towel. All of a sudden they hung up. She looked back at the clock. A record, which must mean she had done something right and that, yes, however incredible it might seem, she was being watched. Yet she had still not done *every-thing* required of her. She decided to try something new: she phoned once more and, while she was standing at the window, raised a hand and tousled her hair. Almost before she had time to finish the gesture, they hung up.

She smiled her agreement in silence, staring down at the street. 'Aha, now I've caught you: you want me not to talk, to stand at the window, to remain motionless, and . . . what else?' Bassan sometimes told her that her face could look kind and heartless at the same time, 'like an angel who has nostalgic memories of being a devil'. Right now, her expression was more devilish than angelic. 'What more, eh? What more do you want?'

It was always the same when she took the first steps in the strange temple that was art, at the beginning of a new work: she felt aroused. It was the greatest feeling in the world. How could anyone want to work in anything else? How could there be people like Jorge, who were not works of art or artists?

She amused herself by imagining what might come next; her imagination always raced in situations like this. The silence on the phone would last ten minutes if she leaned over her balcony, fifteen if she put one leg down on the ledge, twenty-five if she put the other one there, thirty if she stood up on the ledge, thirty-five if she took a step forward into the void . . . perhaps then someone would respond . . . But that would be ruining the canvas, not stretching it.

She chose another, more modest option. She looked over at the clock again, and then, still standing at the window, dropped the towel to the floor. She dialled the number. Heard the same reply as always. Waited.

The silence went on and on.

When she calculated that a good five minutes had passed, she wondered what else she would need to do if they hung up again.

She did not want to have to think about it. She stood at the window without moving. The silence in her earpiece persisted.

The black cat was to blame.

She saw it for the first time in Ibiza, beneath a blazing sun. The cat was staring at her in that strange way all cats do, opening its quartz-crystal eyes wide and challenging her to discover its secret. But she was fourteen years old, was lying on her stomach on a towel with the top half of her bikini undone, and at that moment secrets did not mean much to her. She won the animal's confidence by calling gently to it. Or perhaps the cat was won over by her beauty. Uncle Pablo, who had invited her to spend the summer in Ibiza, used to ask her jokingly who her image consultant was. Someone as beautiful as you must have one, he said. With her long blonde hair, eyes like two tiny marine planets with no shoreline in view, her taut adolescent silhouette perfectly set off by her blooming skin, Clara was well accustomed to admiring glances.

As a child, the father of a school friend called Borja had given her father a business card, saying he was a TV producer and wanted to offer Clara a screen test. He had never seen anyone like her, he said. Her father got very angry and didn't want to hear any more about it. That night there was a violent argument at home, and Clara's TV career was cut short before it began. This happened when she was seven. At nine, when her father died, it was already too late to disobey him. From then on, life was hard, because his death had left the family unprotected. The draper's store her mother ran, where Clara helped as soon as she was old enough, enabled them to get by, and provided the funds for her brother José Manuel to finish school and enrol to study Law. They could also count on Uncle Pablo's help. He was a businessman married to a young German woman and lived in Barcelona. It was his idea to rescue Clara every summer and take her to his apartment in Cortixera on Ibiza, with her cousins. They were girls, too, but older than Clara and so often left her on her own, but she didn't mind: the mere fact of being able to leave her sad home in Madrid to spend a month in that tiny but immense space, painted bright blue by the sun, was wonderful enough.

43

Nevertheless, nothing would have happened but for the black kitten.

Or perhaps it would, but in a different way: Clara was a believer in the hand of fate. The kitten came over to her, and from being suspicious at first was soon converted into a gleaming velvet ball with deep blue reflections in its fur. This was in the glorious summer of 1996, with its smell of chlorine and sea breeze. But the kitten itself smelt of soap, and it was obvious it belonged to someone because it was too well groomed to have come directly from the wild.

'Hello, there,' Clara greeted it. 'Where's your master, little kitty?'

The animal meowed between her fingers, its mouth shaped like a tiny heart, or an almond split in two. She smiled at it, completely unafraid. In her house in the mountain village of Alberca, where her father had been born and where they spent every summer while he was alive, she had got used to all kinds of pet animals. She stroked the kitten as she might have stroked a lamp containing a genie who could grant all her wishes.

'Are you lost?' she asked.

'He's mine,' a voice replied.

That was when she first spied Talia's brown legs standing in front of her. When Clara looked up she could see her smiling against the sun, and knew at once that the two of them would become friends.

Talia was thirteen, with round saucer-like eyes and coffee-coloured skin. She smiled and spoke at the same time, and with the same sweetness, as if for her the two actions were identical – as if everything she had to say was happy, and all her smiles were words. Her mother was from Maracay in Venezuela; her father was Spanish. They had a house at the other end of the island, near Punta Galera. Talia was in the resort by chance, because her parents had come to visit some friends. So it was the black kitten that brought them together.

Talia's father had a lot of money – much more than Uncle Pablo, who was far from badly off. The house in Punta Galera was an enormous villa by the sea, with a walled-in garden full of trees and shade, flowerbeds and ponds. When Talia invited her there two days later, Clara was amazed to find that they had servants, not simply someone to do the washing and prepare the meals, but people in uniforms with glazed, expressionless faces. But the most incredible discovery was at the swimming pool. This was a huge blue rectangle of water. It seemed unbelievable that Talia's tiny dark body should have this immense sapphire-coloured space all to herself, those liquid tiles she could float across endlessly. Yet there was something else about it that first impressed Clara.

Talia shared the pool with another young girl. Could it be her sister? Or was it a friend?

But she was older than either of them. She was kneeling on all fours near the edge of the pool. All she was wearing was the tiniest of blue tangas. Her body glistened in a very odd way. She didn't change her position in the slightest as Clara and Talia drew closer.

'It's one of my father's works of art,' Talia explained. 'He paid a fortune for it.'

Clara bent down and peered at the unmoving face, the skin gleaming with primer and oils, the hair waving gently in the breeze.

'I don't believe it!' Talia crowed when she saw how surprised Clara was. 'Haven't you ever heard of HD art? Of course it's made of flesh and blood, just like you and I! It's a hyper . . . work.' Clara did not understand the other word. 'She's not in a trance or anything like that, she's simply posing. And the smell comes from the oil paint.'

Eliseo Sandoval. *By the Pool*. 1995. Oil and sun cream on an eighteen-year-old girl wearing a cotton tanga. Clara read the description on a small piece of card placed on the ground near the figure.

Like most people, Clara had heard of hyperdramatic art and had seen films and reports about it, but she had never actually seen one.

It was like coming under a spell. She knelt down beside the work of art and completely forgot everything else. She examined it avidly, from fingertips to the painted hair; from the neck down to the curve of its buttocks. The two thongs of the tanga made a V shape just like the shape of one of the trees in the garden. She pored over every centimetre of immobile flesh as though it were a film she had been wanting to see all her life. She raised a trembling finger and stroked the thing's right thigh. It was like feeling the outline of a flower vase . . . The thing did not even blink.

'Don't do that,' Talia scolded her. 'You're not to touch the paintings. If my father saw you . . . !'

The day was one long torture. It was impossible for her to enjoy herself. It was not Talia's fault, of course; it was the fault of that *cursed* thing, that *obscene*, cursed thing which refused to move but simply stayed there in the sun, by the water, without ever sweating or complaining, lost in the contemplation of a small square of tiles. That paralysed, magical V-shaped tanga, lifeless but at the same time full of life. That was where the blame lay.

At some point in the day, Clara felt ill. She started choking, felt she was drowning. She ran off and hid in the house. She found the kitten on the sofa in the luxurious living room, and curled up alongside it. Clara's cheeks were burning, and she found it hard to breathe. When Talia arrived at last, she looked up at her imploringly.

'Does it *never* move?' she sobbed. 'Doesn't it eat or sleep?'

'Of course it does. It's only on show between eleven and seven.'

At seven o'clock sharp one of the servants went out to tell the work the time. Clara, who had been anxiously watching the clock all afternoon, went up to the piece. She could see how it came to life, stretching each limb after a long pause and then, like a child being born, uncurled its body and raised its head, eyes still closed. She saw the oil paint flash on its chest when it drew a deep breath, watched as it stood up ever so slowly and before her eyes changed into a woman, a girl, into someone just like herself. On a blue background.

That's what I want to be, Clara thought. Exactly that.

Her teeth were chattering.

A woman drew back the cobalt curtains, leaned out and began to water the blue flowers. Suddenly she looked up and took Clara

46

by surprise. After staring at her for a moment, she nodded in acknowledgement. Then she stepped back in from her balcony, closed the window and shut the curtains. Her window panes reflected Clara's naked body framed in her own window: her smooth figure, face without eyebrows and depilated pubis, breasts like wavy lines, hair already dried by the night breeze, right hand still clutching the telephone, all plunged into the cobalt deep-sea blue of the window panes opposite.

The receiver was still silent. But they had not hung up.

Clara had been lost in her memories when the woman had appeared and brought her back to reality with a jolt. Ibiza, Talia and the unforgettable moment when she had discovered HD art dissolved into the darkest night. She could not tell how long she had been waiting in the exact same position. She thought it must be at least two hours. She could feel that the hand holding the receiver was much colder than the rest of her body, and the muscles of that arm had stiffened. She would have given anything to change position, and yet she continued to stand there motionless with the telephone to her ear; she even tried to breathe as little as possible, just as if she were being a work of art. She did not transfer her weight from one foot to another, but stood upright, her left hand on her hip and her knees pressed against the columns of the radiator under the window.

She was tempted to hang up. It was possible that this absurd wait was all a mistake. Perhaps the idea that she should wait naked and motionless in front of the window, telephone in hand, was simply the product of her own imagination. After all, she had still not received a single indication from the painter, whoever that might be, not a single gesture, not a word. Who would dream of painting with invisible silence? And besides, all this was running up a huge telephone bill. Jorge would laugh.

I'll count to thirty . . . OK, to a hundred . . . if nothing happens, I'll hang up, she decided.

Having stood all day as Bassan's work of art, she felt exhausted, was starving and needed to sleep. She started to count. She could hear a gang of kids laughing on the far side of the street. Maybe they had seen her. She was not worried. She was a professional canvas. It was a long time since she had felt ashamed or timid.

Twenty-six . . . twenty-seven . . . twenty-eight . . .

Art was her whole life. She had no idea where its limits were, if indeed there were any.

She had learnt to show and use her anatomy alone, in front of others, and with others. Not to consider any of its nooks and crannies as sacred. As far as possible, to resist the onset of pain. To dream as her muscles contracted. To see space as time and time as something that extended before her like a landscape in which she could stroll or laze around. To control her feelings, to invent, fake, and imitate them. To go beyond all barriers, leave aside any reservations, cast off the burden of remorse. A work of art had nothing of its own: mind and body were dedicated to creating and being created, to becoming transformed.

It was the oddest yet most beautiful profession in the world. She had ventured into it that same summer she had returned from Ibiza, and had never regretted her decision.

At Talia's she had found out that Eliseo Sandoval, the man who had painted *By the Pool*, lived and worked in Madrid with other colleagues, in a chalet near Torrejón. A few weeks later, she went there, alone and scared. The first thing she found was that she was not the only one taking this step, and that HD art was more popular in Spain than she had imagined. The house was teeming with painters and adolescents who aspired to becoming works of art. Eliseo, a young Venezuelan artist with the looks of a boxer and a fascinating cleft chin, charged a few euros to give rough-and-ready classes to underage models. He did this in secret and with no hope of selling any of the works, because HD with minors had not yet been made legal. Clara dipped into her scant savings and began to attend every weekend. Among other things, she got accustomed to being on show naked, both inside and outside the house, on her own or with others present. And was able to spend hours with paint on her skin. And the basics of hyperdrama: the games, rehearsals, the different kinds of expression.

Her brother got wind of these visits, and the conflicts and prohibitions began. Clara discovered that José Manuel wanted to replace her dead father as her guardian. But she would not permit it. She threatened to leave home, and, when the situation became unbearable, did so.

At sixteen she started to work with *The Circle*, an international society of fringe artists who prepared young people for great painters. She got her body tattooed, dyed her hair red, perforated her nose, ears, nipples and navel with studs and was able to study with Wedekind, Cuinet and Ferrucioli. At eighteen she was living with Gabi Ponce, an up-and-coming painter she'd met in Barcelona: her first love, her first artist. By the age of twenty she was getting calls from Alex Bassan, Xavier Gonfrell and Gutiérrez Reguero to create original art works. Then it was the turn of the really well-known ones: Georges Chalboux painted a spirit with her body, Gilberto Brentano turned her into a mare, and Vicky brought out expressions in her face she never thought she was capable of.

Until now though, she had never been painted by a genius.

But, she wondered, what would happen if nobody replied, what would happen if they stretched her to an unreasonable extent, tried to take the situation to its limit, what would happen if . . . ?

The night had turned a deep midnight blue. The breeze that had refreshed her earlier now chilled her to the bone.

She had counted to a hundred, then another hundred, then another. In the end, she had given up counting. She did not dare hang up, because the more time passed the *more important* (and difficult) whatever might be behind this seemed to her. The most important and difficult, the toughest and most risky.

She contemplated the silence, the sparse light, the kingdom of cats. She saw how the early hours in the city passed by, as if she were staring at the imperceptible movement of the hands of a watch.

What would happen, she wondered, if they did not speak to her? When, at what precise moment would it be necessary to conclude that the game was over? Who would yield first in this completely unequal test of strength?

All at once she heard the woman's voice. Her ear had been pressed against the receiver for so long the sound hurt, just like

49

when a blind person is suddenly brought into the light again. The voice was short and sharp. It mentioned a place: plaza Desiderio Gaos, no number. Just a name: Friedman. A time: nine o'clock precisely, the next morning. Then the phone went dead.

Clara wanted to remain in the same pose, holding the receiver up to her ear, for a few moments longer. Then she grimaced and returned to life and its inconveniences.

That was in the early hours of Thursday 22 June, 2006.

The attic. The house in Alberca. Father.

The sun was shining brightly in the garden. It was a wonderful sight: the grass, the orange trees, her father's blue check shirt, his straw hat and thick square glasses. Manuel Reyes was short-sighted, almost obstinately so, or at least resigned to the fact, and was someone who did not mind having to wear such heavy, outdated, tortoise-shell contraptions. He insisted that his glasses added a weight of authority to the detailed descriptions he gave tourists of the paintings in the Prado museum. That was his job: to show people round the galleries, explaining with quiet erudition all the secrets of *Las Lanzas* and *Las Meninas*, his favourite works. Father was pruning the orange trees while her brother José Manuel practised at his easel in the garage – he wanted to be a painter, but Father advised him to study for a career instead – and Clara waited in her room to go to Mass with her mother.

That was when she heard the sound.

In a house like her home, where there were so many, one more was unimportant. But this particular one had intrigued her. Her eyebrows raised in a questioning V. She left her room to discover who or what had made it.

The attic. Its door was ajar. Perhaps her mother had gone in to put something away and had not shut it properly afterwards.

The attic was a forbidden room. Their mother never let them go in there for fear that all the accumulated junk might fall on them. But Clara and José Manuel thought something terrible must be hidden in there. They both agreed on that, and only differed as to what that meant. For her brother, it was something

50

bad; for Clara, it could be good or bad, but above all, it was attractive. Like a sweet, which could taste horrible but still look tempting. If something dreadful had appeared in front of them, José Manuel would have recoiled in horror, whereas Clara would have approached it fascinated, as stealthily as a child at Christmas. Horror would have provoked this contradictory movement: something truly *horrible* would have sent José Manuel running, whereas Clara would have been drawn to it like a possessed woman, as calmly and naturally as a stone dropping into the dark depths of a well.

Now, at last, the horror was calling out to her. She might have shouted to her mother – she could hear her busy in the kitchen – or run down into the garden to seek her father's protection, or gone down still further to the garage to ask her brother for help.

But her mind was made up.

Trembling as she had never trembled before, not even on the day of her first communion, she pushed open the ancient door, and immediately breathed in a swirl of bluish dust. She was forced to step back, coughing and spluttering, which rather took the edge off her adventure. There was so much dust and such a horrible smell, like things fermenting, that Clara feared she would not be able to stand it. And worse still she would get her best Sunday dress filthy.

But, what the heck, it takes a sacrifice to confront horror, she thought. Horror does not grow on trees, within easy reach. It's hard work finding it, as her father always said about money.

She took two or three deep breaths outside the room, then went in again. She took a few timid steps into the evil-smelling darkness, blinking to get used to the unknown. She stumbled over bodies tied up with string, and realised they were old coats. Piles of cardboard boxes. A buckled chess board. A doll with no clothes and empty eye sockets, propped on a shelf. Cobwebs and blue shadows. All of this took Clara by surprise, but did not frighten her. She had been expecting to find this kind of thing.

She was on the verge of feeling completely defrauded when all of a sudden she saw it.

Horror.

It was to her left. A slight movement, a shadow lit by the brightness outside the room. She turned to face it, strangely calm. Her sense of terror had grown to such a pitch she felt about to scream. This must mean she had at last discovered true horror and was face to face with it.

It was a little girl. A girl who lived in the attic. She was wearing a navy-blue Lacoste dress, and had lank, neatly combed hair. Her skin shone like marble. She looked like a corpse, but she was moving. Her mouth opened and shut. She was blinking continuously. And she was staring at Clara.

Her flesh crawled with terror. Her heart pounded violently inside her chest until it was almost choking her. It was an eternal moment, and yet a fleeting but definitive fraction of a second, like the moment of death.

In some inexplicable but powerful way, she realised in that split second that the girl in the attic was the most dreadful sight she had ever seen, or would ever see. It was not only horrible, but unbearable.

And yet, at the same time her happiness knew no bounds. At last she was face to face with horror. And that horror was a girl her own age. They could be friends and play together.

It was then it dawned on her that the Lacoste dress was the one her mother had helped her into that Sunday, that the girl's haircut was just like hers, that her features were the exactly the same, that the mirror was huge, with a frame hidden by the darkness.

'You got scared over nothing,' her mother told her, running up when she heard her cry out, and folding her into her arms.

Dawn was painting the deep indigo of the roof a lighter blue. Clara blinked, and the images of her dream dissolved in the light streaming on to her walls. Everything around her was as it should be, but inside she still felt the swirling memory of her distant childhood, that 'scare over nothing' in the attic of their house in Alberca, a year before her father died.

The alarm clock had gone off: half past seven. She remembered her appointment in plaza Desiderio Gaos with the mysterious Mr Friedman and leapt out of bed.

Since becoming a professional work of art she had learnt to look on dreams as strange instructions sent by an anonymous artist inside us. She was puzzled as to why her unconscious had chosen to place this piece from her life long ago on to the board again.

Perhaps it meant that the door to the attic was open once more.

And that someone was inviting her in to confront horror.

4

Paul Benoit's eyes were not violet, but the lights in the room almost made them look it. Lothar Bosch studied them, and not for the first time knew he had to tread carefully. Where Paul Benoit was concerned, it was always wise to be cautious.

'Do you know what the problem is, Lothar? The problem is that nowadays everything valuable is ephemeral. I mean that in days gone by solidity and the ability to last were what gave value: a sarcophagus, a statue, a temple or a canvas. But now everything of value is consumed, used up, disappears – whether you're talking about natural resources, drugs, protected species or art. We've left behind the era when scarce products were more valuable precisely *because* of their scarcity. That was logical. But what's the consequence of that? Today, for things to be more valuable, they *have to* be scarce. We've inverted cause and effect. We tell ourselves: Good things are rare. So let's make sure bad things are rare, and that will make them good.

He paused and stretched out his hand almost without looking. The Trolley was ready to hand him his porcelain cup, but his gesture took her by surprise. There was a fatal hesitation, and the head of Conservation's fingers knocked against the cup and spilled some of the contents on to the saucer. Quickly and efficiently, the Trolley substituted another saucer and wiped the cup with one of the paper napkins she was carrying on the lacquer table attached to her midriff. The white label hanging from her

53

right wrist described her as Maggie. Bosch did not know Maggie, but of course there were many ornaments he had not come across. Although she was kneeling down, it was obvious Maggie was very tall, probably almost two metres. Perhaps that was the reason why she had not become a work of art, Bosch reflected.

'Nowadays there's no money in buying or selling a painting on canvas,' Benoit went on, 'precisely because they are not consumed quickly enough. Do you know what the key to the success of hyperdramatic art has been? Its short shelf life. We pay more, and more readily, for a work that lasts only as long as someone's youth than for a work that will carry on for a hundred or two hundred years. Why? For the same reason we spend more during the sales than we do on a normal shopping day. It's the "Quick, it'll soon be over!" syndrome. That's why our adolescent works of art are so valuable.'

Perfect result the second time, thought Bosch: the Trolley was carefully following Benoit's movements, and he helped by carefully grasping the second cup she held out to him. 'Try some of this concoction, Lothar. It smells like tea, and tastes of tea, yet it isn't tea. The thing is, if it smells and tastes like tea, to me it *is* tea. But it doesn't make me nervous and it soothes my ulcer.'

Bosch caught hold of the delicate imitation porcelain cup the Trolley was offering him. He looked down at the liquid. It was hard to make out its real colour in the funereal violet light of the room. He decided it might be violet as well. He lifted it to his nose. It was true, it did smell like tea. He tried it. It tasted like nothing on earth. Like caramel liquidised with cough medicine. He stifled a grimace and was pleased to see Benoit had not noticed. Better that way. He pretended to drink some more.

The room they were in was part of the MuseumsQuartier. It was large and rectangular, soundproofed and dotted with violet-coloured lights: in the ceiling the lights were a soft purple, in the floor a cobalt-blue colour, while the square wall lights were a pale lavender, so that they all seemed to be floating in a violet fish tank. Except for the Trolley, there were no other ornaments. The far wall of the room was like a TV gallery. Ten closed-circuit monitors were grouped together; they were all switched off, and reflected crescent moons of violet light.

Sitting in front of them were Willy de Baas and two of his assistants. They were about to begin the psycholgical support session held every Saturday night. This came under the Conservation department, which Paul Benoit was directly responsible for. It was obvious De Baas felt nervous at having his boss breathing down his neck.

With an expression of pure pleasure, Benoit put the cup back on its saucer. He licked his lips and looked across at Bosch. The wall lights made his pupils look red; his bald patch glowed like a cardinal's cap, and his feet and the lower half of his trousers gave off violet gleams.

'All of which explains why what happened to *Deflowering* is so dangerous, Lothar. Adolescent works of art like that are extremely valuable. Fortunately, we have managed to keep the news quiet in Amsterdam. Only those at the highest levels know about it. Stein made no comment, and Hoffmann could scarcely believe it. And, of course, they haven't informed the Maestro. 'Rembrandt' is due to open on 15 July, and some of the canvases are still being stretched or primed. So the Maestro is unreachable. But it's said heads will roll. Not yours or April's of course . . .'

'It was nobody's fault, Paul,' Bosch said. 'We were just caught out, that's all. Whether it was Oscar Díaz or not, it was a good plan, and they caught us out.'

'The thing is,' Benoit insisted, holding out his cup for the Trolley to refill it, 'that we have to make sure it's we who find him. We need to interrogate him ourselves – the police wouldn't know how to get all the information we need out of him. You understand, don't you?'

'I understand perfectly, and we're working on it. We've searched his apartment in New York and his hotel room here in Vienna, but we haven't found anything unusual. We know he's a keen photographer and likes the countryside. We're trying to find his sister and mother in Mexico, but I don't think they'll have much of interest to tell us.'

'Didn't I hear he had a girlfriend in New York . . . ?'

'Yes, by the name of Briseida Canchares. She's Colombian, an art graduate. The police don't know about her: we preferred not to tell them, and to look for her ourselves. Briseida met Oscar in

Amsterdam a month ago. Several of Oscar's colleagues saw them together. She got a grant from Leiden University to study classical painters and lived there from the beginning of the year, but she's vanished too . . .'

'That's a remarkable coincidence.'

'Of course. Thea talked to her Leiden friends yesterday. Apparently, Briseida went off to Paris with another boyfriend. We've sent Thea there to see if it's true. We're expecting news from her at any moment.' Bosch wondered whether Benoit would be offended if he realised he was not going to drink any more of his horrible concoction. He carefully concealed the cup under his left hand.

'We have to find her and make her talk, Lothar. By whatever means necessary. You do realise the situation we're in, don't you?'

'Yes, I do Paul.'

'*Deflowering* was going to be sold at Sotheby's in the autumn. The sale would have made even the sports pages. Headlines like: Naked teenager sold at auction; The most valuable adolescent in history . . . well, the sort of nonsense you always find on the front pages . . . except, that in this case, the nonsense would have been accurate. *Deflowering* was the most valuable piece in the 'Flowers' exhibition, and we haven't found a replacement. The offers we were receiving were far higher than those we got in the past for Purple, Marigold or Tulip. In fact, the bidding had *already* started. You know how we like to play people off against each other.'

Bosch nodded as he pretended to take another sip of tea. All he did was wet his lips.

'You'd be astonished if you knew how much people were willing to pay for the monthly rental of that work,' Benoit went on. 'Besides, I knew how to put pressure on the most interested collectors. *Deflowering* had been very sad recently. Willy thought she might be entering a depression, but I had an idea of how we could use that to our advantage.' Benoit's eyes glinted triumphantly. 'We spread the news that the cost of psychotherapy would make the rental of the painting even more expensive. And then any buyer had to bear in mind that the work was only fourteen and so needed to go out, travel, have fun, buy herself lots of things . . . in short, that they would have to spend a fortune if they didn't want to pay three times more for a restoration. Stein told me it was a masterstroke.' He pursed his lips and rolled back his eyes in a typical gesture. Bosch knew he was listening to echoes of the praise he had received. He loves reminding himself of his triumphs, thought Bosch. 'In two years we would have recouped the cost of the work from the rental fees alone. Then we could have negotiated a replacement, if the Maestro had agreed to it. The original canvas wouldn't have been so young any more, so we'd have got rid of her. But there would have been another one. We'd have had to lower the rent a bit, of course, but we could have used the difficulty we found in substituting the original to cream off another substantial profit. *Deflowering* would have gone down in history as one of the most expensive works of art ever. But now . . .'

The TV monitors started to hum, and came alive. The support session was about to start. De Baas and his assistants were ready to hear complaints from works with problems. Benoit did not appear to notice: he was pursing his lips again, but this time his expression was far from triumphant.

'But now all that's down the drain . . .'

One of De Baas' assistants gestured towards the Trolley. It would have been no use trying to shout at her, because the Trolley was wearing ear protectors, as all ornaments did to prevent them hearing any private conversations. The Trolley got delicately to her feet, padded barefoot across the violet floor carrying the teapot and cups, and began to serve De Baas tea. Who could Maggie be, Bosch suddenly asked himself; from what remote part of the world could she have come, and with what remote hopes? What was she doing naked in a room like this, her head shaved, wearing ear protectors, her skin painted mauve with black flourishes, and a board strapped to her waist for a table? He would never get an answer, because ornaments did not speak to anyone, and no one ever asked them anything.

'What I'd like to know, Lothar,' Benoit suddenly said, 'is if all this might be some kind of . . . if there's any suggestion it might have been staged.' As he said this, he waved his right hand in the air. 'Do you follow me?'

'You mean that . . .?'

'I mean could it all be a . . . I shudder even to say it . . . a piece of theatre?'

'Theatre.' Bosch echoed him.

At that precise moment the face of *Jacinto Moteado* appeared on the TV monitors. This was the first work to have asked for support, and had obviously just had a shower and washed the paint off. The smooth skull and primed skin, devoid of eyebrows and lashes, stood out against a black background. The eyes were as expressionless as milky marbles. The label around the neck was just visible.

'*Buona sera*, Pietro,' De Baas said cheerfully, speaking into the microphone. 'How can we help you?'

'*Hello, Mr De Baas.*' The voice of the Italian work boomed out through the loudspeakers. '*The usual problem. The dioxacine brings me out in a rash. I don't know why Mr Hoffmann insists on using it for the indigo on my arms . . .*'

Benoit only followed the conversation between De Baas and the canvas for a moment. Then he spoke to Bosch once more:

'Yes, a piece of theatre. Let me explain. At first sight, Oscar Díaz is a psycho-whatever, isn't he? He's looked after the painting several times and while he was doing so, he was getting his kicks imagining how he was going to destroy it. He plans everything carefully, and decides to make his move on Wednesday night. He is the van driver, but instead of heading for the hotel, he goes to the woods. There, he's got everything prepared. He forces the work to read an absurd text and records her voice, then slices her up and performs his crazy rituals, whatever they might have been. That's the theory, isn't it?'

'More or less, yes.'

'Well now, just imagine it was all stage-managed. Imagine that Díaz is no crazier than you or I, and that the recordings and all the sadistic paraphernalia are a piece of theatre aimed at throwing us off the scent. To make us think it was the work of some serial killer when in reality it was our competitors who paid him to destroy the painting just before the auction.' He paused, raised an eyebrow. 'You used to be a policeman, Lothar. What do you make of the idea?'

Ridiculous, Bosch thought to himself. Fortunately for him, he did not have to conceal his thoughts as he had done the cup to prevent Benoit guessing what he was thinking.

'I find it hard to accept,' he said finally.

'Why?'

'Because I simply cannot believe someone was capable of doing that to a girl like Annek simply to spoil our multi-million dollar sale, Paul. You have more experience in that area, but . . . just think – if they wanted to destroy the canvas, there are a thousand quicker ways of doing it . . . and even if they wanted to imitate a sadistic act, as you say, there are other ways to go about it . . . she was a fourteen-year-old girl, godammit. They cut her up with . . . with a sort of electric saw . . . and she was still alive while they were doing it . . .'

'She was not a fourteen-year-old girl, Lothar,' Benoit corrected him. 'She was a painting valued at a starting price of fifty million dollars.'

'OK, but . . .'

'Either you see it that way, or you'll be on completely the wrong track.'

Bosch nodded. For a few moments all that could be heard was the dialogue between De Baas and Speckled Hyacinth.

'Dioxacine helps create a deeper violet-blue colour, Pietro.'

'You always say the same thing, Mr De Baas . . . but it's not your arms that itch the whole time.'

'Please, Pietro, don't get so upset. We're trying to help you. I'll tell you what we'll do. We'll talk to Mr Hoffmann. If he says the dioxacine is essential, we'll find some way to anaesthetise your arms . . . just your arms – what do you think? . . . It could be done . . .'

'Fifty million dollars is a lot of money,' said Benoit.

At this, Bosch's semblance of calm evaporated. He stopped nodding and glared at Benoit.

'Yes, a lot. But just you point out to me the person capable of doing that to a fourteen-year-old girl in order to spoil our million-dollar auction. Point that person out to me and tell me: He's the one. And let me look him in the eye and see for myself there's nothing but money, works of art and auctions on his mind. Only then will I admit you're right.'

A clink of china. One of De Baas' assistants was putting the empty cups back on the Trolley, who was waiting on her knees to receive them.

'Of course I'm not saying the person who destroyed the canvas was a Saint Francis of Assisi, if that's what you mean . . .'

'He was a sadistic bastard.' Bosch's cheeks flamed a colour that the lights in the room turned to a deep maroon. 'I can't wait to lay my hands on him.'

The two men fell silent. 'Getting mad with Benoit won't get you anywhere,' Bosch told himself. 'Calm down.' He glanced over at the screens. The canvas was busy agreeing with De Baas' advice. Bosch remembered that Speckled Hyacinth was displayed with the right calf lifted over the shoulder and the head resting on the sole of the foot. He could not imagine himself twisted into such a contortion for even a split second, but Hyacinth put up with it for six hours a day.

Bosch realised Benoit was also looking at the screens.

'My God, what it takes to conserve these works. Sometimes I dream of destroying them, too.'

Hearing words like this from the Head of Conservation took Lothar Bosch aback. Benoit often spoke harshly when there were no canvases or luxury ornaments who could hear him, but he did not usually show any weakness. At least, not in public. He gave the false impression of being a gentle old age pensioner one could trust. His bald, round head looked like an anti-stress ball: you looked at it, and it seemed you could squeeze it to help you relax. In fact, it was he who squeezed yours without you being aware of it. Bosch knew that before joining the Foundation he had been a private clinical psychologist in an upper-class district of Paris, and that his previous profession was very useful to him in dealing with the canvases. A very special therapeutic coup had led the doctor to change jobs overnight. Valerie Roseau, a young French canvas Van Tysch had used to paint his early masterpiece *The Pyramid*, had one day refused to continue to be shown in the Stedelijk. This provoked a multi-million dollar crisis. Valerie had been in treatment for years for her neurosis. The specialists knew this was at the root of her refusal to be exhibited, and tried all they could to cure her. Benoit adopted a different strategy: instead of trying to cure Valerie's neurosis, he convinced her to carry on in the museum. Stein immediately offered him the post of Head of Conservation.

The canvases, especially the youngest ones, all loved talking to Benoit. They poured out their fears to this bald grandfather who spoke with a French accent, and invariably decided to struggle on. It was a wonderful act. In fact, Benoit was a dangerous individual: more dangerous, in his own way, than Miss Wood. Bosch thought he was the most dangerous of them all.

Except, of course Stein and the Maestro.

'They're young and rich,' Benoit said scornfully, staring at the monitors. 'What more do they want, Lothar? I can't understand them. They have clothes, jewellery, human ornaments and toys, cars, drugs, lovers . . . if they tell us of somewhere in the world where they'd like to live, we buy them a palace there. So what more do they want?'

'A different kind of life, perhaps. They're human, too.'

Benoit's forehead furrowed. The frown stayed for several moments while Bosch smiled wearily but stubbornly at him.

'Please Lothar, don't say such things while I'm drinking my tea substitute. My ulcer has been worse recently. What Van Tysch has offered them is something far greater than they themselves are, or their wretched lives. He's offered them eternity. Don't they realise it? They are incredibly beautiful works of art, the most beautiful a painter has ever created, but that's not enough for them: they complain of backaches, of itchy backsides or of depression. Please, Lothar, please . . .'

'All I meant was . . .'

'No, Lothar, don't give me that.' Benoit lifted his hand. It was as though he were waving away a plate of disgusting food. 'Beauty requires sacrifice. You've no idea what it costs us to keep these little flowers in good condition. So don't give me that. Let's drop it.'

He waved his cup angrily in the air. The Trolley rushed over, arching her back so that her stomach, with the tray attached, stuck out beneath it. She was almost bent over double backwards, because Benoit had barely raised his arm. Her depilated, mauve-coloured sex pointed straight at Bosch.

'Would you like some more, too, Lothar?' Benoit asked, signalling to the ornament to serve him another half cup.

'No thanks,' Bosch said, taking the opportunity to get rid of his still almost completely full cup on to the Trolley.

'Did you like it?'

'It was delicious.'

'It is, isn't it? I order it personally from a firm in Paris. They have substitutes for almost everything you could think of, even substitutes of substitutes.'

There was another silence. Purple Tulip appeared on the screens.

'Will you be staying long in Vienna, Paul?' Bosch asked eventually.

The question caught Benoit just as he was sipping his tea. He drank greedily as he shook his head.

'Only as long as is necessary. I want to be sure the information about the case is kept out of the news. That's proving quite difficult. For example, yesterday I had a telephone conversation with a bigwig in the Austrian Ministry of the Interior. Those people make your blood boil. He was trying to put pressure on me to make it public. My God, what's happening in this crazy country just because at the end of the last century a neo-Nazi party raised its head? They treat everything as if it were breakable, they use tweezers all the time . . . All they think of is covering their backs . . . He even had the nerve to accuse me of putting the population of Vienna in danger! I told him: "As far as I'm aware, the only things in danger at the moment are our works of art." The idiot! Well, I didn't say that to him, of course.'

Bosch laughed soundlessly, simply opening his mouth and tilting back his head.

'Paul, you need intravenous injections of that tea substitute of yours.'

'I don't like Austrians. They're too twisted. That swindler Sigmund Freud was Austrian. I swear that . . .'

There was a noise at the door and Miss Wood burst in.

'Did that policeman we talked to yesterday get in touch with you?' she asked Bosch directly.

'Felix Braun? No. Why?'

'I left a message on his answering machine demanding he call us at once. His men found the van early this morning, but they didn't tell us a thing. I only found out because a little bird told me so. Oh, hello there, Paul. I'm glad you came. We can all have a good laugh together.'

'The van?' Benoit said. 'What about Díaz?'

'Not a trace.'

The two men looked concerned at the news. For a moment all that could be heard was the dialogue between De Baas and the purple *Flower*. An assistant brought up a chair. Miss Wood's slight frame collapsed into it. She crossed her legs, revealing a pair of jodphurs and a pair of pointed leather boots. Her slender neck rose high above her shoulders, where she was wearing a purple-coloured silk scarf. The badge in her lapel matched the scarf. She looked like a pretty adolescent, an effeminate daddy's boy who had just been expelled from university for the third or fourth time. There was something dispiriting about her: it was not the way she sat, nor the ironic smile on her lips, not even the way she looked at people – although Bosch preferred seeing her in profile to having her stare at him – or the striking clothes she wore. Taken one by one, each of the components that made up Miss Wood was attractive: it was when they were all put together that they became somehow disagreeable.

'Would you like some tea substitute?' Benoit said, pointing to the Trolley.

'No thanks, Paul. You have it, you're going to need it. Because I still haven't told you the best bit.'

Bosch and Benoit looked at her.

'The van was found hidden in trees forty kilometres north of the area where they discovered the work of art. As we suspected, the tracking device had been disconnected. In the back was a bloody sheet of plastic. Perhaps he used it to wrap the work in after he had cut her to pieces, so he could drag her across the grass without getting stains on him. And by the side of the road there were other tyre tracks, apparently from a saloon car. He had another car waiting for him. Our Mr Fixit planned it all very thoroughly.'

It hurts, Mr De Baas. It really hurts. I can bear it, but it does hurt.'

It was the voice of *Imaginary Orchid*. She was in the gym for canvases in the MuseumsQuartier and had adopted a classic stretching pose: standing with her head between her feet with her hands clasping her calves. In order to film her face, the camera was behind her back almost at ground level. And the *Orchid*'s face appeared upside down on the screen.

'Does it only hurt when you adopt the pose, Shirley?' De Baas wanted to know.

Benoit was looking not at the screens but at Wood. He seemed suddenly irritated.

'April, for the love of God, where has Díaz got to? He is only a guard. He can't have dreamed up a plan as sophisticated as this! Where is he?'

'Spin a globe and stick your finger in it, Paul. You might get lucky.'

'I warn you, I'm not in the mood for jokes just now.'

'It's not a joke. Several hours went by between the moment he destroyed the canvas and when we started to look for him. If we bear in mind that he had another car, and calculate he also had false papers, by now he could be anywhere in the world.'

'Now for example, the pain is . . . ow!'

'Don't keep it in, Shirley. Don't try to suppress it, because that way we won't know how much it is hurting you . . . I can see the effort you're making . . . let yourself go. Express the pain you're feeling . . .'

'We have to find that Colombian girl,' Benoit said between clenched teeth.

'That seems easier,' Miss Wood said. 'Thea has just called me from Paris. Our dear Briseida Canchares is with Roger Levin, Gaston's eldest son.'

'The marchand?' Benoit drew his hand across his face. 'Everything is getting more and more complicated . . .'

'I have to get through it . . . Mi . . . ster De Ba . . . aas . . . I am a work of a . . . art, M . . . ister De Ba . . . a . . . aaaaas'

'No, no Shirley, that's a mistake. You can't get beyond your pain. I want you to express it . . . Come on, Shirley, don't hold it in, you can scream if you need to . . .'

'Roger and the girl are going to one of those surprise parties the Roquentins organise to attract clients and deal in illegal works. But the real surprise will be when they get home.' Wood glanced at her watch. 'Thea is going to call me at any minute.'

'Shout, Shirley. As hard as you can. I want to hear how much your back hurts . . .'

'N-n-n-n- . . . N-n-n-n-n-n-n-nnnnnn . . .'

Bosch was observing the screens. The canvas' forehead was racked with dry sobs – she was primed and had no tears to cry. Her knees, on a level with her face, were trembling. Benoit and Wood were the only people in the room paying absolutely no attention to what was happening on the televisions. The Trolley was not looking either, but then she was only an ornament.

'April, scare her as much as is necessary,' Benoit said. 'Her and that idiot Levin boy, if need be.'

Wood nodded.

'We plan to scare them so much they'll piss themselves, Paul.'

'Is Romberg in Vienna?'

'No, Romberg is in Czechoslovakia looking into that fake copies business. Last week we found a false sketch of one of the figures from *Couple*. We convinced him he didn't want to have anything to do with fakes any more. I don't think he'll blab, but it's still a delicate matter.'

'Can't you see, Shirley? It hurts *too much*. I'll count to three, then you shout as loud as you like, OK?'

'April, forget the fakes for a moment. This has priority.'

'Since when have you also been Head of Security, Paul?'

'It's not that, April, it's not that . . .'

'As hard as you can! . . . A real *howl*, Shirley.'

'The Austrian police are searching for Díaz even under the Minister of Interior's carpet,' said Wood. 'I don't think there's any need to invest more men or money in a job they can do for us. The fact that the dogs bring us our prey doesn't make them the hunters, Paul.'

'Two . . .'

'OK, let's do it your way, April. All I want is . . .'

'Three!'

'*AaaaaaaaaAAAAAHHHH . . .!*'

It was strangely fascinating to see a face shouting upside down: at the top, beneath the tiny pyramid of a forehead, a huge blind eye with a pink tentacle; at the bottom, two slits sunk into furrows. Except for the Trolley, everyone raised their hands to their ears.

'Shit, Willy!' Benoit shouted. 'Can't you put a gag on that idiot? It's impossible to talk!'

Willy De Baas moved away from the microphone and turned down the loudspeakers.

'I'm sorry, Paul. It's Shirley Carloni. In April she came apart and we had to operate, do you remember? But she's still not right.'

Bosch remembered that the expression 'came apart' had become popular among the Conservation staff for 'Flowers'. It described the worst problem the works of art faced: damage to their spines.

'Pull her out for a week, suspend the flexibility drugs, give her more painkillers and call the surgeons,' said Benoit.

'That's exactly what I had in mind.'

'Well do it then, and keep the volume of your wonderful speaker down, would you? . . . What was I saying? April, I have no wish to supervise your work, far from it. You know how much we all trust you. But this problem is . . . let's just say . . . a bit special. This bastard has destroyed not merely an adolescent, but part of the world's heritage.'

'I'll take the responsibility, Paul,' said Miss Wood with a smile.

'You'll take the responsibility, fine. I do as well, and so does everyone else in this artistic enterprise, April. That's what we can tell the insurance companies, if you like: "We take the responsibility." We can also say the same to our investors and private clients: "Don't worry, we take the responsibility." Then we organise a dinner in a salon with ten Rayback nudes in it, and fifty wonderful ornaments as tables, vases and chairs à la Stein, we leave them all open-mouthed in astonishment, and then ask them for more money. But they will reply, quite correctly: "You put on a wonderful display, but if a guard from your own security team can destroy such an expensive work of art and get away with it, who on earth will want to insure any of the works in future? And who will pay to have them?"

As he spoke, Benoit waved the empty cup in the air. The Trolley had been waiting for him to replace it on her table, but Benoit had been too carried away to notice. The ornament did not say or do anything beyond crouching there attentively, trying to keep her balance. As she drew breath, her stomach made the teapot tremble. As he observed her antics, Bosch could scarcely stop himself laughing.

'This business is built on beauty,' Benoit was saying. 'But beauty is nothing without power. Just imagine if all the Egyptian slaves had died, and the pharoah had been forced to carry all those blocks of stone himself . . .'

'He'd come apart,' Bosch quipped.

'So art is power,' Benoit declared. 'A wall has been breached in our fortress, April, and it's up to you to plug the hole.'

He finally appeared to realise he was still holding the cup, and quickly moved to replace it on the Trolley, who stood up nimbly.

At that moment, as if a black cloud had passed over the room, it turned a darker shade of purple.

'*I'd like to know what's happening to Annek,*' a voice with a Haarlem accent said.

They all turned towards the screens, though they knew it was Sally before they saw her. She was leaning against one of the bars in the gym for the canvases, and the camera was filming her to halfway down her thighs. She was wearing a T-shirt and shorts. The shorts cut into her groin. She had removed the paint with solution but even so her ebony skin had dark purple highlights. The yellow of her neck label stood out between her breasts.

'*I don't believe the story about flu . . . the only reason for withdrawing a work from this fucking collection is if they come apart, and if Papa Willy can hear me, let him deny it . . .*'

Willy de Baas had switched off the microphones, and was whispering hurriedly to Benoit.

'We told the works that Annek has the flu, Paul.'

'Fuck,' growled Benoit.

Sally smiled all the time she was talking. In fact, she looked very happy. Bosch thought she must be drugged.

'Look at my skin, Papa Willy: look at my arms and here, on my stomach . . . If you switch the lights off, you'll still be able to see me. My skin is like a raspberry past its sell-by date. I look at it and feel like eating plums. I've been like this since last year, and I haven't been withdrawn even once. If you don't come apart, you're on show, flu or no flu. But Annek and I will never come apart, will we? . . . Our postures with our backs straight are easier than most. How lucky we are, they all say. We're the lucky ones, apparently. But I reckon it depends on how you look on it . . . it's true, the other works are carried out on stretchers at the end of the day . . . and they are jealous of us because we can walk without any back problems and we don't need any of those flexibility implants that mean you can kick yourself in the shin with the same foot, isn't that so, Papa Willy? . . . But it also means we're on the outside, we aren't part of the group of those who have officially come apart . . . So cut the crap. What's wrong with Annek? Why have you withdrawn her?'

'Fuck,' Benoit said again.

'She could cause real trouble,' De Baas said, twisting his head towards Benoit.

'She will cause real trouble,' one of his assistants insisted.

'What's happening, Papa Willy? Why don't you reply?'

Benoit swore indignantly again, and stood up.

'Let me deal with her, Willy. Why on earth did you tell her that nonsense about flu?'

'What else could we do?'

'Papa Willy? Are you there . . .?'

Benoit scurried over to De Baas, talking all the time.

'This is a work of art valued at thirty million dollars, Willy. Thirty big bricks and a monthly rental I prefer not to mention . . .' He took the microphone from De Baas, 'And she has become indispensable: the owner will only have *her*. We have to tread carefully . . .'

Benoit's voice suddenly became mellifluous.

'Sally? It's Paul Benoit.'

'*Wow!*' Sally unhooked her thumbs from her shorts and stood with arms akimbo. '*Grandpa Paul in person . . . I'm truly honoured, Grandpa Paul . . . Grandpa Paul is always the one who comes to the phone when things go wrong, isn't he? . . .*'

I'm sure she's drugged, Bosch thought. Sally was slurring her words, and her plump lips stayed open when she fell silent. Bosch thought she was one of the most beautiful pieces in the collection.

'That's right,' Benoit said gently. 'That's how things work with us: they pay Willy less than me, so he spouts more nonsense. But this is pure chance – I happened to be in Vienna and wanted to come and see you all.'

'*Well, make sure you don't come down to the gym, Grandpa. Some of the flowers have turned carnivorous. They say you look after those dogs of yours in Brittany better than you do us.*'

'I don't believe that for a minute. You're wicked, Sally.'

'*What happened to Annek, Grandpa? Tell me the truth, just this once.*'

'Annek is fine,' replied Benoit. 'The thing is that the Maestro has decided to withdraw her for a few weeks to work on some details.'

This was an absurd excuse, but Bosch knew that Benoit had a lot of experience in fooling the works of art.

'*Work on some details . . .? Come off it, Grandpa! Do you think I'm an idiot? The Maestro finished her two years ago . . . If he withdrew her, it's because he wants to substitute her . . .*'

'Don't get mad, Sally, that's what I've been told, and I'm usually told the truth. There isn't going to be any substitute for *Deflowering* for two years at least. The Maestro has taken her to Edenburg to correct a few details of her body colour, that's all. In theory, he's within his rights – *Deflowering* hasn't been sold yet.'

'*Are you telling me the truth, Grandpa?*'

'I couldn't lie to you, Sally. Doesn't Hoffmann do the same with you? Doesn't he renew the purple every now and then?'

'*Yes, he does.*'

'She's falling for it . . .' one of the assistants whispered admiringly. 'She's falling for it!' De Baas hissed to silence him.

'But why didn't you tell the truth from the beginning, Grandpa? Why invent the story about the flu'?'

'What else could we say? That one of the most expensive of Bruno van Tysch's works was not properly finished? And I need hardly tell you, Sally, that this has to be kept between you and me, right?'

'I'll keep the secret,' Sally paused for a moment, and her expression changed. This made Bosch forget about works of art and suddenly see a solitary, fearful young woman on the TV screens.

'Well, I guess I won't be seeing the poor girl for some time . . . I feel sorry for her, Grandpa. Annek is a child, and she has no one . . . I think that's why I liked her, because I'm all alone too . . . Do you know I invited her to go out to the Prater this Monday? . . . I thought that might help her . . .'

'I'm sure you did help her, Sally. Annek feels better now.'

Cynicism three times a day after meals, thought Bosch.

'When am I going back to Mr P's house?'

Bosch recalled that *Purple Tulip* had been bought almost fifteen years earlier by someone called Perlman. He was one of the Foundation's most valued clients. Sally was the tenth substitute for the work. Both she and all her predecessors called him 'Mr P'. Lately, it seemed Mr P had taken a fancy to Sally, and was demanding that she remain with him after the end of the year. Since he paid an astronomical price for renting her, his wishes were commands. On top of that, Perlman had graciously allowed *Tulip* to be lent for this European tour, so he was owed this favour.

'The person who can tell you about that is Willy. I'll put him on. Take care!'

'Thanks, Grandpa.'

As De Baas took up the conversation again, Benoit seemed to be removing a mask in the cold violet wall lights. He took a handkerchief out of his jacket and mopped his face, giving vent to his frustrations.

'Believe me, I'm so sick of those dumb paintings . . . shitty little girls and boys raised to the level of works of art . . .' his voice altered as he copied Sally's accent: '"I feel so alone too" . . . she's been plucked out of a black ghetto, she earns more in a month than I earned in a year at her age, and still she moans on about how "alone" she is! How stupid can you get?'

A single mosquito whine of a laugh greeted this tirade – it was Miss Wood. No joke in any language ever made her even smile, but Bosch had often seen her laughing like this when someone was spilling their bile.

'You were great, boss,' an assistant said, giving Benoit the thumbs up.

'Thanks. And don't make any more excuses about flu, whatever you do. We need to be very careful with these canvases, and to keep them in good condition, we have to be subtle. They're all drugged, but they're still smart. If we substituted them earlier, we'd save a lot on conservation. Of course though, I prefer to keep on the "Monsters".' He paused, then puffed, 'This art business is getting crazier and crazier . . .'

'Thank Heavens we have "Grandpa Paul" to restore all the paintings,' said Miss Wood.

Benoit pretended not to hear. He walked towards the door, but stopped halfway.

'I have to go. Believe it or not, this morning I have to go to a private concert in the Hofburg. A top-level meeting. Four Austrian politicians and me. An eighteen-year-old countertenor is going to sing *Die Schöne Müllerin*. If I could get out of going, I'd be a happy man.' He wagged a finger in the air. 'Please, April, we need results.'

He continued wagging his finger after falling silent, then left the room.

Miss Wood's mobile phone began to ring.

'We've got the Colombian girl,' she said to Bosch after the call ended.

They both hurried out of the violet room.

5

Flesh tints. She could see a flesh-coloured figure split into five by the mirrors as she did her exercises on the tatami. They were strange exercises, typical of a professional canvas: arching her back, rolling into a ball, standing immobile on tiptoe. Afterwards, she took a shower, ate a vegetarian breakfast, made up eyebrows, lashes and lips, then chose a cotton trouser suit with a zip and a large belt buckle, all in the same pink flesh colour. That and light beige went very well with her pale body and her blonde, almost platinum hair. She dialled Gertrude at the GS gallery and left a message on her answerphone. It was impossible for her, she said, to go to the gallery that day because she had an urgent appointment. She would call again. She knew the German woman would raise hell, but she couldn't care less. She picked up her bag and her car keys, and left her apartment.

Finding the place was easy. The plaza Desiderio Gaos was in Mar de Cristal. It was an empty oval surrounded by new, symmetrical buildings built of pink brick. The only building that had no number was an eight-storey-high office block. There were no nameplates at all on the shiny metal entrance doors. She pressed the button and received a low hum in reply. She pushed open one of the doors and found herself in a spacious, aseptic reception area that smelt of leather upholstery. Scattered here and there were low tables filled with catalogues and fleshy three-piece suites. The walls were as bare and smooth as she was under her clothes. The floor looked slippery. There was nobody to be seen. Or perhaps there was. In the centre of the hall was a tall reception desk, and in the centre of that was a head. Clara walked over towards it. It belonged to a young woman. Her hairstyle was striking, but even more eyecatching was the clasp holding it up: it was a small plastic hand, with the fingers spread like claws. The locks of hair flowed up and over the fingers. She was wearing heavy make-up, her eyes almost hidden in all the beige colouring.

'Good morning.'

'Good morning. I'm Clara Reyes. I have an appointment with Mr Friedman.'

'Yes.'

A waft of perfume enveloped the girl as she got up from behind the desk. She was wearing a crêpe de Chine dress, platform shoes and a velvet choker. Clara wondered whether she was an ornament, but she could not see any labels on her wrists or ankles.

'This way.'

They went down a short corridor. The tasteful fitted carpet muffled their footsteps, so there was a sudden gap of silence as they walked along. Another door. A gentle tap. Opening. An office with walls the colour of a fresh-cheeked baby. Fresh orchids in one corner. Mr Friedman was standing in the middle of this tranquil world. There were two white chairs on either side of the desk, one of them with no back, but Friedman did not ask her to sit down. Nor did he greet her, smile, say or do anything. The silence was as cruel as that which greets bad news. When the receptionist left them, Clara and Friedman stared at each other.

He was a strange sight. He was wearing a well-cut worsted suit, a silk tie and Italian shirt, all of them a slightly darker version of Clara's suit. But his features looked odd: the two halves of his face did not match. It was as if God's hand had trembled when he was creating the shape. He was so still and silent that Clara even thought this must be a latex model of Friedman, and that the real person would appear at any moment through one of the doors. Just then, he moved. He turned on his heel, and with a swooping gesture picked up the paper and pen that had been hidden on the table by his body until now. He picked up the sheet of paper between two slender fingers and held it at shoulder height.

'Let's start with this. Read it carefully. There are six clauses for you. If you agree to them, sign it. If not, get out. If you have any doubts, ask. Understood?'

'Perfectly, thank you.'

There were about three metres between them, but Friedman made no attempt to come any closer. He was still standing next to his desk holding the piece of paper aloft. Clara thought of a dolphin trainer holding out a little fish for his pet to grasp. She sighed, walked over to Friedman, and took the contract. Then she stepped back again to read it.

It was a typical official contract. The letterhead was a design: a hand on a thigh, a foot on the hand, an elbow on the foot: together they formed a light-beige-coloured star. She recognised it at once. It was the logo of F&W, one of the best priming work-shops in the world, along with Leonardo and Double I. She had not realised they had a branch in Spain, and to judge by how new the building was, perhaps they had just moved there.

She felt a surge of pure joy. She had never been primed by F&W before (nor by Leonardo, or Double I) because they were very expensive and most of the artists who had painted her could not afford the outlay. Chalboux and Brentano were different, but they had their own priming companies. Vicky had had her primed once for the *White Queen* performance by the Spanish company Crisálida. Gamaio had used Crisálida too. All the others had decided to paint her without primer, even though it was essential to produce a work of the highest quality. The fact that the artist who was contracting her had chosen F&W rein-forced her conviction that it must be someone very important.

There were six clauses, all of them typical in a priming com-pany contract. She, Clara Reyes Pijuán, was the canvas, with such and such number in the international classification of can-vases. F&W was the priming company. It would not accept any responsibility for damage caused by the canvas' failure to follow procedures. The canvas was to submit to all the tests the com-pany considered necessary. The canvas is duly warned that some of these might involve physical and/or psychological risks, or cause offence to her morals, customs or education. The priming company considers the canvas as 'artistic material' for all pur-poses, although the following will *not* be considered as part of the canvas – her clothes, home, family and friends. However, her body and everything in it is to be regarded as part of the canvas. The canvas is to be insured before any of the stages of priming are begun. Beneath this, room for two signatures. Friedman had signed on behalf of F&W. Clara picked up the pen, leaned on the desk and was just about to add her signature under 'the canvas'. But as she put pen to paper, Friedman surprisingly halted her.

'I would like you to know that the artist has given us the authority to reject the material if it seems to us in any way not to meet certain quality standards.'

'I don't understand.'

Friedman's lopsided face showed his impatience.

'You should listen more carefully.'

'Sorry.'

'I'll say it again, in simpler terms you can understand.'

'Thank you.'

Clara did not get upset. She knew it was typical of a man in his position to treat her with scorn: priming companies did not regard canvases as human beings, but as mere objects with holes and shapes they had to work with.

'The priming process is going to be tough. If you don't come up to our standards, we'll reject you.'

'OK.'

'Think about it.' Friedman's expressionless gaze took in Clara's thin arms. 'You don't seem very strong. Your complexion is too delicate. So why waste your time and ours?'

'I've been through very hard priming sessions. Last year with Brentano . . .'

Friedman cut her short with a twist of his lips.

'This has nothing to do with the Venetian school, extimacy or 'dirty' canvases . . . we're not talking about leather hoods, whips or bondage. This is a professional priming company.' He seemed offended. 'We only accept first-class material. Even if you sign this document now, we can reject you tomorrow, the next day, or five minutes from now. We can reject you whenever we like, without any explanation. Or we might put you through the whole priming process and then turn you down.'

'I understand,' Clara said calmly.

In fact she did not feel calm at all. She was shaking deep down in her bones. But it was not fear or anger she felt, it was the desire to take on the challenge Friedman was offering. That excited her. So much, she was sure Friedman was bound to notice.

There was a moment's silence.

'You'd better not sign,' Friedman said. 'Take my advice.'

Clara looked down at the sheet of paper.

The pen traced a flourish.

Friedman's asymetrical face twisted in a strange gesture – was he pleased? put out?. He was one of the ugliest men Clara had ever seen, but at that moment she found him imbued with a mysterious kind of attraction.

'Don't say later that we didn't warn you.'

'I won't.'

'Sit down.'

Clara sat down on the chair with no back, and Friedman settled behind the desk. His Spanish accent sounded neutral, as if he were neither Spanish nor a foreigner, as if he were from nowhere in particular or from everywhere. He spoke Spanish as precisely as a computer. Although he never smiled, he never seemed completely serious.

'It's a quarter past nine,' he said, without looking at his watch. 'You have eight hours to organise your life as you see fit. At a quarter past five you should be back here again. You may shower, but don't put on any make-up or use any creams or perfume. Come dressed however you like, but I must warn you that whatever you are wearing or carrying will be destroyed.'

'Destroyed?'

'It's one of our rules. We do not want to take responsibility for any of your belongings, because that could lead to claims later on. F&W will not pay any compensation for the clothing or any other objects you lose, so do not bring anything of value. Or rather: bring only things you do not mind losing. Is all that clear?'

'Yes.'

'The remainder, in other words you, will be photographed and filmed so we can draw up an insurance policy. Once that is done, your body will become the property of F&W until the priming is finished. You won't be able to go home, to go anywhere else, or to get in touch with anyone. If all goes well, the process will be completed within three days. After that, providing we consider you top-class material, we will hand you over to the artist. If we don't, we'll get rid of the priming and send you home.'

'Fine.'

'If you break the rules, express your opinions or your own desires, if you put any obstacles in the way of the priming, or act on your own initiative, we will consider the contract null and void.'

'You mean I'm not allowed to speak at all?'

'I mean,' Friedman replied with a self-satisfied smirk, 'that if you carry on asking questions, I'll tear up the contract.'

Clara said nothing.

'We will not accept any questions, opinions, wishes or reservations from you. You are the canvas. In order to create a lasting work, an artist needs to start from zero with a canvas. Here at F&W we specialise in *converting* canvases to that *zero*. I hope I make myself clear.'

'Perfectly.'

'We usually work in stages,' Friedman went on. 'There are four of them: the cutaneous, the muscular, the insides, and the mental. Each of these is carried out by the corresponding specialist. I will be in charge of the first stage. I will check the state of the different levels of your skin, the existence of any natural or incidental blemishes, any hard patches or peeling. I will observe whether you can be painted inside as well. Have you ever been?'

Clara nodded.

'The back of my retinas with optic pencil and the inside of my mouth,' she said. 'And of course, my navel, vulva and anus.'

'Under your nails?'

'No.'

'Your ears? By that I mean inside, in the hearing canal?'

'No.'

'Your nostrils?'

'No.'

'The underside of your eyelids?'

'No.'

'Why the smile?'

'I'm sorry, but I can't imagine why it's necessary to paint the hearing canal or inside a nostril . . .'

'That shows how inexperienced you are,' said Friedman. 'I'll give you an example. A nocturnal outdoor piece, painted black but with drops of extra-intense phosphorescent red in the eardrums, nostrils, the underside of the eyelids and the urethra to produce the effect of the work burning inside.'

It was true, and Clara was angry at having shown her ignorance.

'The vagina, urethra, rectum, tear ducts, retinas, follicles, sweat glands,' Friedman reeled off the list. 'Every part of the body of a

77

canvas can be painted. And the latest laser techniques permit us to drill into teeth, paint the roots and then, when the work is substituted, to repair any damage. A body can become a *collage*. Sometimes, in the most violent art-shocks, the veins and blood may be painted so that if there is an amputation, they will produce a striking effect. And in the final stages of a dirty canvas, the viscera can be painted after they've been taken out, or even while they are being removed: the brain, liver, lungs, heart, breasts, testicles, the uterus and the foetus it may contain. Were you aware of that?'

'Yes,' Clara whispered, trying not to shudder. 'But I've never done anything like that.'

'Yes, but we cannot know what this artist is going to do with you. We have to prepare you for everything, to expect everything, offer everything. Is that clear?'

'Yes.'

Clara found it hard to breathe. Her mouth was half-open, and her cheeks were flushed. The possibilities Friedman had mentioned seemed to her no worse than her own decision to accept them, to submit herself to whatever the artist wanted to do with her. The key thing was the genius of the artist. Someone had once told her that Picasso was such a genius he could do anything. Clara was sure that in the hands of a Picasso she would allow *anything* to be done to her.

She thought about it for a moment. Absolutely *anything*?

Yes. Without reservation.

But the artist would perhaps have to be a bit better than Picasso.

'Are you regretting having signed?' asked Friedman, misconstruing her expression.

'No.'

The two of them looked at each other for a moment.

'If you have any questions, ask them now.'

'Which artist is going to paint me?'

'I'm not permitted to tell you. Any other questions?'

'No.'

'Then we'll expect to see you here at a quarter past five precisely.'

*

Eight hours to organise a life are almost too much. Or so Clara thought. Her life was very simple: there was work and leisure. To sort out the first of these, all she had to do was phone Bassan; the latter implied a call to Jorge. To make it even simpler, when she got home she discovered Bassan had left her a message on her answerphone. He did not seem too upset, but it was not his usual affectionate tone. Gertrude had called him to let him know Clara was not going on show that day, and he wanted to know why. 'You know I approve of everything you do, Clarita, but please tell me before you do it.' She could understand he might be a bit put out, but nevertheless was annoyed at his reproach. She called him in Barcelona, but only got his answering machine.

'Alex,' she said into silence, 'it's me, Clara. Something important has come up and I'm not going to be able to continue with *Girl in Front of a Looking Glass*. I'm sorry. Anyway, there was only a week left at the GS gallery, and I seem to remember you had a substitute ready . . . Really, I'm sorry if this causes you problems, but there's nothing I can do about it. A big hug.'

Then she thought about the call to Jorge. Once she was sure what she wanted to say, she dialled his mobile number. All she got was his voicemail. It seemed to her that all of a sudden her life had become a dialogue with silence. She decided to leave another message.

'Jorge, this is Clara. I'm going to be away for a few days on a job that's come up.' She paused. 'It looks like a good opportunity.' Another pause. 'A very good one. I'll call you some other time, if possible. Big kiss.'

It was just gone half past ten but her eyes were heavy as lead. She folded down the bunk in her bedroom, undressed and threw herself under the sheets. She needed to catch up on her night's sleep. She set her electronic alarm for two in the afternoon and fell straight asleep. She did not dream of Alberca or her father, but of an outdoor painting she had been for Gutiérrez Reguero three years earlier, called *The Tree of Science*. When she woke up, she had forgotten all about it. She got up, ran to the bathroom and plunged under the jet of water from the shower. Following her instructions, she put no creams on her body afterwards. She stared at her naked body in the mirror and said goodbye to it: she knew this would be the last time she saw it in its normal state. Then she wrapped herself in a bathrobe, went into the living room, put on a jazz CD and let herself be carried away by the dark notes of the tune as she rummaged through her wardrobes.

The problem was that she liked everything she had. Buying clothes and accessories was one of her chief pleasures. Friedman's announcement that everything she wore or took with her would be destroyed had not seemed to present much of a problem, but now as she gazed at her beautiful, expensive wardrobe, she hesitated. There were clothes by Yamamoto, Stern, Cessare, Armani, Balmain, Chanel . . . it was not so much what all this had cost her as the pleasure she got from the softness of this woven flesh and blood. Every dress, every suit had a different personality for her. They were like new and special friends. She could not do this to them.

What if she wore the tracksuit she went to work in? But as she considered it laid out flat and obedient on the bed, its empty sleeves just waiting for her to fill them, she understood it would be like condemning the faithful old family dog to a sudden death.

Nothing she could sacrifice in the wardrobes then. She stood on a chair and looked in the cupboards on top. Unfortunately, she was in the habit of throwing away old clothes. She did though store some winter items, and the first things she came across were a dark velvet suit and a pink, flesh-coloured rollneck jersey.

The catlike feel of the velvet brought back a sudden phantom, and reminded her of the first time she had worn it.

Vicky.

Vicky was young, scarcely a year older than Clara. She was pretty, slim, with straw-coloured short hair. She took drugs and was a great talent. In a very short time she had become the most important hyperdramatic painter in Spain. Thanks to a grant, she had been able to broaden her studies, first with Rayback in London and then at the Van Tysch Foundation in Amsterdam with Jacob Stein. She had even received the oracle from the lips of the great Maestro himself. She did more than merely admit her lesbianism: she unfurled it like a banner. Her works denounced the way homosexuals were marginalised, or mocked men and women repressed 'by a Roman, Vatican, class-ridden society, a parody of what the Greeks had hoped to create'. The great loves of her life had been two Anglo-Saxon women, two exuberant and beautiful paintings by the name of Shannon Coller and Cynthia Bergmann. Early in 2004 she had chosen Clara for an interior duo with Yoli Ribó that she was thinking of calling *Sit Down*. The two of them met on a grey, freezing afternoon. Clara decided to wear the velvet suit she had just bought to visit the artist in her Las Rozas villa. Vicky received her in shirtsleeves, smeared with paint, and showed her upstairs to the studio. A slender blonde sketch she had poured several cans of paint over was standing naked on tiptoe in one corner. There were also several illegal ornaments, almost all of them obscene. A male Table designed in London served them tea, pastries and marijuana cigarettes. A Japanese toy, also masculine, his body painted quinacridone red, made her more exciting offers, but Clara was not in the mood to play with him, although Vicky insisted she could have him.

'He's not my style,' Vicky told her, 'but he was given to me as a present. Keep him if you like.'

Before she talked about the proposed work, Vicky carried out one of her famous quick interviews.

'What sign are you?'

'Aries,' Clara said. 'I was born on 16 April.'

'We won't get on then,' the artist said, scratching the air. 'I'm a Leo.'

But they did get on, at the beginning at least. She told Clara the idea she had for *Sit Down*. Yoli and Clara would be six metres up on a scaffolding, painted in flesh colours and locked in an embrace. The work was a commission for a mansion in Provence already stuffed with art. Vicky thought that by putting her work high up near the ceiling, it would stand out above the rest. The two women would spend a month in the mansion, and there was a possibility that the work could become permanent. It would require a great effort and would need a first-rate maintenance team, but it would mean a real fortune for all three of them. She's a great saleswoman, Clara thought. She accepted the offer, and Vicky started to sketch her the next day.

A fortnight after that first meeting, during one of the sketching sessions, something happened. Vicky was drawing her outline, and was gently moving her hand soaked in flesh-coloured paint down the outside of Clara's thigh. When she reached the knee, Clara could feel the pressure of her hand, the protracted silence, the tingling sensation on her painted skin.

'Do you like women, Clara?' Vicky asked all of a sudden, calm as could be.

'I like some women,' Clara replied, equally calmly.

She was naked, half-painted in a variety of colours as she squatted on her haunches in Vicky's studio. Vicky was wearing her work clothes: an unbuttoned, paint-covered shirt and track-suit bottom.

Her hand was still on Clara's knee.

'Have you had any experience with women?'

'Aha,' said Clara. 'And with men.'

There was nothing strange about this for a canvas, and both of them knew it. It was easy for a painting to love another body, whoever it belonged to: the barriers were unclear, the limits became blurred.

'Would you like to sleep with me?' Vicky asked.

Clara liked the soft guttural tone of her voice, and the way Vicky's cheeks fired up much more than her own.

'Yes,' she said.

Vicky looked at her and went on painting. Her hand moved smoothly distributing the flesh colour on Clara's knee. Clara had no idea when it happened. One moment there was art, tech-nique, a painter at work; the next, there was feeling, heavy breathing, a lover's embrace. And the brushstrokes suddenly became caresses.

Later on, when the relationship between the two women was a reality, Vicky reproached her for having responded so matter-of-factly. She used it against Clara whenever she was angry with her. 'You said yes as though you were being asked to go hang-gliding at night. You said yes as though you were being asked to meet a Physics Nobel laureate. OK, let's give it a try, you said. There was no real love or sincerity in your declaration.' 'Maybe there was no real love,' Clara retorted, 'but I was being sincere.'

82

'You have no feelings,' Vicky declared. 'I try to hide them: I'm a work of art,' replied Clara. And added, 'And you are an artist, so you find it impossible to hide them. You even invent them if you don't have any.'

Sit Down went on permanent exhibition in Provence. It was an exhausting period: they only had a few hours in which to rest, eat and recover before they had to climb up on the scaffolding again. The length of time they had varied, because it depended entirely on the life of the purchaser, on the visitors or the parties he had organised. The maintenance team was excellent, but the two women ended up completely exhausted. Nevertheless, it was a wonderful experience for Clara. That same year, Vicky painted her in another five works, the early ones with another woman, then on her own: *The Kiss, Double or Quits, Sweet Nothings,* and *The Black Dress*. Outside work, Vicky's obsession with Clara knew no bounds: she called her in the morning, at night, cried on her shoulder, revealed intimate secrets about how cold her father was (he was a surgeon) or her mother's (a university professor) lack of interest in her career as a painter. Some days she considered herself 'a crappy daddy's girl'; on others she was the unfortunate victim of a 'marriage of snobs'. But all that was forgotten as soon as she began to work. In bed she might be a vulnerable soul, but with her hands covered in paint she became a firebird who could draw wonderful things on a woman's body. But Vicky the human being and Vicky the artist were not in watertight compartments. While Vicky the human being fell in love with the models for her works of art, Vicky the artist used that love to paint them. It was characteristic of her, but Clara could not fathom out which came first: her temperament or her way of working.

2004 was the year of Vicky, for Clara at least: a rushing torrent she either had to escape from or let herself be carried away by. Vicky was one of those people who, like candles, consume themselves the more light they give off. The worst of it was her jealousy. Especially since at that time, there was no reason for it. Clara had left Gabi Ponce, her first love as well as her first painter, and was living alone in the loft in Augusto Figueroa. She was no longer seeing either Alexandra or Sofia Lundel, two women friends she had occasionally shared a bed with. And she had not yet met Jorge Atienza. Yet Vicky was capable not only of inventing feelings but motives as well. One night she created a scandal in a restaurant where they were dining because an Italian woman painter had asked Clara to work in an art-shock together with three other female canvases. Vicky told her not to accept, and when Clara refused she threw her cutlery on the floor and attacked the maître, who, like a good shepherd looking after his flock, had come over attentively. A few hours later, she called Clara to make up: 'I was drunk, forgive me.' Then, without warning, it was Vicky the artist who took over: 'I wanted to tell you that your face today in the restaurant . . . My God, you were so pale when I shouted at you . . . Clara, please let me *use* that pallor . . . Those eyes of yours when you were staring at me today . . .'

She was inspired. She finished her new painting in three weeks. It was Clara, painted in ivory white with cerulean shadows, lying face down on a velvet cloak, exactly the same material as the suit she was wearing that first afternoon they met, with her face the natural shade of her disgust. Vicky was thinking of calling the work *Sweet Nothings*. During the hyperdramatic rehearsal they played out the scene in the restaurant as they remembered it. The painter wanted to recapture the fleeting paleness of Clara's cheeks, but Clara was uneasy about mixing art and real life. In the end, Vicky got angry again and started to insult her. All of a sudden she stopped in the middle of her insults and clasped Clara's face in her hands. 'That's it! You've gone pale again! That's exactly what I'm looking for!' she shouted, beside herself. Vicky the artist was back in control.

One day, Clara complained about the way she abused real emotions to paint with. Vicky gave a strange smile.

'I'd do anything for art, sweetie,' she told her. 'Anything. I couldn't care less about anything but art: not emotions or justice, or pity, family health, love or money . . . Well . . .' she hesitated, 'perhaps money is an exception. Art is money.'

Sweet Nothings was bought by a Madrid collector at double its list price. Clara was on show in his house for a whole month.

Early in 2005, Vicky tried to kill herself with a heroin overdose.

This was not Clara's fault, but that of her new love, Elena Valero, who Clara had worked with on *Instant*. The day they were taking her into the intensive care unit in La Paz, it was announced that the Van Tysch Foundation had awarded her their Max Kalima prize for the totality of her work. Groggy from the effects of her oxygen mask, Vicky heard the news from a nurse. When she recovered, she declared she had also rediscovered her emotional stability. Although she was planning another work with Clara for the end of the year, she no longer phoned her as often. Then after *Strawberry* they had not seen each other again. Clara was unsure what she felt about her: was she in love with Vicky, or was it admiration for her talent? The truth was that although she wanted to, she could not forget her. Sometimes she pictured herself lying on the velvet cloak in the *Sweet Nothings* collector's room, one knee drawn up under her stomach, with the heel pointing down to her sex, her eyes shut and face livid with that 'pallor the colour of disgust' that Vicky had managed to produce in her. Perhaps this was all the painter had left her when she disappeared from her life: the feel of velvet, and her bloodless cheeks.

So she pulled the velvet suit out of the cupboard and threw it on the bed. Then she found another beige jersey and trousers, which reminded her more of Jorge because she had worn them during the early days of her relationship with him.

She hesitated for a while, looking at the two sets of clothing as if judging them (Vicky or Jorge? Jorge or Vicky?), before finally condemning Vicky Lledó to destruction. She would be too hot during the journey, but that did not matter.

It was almost three in the afternoon when she realised she should eat something. She threw together a salad and a couple of sandwiches, and polished them off with a bottle of mineral water.

Then as she still had some time left, she decided to prepare herself for what was to come. Rummaging in her medicine cabinet, she chose a couple of muscle toner tablets and a pill that would hold back her period, and swallowed them with the last of the bottled water. She took off her bathrobe, went into the kitchen for a salt cellar, an airline passenger's mask that she found in one of the drawers, and several weights. She started exercising in a

85

very different way from her usual routine on the mat. She stood motionless on tiptoe, with salt on her tongue. She walked around her apartment with the mask on. She rolled herself into a ball, placing a weight on the highest part of her body. The exercises were designed to curb her will without breaking it, to help her see herself as a blind object, something that could be used, transformed. She had become used to this kind of preparation since her days with *The Circle*. It was the only way she had been able to bear the work Brentano did with her.

At a quarter to four she pulled the flesh-coloured jersey over her head, put on the velvet jacket and trousers, and chose a pair of sandals from the dim and distant past. She considered herself in the mirror. None of what she was wearing really suited her: she looked like a beautiful young girl disguised as a hippy, which was exactly the effect she wanted to create.

The remaining details, which she had not thought of, caused her the most problems. What should she do with her house keys? She could not take them with her. Jorge had a set, but she did not want to have to depend on him to get in when she returned, whenever that might be. She did not trust her neighbours, and the building had no porter.

She decided simply to do nothing. It seemed logical to her to shut the door behind her and be unable to get in again. She called for a taxi, calculated how much it would cost her, and put the money in her jacket pocket.

It was then she found the keyring.

She realised she had put the suit on without checking the pockets. Old clothes are the graveyard of memory. In one of the jacket pockets she dug out her father's keyring. For a long time, she had used it with the kind of blind devotion we show to objects that once belonged to the dead. When it snapped, she had to transfer her keys to a new ring. She could not recall why it was in this particular pocket, or why she had not thrown it away. Perhaps because of its sentimental value. The thought amused her.

The keyring had a chess queen on it, a present from the club where Manuel Reyes played. Her father was passionate about chess, and her brother had inherited his love of this sober pastime. It was a black queen. Clara could hear her father saying,

'This is Reyes' queen. They gave me the black one because it's on the losing side.'

She considered whether to save it, but put it back in her pocket. 'I'm sorry, your majesty, but if that's where you were, that's where you'll stay.'

So, dressed in Vicky's suit, wearing her adolescent sandals, and with the weight of her father's keyring in her pocket, Clara left her apartment and shut the door behind her.

As she reached the street, she felt a strong sensation. It was so intense she had to look all round to make sure it was a mistake. She was convinced she was being watched. Perhaps she was wrong.

This was the afternoon of 22 June, 2006. The sun was shining the colour of pink flesh.

6

Briseida Canchares woke up with a gun to her head. Seen from so close up, the barrel looked like a small metal coffin pressed against her temple. The finger on the trigger had its nail painted viridian green. Briseida looked up the bare forearm and discovered it belonged to a blonde woman. It was the emerald-eyed cat dressed in the tiny camouflage outfit who had asked Roger for a light at the Roquentins. It had happened while she was looking at the painting *Invisible Orbit* by Elmer Fludd, and a guard had immediately come over and warned the woman: 'You can't smoke here, miss. The smoke gets in the paintings' eyes, and makes them cough.' She had given Roger a crooked smile as she handed him back his lighter. Then she had vanished into the crowd and Briseida had not seen her again.

Until now.

The blonde woman was dressed in the same combat gear, and smiled in the same way. The only difference was the gun. She raised a finger to her lips, still training the pistol on Briseida (I'm not to speak, Briseida translated this to mean) then signalled with her other hand (I'm to get up). She suspected it was all a dream, so she obeyed, because she liked doing fascinating things in her dreams. She pulled back the sheets and stood up. The gun pressed to her temple moved as she did, as if her head were made of metal and the pistol were a magnet. Briseida turned to the side and placed her feet on the cool carpet of Roger's apartment floor as delicately as a space module landing on the moon. She was completely naked, and felt a bit chilly. It was still night (she didn't know the exact time, because the alarm clock was on Roger's side of the bed), and the room was lit only by the bedside lamp. She remembered having gone to bed very late and sharing moments of enthusiasm and struggle with Roger (that mouth of his, with its aftertaste of vintage champagne and velvety Havana cigar, his tongue a green marijuana rug) before night covered them in its cloak of drunkenness and . . .

That's right.

Where was Roger?

She discovered him sitting at the far end of the room. All he was wearing was the ring on the little finger of his left hand. The same ring that had left marks on Briseida's backside, but which he said he could not remove because that brought bad luck. He had got it in some remote corner of Brazil, stealing it from a shaman who could tell people's secrets. It contained a tiny emerald that glinted in its setting like a jungle-green drop of pus. According to Roger, it had great powers, although he was not sure exactly what they were. He claimed there were only five or six jewels like it in the whole world. What an incredible guy Roger was. A bit of a bastard too, of course, but Briseida had never met anyone with that amount of money who wasn't also a bastard.

At that moment it seemed not even the ring's powers could help him. A pincer in the shape of a hand was clamped so fiercely on his jaw his cheeks were puffed up. The pincer-like hand belonged to a spectacular woman, similar to the blonde but much more impressive, like the ones Roger liked to fuck only at weekends. She was jabbing a silver-plated military pistol into his throat. Its barrel made his Adam's apple stand out starkly. This woman was wearing baize-green jacket and trousers, olive-green kerchief and beret, and pistachio-coloured gloves. One of her legs was thrust between Roger's thighs (perhaps her knee was crushing his genitals, and this was causing the look of desperation on his face), the other was firmly planted on the floor in shooting position. She was not looking at Roger but at Briseida, as if it were up to her to decide what she should do next. Her eyes were of the kind it is hard to forget. The kind, thought Briseida, you stare into a second before you see nothing any more.

Even so, she had to admit that the make-up and the combination of greens (jacket–trousers, gloves–beret, eyes–shadow) were perfect. A paramilitary catwalk! *Prêt-à-porter* terrorism! What prevented police SWAT teams, army commandos or any other *ad hoc* armed group keeping up with the demands of fashion? Briseida wondered.

The blonde woman was still signalling to her to stand up. She glanced over at Roger, who raised his hand as if to say: Do as she tells you, so she got up from the bed, still keeping her eyes on everyone in the room.

Are they burglars or cops? Have they come to kidnap Roger? Let's see. What did we get up to? Last night we were at that party . . .

God, how her head hurt. She could not think straight. Perhaps that was because of the mix of alcohol, hashish and pills she had taken at the Roquentins. Besides, the scene before her was so odd that the terror she could feel starting to beat in her chest was still muffled. It looked as if it had all been set up by the God of Art: a combination of the fascinating – the blonde in her camouflage outfit; the ridiculous – Roger and her stark naked, still clammy from their dense dreams; and the absurd – the heavily made-up model in her combat gear. It was like a Cézanne painting in green – cobalt green, military green, turquoise green, green carpet, apple green of the bedroom walls. If she were to die young, thought Briseida, she would choose exactly this green moment.

It was a shame this aesthetic impression faded a little when the blonde woman pushed her towards the men waiting in the dining room.

They pinioned her arms, and pushed her down on to a chair in front of what appeared to be a blank computer screen. Briseida had shouted out as she was being hustled into the room, and had apparently broken some code of silence, because a few seconds later she heard noises and words in Dutch from the bedroom, then more noises in the corridor. But the next words were in English and were directed at her.

'Don't do that again,' Fascinating Eyes Blondie said, bending over her. 'And don't try to stand up.'

She could not have done so even if she had wanted to: two pairs of iron gloves were forcing her down on her seat.

'Here's a glass of water. Drink some if you like. I'm going to press a key on the computer and a person will appear on the screen to ask you some questions. Reply loudly and clearly. Don't avoid any of the questions, and don't take too much time over them. If you don't know the answer, or want time to think about it, say so. We know you speak good English, but if there's something you don't understand, say so too.'

The blonde pressed a key, and the face of an elderly man, bald except for some white tufts above the ears, appeared on the screen. In the top left-hand corner there also appeared an insert of a young woman with tanned brown skin, hair the colour of coal, prominent cheekbones and plump lips, gripped by the shoulders and arms by four gloved hands, and with naked breasts. Briseida realised it was her. They were filming her and sending the images in real time to heaven knows what damned spot on the planet. Diagonally across the screen from this, a timing device ticked off the seconds.

Hallucinatory effects produced by the chaotic consumption of toxic products: that was how Stan Coleman, her unforgettable, wealthy (and asshole) professor of Contemporary Art at Columbia described all the strange things that happened after an orgy of soft drugs. That was what this must be. It could not really be happening to her.

'Good morning. I'm sorry if we've disturbed you, but we need to know something urgently, and we're counting on your generous cooperation.'

The man spoke English with an undeniable continental accent, perhaps German or Dutch. At the bottom half of the screen, his

90

neck and the knot of his tie were obscured by subtitles of what he was saying in French and German. Briseida did not need any more languages to feel terrified.

'We know a lot about you: you're twenty-six, born in Bogotá, have an art degree from a New York university, you father is his country's cultural attaché at the United Nations . . . Let's see, what else?' The man bent forward, and for a few seconds the screen became a globe featuring his polished bald head. 'Ah yes, you're engaged on a research project for the university about painters and their collections . . . this year you have been in the Netherlands to study the objects Rembrandt collected in his house in Amsterdam. And now you're in Paris, with our good friend Roger Levin. Last night you went with him to a party at Leo Roquentin's. All this is correct, isn't it?'

Briseida was about to answer yes when the fairy godmother of computers dissolved the image with an explosion of green flashes and replaced it with another face: a thin woman with her hair cut in a boyish bob, wearing dark glasses. Her subtitles were in green.

'Hello there, I'm the bad cop.' Her accent was more English than the man's, and her voice was more disturbing. Her smile was like a scythe blade. 'I just wanted to say hello. Some place Leo Roquentin has, doesn't he? I think the salon is from the eighteenth century, and the ceiling frescoes were painted by the maestro Luc Ducet and tell the story of Samson and Delilah. In the west wing, in a room with two ceiling roundels, the story of the Flood is depicted, from the building of the Ark to the return of the dove with the olive branch in its beak. We know Leo Roquentin very well . . . His HD collection is also excellent, especially the Elmer Fludd paintings in the main room. But they are just the tip of the iceberg. Did you take part in the art-shock that was going on in the huge basement underneath the mansion? It was called *Art-Chess*, and was created by Michel Gros. Twenty-four young people of both sexes, and plastic material . . . the figures, completely naked and painted in various shades of green, are pieces on a thirty-metre-square chessboard. The guests suggest the moves they should make. Any piece that gets taken is handed over to the guests to do what they like with. You didn't play the game? Of course, your little friend Roger mustn't have told you anything about it. You would have simply seen the paintings upstairs: the art-shock was for a select few. Leo astonishes them with these interactive performances, then offers them irresistible deals with even more prohibited works.'

Was what that woman was saying true? It was certainly true that Roger had disappeared for a long while to talk with Roquentin while Briseida wandered from one corner to another across green carpets, on the billiard table of guests, contemplating the magnificent oils by Elmer Fludd. Then when he returned she had told him he looked a bit nervous. And his shirt collar was undone. An art-shock consisting of a game of chess with human pieces . . . she said to herself. Why hadn't Roger told her anything? What was going on in the basement of the world, beneath the feet of all those rich people?

The woman paused, and gave another of her unpleasant smiles.

'Don't worry, men are always the same. They like to keep secrets. We women are more sincere, aren't we? At least I hope you are, Miss Canchares. I'm going to leave you with my friend the Good Cop, who's going to ask you some questions. If your replies are convincing, we'll unplug the computer, go home and we'll all be good friends. If they're not, it'll be the Good Cop who'll leave, and the Bad Cop, i.e. me, who will be back. Understood?

'Yes.'

'I'm delighted to have met you, Miss Canchares. I hope we don't meet again.'

'My pleasure,' stammered Briseida.

She didn't know what to think about the woman's warnings. Were they just idle threats? And what about all this fantasy with military uniforms? Were they trying to stir up her atavistic fear of guerrillas? All of a sudden she thought she was in the midst of a carnival, an artistically organised farce. What was the neologism Stan had invented? An *imagic,* a magical image, a cultural archetype to project our fear or passion on to, because – according to Stan – nowadays everything, absolutely everything, from publicity to massacres, from food aid for Third World countries to torture, is done with a sense of style.

Carnival or not, this performance was achieving its objective: she was terrorised. She felt close to pissing on Roger's sofa, to throwing up on Roger's carpet.

A green explosion. The man again.

'This is the question . . . listen closely . . .'

Briseida stiffened as much as she could under the grip of the claw-like hands on her shoulders and arms. Her thighs were aching from the effort she made to press them together to conceal her sex from view. All at once she was conscious of her total nudity.

'We know you are a close friend of Oscar Díaz. I'll repeat the name: Oscar Díaz. The question is: where is Oscar now?'

Some part of the cerebral cortex of Briseida Canchares – twenty-five years old (the man had been mistaken, she would not be twenty-six until 3 August) with a degree in Art History – carried out a swift calculation and came up with a list of provisional conclusions: Oscar Díaz; something to do with Oscar; Oscar has done something bad; they're going to do something bad to Oscar . . .

'Where is you friend Oscar?' the man repeated.

'I don't know.'

Immediately, the screen was covered in a green slime that reminded Briseida of the time she had carried out chemical experiments for the restoration of paintings. A set of teeth emerged out of the green. A smile. The face of the woman in dark glasses.

'Wrong answer.'

A tuft of her scalp suddenly seemed to spring to life. She screamed, and her eyes imagined a fiesta with firecrackers, a New Year's Eve party in a hotel somewhere in the green jungle. Her neck was twisted back; her vertebra only escaped destruction thanks to the aerobics she practised every day. Two strange green planets swam into her universe (Venus was always green in the pulp science-fiction books Stan Coleman read by the sackful), and she found herself staring at a stylish and undoubtedly very expensive instrument. It was a chrome metal pencil with a sharpened tip on the end of which glistened a drop of martian blood.

'This toy is an optical laser brush,' the blonde said, an inch away from her face. 'I'll not bore you with all the technical details. Let's just say it's an improved version of the brushes painters use to work on the retinas of their primed canvases. The retina is the pigmented layer on the back of our eyes, which among other things allows us to distinguish colours. Usually it is very boring, but it's very useful when we want to see the world. I'm going to paint your retinas dark green. First your left eye, then the right one. The problem is, I'm going to use permanent paint, which is totally unadvisable in this kind of situation. You won't have any scars or external bruising, it will all be very aesthetic and so on. But by the time I've finished, you'll be so blind you'll have to suck your fingers to be sure they're yours. But it will be a very beautiful blindness, everything will look a wonderful bottle-green colour. Now, don't move.'

The order was not necessary. All Briseida could move was her mouth and her right eyelid. Something was forcing open her left eyelid to the point where she was on the verge of tears. It smelt of imitation leather: a glove. Leather vultures had seized her wrists, knees, ankles, throat, and hair. She wanted to say something in English, but all that came out was mangled Spanish. But she had to speak English. English is vital in situations like this, when you are being tortured by a foreigner. *OK, Johnson family at holidays. Mary Johnson is in the kitchen. Where's Mary Johnson?* Then, along the left-hand side of her optic nerve there appeared a spectacular universe of such a kitsch green and red colour it reminded her of a phosphorescent buddha she had seen in a street market. Or the postcards by Pierre & Gilles she used to send her parents from Europe. She thought she was going blind.

At that point the hand pulling her hair back let go, and another one pressed down on the back of her neck forcing her head forward as though wanting to smash it into the computer screen. She found herself with her nose pressed up against the French and German subtitles. She fought back a sudden wave of nausea.

'Your second opportunity.' It was the woman again. 'Our colleague simply brought the brush close to your pupil . . . Listen, and don't scream . . . if you give the wrong answer again, she will draw a comma on your retina . . . after she's done that, you'll be able to see a green crescent moon even in the light of day. A curious aesthetic effect, don't you agree? Stop snivelling and pay attention . . . After this second session, you might as well keep your left retina in a jar. I can assure you, it will glow green in the night like one of those virgins of Lourdes . . . So please, concentrate. The prize is your eyesight.'

'The same question again.' It was the man once more.

Since the hands clasping her shoulders and arms were still there, and the one on the back of her neck was still pressing her down, Briseida was convinced her cervical vertebra was about to crack apart like rotten wood. She decided that would be the best thing that could happen.

'I don't know, I swear, please, I don't know, I swear I've no idea, in Vienna, yes, in Vienna, but I don't really know, *I swear, I swear* . . . !' Saliva, tears and words came pouring from her face as if her glands were secreting them: *'I've no idea where, it's true, I've no idea where, I swear it, please, please, please, plea . . .'*

A bout of vomiting cut her off.

Seated at his portable computer in the MuseumsQuartier office, Lothar Bosch pressed a button on his mobile memory and called the number that appeared. He had a brief but forceful discussion with one of his men in Paris. Miss Wood had her back turned to him, and was staring out at the Vienna dawn through the glass wall. Bosch noticed she was smoking one of her disgusting ecological cigarettes, the mentholated green smoke formed halos on the window round her head.

'Mr Lothar Bosch, always a gentleman where ladies are concerned,' he heard her say.

'Don't you think we've scared her enough with that game of the optical brush?' Bosch snapped back, wounded by his colleague's cold irony. 'That's no way to start a conversation. We won't get anything out of her like that.'

Her eye was undamaged. They were quite kind to her, really. They had even let go of her so she could vomit more easily.

Briseida was sick as she used to be as a child: with one hand on her forehead, and the other clutching her stomach. That was how it always was with her. Strange moment this bilious *déjà vu*. According to her mother, she threw up like a cat. Her grandmother said it was because she didn't know how to be sick. The little kitten would suffer all her life because she did not know how to vomit properly. She didn't take after her father in that, especially after he had been boozing. Stan was also an expert in vomiting, it was easy, prolonged and abundant. The same was true of most of the fluids emanating from her Art Professor. The same could not be said of Luigi, her Aesthetics Professor, whose stomach was toughened by a diet of pizzas laced with chilli: he was stiff, repressed and impotent. By their vomit shall ye know them, not by their ejaculations. Sneezing, vomiting and death were the only three truly unforeseeable, uncontrollable and instantaneous reactions of the body. Semi-colon, fullstop; new paragraph, full stop, end of dictation about life: as a teacher at her Swiss school had once told her.

She stemmed her retching with a sip of cold water. God, what a state she had left Roger's dining-room carpet in. A man with such an aesthetic sense as Roger (could it be true he had played chess last night with twenty-four human pieces?) and just look what she had deposited on his carpet, it looked like radish juice all over his spotless Italian floor. Briseida was forced to separate her knees to avoid the pool, and in doing so opened her thighs. But since they were no longer holding her down, she could cover her sex with her hands. The Good Computer (or was it the Good Cop?) was waiting, a gold Montblanc pressed against the side of his head. The blonde and the soldiers had retreated to behind the chair, ready to swing into action at any moment. A Windows icon called 'Bad Cop' crouched in the opposite corner to Briseida's. But Good Cop had told her that, for the moment, Baddie wanted a rest.

'Feeling better?'

'Yes. Can I put some clothes on?'

A moment's hesitation.

'This will soon be over, I promise you. Now tell me all you know about Oscar.'

She began to talk freely. A string of unemotional, technical terms about art (this helped her relax). She did not look at the screen as she spoke, nor at the floor (the vomit), but at a fruit bowl on the table behind the computer: green apples and pears as calming as an infusion.

'I met him at MoMA in New York last spring. He was looking after *Bust*, a Van Tysch etching. I suppose you know the work I'm talking about, but I can describe it for you . . . it's a preparatory study for *Deflowering*. A twelve-year-old girl in a black-painted box with a slit at the top. The slit allows you to see only her face and shoulders, painted in faint greys on her skin primed with acids, like a human etching. To see the work, the public have to file in one by one, climb the two steps in front of the box, and stand only a hand's breadth away from her face. The girl stares out without ever blinking, her eyes painted coal black; her expression is almost . . . almost supernatural . . . it's an incredible work . . .'

'The sensation is like going into a confessional and finding that the priest has the features of your sins,' a Spanish critic had written about *Bust*, but Briseida left out that comment because she did not want to appear to be giving an art lecture. The work had made a huge impression during its American tour, especially because *Deflowering* had been banned by a censorship committee in the United States.

'Oscar was in charge of the security for *Bust*. One day he saw me waiting my turn at the end of a long line of people. I had gone to MoMA to study an Elmer Fludd on show in the next gallery, but I didn't want to leave without having a look at Van Tysch's etching. The previous weekend I had fallen badly playing basketball and was on crutches. When he saw me, Oscar came over and offered to take me to the front of the queue. He led me up and into the box. He was a real gentleman.'

'So you became friends?' asked the man.

'Yes, we began to see each other quite often.'

They started to go for long walks, which almost invariably ended up in Central Park. He loved trees, fields, all of nature. He was expert at photographing landscapes, and had all the equipment: a 35mm Reflex, two tripods, filters, zoom lens. He was very knowledgeable about light, atmosphere, and reflections on water, but had no real interest in any life forms bigger than insects. Oscar was green as a shoot, and perhaps as unripe.

'He took photos of me everywhere: by the ponds, the lakes, feeding the ducks . . .'

'Did he ever talk about his job?'

'Not often. He said he had been a guard in the Brooke's chain before he was taken on by the Van Tysch Foundation in New York, based on Fifth Avenue. His boss was a woman called Ripstein. He earned a fortune, but lived on his own. And he said he hated the Foundation's aesthetic mania: that they forced him to wear a toupee for months, for example.'

'What did he say about that?'

'That if he was bald, or starting to lose his hair, that was nobody else's business. Why on earth had they told him to wear a toupee. "All the big bosses are bald, except for Stein, and nobody cares," he told me. "But the rest of us have to look good." And he said the Van Tysch Foundation was like a meal in a designer restaurant: bags of image, taste, very expensive, but when you left you still had room for a couple of hotdogs and a bag of French fries.'

'He told you that?'

'Yes.'

Was that a smile on the man's face, or simply a distorted image?

'He also said he could never consider the people he was looking after as works of art . . . to him, they were human beings, and he felt very sorry for some of them . . . he told me about one in particular . . . I don't remember her name . . . a model who spent hours crouched in a box, an original painted by Buncher, one of the 'Claustrophiles'. He said he had been her guard several times, and that she was an intelligent, pleasant young girl who used to write poems like Sappho of Lesbos in her free time . . .'

'"But who the fuck is interested in that aspect of her?" Oscar would complain. "To the public, she's no more than a figure on show in a box for eight hours a day." "But it's a *beautiful* work, Oscar," I'd reply. "Don't you think the 'Claustrophiles' are beautiful? And what about *Bust*? A twelve-year-old girl shut into that dark cubicle . . . when you think about it, you say: the poor girl, what a travesty. But when you get up close to her and see her grey-painted face, that expression of hers . . . My God, Oscar, that's *art!* I also feel sorry at shutting up a girl inside a box like that, but . . . what can we do if the result is so . . . so *beautiful?*"'

'Those were the kind of discussions we had. I ended up asking him: "So why do you carry on guarding paintings, Oscar?" He replied: "Because they pay me better than anywhere else." But what he really liked was to learn things about me. I told him about my family in Bogotá, my studies . . . he was pleased we might be able to see each other again this year in Amsterdam, because he was working in Europe . . .'

'Did he say what kind of work?'

'Looking after paintings on the tour of Bruno van Tysch's 'Flowers' collection.

'Did he talk about that?'

'Not much . . . he saw it as just another job. He told me he'd be in Europe a year, and that he'd be spending the first months between Amsterdam and Berlin . . . he wanted me to talk about my research . . . he was thrilled when I told him that Rembrandt collected things like dried crocodiles, families of shells, tribal necklaces and arrows . . . and I was hoping he could get me a pass to visit Edenburg castle.'

'Why did you want to visit Edenburg?'

'To see if it was true what they say about Van Tysch: that he collects empty spaces. People who have been inside Edenburg say there is no furniture or decoration, just bare rooms. I don't know whether it's true or not, but I thought it might make a good . . . a good appendix to my thesis . . .'

'You went on seeing Oscar in Amsterdam, didn't you?' the man asked.

'Just once. The rest were phone calls. He was constantly on the move with the collection, from Berlin to Hamburg, Hamburg to Cologne . . . He didn't have much time off.' Briseida rubbed her arms. She felt cold, but tried to keep her mind on the questions.

'What did he say on the phone?'

'He wanted to know how I was feeling. He wanted to see me. But I think that our relationship, if there ever was one, was finished.'

'What about when you met?'

'It was back in May. Oscar was in Vienna. He had been given a week off and called me. I was living in Leiden, and we arranged to meet in Amsterdam. He stayed in a small hotel off Dam square.'

'That was a bit of a rushed trip, wasn't it?'

'He was bored in Europe. All his friends were in the United States.'

'What did you do in Amsterdam?'

'We walked along the canals, ate in an Indonesian restaurant . . .' Briseida decided it was time to lose her patience. 'What more do you want me to tell you! I'm tired and nervous! Please . . .'

The Bad Cop's window turned into the woman in black glasses. Briseida nearly jumped out of her seat.

'And I supposed you fucked as well, didn't you? I mean, in between all those interesting conversations about art and landscape photography . . .'

No reply.

'Do you know what I'm talking about?' said the woman. 'The old whambang males and females get up to, sometimes the males on one side and the females on the other, sometimes together.'

Briseida decided this unknown woman was the most unpleasant person she had ever seen. Even at the distance of a computer screen from her, with her squashed, two-dimensional, luminous face, her head shrunken by the *jíbaros* of software, the woman was unbearable.

'Did you fuck or not?'

'Yes.'

'Was it an investment, or on current account?'

'I don't follow you.'

'I'm asking if you got anything in exchange, such as entrance tickets to Edenburg, or if you did it because you were fascinated by the lower half of Oscar's body.'

100

'Get lost.' The words poured out of Briseida effortlessly, fearlessly, like a pair of desperate lovers. 'Get lost, will you? Burn my eyes if you like, but get lost.'

She was expecting revenge, but to her surprise, nothing happened.

'Was there love? Between Oscar and you?'

Briseida looked across at the green walls of Roger's apartment.

'I've no intention of responding to that question.'

This time there was a reaction, so quick that her eyes flitted from the green of the wall to the green brush in one movement. All of a sudden she found herself immobilised and open, like a woman giving birth for the first time. Thick gardening gloves smothered her face. Her jaw was held so firmly she could scarcely shout that yes she would answer, of course she'd answer all the questions they wanted to ask, please, please . . . She heard a click, a tiny buzzing sound, and once again could feel her eye was intact.

'No! There was no love! I don't know! I don't know if he loved me! . . . I just thought of him as a friend! . . .' The soles of her feet felt wet and sticky. She realised she had trodden in her own vomit, but what did that matter now she was in tears, and that woman (an unmoving bust on the screen, splintered by her tears) was watching her cry. 'Please, let me go! . . . I've told you all I know! . . .'

'Come on, admit it,' the woman said. 'There was an ulterior motive, wasn't there? Otherwise, what kind of attraction would you feel for a bald guy who had been forced to wear a toupee at work, and who talked to you about landscapes and Sappho of Lesbos? As far as I can see, you don't have problems with men: you only had to wiggle your ass a bit in Amsterdam for Roger Levin to notice and invite you to stay at his place. Isn't that right?'

It was a cruel way to describe what had happened. A week earlier, in Amsterdam, Briseida had gone to see the 'Pleasures' exhibition by Maurice Marchal. He was a painter who interested her because he collected fetishes and only painted men with erections. That afternoon, Roger Levin was also in the gallery by chance, as he explained to her later. He had gone to Amsterdam to

101

try to interview the Foundation bosses to get information on the much-awaited launch of the 'Rembrandt' exhibition scheduled for 15 July. While he was there, he was thinking of buying a Marchal for a girlfriend of his. According to Roger, what first attracted him to Briseida was the dark mane of hair spreading across her pert buttocks. Briseida had bent down to get a closer look at one of the works, a muscular young man squatting with a perfectly vertical penis, painted Veronese green. Roger had made use of the symmetrical effect to come over and comment in English that her posture was exactly the same as the work of art. It was not a particularly smart comment, but it was a lot better than most of the chat-up lines she had heard. Levin had a pleasant, childish face and was wearing a suit with a waistcoat. His hair looked like a nursery of gelled snails. He was irresistible, even in the context they found themselves in, with more than a dozen painted, naked young men standing there with their penises in the air. But Roger's chief attraction was his father, whom he mentioned soon enough. Briseida knew that Gaston Levin was one of the most important dealers in France. With the same spontaneity that seemed to characterise everything he did, Roger suggested that Briseida might like to go back to Paris with him and stay for a few days at his chrome-plated home on the *rive gauche*. Why not? she thought. It was a unique opportunity for her to get a close look at a great family that dealt in works of art.

Luckily, the Bad Cop had vanished again.

'Did you not see Díaz again after Amsterdam?' the man went on.

'No. The last time he called was a fortnight ago . . . on Sunday the eighteenth, I think . . .'

'Did he have any news?'

'He wanted to ask me how you obtained a residency permit for a country in the European Union. He knew I'd got one thanks to the grant from my university.'

'Why was he interested in that?'

'He said he had recently met someone who had no papers, and he wanted to help them.'

Briseida sensed she had said something important to them. The tension of the man on the screen was well-nigh tangible.

'Did he say who this person was?'

'No. I think it was a woman, but I'm not sure.'

'Why do you think that?'

'That's the way Oscar is,' Briseida said with a smile. 'He loves helping ladies.'

'What were his exact words?'

'It's an immigrant, but they have no papers,' was what Oscar had said. 'Since you've been living in Europe for several months, I thought you might know how to get some kind of visa.' He hadn't wanted to give any further details, but Briseida was almost certain it was a woman he was talking about. And that had been all.

'Did you say you would call each other again?'

'He said he'd phone me, but didn't say when. When I left Amsterdam, I left Roger's number with my friends so that Oscar could find me, but he hasn't called yet.'

'Did you try to find out any of the information he was asking for?'

'I asked at my embassy, but I didn't get very far with it . . . can I blow my nose, please?'

'That's all we're going to get from her. Tell Thea to make sure everything is cleaned up, the kiddies are given some sweets as reward, and then everyone gets out of there,' Miss Wood muttered, slamming her computer shut.

Giving the kiddies their sweets would not be that easy, as Bosch knew very well. Roger Levin was a cretin, but by now he must be incensed at having been hauled out of bed while he was busy enjoying his latest conquest, and had probably already called that wonderful father of his. It was true that while his son was playing chess in the basement of the Roquentin mansion (and was trying his hardest to take the white bishop, one Solange Tandrot, eighteen years old, a bony blonde with curls and an anorexia problem – unsuccessfully, as it turned out – and in the end having to console himself by taking Robert Leyoler, a sturdy nineteen-year-old pawn) Gaston had been told on the phone what was going to happen. Bosch had explained to him they were only interested in the

Colombian girl, and that they were not going to touch his son (this was a lie, of course; they wanted to interrogate them separately). Levin Senior had given his consent, but even so they had to be very careful. Levin's influence was something to take into account. He was a second-grade dealer, but he was very astute, and lived in luxury in an Art-Deco building on the *Quai Voltaire*. It was said his wife hung her clothes on the outstretched arms of a Max Kalima original, *Judith*, which Annie Engels modelled next to the fireplace in the salon. But the Levin family was not to be taken lightly. Fortunately, Bosch knew his weak point. Levin was in love with some originals from the Maestro's early period. He claimed he wanted to acquire them at a special price so that he could sell them on in the United States. Negotiations with Stein had stalled: Levin knew that if he did not behave, Stein would block the sale. The Van Tysch Foundation was not to be taken lightly either.

'Who were they, Roger? They weren't the police, were they? Did you know them?'

Roger was staring in the mirror at a huge bruise on his shoulder blade, probably the female soldier's handiwork. It hurt, whoever had done it. He felt humiliated by what had happened, and his legs were still shaking, but he consoled himself with the thought that it had not been – as he had at first feared – a raid by real cops (he had a sealed room downstairs where he kept his collection of illegal ornaments, which even his father was unaware of) and that they had not ruined any of the beautiful paintings he kept upstairs.

'They were . . . they were people from my world,' he replied. His father had forbidden him to talk to the girl about the incident.

'From your world?'

'Yes, like the people you saw yesterday at the Roquentin mansion! Assholes who get paid to carry guns and guard paintings! Anyway, what does it matter who they were!'

'They were looking for a friend of mine who works in the Van Tysch Foundation . . . Why . . . ?'

'How should I know!'

104

'We must go to the police.'

'No, better to let things lie,' said Roger. 'Business is business, you know . . .'

Briseida went on drying herself without another word. She had just taken a shower and been able to check that she was unharmed after the incredible painting session. Or torture session. She was thinking that as soon as she got dressed, she would pack her things and get out of Roger Levin's apartment. Accepting his invitation had been a mistake. She was almost sure the responsibility for what had gone on lay mostly with Roger and the gangsters surrounding him.

What about Oscar? She sincerely wished nothing had happened to him, but a sense of foreboding she could not shake off told her she would never see him again.

'I'm increasingly convinced Díaz had nothing to do with this,' said Miss Wood.

'So why has he disappeared?' Bosch asked.

'That's what I can't understand.'

Stubbed out in the ashtray, her ecological cigarette was a mass of green wrinkles.

7

'What's this?' asked Jorge.

'It's me,' Clara said.

He could not believe it. The creature staring at him out of all that yellowness was a being from another planet, a devil from a traveller's tale, a sulphurous spirit. It was Clara, but less than her. Clara the egg yolk. Or a *corrected* Clara: because he could remember that the curve of her collar bones had never been quite so gentle, the shadow under her cheekbones so ill-defined. And her muscles looked different. And her silhouette. It was her, but not her. And whoever had drawn her like this did not have flesh-coloured pencils, but very pale lemon-yellow ones. He was used to seeing her in an unending carnival of works of art, and so part of his brain did not react. But this *thing* went beyond painting.

'If you like, I'll take my clothes off,' she said. Even her voice sounded odd – was there a distant crystal echo? 'But I warn you, the rest is more of the same.'

Jorge went cautiously over to her. In the creature's face, the slit of the lips curved upwards.

'I don't bite, you know. And I'm not contagious.'

She was standing there like a well-behaved schoolgirl, hands behind her back. Her clothes – a top with crossed straps that left her midriff bare, and a creased miniskirt, looked youthful and normal. 'But it's padding,' she explained, 'for works of art to be despatched.' Her shoes were flat enclosed sandals like bedsocks.

'What have they done to you?'

'They've primed me.'

'Primed you?'

'Aha.'

Jorge knew of the word, just as Clara knew what an endoscopy or a cardiac scan were. Your partner's language is the first thing you pick up, sometimes the only thing. But there was a slight difference. He always grimaced when he heard her mention things like hyperdramatic, prime or quiescence. He knew it was a bit unfair of him, but unfortunately it was unavoidable. Clara's profession was too much for him. His ex-wife Beatriz also had a job that did not exactly enthuse him (watching bacteria copulate, for God's sake), while that of his sister Arabia (interior design), not to mention his brother Pedro's (an art critic) seemed to him merely eccentric, but biology, design and art criticism are professions one can understand. Being a work of art, though, was beyond his comprehension.

'I'm sorry, but I seem to remember you've been primed before, or at least that's what you've told me, and it wasn't . . .'

'No, it was never like this Jorge, never like this. This is the work of specialists. It was done by F&W, the top people. If I told you all they have done . . .'

'Even your eyes . . .'

'Yes, the irises, the conjunctivae, and the retinas. And all the rest of my body, including the holes and uumm . . . cavities,' she ended, sticking out her tongue.

A quivering stamen poking out from the flower of her lips. Jorge had seen orchids with reproductive organs the same colour as this thing. It was not just her tongue – it was her entire palate. Will it ever come off? was the macho worry that flashed through his mind. She loved producing astonishment like this.

'Don't worry, the priming is never permanent. I'm the same as ever underneath. But you still haven't seen the best.'

What else could there be? He blinked, and moved closer.

'It's not my skin, it's what I've got hanging here,' Clara helped him.

It was then he saw it. A label dangling between her breasts, hung round her neck by a black thread. Another one similar on her right wrist, and a third round her right ankle. A strong, orange-tinged yellow, the yellow of a Chinese emperor. She had once told him that this colour, this and no other, belonged to labels from . . .

'Aha.' Clara smiled gleefully when she saw he had got it at last. 'I've been contracted by the Van Tysch Foundation!'

A suitcase – Jorge reasoned – also carries labels of the airline company it is being sent with, but after all, it is a suitcase, so that surprises no one. But what would anyone think if they could see this girl in her pearl-white top and skirt, her hair and skin like a plastic doll's, stripped of her eyelashes and brows, almost completely devoid of facial features, but attractive despite all that, yes, for some morbid and inexplicable reason even more attractive because of the three yellow labels hanging from her. The latest generation of Japanese toys? A female entertainer for long-haul flights? She could be anything, thought Jorge. A bell-flower with no dragonfly wings; a faery creature freshly painted by one of those Pre-Raphaelites Pedro hated so much, dressed in her summer best.

'Don't worry,' she reassured him, 'No one is going to see me. I was brought to Barajas in an armour-plated van, and we came in at the freight terminal rather than the one for passengers. They always treat their primed paintings as fragile freight items when they have to travel.' Her eyes gleamed yellow. 'This room is exclusively for artistic material transported by KLM. I have to wait here until they tell me it's time to get on the plane to Holland.'

There was not much furniture in the room: a yellow bench (where she had been resting before Jorge arrived) and a shelf like a narrow bar all along one wall. They preferred to lean against the shelf.

'So who's going to paint you . . . ? Jorge muttered, as if he were dreaming, too frightened to pronounce the magic word. 'Will it be Van . . . ?'

Clara, busy fixing her top, stretched out a yellow finger and placed it on his lips, in the centre of his grey moustache. Jorge smelt of chemicals.

'Don't say it. If you do, it'll be sure to bring me bad luck. Anyway, I'm still not sure. Remember, there are many artists in the Foundation. It could be Rayback, Stein, Mavalaki . . .'

'What about the "Rembrandt" collection . . .'

'Yes, yes that's it! It's *his* collection and there's still time for me to be one of the paintings. But please, don't talk about it! I'm so happy with what I've got that I don't want to think of anything else . . .'

They stared at each other. Clara was radiant under the neon lights. Jorge felt dull in comparison. There was nothing he shared with that tiny alien figure, that half-finished piece of porcelain (God, it set his eyes on edge just looking at her, all that yellow was like scraping a fingernail on a blackboard; how he would have loved to be able to add the missing layer of flesh pink). He could understand how excited she was, but he could not go along with her. Who could blame him? He was a forty-five-year-old radiologist, with hair as white and fluffy as the cottonwool used for snow in Christmas cribs. This was, in fact, one of only a pair of bright spots in his life. His moustache, for example, was grey. And five years of a failed marriage to biologist Beatriz Marco had been enough to convince him that his life was no brighter than his moustache. Clara was the other exception. He had met her the previous spring, on a day when it seemed the sun was determined to paint everything yellow. His brother

Pedro had invited him to a cocktail party of a collector, a Belgian woman who had settled in Madrid by the name of Edith, who was anxious to show everyone her most recent acquisition: *The White Queen*, the latest work by Victoria Lledó. At that time, Jorge was preoccupied with his divorce proceedings. He had no shortage of work (his radiology practice was satisfyingly busy) but he was more lonely than the losing chess king. He had no idea that meeting *The White Queen* would change his life completely. An infallible sixth sense ('You inherited it from your father,' his mother used to say) led him to accept the fateful invitation his brother had made simply to take his mind off things.

Edith Whatever-weke, resplendent in tunics and perfumes, showed them round her hovel in La Moraleja, pointing out her complete collection of HD works: painted men and women in poses in the living room, the library, on the balcony. What on earth are they doing standing there like that? Jorge wondered, fascinated by the weary beauty of their faces. What are they thinking of when we are looking at them?

Then she led them out to the garden, where the work by Vicky Lledó was on show.

'It's an outdoor performance,' Edith explained.

'What does that mean?' Jorge wanted to know.

'They are HD works in which the figures move and carry out actions planned by the artist,' Pedro said, adopting a professional tone. 'They are called *outdoor* because that's where they take place, and *performance* because they follow a plan and are repeated in a continuous cycle with or without the presence of the public. If they were shown like any other dramatic work and the public had to arrive at a certain time to see them, then they would be *reunions*.'

'So is this a kind of *art-shock*?'

Edith and Pedro exchanged knowing smiles.

'Art-shocks, dear brother, are interactive reunions, that is, dramatic works put on at a specific time and in which the owner of the work or his friends can take part if they so wish. Most of them involve sex or violence, and are completely illegal. No, don't pull that face, Jorge, because you're not going to be that lucky today: *The White Queen* isn't an art-shock, it's a noninteractive performance. In other words, a work that will perform an action according to a schedule, but the public will not take part in any direct way. As innocent as can be, isn't that right, Edith?' The Belgian woman agreed with a giggle.

Jorge got ready to be bored. He had no idea of what he was about to see.

It was a big garden, protected from prying eyes by a high wall. The work was to take place on the lawn. It consisted of a roofless box with three white walls and a floor of black-and-white tiles. At ground level on the back wall, there was a rectangular opening through which the green grass could be seen. Inside the cubicle were a table, chairs, sandwiches, water and a clothes hanger, all of them painted white. A girl with a glorious mane of blonde hair, wearing a starched white wedding dress, was lying sprawled on the floor tiles. Her face and arms glowed with an ethereal brightness. All of a sudden, as Jorge was taking all this in, the work turned onto all fours, crawled over to the slit in the back wall, put her head into it, withdrew it, put it back again. All this produced a very striking image, like a surrealist film.

'See?' Edith explained. 'She wants to get out through the hole, but she can't, because her bride's dress won't let her . . .'

'It's a simple metaphor,' Pedro added. 'She's tired of living a bourgeois marriage.'

More fruitless attempts to push the flounces of the dress through the hole. Back again. Another push. Her waist wriggling, backside in the air, hips stuck in the frame. Looking at her, Jorge felt a stab of sympathy – he could identify with how Beatriz felt.

'Now the girl understands,' Edith went on, 'that to get out she has to take off her dress . . . yes, there she goes, she's taking it off and hanging it on the hanger . . . she's overcome her prejudices, she's stripped naked and can escape.'

She paused to speak to all her guests: 'Let's go to the other side, shall we, to see what happens next?'

Jorge's brother had to prod him with his elbow.

'He's never seen a real live performance,' he laughed.

'It's good, isn't it?' Edith said, winking at him.

Jorge felt he was sleepwalking as they moved to the far end of the garden, behind the cubicle. Here there was a square patch of wet sand which was also part of the work. The girl was stretched out on it. She looked happy. The sun sparkled on her painted body like a pointillist painting by Seurat. An open-mouthed Jorge had never seen such a perfect nude. The breasts were not especially large, but they were in perfect harmony with the body and the gentle staircase of her ribcage. The gentle curve of her stomach was real, not the effort of her holding it in. He thought he could encircle her whole waist in his two hands. Her legs went on and on: it is easy to be mistaken when glancing at a pair of legs, but Jorge explored them in slow motion with a radiologist's trained gaze, and could find no fault as they stretched out endlessly like a highway. Not even feet and hands (always so difficult for a painter or for genetics to get right) sounded a jarring note: long, tapering finely, with tendons that stood out to emphasise they were alive, and nothing more. Her cultural archetypes, perfectly in tune with the ideas of beauty held at the end of the twentieth century and early in the twenty-first, were unanimous: it was a masterpiece.

But beyond the shape were the gestures Clara made: the contradictory effects produced by a face that was mischievous and disingenuous at the same time; the highlighted joint movements, and the use of muscles which in bodies like Jorge's lay dormant all their lives until finally awakened (perhaps) in death throes. It was the most harmonious composition Jorge had ever seen. The girl was rolling in the wet sand. She stood up and began a wild dance – her hair converted into a frenzy of whipcords – and then began to make a loincloth out of mulberry leaves, placing it round her sinuous waist. Throughout all this furious activity, her body gave off flashes of paint: the light, shiny colour of squeezed lemons which his brother defined as 'gamboge yellow'. In Jorge's feverish state, the word made it sound like a sacred dance. As they went back into the house for a drink before returning quickly to see what was to come next, he muttered to himself: Gamboge. Gamboge. It became an obsessive beat.

Evening was drawing in. The work had been performing for an hour and a half. As an appendix to her private bacchanal, the girl masturbated: slowly, imperiously, on her back on the sand. Jorge did not think she was pretending.

'So then,' Edith continued her commentary in her foreign, musical Spanish, 'after the ecstasy she starts to feel hungry and thirsty. Cold as well. She remembers the food, water and her dress are back in the room. So she crawls back through the slit, gets into the cubicle, eats, drinks, puts her wedding dress on again, and becomes the chaste, well-educated young woman she was at the start. It's full of meaning, isn't it?'

'A typical Vicky Lledó piece,' Pedro gave his verdict, stroking his beard. 'Women's liberation will not be complete while men keep on blackmailing them with the apparent benefits of the welfare state.'

That night, the canvas was returning to Madrid by taxi. Jorge offered to take her instead – fortunately, Pedro preferred to go on his own. Dressed in jersey, jeans and with a scarf round her neck, she seemed to him just as exciting as when she had been naked, dishevelled and glistening with sweat and sand. Her lack of eyebrows and the sheen of her skin caught his attention. She explained that she had been primed. It was the first time he had heard this expression. 'To prime means to prepare a canvas for painting,' she told him. During the journey, with his hands tight on the wheel, he asked many questions, and obtained a few answers: she was twenty-three years old (about to be twenty-four), and had been an HD model since she was sixteen. Jorge was delighted at her self-assurance, her intelligence, the way she waved her hands as she spoke, the gentle but determined edge to her voice. She told him some extraordinary things about her work. 'Don't get it wrong: the HD models are not actors: they are works of art and do *everything* the artists decide they should do – yes, everything, without exception. Hyperdramatism is called that precisely because it goes *beyond* drama. There is no make-believe. In HD art, everything is real, including the sex when there is sex, and the violence.'

How did she feel doing all this? What she was supposed to feel, what the painter wanted her to feel? When she was doing *The White Queen* it was claustrophobia, complete freedom, unease, then claustrophobia once more. 'It's an incredible pro-

fession,' he admitted. 'What do you do for a living?' she asked.
I'm a radiologist, he told her.

After that there were dates, evenings out, shared nights.

If anyone had asked him to define their relationship, he would
have responded without hesitation: strange and exciting.

Everything about her fascinated him. The way she sometimes
made up. The exotic essences she occasionally used as perfumes.
The rich elegance of her wardrobe. Her complete indifference
when it came to showing herself off naked. Her unabashed bisex-
uality. The scandalous exercises she had to do for some painters.
And in spite of all this, her incredible naiveté. Contradictions
were the norm for her. He savoured her qualities until he was full
of them, and then found himself wishing for a little bit of simplicity. After spying on her copulating bacteria, Beatriz became
simple again. Why couldn't Clara be the same after she had
wiped all the paint off? Why did he always have this terrible
sense of fetishism, as if sleeping with her was like kissing a
luxury shoe?

Recently he had been forcing her to argue with him – it was
his way of trying to rediscover this simplicity. All couples argue.
We do too. Conclusion: we are like all couples. The logic of this
argument seemed to him watertight. Their last fight had been on
her birthday, 16 April. They went out to eat in a new restaurant –
candelabra, accordeons and dishes their tongues had to do yoga
to pronounce – he had discovered. Jorge closes his eyes and can
see her just as she was that night: a Lacroix leather dress and a
choker with the designer's name on a silver ring. This and nothing more – no underwear, because in the morning she was
appearing naked in a work by Jaume Oreste. Jorge kept glancing
from the ring to the curve of her breasts pressed together by the
dress. As she breathed, her breasts looked like two white whales,
and the ring swung to and fro like a ship's porthole. He was
excited of course (he always was when he went out with her),
but he also felt a strange desire to destroy all this magnificent
harmony. Like the temptation a child feels to smash the most
expensive piece of crockery. He began stealthily, without revealing his real intentions.

'Did you know "Monsters" was the most popular exhibition

the Haus der Kunst in Munich has ever had? Pedro told me so the other day.'

'I'm not surprised.'

'And in Bilbao they're wetting themselves trying to get "Flowers" to the Guggenheim, but Pedro says it'll cost them an arm and a leg. But that's nothing: everyone is saying that the new collection they're putting on this year, "Rembrandt" by Van Tysch, is going to top "Flowers" and "Monsters" both in visitors and in the price of the works. Some are even saying it's going to be the most important exhibition in history. In other words, your Maestro has succeeded in making hyperdramatic art one of the most lucrative businesses of the twenty-first century . . .'

A good line to throw, Captain Achab! The two symmetrical whales rise up as one. The silver ship trembles.

'And you, as always, reckon the world has gone mad.'

'No, the world always has been mad, it's not that. The fact is, I don't agree with the opinion most people have about Van Tysch.'

'Which is?'

'That he's a genius.'

'He is.'

'I'm sorry, Van Tysch is very smart, but it's not the same thing. My brother says that HD art was created by Tanagorsky, Kalima and Buncher at the start of the seventies. They were true artists, but they starved. Then along came Van Tysch, who as a young man had inherited a fortune from a distant relative in the United States. He invented a system for buying and selling the works, created a Foundation to manage his production, and he devoted himself to lining his pockets thanks to hyperdramatism. A brilliant business idea!'

'So what's wrong with that?'

As usual, Clara was imperturbable. She was accustomed to controlling all her impulses, and used this power to her advantage against him. It was hard for Jorge to make her lose her patience, because a canvas' patience is boundless.

'What's wrong is that it's a business, it's not art. Although wasn't it your beloved Van Tysch who once came out with the definition "art is money"?'

114

'And he was right.'

'He was right? Was Rembrandt a genius because today his paintings are worth millions?'

'No, but if Rembrandt's paintings weren't worth millions today, who would care whether he was a genius or not?'

Jorge was about to respond when a dollop of cream (from the dessert-rolled crêpes stuffed with cream) fell on to his tie (*plop!* Captain Achab, a seagull just shat on you), which meant he had to busy himself with his napkin while she carried on.

'Van Tysch understood that to create a new kind of art all you need is for it to make money.'

'That line of argument only applies to business, darling.'

'Art is a business, Jorge,' she declared, unmoved, while the candle flame blinked, photocopied by her blue eyes.

'My God, listen to the opinion of a work of art! So according to you, a professional painting, art is a business?'

'Aha. Just like medicine.'

Aha. That dreadful habit of hers when she spoke. She opened her mouth and arched one of her false, painted eyebrows as she pronounced the symmetrical word: Aha.

'You charge for your X-ray plates just like a painter does for his paintings,' she went on. 'Aren't you tired of always saying that some colleague or other ought to realise that medicine is an art? There you go.'

'There I go what?'

'Medicine is an art, which means it's also a business. Today it's all the same: art and business. The real artists know there's no difference. At least there isn't nowadays.'

'Fine, let's admit art is a business. So then hyperdramatic art is the business of buying and selling people, isn't it?'

'I can see where you're heading, but we models are not people when we are works of art: we're paintings.'

'Don't talk such nonsense. That rubbish is fine to pull the wool over the public's eyes. But people are not paintings.'

'Now you sound like those experts who at the end of the nineteenth century said that impressionist paintings weren't real paintings. But art history finally accepted impressionism, and then cubism, and now it is accepting hyperdramatism.'

'Because it's a profitable business?' She shrugged without saying anything. 'Look, Clara, I don't want to be an iconoclast, but hyperdramatic art consists of putting young women like you naked or semi-naked in "artistic" poses. Young men, too, of course. And a lot of adolescents, children even. But how many mature men or women do you see in HD works of art? Go on, tell me! Who would pay twenty million euros to take home a painted fat old man, and stand him there in a pose?'

'But the work that gave the title "Monsters" to Van Tysch's collection is of two hugely fat people. And it's worth far more than twenty million, Jorge.'

'What about the HD ornaments? Converting someone into an Ashtray or a Chair, what's that? Is that art too? And what about art-shocks? And "dirty" paintings? . . .'

'All that is completely illegal, and has nothing to do with legitimate hyperdramatism.'

'Let's drop it. I know it's a sin to take the name of God in vain.'

'Would you like another crêpe, or is the one you're dripping down your front enough?' She pointed to her plate, where the rolled-up crêpes lay untouched. This was another consequence of her work: she kept a tight rein over her calorie intake, and controlled her weight with portable electronic gadgets – the latest fad. She often dined only on high-vitamin juices, but never seemed to be hungry.

That night they made love at his place. It was as it always was: a delicately pleasurable exercise. She was a canvas, and he had to be careful. Sometimes he would ask her why she was not so careful with herself in the brutal interactive reunions known as art-shocks she sometimes took part in. 'That's different, it's art,' she would reply. 'And in art anything goes, even damaging the canvas.' 'Ah!' he would say. And go on adoring her.

He was crazy about her. He was fed up with her. He never wanted to leave her. He wanted never to see her again.

'You won't be able to give her up,' his brother Pedro warned him one day. 'It's always the same when we fall for a painting: we've no idea why we like it so much, but we can't get rid of it.'

*

Clara was not sure what she felt for Jorge. It was not love, of course, because she did not believe she had ever felt true love for anyone or anything except for art (people like Gabi or Vicky were facets of that diamond). And she guessed Jorge was not in love with her either. She could understand that for him it was very satisfactory to have made it with a canvas: it was the same kind of status symbol as buying himself a Lancia or a Patek Philippe, having an appartment in Conde de Penálver, or being the boss of a profitable radiological institute. 'Going to bed with a painting is a kind of a luxury, isn't it, Jorge? Something your social class likes to do.'

Naturally she found him attractive: that shock of white hair, and that moustache standing out in his huge frame, those grey eyes of his, his manly chin. It excited her to think he was an older man she was perverting. She loved it when she made him blush. But she also enjoyed thinking the opposite was true: that it was he who was perverting her. Her white-haired master. The sunbed-tanned mentor. And on top of it all, Jorge was not part of the art world – a detail rare enough to make him extra special.

On the other side of the balance was his complete vulgarity. Doctor Atienza was of the ridiculous opinion that hyperdramatic art was a kind of legalised sexual slavery, twenty-first century prostitution. He could not understand why someone might want to buy a naked minor whose body had been painted, simply to put them on show in their house. He thought Bruno van Tysch was a playboy whose sole merit had been to inherit a stupendous fortune. When she heard Jorge's pronouncements, she felt bitter. What she hated above all in this world was mediocrity. Clara longed for genius like a bird longs for the infinite air. But she could understand the reason for all this mediocrity. Unlike her, his profession did not demand he give his heart and soul to it. Jorge had never felt that shudder of emotion, the sense of fragility and fire that a model felt in the hands of an expert painter; he knew nothing of the nirvana of quiescence, the wing-beats of time in a paralysed salon, the gaze of the public like cold acupuncture on the body.

Neither of them was sure where this relationship of dates and shared nights might lead. Probably nowhere. Jorge wanted children, and occasionally said so. She looked at him with pitying compassion, as a martyr might look at someone who was asking: Does it hurt? The only life she wanted to reproduce, she would tell him, was her own. 'Don't you see, every time I'm a painting, it's as if I'm giving birth to myself?' Of course, he couldn't understand her.

Perhaps what she valued most of all in him was his calm nature, his ability to give her good advice. Even when he was asleep, Jorge was therapeutic: he breathed steadily, was not troubled by any nightmares, did not get afraid in dark rooms (she did), was a lesson in the perfect way to rest. His words were like creams prescribed by an amiable doctor, his smile an instantly effective sedative. All this was far removed from her world, and immensely welcome.

Right now, she needed a large dose of Jorge.

'Are you sure you're not being duped?' he asked, trying to appear doubtful.

'Of course I am. This is the most important thing that has ever happened to me. Not only am I going to earn more money than I ever dreamed possible, but I'm going to become . . . I'm sure I'm going to become a . . . a *great* work of art.' Jorge noticed she had hesitated, as if anything she could say would be far beneath the reality of what was to happen to her. 'Today they told me that in another twenty-four thousand years, they would still be talking about *me*,' she added in a whisper. 'Can you believe it? The Foundation woman told me so. 'Twenty-four thousand years. I can't stop thinking about it. Can you believe it?'

She had just given him a brief summary of all that had happened. She told him about the two men visiting the GS gallery, and her interview with Friedman on the Thursday. After that, she had been primed by five experts: Friedman himself examined her hair and skin; a Señor Zumi her muscles and joints; Señor Gargallo prepared her physiology; and the Montforts fine-tuned her concentration and habits. Friedman received her in the basement of the Desiderio Gaos building once they had stripped her, destroyed her clothing, and taken photographs of her for the insurance company. He felt her all over. Her hair, he said, needed cutting. Then it had to be coated with a gel that would allow it to be painted. He did not consider her skin soft enough, so pre-scribed creams she would need to rub on. He noted any abrasions or wrinkles. He observed the movement of her Adam's apple when she swallowed, and how her ribcage showed with her breathing, how her nipples reacted to pressure or cold, the character of all her muscles. After that, he probed each and every hole and cavity with his fingers and light. 'Spare me the details,' Jorge begged her.

Zumi, a mysterious Japanese man of few words, saw her on the first floor once Friedman had finished with her. For hours, it seemed, Clara had to hang from various pieces of apparatus in the gym there. Zumi discovered a certain laxity in her cervical vertebrae, and a tendency to accumulate lactic acid in her legs. Through beads of sweat, she could see him smile silently at each successive torture: balancing on one leg, being strung from the ceiling by the ankles, standing on tiptoe on a bench, bending over backwards, raising her arms with weights attached to her biceps. Two hours later, the exhausted material was passed on to Señor Gargallo on the third floor. Gargallo was an expert in the canvas' physiological reactions. He had a huge collection of his experiments on film, an absolutely repugnant DVD library. He was convinced of his own uselessness.

'The only organ that matters is the one I'm not expert in,' he told Clara, tapping his forehead. 'Fortunately, I am expert in the second most important one.' He pointed to his groin.

He was a plump, affable fellow, with a yellowish complexion, goatee beard and round, smudged glasses. He began by warning her that his job was 'an unavoidable mess'. 'Naturally, we'd like to be a pure work of art like a piece of canvas or a lump of alabaster,' Gargallo philosophised. 'But we are alive. And life is not art: life is disgusting. My task is to stop life behaving like life.'

The exercises he put her through were yet another nightmare: the material – her, naked and immobile – had to put up with drops being spread under her eyelids; feathers tickling her in remote folds of her body; drugs which activated her bowels and her bladder at the same time, or changed her mood, increasing or decreasing her libido or simply gave her a headache; pills that suddenly made her blood pressure collapse, or made her feel

119

cold, hot, or itchy all over (my God, the desire to scratch, forbidden in any painting); the dizziness of intense hunger; the raging curse of thirst; the stinging threat of insects and other creatures – 'in outdoor pieces they often crawl up legs', Gargallo explained; extreme tiredness and sleep, that steamroller of awareness that can flatten the willpower of any permanent work of art. Gargallo tried out further tests, made adjustments here and there when he saw the material was suspect, prescribed a few pills, noted down problems.

She was left to rest for a few hours and then, still exhausted, she was taken up to the fifth floor and handed over to Pedro Monfort. 'I started in a cellar and I'm going to end up in the loft,' she thought, her brain weakened but still determined to fight back. The Monforts were brother and sister: he was very young, she was older. Their speciality was to prime thoughts (a noble enough task, surely) and yet they did not seem happy. In fact, Pedro Monfort regarded Gargallo as the real specialist. He was a badly shaven, intellectual-looking man who liked lengthy silences and stuffing his phrases with obscenities.

'The only things that matter are the cunt and the prick,' he suddenly declared to a weary Clara. 'And I'm telling you that as a brain expert.'

He also insisted that concentration was impossible.

'We can only concentrate by letting our attention wander. I know you canvases are taught differently in the academy, but I couldn't give a fuck about the methods you learn in academies. Just look at children while they're playing. They're completely concentrated on what they're doing. Why? Because they're making an effort to concentrate or because they're playing? Shit, it's obvious: they are concentrating because they are absorbed, because they're enjoying themselves. It's absurd for you to concentrate on quiescence. What you should be doing is enjoying yourself.'

This was his favourite word: 'Enjoy,' he kept saying as he submitted her to yet another mental test.

Marisa Monfort, middle-aged, with dyed hair and eyes buried in mascara, received the last remains of Clara on the seventh floor. Her office was gloomy, and she did not look happy either.

The backs of her hands were tattooed with two snakes, cut up into segments by innumerable yellow bangles. She pressed fingers to her temples as she spoke, as though pressing two bells. 'I'm the memory woman, my girl,' she said. 'The habits anchored in our ego that get in the way of hyperdramatic art so much.' She made Clara come into her office three times, and analysed her gestures. She was concerned by her excessive tendency to repeat the same thing. Fortunately, she did not discover any of the faults 'which ruin good material': a nervous tic, nail biting, a niggling nervous cough, other defence mechanisms. She bombarded her with imaginary situations. Showed her obscene or terrible photos. Praised her for not feeling ashamed. But she was damning over Clara's squeamishness over illegal behaviour.

'My child: to be a great work of art you have to overcome *all* obstacles,' Marisa Monfort reproached her in a voice like an oracle. 'You've no idea of the world you are entering. Being a masterpiece has something . . . inhuman about it. You have to be a lot less involved. Imagine it's a science-fiction film: art is like a being from another planet which manifests itself through us. We may paint pictures or compose music, but neither the picture nor the music belongs to us, because *they* are *not* human things. Art uses us, my child, it uses us in order to exist, but it's like an alien being. That's what you've got to think: you're not human when you are a painting. Think of yourself as an insect. A very odd insect. Think of yourself as an insect capable of flying, sucking flowers, being fecundated by a male proboscis, poisoning a child with your sting . . . Go on, think of yourself as that insect right now.'

Clara tried, but found it impossible to understand what the insect might be thinking.

'When you discover what the insect is thinking,' Marisa Monfort said, 'then you'll be a great work of art.'

On the eighth floor was the priming workshop. It was decorated with blown-up photos of F&W's past triumphs: an aquatic work by Nina Soldelli, the fabulous Kirsten Kirstenman standing in someone's salon, the amazing flame-haired female figure of Mavalaki, an outside piece by Ferrucioli on a cliff top. All of them had been primed by F&W. It was here that Clara

121

finally received Friedman's icy verdict: they accepted her, with reservations. She was good material, but would have to improve. A woman with a South American accent (Clara recognised the voice – it was the woman who had stretched her on the telephone) handed her the contract. Four sheets of turquoise paper, with the letterhead 'The Bruno van Tysch Foundation, Department of Art'. Clara was so overjoyed, she could scarcely believe her eyes. The contract was for one year. The fee (five million euros) was to be paid in two instalments: half had already been put into her bank account, the rest would follow at the end. She would also receive a percentage of the sale price of the work, and of the monthly rent. There was also a comprehensive insurance and two appendices. One of these stated she would work exclusively for the Foundation; the other a commitment that she would not allow herself to be used as a fake. A third appendix required her to leave everything in the hands of the Department of Art. Art could do what it liked with her, because Art was Art. Only Art knew what it was going to do with her, but whatever that might be, she would have to accept it. The painter contracting her was from the Foundation, but she would not discover his identity until the work began. Clara signed the four sheets.

'That's crazy,' Jorge scolded her.

'You haven't the slightest idea of how this scene operates. Everything is kept a complete secret. Rembrandt, Caravaggio, Rubens and other great masters had their professional secrets, didn't they? The way they made their colours, their choice of canvas . . . well, modern painters have secrets, too. It stops others copying their ideas.'

'What did you do after signing?'

'I was free until the final priming session.'

That had been on Saturday. It took all day. A haircut, shower in cleaning acids, then creams applied to her body using huge rotating brushes like in a carwash, the removal of scars and other marks (including Alex Bassan's signature), the shaping and moulding of her muscles and joints with flexing agents and more creams; then the dyeing of her skin, hair, eyes, holes and cavities with the white-coloured base, followed by a thin layer of yellow paint. And finally, the labels, which showed only her name, the Foundation's logo, and a mysterious bar code.

It was Sunday 25 June, 2006, and the priming was finished. Clara was dressed in the padded top and miniskirt, driven to Barajas airport, and stored in the room. They asked her if there was anyone she wanted to say goodbye to. She chose Jorge, who was just back from a radiology congress and had heard her message.

'So there you are,' she concluded.

Jorge interpreted all this from his point of view.

'Five million euros is a lot of money. You'll have no more worries.'

'You're forgetting the percentage on the sale and rent. If they make a masterpiece out of me, I can easily treble my earnings.'

'Goodness me.'

Clara's golden eyes opened wide as she smiled: two Jorges were reflected in the yellow irises.

'Art is money,' she whispered.

He stared this glowing golden apparition up and down. 'She hasn't even been painted yet, and she's already worth a fortune.' In the silence, all they could hear was the muffled distant sound of the airport's loudspeakers.

'Twenty-four thousand years,' said Jorge in a tone which made it sound as though it were negotiable, like a sum of money. 'But can an HD work last that long?'

'All you would need are twenty-four thousand substitutes, one a year. But I would go down in history as the original model.'

What about a million years? A million people, Jorge calculated. Just with the inhabitants of Madrid, at a rate of one person per year, the work could last as long as the life of mankind on Earth, including his anthropoid ancestors. Of course, it would take many generations, but what are three or four million people? All at once it seemed to him he was no longer looking at Clara: he was staring at eternity.

'That's incredible.'

'I'm a bit scared,' she confessed. Then she added, with a shy smile: 'Only a bit, but the highest quality.'

Impulsively, Jorge held out his arms.

'No,' she protested, stepping back. 'Don't embrace me. You could damage me. I feel like crying, but I don't want to. And anyway, they told me I don't have any tears or sweat any more. I've hardly even got any saliva. That's the effect of being primed.'

'But do you feel all right?'

'I feel wonderful, ready for anything, Jorge, anything. Right now I'd be able to do anything with my body, *anything* a painter might ask of me.'

Jorge had no wish to enquire just what that meant. At that moment, a man in a dark-blue pilot's uniform came in. He was tall, attractive, with a sensual mouth, and had slackened his tie.

'Plane now,' he said with a strong Spanish accent.

Clara looked at Jorge. He would have liked to say something earth-shattering, but he was not much good at moments like these.

'When will I see you again?' was all he could think of.

'I don't know. Once I've been painted, I suppose.'

They stood looking at each other for a second or two, and Clara suddenly realised she was crying. She could not tell for certain when it had begun, because there were, in fact, no tears, but the rest of the mechanism continued to function: the lump in the throat, heavy eyelids, irritated sensation in the eyes, but-terflies in the stomach. She told herself the artist would have to add the teardrops if he wanted them – perhaps he could paint them on her cheeks, or imitate them with tiny crystal shards, like in some statues of the Virgin. Then she controlled herself. She did not want to get emotional. A canvas should always remain calm.

She walked away from Jorge without looking back. She fol-lowed the other man down a metallic corridor throbbing with the roar of aeroplanes. With each step she took, the label banged against her ankle.

It was a sudden flash. Perhaps it was his sixth sense ('You inher-ited it from your father') which raised the alarm as he saw her disappear through the door. Clara should not be going, she should not accept the job. Clara *was in danger*.

Jorge hesitated for a moment, thinking he should call her back, but his absurd premonition vanished as quickly and calmly as she had done.

He soon forgot it.

She had never felt such a combination of fear and happiness. Both the feelings were there, distinct and contradictory: an immense fear and an ecstatic sense of joy. She remembered her mother had said something similar about the way she felt as she went into church on her wedding day. She smiled at the memory as she followed the man in pilot's uniform down the deafening passageway. She imagined there were people on both sides watching her as she glided in a silky gauze towards an altar decorated with golden or yellow objects just like her: tabernacle, chalices, the cross.

Gold, yellow, gold.

8

Black.

The backdrop is coal black, the floor a smoky black. Rising from the floor is a metal chair like a bar stool. Annek Hollech is sitting on the stool swinging one of her bare feet. All she is wearing is a black T-shirt with the Foundation's logo on it, and the three labels at her neck, wrist and ankle. Her slender thighs, bare almost to her groin, are like a pair of open scissors with the light glinting on them. Her auburn hair has a tendency to fall like a curtain across her eyebrow-less face, a shadowy face as pure as fresh clay. The fingers of her right hand play with her hair, pulling it back, combing it, stroking a handful.

'Do you really think that?' asked the man from somewhere invisible.

A nod of the head.

'Perhaps you're confusing a lack of time with a lack of interest. You know the Maestro is fully occupied with finishing the works in homage to Rembrandt for 15 July.'

'It's not his work.' Now she was playing with the bottom edge of her T-shirt. 'It's that he doesn't want to see me any more. We paintings all realise that. Eva has noticed it too.'

'You mean your friend Eva van Snell has also noticed that the Maestro has apparently lost interest in you?'

A nod of the head.

'Annek, we know from experience that paintings with an owner feel better, more protected. And Eva has been bought at the moment. Isn't that what's worrying you? The fact that you haven't been bought yet? Do you remember when we sold you as *Confessions*, *Door Ajar*, and *Summer*? Didn't you feel good with Mr Wallberg?'

'That was different.'

'Why?'

She blushed, but the priming prevented her cheeks changing colour.

'Because the Maestro used to say that he had never done any-thing like *Deflowering*. When he called me to Edenburg to start the sketches, he told me he wanted to paint a childhood memory with me. I thought that was so nice. Mr Wallberg loved me, but the Maestro had created me. Señor Wallberg is the best owner I've had, but it's different . . . the Maestro tried so hard with me . . .'

'You mean with the hyperdramatic work.'

'Yes. He took me to the Edenburg woods . . . while we were there, he saw an expression on my face . . . something he liked . . . he said it was incredible . . . that I was . . . was like one of his own memories . . .'

The left foot was tracing slow circles over the black carpet: a graceful needle turning on a vinyl record. As it moved round, the ankle label caught the light.

'I don't mind not being bought. I'd just like . . . him not to suffer because of me . . . I've done everything he asked of me. Everything. I know it's selfish of me to think he owes me some-thing in return, because when he painted me in *Deflowering* he . . . he gave me . . . the best thing in the world, I know, it's just that . . .'

'Tell me,' the man encouraged her.

As she raised her head, Annek's green eyes shone.

'I'd like . . . I'd like to tell him . . . that I can't avoid . . . I can't avoid growing up . . . It's not my fault . . . I'd like my body to be different . . .' She choked with emotion. 'It's not my fault . . .'

At that moment, something incredible happened. Annek's body split down the middle, like a flower, from head to toe. The chair she was on also collapsed in two. Through the centre of the two halves appeared a middle-aged man in a dark suit, bald head with a fringe of white hair. He came to an abrupt halt, and spoke:

'Oh, I'm sorry. You were on the video-scanner. I didn't know.'

Lothar Bosch stepped to one side, and Annek's three-dimensional figure came together again in pure silence, just as water flows back around the void when a finger is withdrawn from it. Miss Wood pressed the pause button, and the adolescent hung immobile in the centre of the room.

'I'd already finished,' Miss Wood said with a yawn. 'It's all much of a muchness.'

She pressed the rewind, and Annek started a strange Saint Vitus' dance. Miss Wood took off her virtual reality visor and left it on the table, dismissing the apparition. The table was a half-crescent moon built out of the wall. It was the only wooden-coloured piece of furniture in this small audio-visual room in the MuseumsQuartier. Everything else was black, including the stiletto-like chair legs. Miss Wood was seated in one of them, her pink cardigan and suit gleaming in the dark. Next to her lay a pile of virtual reality tapes. On the wall to her left, cameras and loudspeakers stuck out like gargoyles.

Bosch, wearing an elegant grey suit in which the red label shone like a wedding carnation in his lapel, sat in a chair opposite her and pulled out his reading glasses.

'How long have you been here?' he asked.

He was concerned about her. They had been in Vienna for five days including this Monday 26 June, working non-stop. They had suites in the Ambassador, but only used them to sleep in. And no matter how early Bosch appeared at the Museums-Quartier, she was already there, working away. The thought suddenly crossed his mind that Wood probably did not go to sleep at night either.

127

'For a while,' she said. 'I still had to check a few interviews Support had done, and my father always told me never to leave work undone.'

'Good advice,' Bosch agreed. 'But be careful not to overdo the virtual reality visors. They can damage your eyesight.'

As Miss Wood sat back in her chair, the cardigan opened like a pair of wings, and Bosch was treated to a wave of perfume. The mounds of her breasts pushed against the pink dress. Embarrassed, Bosch lowered his eyes. He liked everything about this woman: the sudden smell of her perfume, her tiny, cutglass body, even the extremely slender legs of hers, and the knees peeping over the top of the desk. And the sombre gravity of her voice, which he was now listening to.

'Don't worry, I have been taking walks. There is something soothing about Vienna at dawn on a Monday morning. And I've realised something: people here buy a lot of bread, don't they? I've seen several men with a baguette under their arm, like in Paris. I almost thought they were deliberately parading the bread under my nose.'

'In fact, they're Braun's men keeping an eye on you.'

Her smile told him his joke had hit the mark. It was dangerous to talk about food with Miss Wood.

'I wouldn't be surprised,' she said, 'although they'd do better to keep an eye on other things. Our bird has flown, hasn't he?'

'Completely. Yesterday was Sunday, so I couldn't talk to Braun, but my friends in CID tell me no one has been arrested. And don't go thinking the other news is any better.'

'Go on anyway.' Miss Wood rubbed her eyes. 'God, I'd kill for a decent cup of coffee. A cup of black, black coffee, a good Viennese *schwarzer*, hot and strong.'

'An ornament is serving the people in Art this morning. I told her to pass by here.'

'You're a perfect gentleman, Lothar.'

Bosch felt naked. Luckily, his flaming cheeks soon died down. At fifty-five, there's no fuel that can produce a lasting blush, he thought to himself. Old blood is too thin.

'I'm beginning to know your habits,' he said.

The papers were trembling between his fingers, but his voice sounded firm enough. Miss Wood leaned forward on the desk, head in hands, as she listened to him.

'We said the other day that there were three legs to this particular construction, didn't we? The first, Annek; the second, Oscar Díaz; and the third what we could call the Competition.' He saw Wood nod in agreement, and went on: 'Well, the first has produced no results. Annek's life was a mess, but I haven't found anyone capable of harming her for any personal reason. Her father, Pieter Hollech, is a madman. At the moment he's in jail in Switzerland after causing a traffic accident while drunk-driving. Annek's mother, Yvonne Neullern, divorced him and got custody of Annek when she was four. She works as a press photographer, specialising in animals. She's in Borneo. Conservation has been in touch with her to tell her the news . . .'

'OK, so the painting's family had nothing to do with it. Go on.'

'Annek's previous buyers don't offer much either.'

'Wallberg fell in love with the canvas, didn't he?'

'Yes, he liked Annek,' agreed Bosch. 'Wallberg bought Annek in three works: *Confessions*, *Door Ajar*, and *Summer*. The last of these was a performance. Do you recall the meeting we had with Benoit, when he insisted we should find out what Wallberg *really* felt for Annek? . . . No, that's not quite right. "We have to distinguish between Mr Wallberg's artistic and erotic passions" . . .'

The baying laugh (cut short by Wood) pleased him. So his Benoit impression had gone down well. 'My God, I'm making her laugh. That's fantastic.'

All at once the sense of satisfaction drained from Bosch's face: it was as sudden as a dark cloud passing in front of the sun. His grin faded; his mouth turned down at the corners.

'Poor Annek,' he said.

He blinked several times, then shuffled the papers on the table in front of him.

'Whatever the truth, Wallberg is on his deathbed in a hospital in Berkeley, California. Lung cancer. There's nothing suspicious about any of her other purchasers either: Okomoto is in the States, searching for paintings; Cárdenas is still in Colombia, and his record is as dubious as ever, but he didn't bother Annek when she was on show in *Garland*, and he hasn't touched any of the substitutes . . .' He coughed, and his finger pointed to the next paragraph. 'As for all the other madmen . . . according to our information, almost all of them are either in hospital or serving prison sentences. A few are still on the loose, like that crazy Englishman who covered the façade of the New Atelier with stickers accusing the Foundation of dealing in child pornography . . .'

'What's he got to do with this?'

'He used a photo from *Deflowering* on the stickers.'

'OK.'

'His whereabouts are unknown. But we'll continue investigating. So that's all for the "Annek" leg.'

'Nothing there. What about Díaz?'

'Well, there's Briseida Canchares . . .'

'Count her out too. That art nymphomaniac has nothing to do with it. The most interesting thing she said was about that person with no papers. Go on.' Wood was playing with her cigarette lighter – a lovely black steel miniature Dunhill. Her long, slender fingers made it flick over and over like a magician's playing card.

'Díaz's friends in New York say he's a simple, goodhearted sort. The guards on tour with him are more "scientific" as you would call it: according to them, he's a loner. He didn't like making friends, and preferred his own company. Our second search of his New York apartment turned up nothing. Everything to do with photography, but nothing related to any supposed obsession with destroying paintings or even with art. In his room at the Kirchberggasse we found Briseida's address and phone number in Leiden and . . . listen to this . . . a notebook with landscape photos which, in fact, is . . . a diary.'

Miss Wood's head, with its cap of cropped hair shiny as patent leather, snapped back so quickly Bosch was afraid her skull would come loose. He immediately reassured her:

'But it doesn't offer us any leads: Díaz took snapshots of places so he could go back there later on when the light was better. Sometimes he mentions Briseida or a friend, but they are completely ordinary references. He also writes about his love of the countryside. There's even a poem. Plus a few references to his work, along the lines of "I see them as people, not as works of art". The last entry is on 7 June.' Bosch raised his eyebrows. 'I'm sorry: there's nothing about anyone without papers, man or woman.'

'Shit.'

'Exactly. But I do have some good news. We've found a café near the Marriott hotel here in Vienna where the barman remembers Díaz. Apparently, it was one of the places he used to go to when he left the paintings in their hotel. The barman says he used to ask for bourbon, which was unusual for his customers, and that was why he noticed him, as well as because of his American accent and his dark skin.'

'New York completely corrupted our poor landscape photographer,' commented Wood. Her fingers were smoothing down her hair. To Bosch, they looked like the hands of a medium: it was not Wood's mind directing those soft, irreproachably aesthetic gestures that were so typical of her. No, her mind was focused on Bosch's words (not on me, on my *words*, don't get confused, kid) with the look of a shipwrecked mariner who thinks they can glimpse the lights of a ship in the dark night.

'But there is one odd detail,' Bosch said. 'The barman swears that the last time he saw him was exactly a fortnight ago, on 15 June. He remembers the exact date thanks to another coincidence: it was a friend's birthday, and he had made arrangements to leave the bar early. He says Díaz was at the bar chatting to a girl he had never seen before – she was dark, thin, attractive, wore a lot of make-up. He reckons they were speaking in English. The waiters cannot really remember her, because there were a lot of customers that night. Díaz and her left together, and the barman has not seen either of them since.'

'When did Díaz ring his Colombian friend to ask for information about residence permits?'

'On Sunday 18 June, according to Briseida.'

Wood's outline seemed sculpted in stone.

'Three days: more than enough time to get close. Our friend Oscar took pity on our Colombian friend in a lot less.'

'That's true,' Bosch admitted, 'but if we put Unknown Girl into the mix, it could be that Díaz is completely innocent. Just imagine for a moment she is working with accomplices. They manage to get information out of Díaz about when and how he is picking the painting up, then on Wednesday they forced their way into the van and make Díaz drive to the Wienerwald.'

'So where is Díaz now?'

'They've taken him with them, as a hostage . . .'

'And run the risk he might escape and give the game away? No, if Díaz isn't guilty, that can mean only one thing: he's *dead*. That seems to me the obvious conclusion. The fundamental question is: why hasn't his body appeared yet? That's what I don't get. Even if we admit they may have needed him to drive the van, why wasn't he found in it? Where have they taken him? Why would they want to hide Díaz's body?'

'That means you think Díaz is part of this.'

'If we forget about the girl with no papers, what are we left with?'

'In that case, the police's theory is the most likely one: Díaz makes the recording, and cuts Annek up inside the van. Then he drives to a remote spot, wraps Annek in the plastic sheet, dumps her on the grass and strips her. Then he puts the cassette at her feet and drives another forty kilometres north, where another car is waiting for him.'

'I don't buy that theory either.'

'Why not?'

'Díaz is a ninny,' Miss Wood declared. 'He writes little poems, takes photos of landscapes and gets taken in by girls like Briseida. If he's involved in this, he wasn't alone.'

'But he was a very efficient security guard,' Bosch objected. 'Remember, we only choose the best for transporting paintings to their hotels.'

'I'm not saying he was bad at his job. I'm saying he's a ninny. A country bumpkin. He can't have organised all this on his own.'

Soft knocks at the door, and a waft of perfume. The server was not a Trolley or any other proper piece of furniture, but a Decoration, a wretched thing that worked on Mondays (the day off for the works of art in the MuseumsQuartier) one of the objects dreamt up by the Decorative Arts Department to fill an empty room – and the lack of experience showed when it came to him serving their coffee. It took Bosch several seconds to realise it was a young male, about eighteen or nineteen years old. His hair was a

132

symmetrical mass of blue-black scrolled curls pierced by silvery feathers. His long, tubular tunic in black velvet was cut almost too drastically at the back, and revealed the top half of a pair of black buttocks painted chestnut brown as was all the rest of the body. He placed two cups of coffee on the table. His make-up gave no clues as to what he might be thinking or feeling: it was the mask of a Polynesian warrior, a voodoo priest. The white label hanging round his neck read 'Michel'. The signature low down on his back was by someone called Garth. He was wearing ear-protectors.

When he turned towards Bosch, he got a good view of his hands: they glowed a deep bronze colour, with onyx fingernails.

'It's all too perfect, Lothar,' Miss Wood was saying. 'A second car waiting in the Wienerwald, false papers . . . in other words, a carefully laid plan. I could accept he might have been paid to take the painting to the Wienerwald, but even that seems far-fetched to me.'

'So you want us to reject the "Díaz" leg as well. That means the whole construction is in danger of collapsing . . .'

'We can't eliminate Díaz altogether. I think his role was that of scapegoat. What I can't understand is why he's disappeared.'

'They could have hidden his body so that suspicion would fall on him, while the real criminal made his getaway,' Bosch reasoned.

Miss Wood had leaned forward to examine the ornament's lower back and the signature. The ornament stood perfectly still while she did so. The label said he could be touched, so Wood slipped a hand round his waist and down towards his gleaming bronze buttocks. Her expression, with her brows knitted intently, was that of an expert judging the value of a porcelain vase. As she was doing this, she responded to Bosch.

'That's the most likely theory. But my question is: *where is he?* The police have combed several kilometres round the area, Lothar. They've used dogs and all kinds of sophisticated search equipment. So where's Díaz's body? And where did they kill him? The van offered no clues at all: no signs of struggle, not a drop of blood. And consider this for a moment: he destroys the painting, then wastes time taking all her clothes off out in the wood, running the risk of being discovered. On the other hand, whoever it was, worked out a detailed escape plan and managed to divert all the suspicion on to the security guard who was looking after the work. Does that seem logical to you?'

'No, you're right, it doesn't.'

Miss Wood stopped fondling the ornament's backside. She raised her arm, got hold of the neck label and pulled it down towards her, obliging the ornament to lean forward so she could read it. As well as the model's name, the label gave details of the craftsman who made it, and its specifications. Bosch knew that April Wood bought ornaments and utensils for her London house. Despite an official ban on the sale of human handicrafts, it still went on, and many people of a certain social level bought them just as they did soft drugs.

When she had finished reading the information, Miss Wood let go of the label. The ornament straightened up, turned on his heels in the darkness and walked out noiselessly, his bare feet gliding across the thick black carpet. Miss Wood grimaced as she sipped her hot coffee.

'I'm sure Díaz is dead,' she insisted. 'The problem is how his death fits in with everything else.'

'We still haven't considered the Competition and Rivals.' Bosch riffled through his papers. 'I have to admit this is where I get lost, April. I can't find anything. The people behind BAH, for example, are not up to much. You know Pamela O'Connor wrote a book about Annek . . .'

'*The Truth About Annek Hollech*,' Wood concurred. 'Pretentious nonsense. What she does is use Annek as an example to denounce the use of underage models in supposedly obscene works of art.'

'We're also investigating the Christian Association Against Hyperdramatic Art; the International Society For Tradition and Classical Art; the European Society Against Hyperdramatic Art . . .'

'You're leaving out the real competition,' said Wood. 'Art Enterprises, for example, has become a serious enemy. Stein says they would do anything to throw a spoke in our wheels, and, in fact, they are taking investors from us. Just imagine if what happened to *Deflowering* is only part of a master plan to discredit our security system.'

'But that doesn't fit in with what happened. A bullet in the back of the head would have had the same effect. Why all the sadism?'

'What do you mean exactly?'

The question filled Bosch with horror.

'Good God, April, he cut her up with . . . look, here is the autopsy report. Braun sent it to me this morning. Look at these photos . . . the lab tests confirmed it: whoever it was used a portable canvas cutter . . . do you know what that is? . . . a saw with a cylindrical handle and serrated edges that fits into one hand. Artists who still work with canvases and old picture restorers use them to change the size and shape of paintings. It's a powerful gadget – with the right fittings, you can cut a normal tabletop in half in five seconds . . . and he made ten cuts with it, April . . .'

Wood had lit one of her ecological cigarettes. The dark green smoke produced by the vaporising of coloured water that was guaranteed harmless, curled up towards the ceiling. Bosch remembered when it had become fashionable to use these fake cigarettes in order to give up smoking. He had succeeded in giving up thanks to the classic nicotine patches, and regarded this other method as unnecessarily showy.

'Look at it this way,' she said. 'They want public opinion to think that Oscar Díaz was raving mad. So, if they can say we take on psychopaths to look after our most expensive works of art, then no one will be able to trust us, and so on and so forth.'

'But if that was what they were after, why on earth didn't they kill her *before* they cut her up? According to the autopsy report, they sedated her with an intramuscular injection of a neuroleptic drug, probably using a hypodermic pistol to the back of her neck. The dose was strong enough for her not to be able to defend herself, but not to anaesthetise her. I don't get it. I mean . . . and forgive me for insisting, April, but it seems to me . . . if all this was simply a bit of theatre, why go so far? The murder would have been just as regrettable, but . . . it would have been . . . there would have been . . . I mean, imagine I wanted to pretend it was the work of a sadist . . . Well then, first I get rid of her, I inject her with something, anaesthetise her . . . then I do all the other things . . . but there's a limit that never . . . Money has got nothing to do with it, April. I won't make any *more money* by doing *that*. There's a limit which . . .'

'Lothar.'

'Don't tell me they *only* did it for money, April! I may be getting old, but I'm not completely gaga yet! And I am experienced: I used to be a police inspector, so I know about criminals . . . they're not as sadistic as all those films would have us believe. They're human beings . . . I'm not saying there are no exceptions, but . . .'

'Lothar.'

'That guy wasn't trying to fool anyone: he *wanted* to do what he did, and in just the way he did it! We're not facing some underhand ruse by the competition – we're trying to track down a monster! . . . He cut her face and left her writhing while he made ready to . . . to cut her breast off! . . . Would you like me to read you the report . . . ?'

'Lothar,' came the weary, deep voice. 'Can I say something?'

'Sorry.'

Bosch had difficulty recovering control of his emotions. 'Come on, kid, calm down. What's got into you?'

Miss Wood stubbed out the cigarette in the ashtray. She lifted her hand; leaving a green thing there, a steaming, crushed broad bean. She exhaled the last of the green smoke through her nostrils. The Dragon's Poisonous Breath.

'She was a *painting*. There's no need to look any further than that, Lothar. *Deflowering* was a painting. I'll prove it to you.' She pounced on one of Annek's studio photos and thrust it in Bosch's face. 'She looks like an adolescent, doesn't she? She has the shape of an adolescent, when she was alive she walked and talked like an adolescent. She was called Annek. But if she had really been an adolescent, she wouldn't have been worth even five hundred dollars. Her death would not have interested the Ministry of the Interior of a foreign country, or mobilised a whole army of police and special forces, or led to high-level discussions in at least two European capitals, or meant that our positions in the Foundation are on the line. If *this* had been only a girl, who the shit would have been interested in what happened to her? Her mother and four bored policemen in the Wienerwald district. Things like that happen every day in this world of ours. People die horrible deaths all around us, and nobody could care less. But people do care about the death of this girl. And do you know why? Because this, *this*,' she shook the photo in his face, 'which apparently shows a young girl, *is not a girl at all*. It cost more than fifty million dollars.' She repeated the words again, emphasising them with a pause between each one. 'Fifty. Million. Dollars.'

'However much the work cost, she was still a young girl, April.'

'That's where you're wrong. It cost that much precisely because it was not a girl. It was a painting, Lothar. A masterpiece. Do you still not get it? We are what other people pay us to be. You used to be a policeman, and that's what you were paid to be; now they pay you to work as an employee for a private company, and that's what you are. *This* was once a girl. Then someone paid to turn her into a painting. Paintings are paintings, and people can destroy them with portable canvas cutters just as you might destroy documents in your shredding machine, without worrying about it. To put it simply, *they are not people.* Not for the person who did this to her, and not for us. Do I make myself clear?'

Bosch was staring at a fixed point – he had chosen April Wood's anthracite-coloured hair, and in particular the fiercely drawn parting on the right side of her head. He kept his eyes on it as he nodded agreement.

'Lothar?'

'Yes, I understood.'

'Which means we have to keep an eye on the competition.'

'We will,' said Bosch.

'And there's also the anonymous madman,' Miss Wood sighed, and her thin shoulders hunched. 'That would be the worst of all: a freshly baked psychopath, just like all that Viennese bread. Is there anything else in the forensic report?'

Bosch blinked and looked down at his papers. She's not being cruel, he told himself. She doesn't talk like that out of cruelty. She's not cruel. It's the world which is. All of us are.

'Yes . . .' Bosch looked several pages further on. 'There is one curious detail. Of course, the analysis of the painting's skin is very detailed: the forensic experts don't know much about the priming process, so they haven't picked up on this. Near the wound in the breast they found traces of a substance which . . . I'll read you what it says . . . "the composition of which, while being similar to silicon, is different in several fundamental aspects . . ." Then they give the full name of the chemical molecule: "dimethyl-tetrahydro . . ." well it's an enormously long name. Guess what it is?'

'Cerublastyne . . .' said Miss Wood, her eyes wide open.

'Bingo. The report says it must have been part of the painting's priming, but we know that *Deflowering* did not have any cerublastyne on it. We called Hoffmann and he confirmed it: the cerublastyne cannot have come from the painting.'

'My God,' Wood whispered. 'He disguises himself.'

'That seems most likely. A few touches of cerublastyne would have been enough to change his looks completely.'

This news had suddenly made Miss Wood uneasy. She had got up, and was pacing to and fro about the room. Bosch looked at her with concern. Good God, she hardly ever eats, she's a skeleton. She'll make herself ill if she carries on like this . . . A different voice, also part of him, counterattacked: Don't pretend. Look at the light reflected on her breasts, look at that tight arse and those legs of hers. You're crazy about her. You like her just like you did Hendrickje, perhaps more even. You like her the way you liked Hendrickje's portrait later on. Nonsense, the other Bosch replied. And . . . why not say it? the other voice came back. You like her *intelligence.* Her sharpness, her personality, the fact she is a thousand times more intelligent than you.

It was true, April Wood was a precision instrument. In the five years they had worked together, Bosch had not seen her make a single mistake. Stein called her the 'guard dog'. Everyone in the Foundation respected her. Even Benoit seemed cowed in her presence. He often said: 'She's so skinny her soul is too big for her.' Her record was brilliant. Even though she had not been able to avoid all the attacks on the works during her five years as head of security (it was impossible to prevent them all), those responsible had been found and dealt with, sometimes even before the police had heard about the incident. The guard dog knew how to bite. Nobody was in any doubt (Bosch least of all) that now she would also find whoever it was who had destroyed *Deflowering*.

And yet, outside their professional relationship, he scarcely knew her. Black holes in space, according to the scientific magazines his brother Roland collected, cannot be seen precisely because they are black, their presence can only be *inferred* from the effects they have on the other bodies around them. Bosch thought Miss Wood's free time was a black hole: he inferred it from her work. If Miss Wood had managed to rest, everything went smoothly. Otherwise, there were bound to be sparks. But so far, no one had so much as glimpsed what might be hidden in the dark hole that was Miss Wood's time off. Wood without her red pass, Miss Wood outside working hours, Miss Wood with feelings, if such things existed. Could there be a blot on such a perfect character? Bosch wondered about it sometimes.

The truth of it, Mr Lothar Bosch, is that this youngster of hardly thirty, who could be your daughter but is your boss, this soulless skeleton, has completely hypnotised you.

'April,' said Bosch.

'What?'

'I was thinking that maybe Díaz leads a double life. Maybe he has two voices inside his head, one normal, the other not. If he is a psychopath, there would be nothing odd in the fact that he behaved properly with friends and colleagues. When I worked for the police, I had some cases of . . .'

Mozart rang out from the table. It was Miss Wood's mobile. Even though her features did not alter in the slightest as she took the call, Bosch was aware something important had happened.

'All our problems are over,' she said as she switched off her phone, smiling in that disagreeable way of hers. 'That was Braun. Oscar Díaz is dead.'

Bosch leapt from his seat.

'They've caught him at last!'

'No. Two anglers found his body floating in the Danube early this morning. They thought it was the carp of their lives, a *Guinness Book of Records* carp, but it was Oscar. Well, all that was *left* of Oscar. According to the preliminary report, he had been dead more than a week . . . That was why they wanted to keep his body hidden.'

'What's that?'

Wood did not reply at once. She was still smiling, but Bosch soon realised it was a tremendous rage that was paralysing her.

'It was *not* Oscar Díaz who picked up Annek last Wednesday.'

This affirmation threw Bosch into confusion.

'It wasn't . . . ? What do you mean? . . . Díaz turned up at the agreed time last Wednesday, chatted with his colleagues, identified himself, and . . .' All at once he came to a halt, as though forced to brake before coming up against the stone wall of Miss Wood's gaze.

'It's not possible, April. One thing is to use resin to escape the police, but it's quite another to imitate someone so well that you deceive everyone who knows them, who sees them every day, the colleagues who greeted him on . . . on Wednesday . . . the security screens . . . all of them . . . to be able to pass off as someone you'd have to be a true specialist in latex. A real maestro.'

Wood was still staring at him. Her smile froze his blood.

'That bastard, whoever he may be, has made fools of us, Lothar.'

She said these words in a tone Bosch recognised perfectly. She wanted revenge. April Wood could forgive other people being intelligent, just so long as they were not more intelligent than her. She could not bear any opponent to do anything she had not thought of. In the heart of this slight woman burned a volcano of the blackest pride and will to perfection. Bosch understood, with the kind of sudden certainty which sometimes grasps the deepest, most hidden truths, that Wood had slipped her chain, that the guard dog would hunt down her adversary and would not relent until she had him in her jaws.

And not even then: once she had him, she would chew him to bits.

'They've made fools of us . . . fools of us . . .' she went on in an almost musical whistle, scarcely separating her two rows of perfect white teeth, the only white showing in the darkness of the room.

A white slash on a black background.

Second Step

Shaping the Sketch

Points, lines, circles, triangles, squares, polygons . . . these are the terms we should think in when we begin to sketch a human painting. Afterwards we will have to add shading.

BRUNO VAN TYSCH Treatise on Hyperdramatic Art

'If you think we're waxworks . . . you ought to pay, you know . . .'
'Contrariwise! . . . If you think we're alive, you ought to speak!'

LEWIS CARROLL Tweedledum and Tweedledee
in Through the Looking Glass

1

A point is not really a shape. Anyone who thinks a point is round is mistaken. A point exists in so far as interconnecting lines exist. Yet lines and everything else, all other shapes and bodies, are made up of points. A point is the essential invisible, the unmeasurable inevitable. God himself may be a point, solitary and remote in His perfect eternity, thinks Marcus.

Marcus Weiss is holding up an invisible point between his closed fingers. *Friends, this is more complicated than it seems.* The gesture is: left hand held out, palm of the hand facing upward, five fingers forming a little summit. If the tips are close enough together, the hole in the middle disappears in the curves of flesh. And there, right in the middle, is the point Weiss is holding up. *You think it's easy? Think again, friends, it's really complicated.*

When she first started her sketches, Kate Niemeyer put a ping-pong ball on the tip of his fingers. In the next sketch, the ball was replaced by a marble; after that a bean, and then a pea, just like in children's stories. Finally, Kate decided there should be nothing. 'The idea is the ball is still there, but invisible. You're offering it to the public. People will look at you and ask: what's he got between his fingers? That will catch their attention, and they'll come closer.' Marcus understands that curiosity is a terrific bait for any artist who knows how to use it.

That afternoon, he had been holding up the invisible point for several hours. A girl with blonde curls, orange dress and red glasses (one of the last visitors) had stood up on tiptoe to see what Marcus was hiding in his fingers. Weiss was unable to see her expression when she eventually realised there was nothing there – as a work of art, he was forced to continue looking straight out in front of him, his eyes painted white. He wondered what on earth such a small child was doing in the gallery, where the works were meant to be for adults. Marcus would have banned himself to children under thirteen. He had no children of his own (what painting could have?), but he felt a great respect for them, and considered his 'attire' as Niemeyer's work far from suitable for them: he was completely naked, his body spray-painted bronze, his penis and testicles (hairless, visible) a matt white colour, the same as his eyes. A crown of yellow and blue feathers with purple tips, shaped like an Aztec plume or a tropical bird's crest, covered his brow. His crafted muscles, shaped over the years with the patience of a carpenter, shone individually with a metallic bronze, throwing off shifting shadows and glints under the halogen lights.

Tired of holding up nothing, he was pleased it would soon be time to close. He realised the gallery had shut when he saw the maintenance man for Philip Mossberg's *Rhythm/Balance* come into the room. *Rhythm/Balance* was the painting on show opposite him. It was a seventeen-year-old canvas called Aspasia Danilou, painted in gentle, almost washed-out colours, which hid nothing of her anatomy. Her pubic hair was visible, because Mossberg always used non-depilated canvases for his works. Aspasia blinked, stirred, handed the satin sheet she had been holding in her left hand to the technician, and skipped off to the bathroom, waving to Marcus as she left. Until tomorrow, Marcus, see you then; of course you will, we'll be staring at each other all day. Beautiful Aspasia was not a bad canvas. Marcus thought she would go far, but she was only seventeen and this was her first original. When she had arrived in the gallery, he had tried to pick her up, but she had made several excuses and systematically refused his advances, until he was forced to realise that, in some areas of life, Aspasia already had considerable experience.

Marcus was Kate Niemeyer's work *Do You Want to Play With Me?* He was priced at twelve thousand euros, and was not sure he would be sold. He was the last to leave the gallery. There was no technician to help him, no one came to take his plume of feathers off: he had to make his own way out. The hand he used to hold nothing up with hurt a little. The whole arm, in fact.

'*Au revoir*, Habib.'

'*Au revoir*, Mr Weiss.'

He kept his bare black and bronze painted feet well away from the smooth track Habib's vacuum cleaner was making. He got on very well with the cleaning foreman on that floor. Before coming to Munich, Habib had lived in Avignon, and Weiss, who knew and admired that city (he had twice been exhibited in a gallery on the banks of the Rhône), liked to offer the Moroccan cleaner beer and cigarettes, and to practise his French. Habib the Great also went in for Zen meditation, which was guaranteed to endear him to Marcus. The two of them shared their books and thoughts.

That night though all he said to Habib was goodbye. He was in a hurry.

Would *she* be waiting for him? He hoped so, because he could not bear to think otherwise. They had met the previous evening, but Marcus had enough experience to know she was not the kind to take things lightly. Whoever she might be, and whatever she wanted from him, Brenda was *serious* about it.

He walked down the stairs to the bathroom on the second floor. Sieglinde, who was *Dryad* by Herbert Rinsermann, was already bent over the wash basin when Marcus came in. She had her head under the tap and was briskly rubbing her hair. Her athletic figure was like a flesh longbow, without an atom of fat. The fake brambles that were wrapped around her in the work were now propped against the wall, glistening with red points of artificial blood. The intricate swirl of Rinsermann's signature decorated her left ankle. Marcus and Sieglinde had met two years earlier during classes Ludwig Werner had held in Berlin for canvases of all ages. They had been friends ever since. Now they had coincided again in the Max Ernst gallery.

Marcus bent over next to her, taking care not to damage his plume of feathers, and boomed out a greeting.

'Good evening.'

Sieglinde's face emerged from the water, streaked with tiny pearls.

'Hi there, Marcus! How are things?'

'Not too bad,' he smiled enigmatically as he removed his crest.

'You're very pleased with yourself today. Has someone bought you?'

'In your dreams.'

'Another original in sight then?'

145

'Maybe.'

Sieglinde turned towards him, hands and buttocks pressed against the edge of the washbowl. Her short hair was like a wet golden helmet. She looked at Weiss with all the mockery of a smart nineteen-year-old.

'Hey, that's great. I'm fed up with seeing you painted bronze. And might I be allowed to know the name of the artist who wants to go down in history by doing something with you, Mr Weiss?'

'Mind your own business,' Marcus said, only half jokingly.

Sieglinde burst out laughing and carried on drying herself. Marcus went into the shower and hung a bottle of solvent on the taps. The oil paint on his body began to wash down below his knees. He turned and splashed in the welcome, pleasurable jet of water. Through the half-open door he caught glimpses of Sieglinde's anatomy, brief flashes of her youthful muscles. Ah youth, a point of no return, he thought. They buy you more quickly and pay more when you're a young canvas. He recalled that Rinsermann had been able to sell Sieglinde as a seasonal outdoor piece to an ancient Bavarian family. It's never easy to sell a seasonal work, because they are on show for only a few months each year, the summer in *Dryad*'s case. Marcus had seen the work several times. He did not particularly like Rinsermann, but he thought *Dryad* was quite good. It was a sort of wood nymph painted in diluted orange, ochre and pink tones, and covered in brambles whose thorns were apparently caught in the naked body. The expression on the work's face was a triumph: a mixture of fear, surprise and pain. But in Marcus' opinion, the best thing about the work was its owner. One of those a painting only meets once every ten years or so. Not only had he decided to install Sieglinde in his garden for three years before he substituted her (which meant steady work for three months and the possibility of more the rest of the year) but he also saw no problem with lending her for temporary exhibitions in the city, like this one at the Max Ernst, which allowed Sieglinde to earn an extra one thousand five hundred and thirty-two euros a month as a sold work. Weiss was pleased for her, but could not deny feeling a sharp stab of envy. His friend's face radiated with the happy glow of a bought canvas. But no one wanted to play with *Do You Want to Play With Me?* He was convinced Kate would not manage to sell him this time either. Was that Kate's fault or his?

He turned off the shower and looked down at his body, feeling its contours with his hands. He kept fit, of course. His muscles, faithful, well-trained dogs that they were, continued their endless task of construction. People like Kate Niemeyer would go on painting him (or at least, so he believed) for a few more years, but he knew that at forty-three he should be thinking of a different career. The market for human ornaments was growing irresistibly. Collectors privately amassed Chairs, Pedestals, Tables, Flower Vases and Carpets, and firms such as Suke, Ferrucioli Studio or the Van Tysch Foundation designed, sold and used flesh and blood ornaments every day. Sooner or later it was bound to become legal for these objects to be sold openly, because otherwise, where did old canvases and the young ones who did not make it as works of art have to go? Marcus suspected he would end up being sold as an ornament for some merry spinster's home. Why not take a souvenir from Germany with you, madam? Here's Marcus Weiss, with lovely nacreous buttocks, a fine Aryan object that would fit in nicely alongside your chimneypiece.

Weiss had only a few more opportunities left. Opportunities are points too, atoms, interconnecting lines, tiny, invisible dots, the remains of nothingness. How many had he missed? He had lost count. He had been a model from the age of seventeen. He had studied HD art in his home town of Berlin, and had worked for some of the best artists of his generation. Then suddenly it had all gone sour. He started turning down offers, partly because he want to live in peace. He liked being a painting, but not enough to sacrifice all his love life for it. He was well aware that masterpieces live alone, isolated, and don't get married or have children, don't even love or hate, don't enjoy life or suffer. True masterpieces like Gustavo Onfretti, Patricia Vasari or Kirsten Kirstenman could scarcely be called people: they had given *everything* – body, mind and spirit – to artistic creation. Marcus Weiss missed life too much, and perhaps that was the reason he had slowed down. And now it was too late to change things. The worst of it was that he was still on his own. So he was not a masterpiece, but he wasn't the human being he would have liked to have been either. He hadn't achieved one thing or the other.

He got nervous when he calculated that what Brenda was going to propose that evening might well be his last real opportunity.

As he was leaving, he found Sieglinde waiting for him at the changing-room exit. They often left together. They walked down the stairs with their rucksacks on their backs: he was carrying his Aztec headdress of artificial parrot feathers, she had the brambles. The labels on their wrists clinked as they descended the stairs. Sieglinde did the talking: Marcus gave only monosyllabic replies. He felt increasingly nervous. If Brenda had not kept her word, if she was not waiting for him outside as she had promised, he could say goodbye to that last big chance.

He decided he should say something, to avoid any indiscreet question from his friend.

'Guess what? This afternoon a nine- or ten-year-old girl stood looking at me for half an hour at least. I don't understand what's going on. The laws against child pornography get tougher and tougher, but there's no one to prevent any kid walking into an adult gallery.'

'You know we're considered as artistic heritage, Marcus. Kids can go and see Michelangelo's *David*, so why shouldn't they see *Do You Want to Play With Me?* as well? That would be discrimination.'

'I still think children are a special case,' Marcus insisted. 'I don't like them as viewers, but I like them even less as paintings. No painting less than thirteen years old should be allowed.'

'How old were you when you started?'

'OK, lets say under twelve then.'

Sieglinde laughed, then went on:

'I think the question of underage works is difficult. If you ban them, you'd have to ban children appearing in films and plays as well. And what about adverts? I reckon it's much more indecent to use a child's body to sell toilet rolls than to paint it and pose it as a work of art. Hey! Are you listening?'

Marcus did not reply.

148

Brenda was there, standing between two columns.

She nodded at Marcus; he smiled back. His heart was pounding, as if instead of walking down the stairs he had run up them three at a time.

'Hello there,' Marcus said, going over.

The girl nodded again. This time she was not looking at Marcus, but at his colleague. Weiss found himself obliged to introduce them.

'This is Brenda. Brenda, this is Sieglinde Albrecht. Sieglinde can give you a lesson or two about how to be an outdoor seasonal work and get bought.'

'Are you a painting too?' Sieglinde asked with a broad smile, raising eyebrows that were no longer there, and openly examining Brenda from head to toe.

'No,' replied Brenda.

'Well, you should be. You'd be bought very quickly, whoever painted you.'

Marcus was delighted to detect a hint of jealousy in his companion's voice.

'Brenda, you'll have to forgive Sieglinde's twisted mind,' he said with a laugh.

'It was meant as a compliment, you idiot!' said Sieglinde, slapping his shoulder.

Brenda looked like a doll programmed only to nod and laugh at everything said to her. Weiss thought there was no need for her to speak: her extraordinary face said it all anyway.

'You may not believe it,' he explained, 'but Brenda isn't a painting . . . she's more like a . . . dealer.'

'Oh, so it's business, is it?' Sieglinde planted a kiss on Weiss' lips. Then she winked at Brenda with an eyelash-less eye. 'In that case, I'll leave you two to it. I'll see you the day after tomorrow, Mr Weiss.'

'Absolutely, Miss Albrecht.'

Although the gallery was open the following day and Sieglinde had to go to work, Marcus always took Tuesday off. Sieglinde did not know the reason for such unusual behaviour in a work that had not yet been sold, but her sly attempts to find out had met with a wall of laconic replies, so she had not dared

149

enquire any further. She was sure though that Marcus had another job in a much less public (and much more scandalous) venue than the Max Ernst gallery.

Sieglinde's hair became a golden dot quickly disappearing down Maximilianstrasse. Marcus gently put an arm on Brenda's shoulder and steered her in the opposite direction. It was the last Monday in June, and the streets were crowded.

'I thought you weren't going to come.'

'Why not?' Brenda asked.

He shrugged.

'I don't know. I guess because everything happened so quickly yesterday. Look, you're not annoyed I told Sieglinde you were a dealer, are you? I had to tell her something. And besides, Sieglinde is not a nosey person.'

'That's OK. Where are we going?'

Marcus stopped and glanced at his watch. He spoke as if he were unsure of what to suggest, even though he had planned everything out the night before.

'How about having a drink and then going for dinner?'

He took her to a place called the Mini Bar. It was on a street corner near the gallery, but the paintings and sketches preferred to go to the bars on the avenue, so that with any luck the two of them could enjoy some privacy. The Mini Bar sold everything in small sizes: the drinks came in tiny bottles, just as in hotels. The ice cubes were as big as poker dice. It was self-service, and behind the bar (which reached up to the waist of an adult) could be seen an espresso coffee machine as big as a silver shoe box with three handles, shelves as narrow as skirting boards, notice boards advertising the dishes of the day in handwriting not for the short-sighted, and tiny lights hanging from the ceiling which after nightfall gave the bar the air of a puppet theatre. The background music was a tremulous violin solo. But apart from this, Gulliver suddenly found himself in the land of giants: the barmen were unusually tall, and the prices were much higher than average. Marcus knew the Mini Bar was way beyond his budget, but he did not want to skimp on entertaining Brenda: he wanted to impress her so that she would realise he was used to the best.

150

They found a quiet corner with a table and a couple of stools. Marcus had intended to start with a beer, but changed his mind and joined Brenda in a whisky. He ordered two delicious Glenfiddichs and two glasses full of ice so pure and clear it shone transparently. As he was returning to the table he had time to consider Brenda once more. He saw no reason to change the opinion he had formed the previous evening. She was quite slim, but undeniably attractive, and wore her wavy blonde hair in a ponytail gathered on her back like a bushy paint brush. She was wearing a short jacket and a dark-blue miniskirt (the previous day it had been a blouse and a pair of short blue jeans). Her clothing was creased and obviously not new, but this only attracted Marcus all the more. Her shoes had stiletto heels, a style he had never thought of as old-fashioned. He realised she did not have a handbag. Or stockings. He liked to imagine she was wearing nothing more than what he could see.

When he sat down again, he saw she was staring at him without smiling. Her blue eyes did not shine, but reminded him of something he could not quite place: they were penetrating, fixed points. Points like tiny black pools.

'And now,' he said, serving her the Glenfiddich, unable to take his eyes off those two points, 'you're going to tell me the truth.'

'I always tell you the truth,' she replied.

That was the first time he was sure she was lying.

So the questions began. The customers in the Mini Bar came and went constantly without him noticing: he was concentrating on his interrogation. Marcus was an experienced painting, and nobody was going to pull the wool over his eyes, least of all using a doll like this girl. By the time he looked down at his glass, the Lilliputian ice cubes had watered down the taste of his whisky. She had not drunk much either: between answers she raised her glass to her lips, but did not seem to swallow. In fact, she did not seem to do anything. She just sat there crossing and uncrossing her pretty, bare legs and looking straight at Marcus as she replied to his questions.

'Why did your friends think of me for this job?'

151

'I've already told you that.'

'I want to hear it again.'

'They're looking for people. And as I told you, they sent me to Munich to see you.'

She spoke German perfectly, but Marcus could not place her accent.

'That doesn't answer my question.'

'I don't know, I guess they liked you as a painting. You'd have to ask them. I'm just here to try to hook you.'

The girl seemed to be trying to be honest at least. Marcus took another sip of Glenfiddich. The Mini Bar violin began a tinny, musical-box waltz.

'Tell me more about the work.'

'It'll take a month to complete, but I can't tell you where. Then it will automatically be sold. In fact, it's a commission. You're not allowed to know who the buyer is either, but you'll be travelling south. To Italy, probably. It's an outdoor performance. It takes five hours a day, and will carry on until the autumn.'

'How many figures are there in it?'

'I don't know, it's a mural painting. I know there are adults and adolescents. I think it's a mythological subject.'

'Is there anything "dirty" about it?'

'No, it's entirely clean. Everyone is a volunteer.'

'Kids?'

'No, only adolescents.'

'How old?'

'Fifteen and upwards.'

'Fine.' Marcus smiled and leaned closer to her. At times, the bar got so full it was difficult for him to speak softly sitting back. 'You've given me the excuse. Now tell me the truth.'

'What do you mean?'

'Adolescents and adults together in a mural performance that is sold even *before* it's painted . . . and as if that weren't enough, a girl sent to "hook" me.' He tried to give a knowing smile. Listen, I've been in this business a long while. I've been painted by Buncher, Ferrucioli, Brentano and Warren. So I do have experience, you know.'

He did not take his eyes off her face even when he raised his drink vertically to drain his glass. An avalanche of ice buried his nose. Was he a bit tipsy? He didn't think so.

'Let me tell you something. Last summer I worked in a clandestine art-shock in Chiemsee. They painted us in a Berlin workshop, then bought us and put us on show three days a week for the whole summer in a private estate by the lakeside. There were four adolescents and three adults, me included.' Marcus glanced down at the label on his wrist. 'It was a . . . how shall I put it? A terrifying experience. I mean, in the way art-shocks can be terrifying. But there was also a real risk. One of the figures was only thirteen . . .'

'You want more money,' Brenda interrupted him.

'I want more money and more information. Enough of all that mythology crap. From time immemorial, art's excuses have been mythology and religion. The art-shock I did in Chiemsee was meant to be religious . . .' he wanted to laugh, but when he saw the girl was not joining in, he restrained himself. 'But deep down, it's always been about showing nudes and violence, whether it was Michelangelo in the Sistine Chapel or Taylor Warren in his Liverpool cavern. That's always been the best, the most expensive art.' He lifted his forefinger to emphasise his words. 'Tell your friends I want precise information about what I will be required to do. And I also want a clause stipulating the limits beforehand, and another exonerating me from all responsibility. They're not much use when you're accused of molesting children, but they do mean if there are complaints, the artist has to take most of the blame. And I want proof that the painting will be clean and that there'll be no kids, volunteers or not. And I want twice the sum you mentioned yesterday: twenty-four thousand euros. All that's just a start – do I make myself clear?'

'Yes.'

They both fell silent. It suddenly occurred to Marcus he should not have told her about the art-shock in Chiemsee. She was going to think he was only contracted for marginal pieces, which in fact was partly true. At the peak of his career, Weiss had been sold in several great hyperdramatic originals. But nowadays almost all his earnings came from interactive performances and art-shocks.

Works such as Niemeyer's painting (or Gigli's, which he preferred not to bring up) were the exception.

'Shall we go?' he suggested.

When they left the café, almost all the shops still had lighted windows. The galleries along the Maximilianstrasse showed late-evening canvases grouped in paintings with two or three figures. Their outlines, clothes (or the lack of them) and their colours vied for the attention of an innumerable and very mixed public. There were paintings for almost every pocket, from the poor devils who were sketches by unknown artists at three or four thousand euros, to works by the great masters whose price was always agreed over dinner, and whose canvases were on show only for a few hours (and never in gallery windows) before they were accompanied back to their hotels or rented apartments by security guards. Girls on rollerblades were handing out catalogues from fringe galleries, or from portrait painters expert in the use of cerublastyne. Marcus collected whatever he was offered. As they reached the corner where the Nationaltheater was lit up for a first night, he turned to the girl and asked her:

'Well?'

'I'll convey your requests to my friends, and give you the reply soon.'

Marcus leaned down towards her ear to make sure she could hear him above the traffic. It was then he realised she had no smell. Or rather, she smelt like a point: lines of interconnecting smells (it is impossible to smell of nothing: there is always some scent, a faint trace of something). He was delighted at this new discovery. He couldn't bear the complicated olfactory filigree work some women presented him with.

'I wasn't asking you about the work, but about tonight,' he said with his best seductive smile. 'Where would you like to go now?'

'What about you?'

He knew of several things she might enjoy. Some of them, like the reunion in Haidhausen where everyone, model or not, got to be a work of art, were tempting. But his hand on the back of her jacket seemed to have a mind of its own.

'I'm staying at a motel in Schwabing. It's not a great place, but on the ground floor there's a wonderful vegetarian restaurant.'

'Fine,' said Brenda.

Marcus hailed a taxi, even though he usually took the metro in Odeonsplatz. The restaurant was small and packed at that time of night, but Rudolf, the owner and main chef, smiled when he saw Marcus and led them over to a quiet table. There would always be a table for Mr Weiss, and a bottle of wine of course – Marcus was delighted to be received so warmly in front of Brenda. He ordered vegetable strudels and some delicious seasonal asparagus. Throughout most of the meal he talked to her about his love of Zen, meditation and vegetarian food, and of how all this had helped him become a painting. He admitted his was a *prêt-à-porter* Buddhism, a tool, something to help him put up with life, but at the same time he doubted whether there was anyone in this twenty-first century who had more profound beliefs he had. He also told her stories about painters and models, which led to those mysterious, perfect lips of hers relaxing still further. But as the evening wore on, he found himself running out of things to say. This hardly ever happened to him. His friends thought of him as a good talker, and he had an excellent memory for his stories. *Now I'll tell you about a girl called Brenda I met in Munich.* If only Sieglinde could see me now . . . All at once he realised he was crazy with desire for Brenda. This annoyed him, because he knew she had been sent to hook him, and here he was not only taking the bait but savouring it as he did so. And yet he had to admit that her friends, whoever they might be, had made a good choice: Brenda was the most tempting woman he had met in a long while. Her passivity, her way of staying mysterious while suggesting the door was half-open, only inflamed his passion still further. *Listen, I'll tell you what she was like.* He tried to conceal his feelings – he did not want her to know she had achieved her goal so quickly. But could she really not tell? Wasn't that a mocking gleam he could detect in the midnight blue points of her eyes?

'You're not German, are you?' he asked over dessert.

'No.'

'North American?'

She shook her head.

'You don't have to tell me if you don't want to,' Marcus said.

'I won't then.'

'I couldn't give a damn where you're from.'

His lips were trembling. Hers looked as though they were carved in wood.

He settled the bill quickly, and they left. The punk on the desk at the motel seemed to have his key ready and waiting for him. His room was small and smelt of damp, but at that moment they could have been in the salons of the Residenz or a public lavatory for all he cared. He pushed Brenda into the darkness, then sought her mouth with his own. She wriggled out of his caresses, bent her knees and began to slide effortlessly down his body. Marcus groaned with pleasure when he realised what she intended to do.

It was not what he had been expecting. He had hoped to prolong things while she undressed, or while he undressed her, perhaps on the floor the way Kate Niemeyer liked it. The painter was one of his most stable recent relationships, and during her visits to Munich they had made love in his motel, her hotel or even occasionally in a museum, canvas and artist intertwined on the gallery floor. Brenda was in too much of a rush. Marcus was sure he would explode before he was even able to touch her.

'Wait,' he murmured anxiously. 'Wait a minute . . .'

But what he was fearing did not happen. She knew when to pause or to increase the rhythm, and what areas to leave untouched. After the anxious start, Brenda's mouth slipped round his penis like a scorching leather sheath, while her hands grasped his buttocks and drew him towards her. My God, but the girl was a real suction pump. Kundalini, the serpent of sexual energy, raised her bicephalic head inside him and asked what was going on. Marcus groaned, clawed at the whitewashed wall, bit his lip in a moment of complete loss of control. When it was all over, the two of them were still in the same position: he was standing leaning his forehead against the wall, the unmistakable taste of his own blood in his mouth – his lips were cracked from the solvents he had used, and he had bitten them raw – and she was on her knees, also tasting something belonging to Marcus.

This synchronisation of fluids in their mouths struck him as having a kind of artistic symmetry.

Brenda stood up, and Marcus switched on the lights.

'Christ,' he said. 'That was good.'

There was no reply. *Friends, you can't imagine how silent this girl is.* Brenda's eyes were staring at him without blinking: black round points in a circle of blue nothingness. There was no stain on her lips. Her features – perfect, etched – had a strangely detached air to them, seemingly so independent of all emotion and involvement that Marcus could find only one word to define them: symbol. All of a sudden Marcus thought of her as symbolic, a sort of archetype of his desire. He missed only one thing in her: some slight sign of individuality, of imperfection. Questions he could find no answer to flitted through his mind: was the individual better than the archetypical? Imperfection better than perfection? Emotional than intellectual? Natural than artistic? When he realised all these musings had been provoked by having his cock sucked by her, he could almost believe he understood the tragic destiny of mankind.

He tried to kiss her again, but she turned her head away.

'Shall we sit down?'

Before she moved away, Marcus' fingers had finally managed fleetingly to touch her wonderful skin. He realised with a shock that this was the first time he had felt her naked flesh. Its texture was like a baby's, a little firmer than normal. A rather grown-up baby. On his fingertips there was a point (because that is what everything finally ends up as) of smooth oil, a viscous nothing. He did not think it was a skin cream: Brenda must have greasy skin, that was all. He had known several people like that: they always stayed young. The secret of eternal youth and of early death are one and the same: grease. Perhaps this simple, tiny reason is the origin of the sad fact that the only people who stay young forever are those who die young.

Yet the world could not be such a bad place after all, if nature could produce beings like Brenda. Marcus promised himself he would enjoy every inch of her through that endless night.

He remembered he had a small bottle of Ballantine's. He busied himself preparing two whiskies. Brenda sat back in the only armchair in the room, and crossed her legs. She was sitting beside the bedside table where Marcus kept all his daily requirements: firming lotions, cosmetic creams, disposable lenses, sprays and hair dyes. Next to all these tubs lay a black mask. Brenda picked it up.

'Be careful with that, I need it tomorrow,' Marcus said. He was bringing over the whiskies when he suddenly came to a halt. 'Oh, shit . . . !'

He had just realised he had left his bag of paints (together with the catalogues and the feather headdress) in Rudolf's restaurant. Too late now to go and get them. Oh well, he told himself, Rudolf will keep them for me.

Brenda put the mask back where she had found it.

'I thought you were only on show at the Max Ernst.'

Still half-thinking about the bag he had left behind, Marcus replied in an offhand way:

'No, I'm in a work by Gianfranco Gigli as well, but I'm only a substitute on Tuesdays. I'm due there tomorrow afternoon. In fact, it's mostly thanks to Gigli that I'm here in Munich. Like some more?'

'I'll have whatever you're having.'

Marcus liked her reply. He poured two large glassfuls. This was going to be a long night. Tomorrow morning I'll drop into the restaurant and pick up my bag, he thought. It's no problem.

'What gallery are you on show at for the Gigli?' Brenda wanted to know.

He was about to tell the usual lie (I go from one to another) but when he saw how untroubled she looked, he decided he had nothing to hide.

'None.'

'Have you been bought?'

'Yes, by a hotel,' he smiled (my big secret he thought, with a stab of shame). 'The Wunderbar, do you know it? It's one of the newest and most luxurious hotels here. And its main attraction is that the decorations are hyperdramatic works. That may be common enough nowadays, but when the hotel opened it was just about the only one of its kind in all Germany. I'm the painting in a suite. What do you think of that?'

'That's OK, if you're well paid.'

She was perfectly right. With that one comment, Brenda had shown him there was nothing to be ashamed of.

'I'm very well paid. And the truth is I don't in the least mind being in a hotel. I'm a professional painting, so it's all the same to me where I'm on show. The problem is the guests staying in the suite.' He twisted his mouth, then took a sip of whisky. 'How about if we change the conversation?'

'Fine.'

Brenda did not want anything, did not ask for anything, did not show the least curiosity. She was like a hermetically sealed box, and this completely disarmed Marcus.

'Well, I guess there's no harm in your knowing. But don't tell anyone – nobody would be interested anyway. Do you want to know who those guests are? . . . It may sound ironic, but they're considered one of the greatest paintings in the history of art.' He had said the words with calculated disdain, dripping with irony. 'They are no less than the two figures in *Monsters*, by Bruno van Tysch.'

If he had been trying to provoke some reaction from the girl, he was disappointed. Brenda was as quiet and calm as ever, her legs crossed; the perfect gleam of her naked thighs, just like the shine of her shoes. Nature is more artistic than art when it imitates art, isn't it, Marcus?

Marcus was giving in to long-suppressed emotions. Now he had revealed the unpleasant side of his work to someone, there was no stopping him.

'Sometimes an odd thing happens to me, Brenda. I don't understand modern art. Can you believe it? That exhibition . . . "Monsters" . . . I suppose you've seen it somewhere, or heard about it. It's on now at the Haus der Kunst. To me, one of the great mysteries in art is trying to figure out how the creator of "Flowers" could then devote himself to creating a collection like that . . . live snakes in a girl's hair, a terminally ill patient, a cretin . . . and those two slimy criminals I am a painting for.' He paused, took another sip of his whisky. 'It's wrong for a work of art not to understand art, don't you think?' She smiled fleetingly with him, but then Marcus' face turned serious again. 'But it's not that. It's those two pigs. I only have to put up with them one day a week, but I find it harder and harder . . . Just listening to them makes me want to . . . to throw up . . . I find it unbelievable that those two degenerates can be one of the greatest paintings of all time, whereas canvases like me end up having to act as ornaments in the rooms they stay in.'

The thought so outraged him that he raised the glass to his lips again, only to discover it was empty. Brenda was listening to him without moving a muscle. Marcus was slightly ashamed at having poured his heart out to a stranger (however hard it was for him to believe it, Brenda was still a stranger, after all). He looked down at his glass, then up at her.

'Well, we're not going to spoil a night like this by talking about work, are we?' he said. 'I've still got paint all over me. I'll have a shower and be back straightaway. Pour yourself some more whisky. Get comfortable.'

Brenda smiled faintly.

'I'll wait for you in bed.'

Under the shower, Marcus suddenly recalled what Brenda's eyes reminded him of: she had the same gaze as Dante Gabriel Rossetti's *Venus Verticordia*. He had a framed copy of the Pre-Raphaelite painting hanging in the living room of his Berlin apartment. Holding an apple and an arrow, the goddess was staring straight at the viewer, one of her breasts uncovered, as if suggesting that love and desire can sometimes be dangerous. Marcus liked Burne-Jones, Rossetti, Holman Hunt and the other Pre-Raphaelites. He thought there was nothing to match the mystery and beauty of the women they had painted, the sacred aura they gave off. But as Marcus knew, or thought he did, art is less beautiful than life, even though he had rarely found such convincing proof of this assertion as Brenda. No Pre-Raphaelite could ever have invented Brenda, and that was the reason – he suspected – why life would always have the advantage over art in their race towards reality. Who knows? Perhaps for him it was not too late for life, even if it already was for art. Perhaps life was waiting somewhere: children, a partner, stability, the bourgeois nirvana were he could find eternal rest. *Let's enjoy life, friends, for this one night at least.*

He came out of the bathroom and picked up a towel. He had taken off the Niemeyer label – he would not need it the next day. He experienced another fierce erection. He felt, if anything, even more aroused than before, when they had rushed into the room. And the drink had not affected him either. He was sure he could keep going until dawn, and with a girl like Brenda, that should be no sacrifice.

The room was in darkness again, apart from the faint light from the neon signs outside that filtered through the blinds. In the flashing gloom Marcus could make out Brenda's shape, waiting for him in bed as promised. She had pulled the sheets up to her neck, and was staring at the ceiling. *Venus Verticordia.*

'Are you cold?' Marcus asked.

No reply. Brenda still did not move, staring up at a point in the darkness. This seemed like a strange way to start another love-making session, but by now Marcus was well accustomed to her odd behaviour. He went over to the bed and knelt on it.

'Do you want me to uncover you bit by bit, like a surprise package?' he smiled.

At that moment something happened that Marcus could not comprehend at first. Brenda's face trembled and turned, twisting itself at an impossible angle, like a shroud sliding off a corpse. Then *it moved.* It crawled towards Marcus' hand like a limp rat, a dying rodent. A second or two of panic, enough to provide Marcus with more than enough material for another of his anecdotes. *Now I'll tell you about the day Brenda's face came off and started moving towards my hand. It was some sensation, let me tell you, friends.* As though in a trance, Marcus stared at the deflated nose, lips and empty eyes scurrying across the pillow to his fingers. He drew back his hand as if he had been burnt, and gave a strangled scream of horror before he realised he was looking at some kind of mask made from a plastic material, probably silicone. The mass of blonde hair and its ponytail lay empty across the pillow, like a roof without walls.

I'm going to tell you about the day Brenda became a marble, a green pea, a nothing. I'll tell you about the horrible day when Brenda became a point in the microcosm.

He pulled back the sheets, and discovered that what he had

first thought was the girl's body was nothing more than her clothing (jacket and skirt, even the shoes) twisted and screwed up. Like a schoolboy joke to make you believe someone was asleep in the bed.

But the mask . . . *The mask* was what he could not understand.

He shuddered repeatedly, and his teeth chattered.

'Brenda . . .' he called out in the darkness.

He heard the noise behind his back, but he was kneeling naked on the bed, and his reaction came too late.

2

Lines.

Her body was a sheaf of lines. Her hair for example: gentle curves down the nape of her neck. Or her eyes: ellipses containing circles. The concentric rotundity of her breasts. The faint line of her navel. Or the seagull print of her sex. She stroked herself. She raised her right hand to her neck, drew it down between her breasts and the tight knot of her stomach muscles. She embraced the curve of her biceps. As she touched herself, her body felt different. Life returned: soft surfaces she could press, change the shape of; outlines where her hand could pause, sweet labyrinths for fingers or insects. She recovered her own volume.

She felt like crying, as she had done when she said goodbye to Jorge. What could she see? A yellow mother-of-pearl skin. She guessed that any hypothetical tear, flowing down vertically from her eyelid to the corner of her mouth, would also trace a line. She was not sad, though she was not happy either. Her wish to cry came from a colourless feeling, a linear sentiment that the future would doubtless find a way of painting more clearly. She was at the beginning, at the starting *line* (the exact word for it), a twisted figure waiting in the world of geometry for an artist to select her and provide her with shading and definition. And then what? She would have to wait to find out.

Apart from that, her current state could be defined as gravity-free. The priming process had freed her of all ballast. She was barely aware of her own self. She was completely naked, and did not feel cold or even cool; she did not feel anything that might be called 'temperature'. Despite the discomforts of the journey, she still felt awake and energetic: she could have rested equally well doubled up on herself or standing on tiptoe. The mysterious combination of pills she had started to take on F&W's instructions had made her bodily needs almost vanish. It seemed wonderful to her not to be at the mercy of any of her inner organs. It was more than twelve hours since she had needed to go to the bathroom. She had not eaten – or felt like eating – anything solid since Saturday. She was neither nervous nor calm: she was merely *waiting*. Her whole state of mind was projected towards the future. For the first time in her life, she felt like a real canvas. Or not even that. Like a tool. A hammer, a fork or a revolver, she deduced, could understand her feelings better than another human being.

Her mind was clear and empty. Incredibly clear. For her, to think was like contemplating sand dunes in the desert. This too made her happy. It was not amnesia: she could remember everything, but none of her memories got in the way. They were there, in the library, lined up and within reach (if she wanted them, she could remember her parents, or Vicky, or Jorge) but she had no need to flick through her past to be alive. It was a tremendous sensation to feel she was someone else while still being herself.

The house was plunged in silence. She had no idea where they had taken her after the plane had landed at Schiphol. She guessed she must be somewhere not far from Amsterdam. The flight had lasted an hour or a little more, but an hour can be very long when you are blindfolded and unable to move. But time and Clara's body had got on well, and she had not experienced any discomfort.

She had been transported as artistic goods. This was the first time this had happened to her. Well, occasionally when she was in *The Circle* as an adolescent, she had been tied up with nylon string, had had her eyes blindfolded, been wrapped in padded paper and then put in a cardboard box. This was called the 'Annulling Test', intended to help the future canvas accept its

163

condition as an object. But this was different: it was a real trans-fer. According to international law, any canvas that had been primed and given labels was considered artistic goods, even if it had not yet been painted. All the previous journeys she had made for work purposes had been as a person: she had been primed at her destination. This meant the artist saved on trans-port costs, any risk of damage, and on customs duties. Evasion of these payments by works of art who travelled as normal passen-gers and then were repainted in another country had not yet been classified as an offence: legislation was definitely needed. But Clara had been transported as artistic goods, with all the required paperwork.

She could not make out the shape of the ten-seater jet she climbed aboard at the end of the tunnel down which she had fol-lowed the uniformed man. Inside the cabin, a mechanic dressed in an orange overall was waiting for her. He never spoke to her by name. In fact, he hardly said anything at all (and besides, he did not speak Spanish). He led her with gloved hands (everyone used gloves to handle her once she had been primed) and helped her lie down on a padded couch with its back raised forty-five degrees and the word FRAGILE written in large letters on the leather. There was another lifted rail for her feet, which forced her to keep her knees bent. There was no need for her to take her top or miniskirt off. On the contrary: the workman wrapped her in another layer of plastic, this time a loose sleeveless tunic, and stuck warning labels in Dutch and English all over it. The only thing he removed were her shoes. She was strapped in her seat by eight elastic belts: one across her forehead, two under her arms, another round her waist, and a further four at her wrists and ankles. They were all amazingly soft. As he tightened them, the mechanic made sure they did not trap the labels on her right wrist and ankle. The only time he spoke was when he put her mask on.

'Protect eyes,' he said.

Those were the last words she heard until they landed.

There was a brief interval without darkness during the flight: the mask was lifted and she was offered a tall vertical line inserted in a hermetically sealed glass. She drank from it, though she was not thirsty. It was a fruit juice. She was able to see that outside, in the cabin and the rest of the world, night had fallen. While he held the glass up for her to drink, the mechanic also checked that none of the straps was too tight. He moved the labels around to avoid them chafing. Another man used a doctor's torch to check her stomach, and then they slightly loosened the central strap. She did not move (although she could have if she had wanted to) because she was not worried about having to stay in the same position the whole day if necessary. When they had finished all their adjustments, the two men put her mask back on.

She felt the landing as a foetus might experience being born on a fairground big wheel. It helped her understand there must be something intangible within us that gives us a sense of direction, of above and below, of acceleration and braking. The awareness that an arrow or a line might have. Inertia gripped her like a powerful dance partner, pushing her forward, then backwards. Then the violent rubber stamp of wheels on the ground.

'Careful . . . step . . . careful . . . step . . .'

They held her arms as she descended the steps. A wave of Amsterdam night air greeted her. Holland caressed her legs, lifted the edges of her plastic shroud, stroked her stomach and hot back. She felt encouraged to be received in this way by an unabashed, cool Holland that smelt of gasoline and jet engines. A gust of wind made her neck label swing out to the left.

They came to a stop in a distant zone of Schiphol airport. Flashing lights were the only decoration. At the foot of the steps another mechanic was waiting with a transport trolley. They were called 'capsules', and Clara had seen them before, but never travelled in one. It consisted of another stretcher like the one on the plane, with the back raised, and a plastic cover with holes in for her to breathe, covered in more warning stickers. When they zipped the cover over her head, she could hear no more noise, but could still see out through the plastic. They had removed her mask, and she felt a lot more comfortable than she had in the plane (she could stretch her legs, for example) although this did not mean much to her. The mechanic walked round behind her and started to push the trolley.

165

They went towards a long, low building beyond which she could see the tall, cool lines of the control tower. A sign – *Douane, Tarief* – flashed electronically. Muscular figures in tunics, others showing bare flesh, necks bearing orange or bright blue tags, faces with no eyebrows, their skin primed and shiny, a rainbow of hair colours, others again with bald, gleaming heads, youngsters of both sexes, adolescents, little boys and girls, beautiful monsters waiting in the intermittent lights in the darkness, canonic but unfinished images, models not yet sketched (she was particularly struck by one ineffable shaven and primed work in a wheelchair who turned its head to stare after her like a drugged alien being), all of them waiting in line to go through the customs. Many of them had been brought here on luggage trolleys, often without guards, because they did not need any special transport requirements. Clara was fascinated at the amount of trafficking in works of art that obviously went on in Holland. There was nothing like it in Spain, where artistic immigration, like so many other kinds, was strictly controlled. How much could each of those works cost? Even the cheapest must be worth more than a thousand dollars.

Her capsule went straight into the building without having to queue. Inside it was like a hangar with conveyor belts and long customs tables. Employees in blue uniforms raised their arms and reeled off precise instructions. Everything was studied, regulated, listed, considered. They wheeled her to a desk. Forms were stamped, labels checked. Then she was taken into an adjacent room, where they unzipped her cover. As they did so, a mixture of male and female perfumes overwhelmed her sense of smell. A silent, smiling couple wearing surgical gloves that matched the colour of their suits and with blue tags in their lapels (she remembered this was what the Conservation department wore) were waiting for her. The room was an office: a desk, two exits, an open door. Someone shut the door, and to Clara it seemed that for a second she had gone deaf.

'How are you feeling? OK? My name is Brigitte Paulsen, and my colleague here is Martin van der Olde. Can you get up? Slowly, there's no need to rush.'

This sudden burst of musical Spanish surprised Clara at first.

She had thought they would treat her as they had until now, as simply art material. Then she understood her reception. They were part of Conservation, and in Conservation they always tried to make the works feel at ease. She swung her bare feet down to the floor – the primed toenails reflected the strip ceiling lights – and stood up without help or any difficulty.

'I'm fine, thank you.'

'Mr Paul Benoit, director of Conservation at the Bruno van Tysch Foundation, is sorry he cannot be here in person, and has instructed me to welcome you to Holland,' the woman said with a smile. 'Did you have a good trip?'

'Yes very good, thanks.'

'I little Spanish,' the blond man said, blushing slightly.

'Don't worry,' Clara reassured him.

'Do you need anything? Want anything? Want to say anything?'

'No, I'm fine at the moment, and there's nothing I need,' said Clara. 'Thanks all the same.'

'May I?' the woman took hold of the label round Clara's neck.

'Excuse me,' said the man, lifting her arm with his gloved left hand, and catching her wrist tag in his right.

'Sorry,' a third man she had not noticed until now said, as he knelt on the floor to grasp her ankle label.

It's comforting when they treat you like a human being occasionally, thought Clara. Every being in the universe, as well as the majority of natural and artificial objects, likes being treated kindly, so Clara did not feel ashamed to think as she did. The parallel red claws of their laser beams sneaked out over the lines of the bar codes on her three labels. She kept her silent smile throughout their inspection, examining the woman closely. She decided she was pretty, but was wearing too dark a shade of make-up. She had also put too much rouge on: it looked as though she had been slapped hard on both cheeks.

Then they stripped her: they lifted her padded plastic tunic over her head, and removed the top and miniskirt. The ceiling lights rippled across her body like luminous eels.

'Are you feeling all right? Not nauseous at all? Tired?'

While the woman practised her Berlitz Spanish, she felt

Clara's pulse with fingers as delicate as a pair of tweezers. In the pauses, Clara could hear echoes of questions in another language from a nearby room. Had more artistic goods arrived? Who could it be? She was dying to know.

The Conservation team changed instruments and started to examine her with a sort of mobile phone that gave off a loud hum. She guessed they must be checking she was all of one piece. Armpits, ribs, buttocks, thighs, backs of her legs, stomach, pubis, face, hair, hands, feet, back, coccyx. They did not touch her with their instruments: these were like red-eyed crickets all chirruping on the same note a couple of centimetres from her skin. She helped them by raising her arms, opening her mouth, spreading her legs. She felt a sudden surge of panic: what would happen if they found something wrong? Would they send her back?

Another man had joined their group, but he stayed in the background, near the exit, leaning against the wall with his arms folded, as though waiting for the others to finish before it was his turn. He was a platinum blond with a firm jaw and reflecting glasses. He looked like a bad-tempered Aryan, and perhaps that is what he was. A mobile phone cable sprouted from his right ear. Clara saw the red tag in his lapel: he was a security guard. I should start recognising them: the dark blue label is Conservation, the red one is Security; Art is turquoise . . .

'All done,' said the woman. 'In the name of the Bruno van Tysch Foundation, I wish you a happy stay in Holland. Please, if you have any doubt, any problem, or if there's anything you need, call us. You'll have a number you can call Conservation on. You can ring at any time of the day or night. Our colleagues will be delighted to help.'

'Thanks.'

'Now we'll leave you in the capable hands of the security people. I should warn you that Security will not speak to you, so don't waste time asking them questions. But you can always talk to us.'

'What about Art?'

These simple words had a surprising effect. The woman's eyes opened wide; the men turned towards Clara and gesticulated; even the guard appeared to smile. It was the woman who spoke.

168

'Art? . . . Oh, Art does what it likes. Art has its own agenda, none of us knows what that is, and there's no way we could know.'

Clara recalled the long silences on the phone while she was being stretched, the clauses of the contract she had signed.

'I understand,' she said.

'No, no,' the woman responded unexpectedly. 'You'll never understand.'

They gave her some plastic slippers which she hurriedly put on. So far she was not damaged, so why run any risk at the last moment? Then they put the plastic tunic back on. She realised they had not returned the top and miniskirt, but that was not important. The tunic moulded itself around her naked body. The security man set off and Clara followed him slowly, the plastic swishing as she walked along. They left by the back door. As they passed the next room, she thought she caught a swift glimpse of a naked old man with a primed body and yellow labels. His eyes were gleaming. Clara would have liked to pause for a moment and say hello to him, but the security man was striding off unconcerned. They soon came out into a silent private parking lot. The vehicle waiting had more than enough room for her. It was a dark-coloured van with a back door and two more up by the driver. There were no windows in the rear part, so that the canvas was protected from prying eyes. The back section had optional seating, but all of them had been removed except for one, to give her even more space. Clara could have stretched out on the floor easily without reaching the driver's seat, but instead she was strapped in by four seat belts that the driver snapped shut with his gloved hands. Clara found she was pinioned to the seat back.

The journey was as brief as a dream. Through the front windscreen she could make out green road signs: Amsterdam, Haarlem, Utrecht; arrows, lines; phosphorescent signs. The night was streaked with power pylons, or perhaps they were telegraph posts, which caught the van's speeding headlights. The security man drove in silence. Clara soon realised they were not heading for Amsterdam. The lights she had seen when they left Schiphol airport began to die away, which must mean they had turned off the main highway. Now they were in the countryside. A sudden cold sensation gripped her. For just a moment she was filled with an absurd thought. Could they be heading for Edenburg? Would the Maestro receive her that very night? But what if all this was a dream, and it was not Van Tysch who was going to paint her, as she had been imagining since she found out who had contracted her? She scolded herself for thinking this way. A good painting had no right to get emotional. She had too much experience for that. She was a twenty-four-year-old canvas, for goodness' sake. She had started out with *The Circle* and Brentano had painted her on three occasions. Eight years in the profession was too long for her to give in to her nerves, wasn't it? I'll try to stay calm. You *must* feel *distant* from everything that happens to you. What was it that Marisa Monfort always said? Be like an insect. Like someone who has forgotten their own name. A linen canvas plaited with white lines. Someone once told her memories are lines on white nothingness: we have to rub them out, we have to be different, we have to *not be*.

She had no idea how long it was before she began to notice the van was slowing down. The headlights picked out scrawny trees. A track. She caught sight of wheelbarrows, rakes, buckets, objects that reminded her of the garden tools which helped her father enjoy the summers in Alberca. The man from Security drew up outside a hedge. He got out, opened the gate, then drove the van inside. Soon afterwards he had parked and undone Clara's seat belts. As soon as she stepped down on to the gravel in her plastic slippers, she realised this could not be Edenburg. But it did not seem to be any other town either. The lights showed it was some kind of market garden. To the right and left, she could see the night was not invulnerable, there were signs of civilisation, a row of lines which perhaps betrayed the presence of houses or factories, or even some kind of airport or small village. It was cool, and the wind was tugging at the edges of her tunic. The moon was a curved, clipped length of wire. She sniffed the air: it smelt of woods and marsh. The smell of the earth became distinct in her mouth, as if she were tasting it. She pushed back a fleck of hair from her eyebrow-less face. At her feet, her shadow on the gravel was dark and twisted.

The man from Security waited for her, and then the two of them walked towards the house. It was a small, one-storey affair, with a porch and little else of note, as though it were waiting for her to arrive to start to exist. The crickets were tapping out their night-time morse code. I'm sure all this will be very nice in the morning, but at the moment it's a bit scary, Clara thought. As they climbed the few steps up to the front of the house, the sound of the man's shoes on the wooden boards reminded her of a horror movie she had seen years earlier with Gabi Ponce.

There was a glint of keys. The inside of the house smelt of bathroom fresheners. There was a small hallway, with a staircase on the right and, to the left, a closed door. Clara suddenly noticed that the light switches to all the rooms were in the hall. The man flicked them on, and light filled the house, revealing what appeared to be part of a living room on the far side of the staircase: white walls, cream doors, a full-length mirror on a mobile frame, and a floor of white wood. Clara later discovered the whole house had the same parquet. The black lines of the gaps and the white of the boards made the floor look like a sheet of paper for calligraphy or for a study of perspective foreshortening. The closed door on the left opened into a simple kitchen. The other half of the living room stretched to the back of the house, parallel to the kitchen. A sofa, a faded carpet (once a crimson colour?), a small chest of three drawers that had a telephone on it, and another full-length mirror, were all the furniture she could see. Placed opposite each other, the two mirrors suggested infinity. There was only one ornament on the walls: a framed, medium-sized photograph. It was a very odd one. It showed the head and shoulders of a man facing away from the camera, on a black background. His dark, well-cut hair and his jacket blended in so well with the surrounding shadows that only his ears, the half-moon of his neck and the shirt collar were visible. It reminded Clara of a Surrealist painting.

The bedroom was on the right. It was a big room, with a mattress on the floor and no other furniture. The mattress was a bright blue. A door led to the bathroom, already equipped for

171

hyperdramatic needs. A couple of bathrobes were hanging on the back of the door.

The man had gone into all the rooms. Rather than showing her the house, he seemed to be inspecting it. Clara was looking at all the things in the bathroom when she saw a shadow over her shoulder. It was him. Without a word, he bent down and started to lift off the plastic tunic. She understood what he was trying to do, and raised her arms to help. The man finished removing the tunic, folded it up, and put it into a big bag. Then he bent down again and took off her slippers, which he stored in the same bag. Then he left the room, bag under his arm. She heard his footsteps across the floorboards, the door, the lock. She breathed in deeply as she heard the sound of the van engine fade into the distance. She left the bedroom and went to the front window just in time to see the pen of light drawing parallel lines across the darkness. Then everything was black again.

She was alone. She was naked. But she didn't feel at all bothered by this.

She went up to the front door and examined it. Locked. She tried the window and found it was locked too. She tried all the windows in the house as well as a back door she discovered in the living room, and found that none of them would open without keys. She preferred to think of it another way: she was not locked in, she was *in storage*. She was not alone, she was *unique*.

Unique and stored in a locked house.

She was a precious object.

She went into the living room and looked for the phone. It was cordless. She picked it up. A dead silence. She saw a dark blue rectangle next to the receiver, a card with a number on it. She guessed it must be Conservation's details ('You can ring at any time of the day or night') but it would be useless if the phone was not working anyway. She followed the cable back and saw it was properly connected. She tried again, tapping in numbers haphazardly. The phone was dead. She dialled the number on the card. As her finger touched the last digit, she heard the call go through. So it worked in certain cases. She hung up. She immediately knew what was going on.

You can ring us, *but only us*.

Of course.

She gazed around at the silence, the emptiness of the lined floor. The house was anonymous and naked, just like her. She ran her hands over the incredible smoothness of her primed thighs, the harsh rigidity of the labels attached to her body, and looked all around her. She needed to start from scratch, and that was where she was, at the start of *everything*, polished, smooth, reduced to a minimum, labelled.

Having nothing better to do, she approached one of the mirrors.

It was then that she discovered her body was nothing more than a sheaf of lines.

Her father's scrawny, angular features bent over her, distorted by their proximity: the majestic nose, the big square glasses in which she could see the reflection of an oblong copy of herself. He spoke to her in a voice that seemed to come from a long-lost recording:

'What a sad life, a sad life; the fact is, I've no idea why I was born. How I wish I had an objective, a goal in life like you do, that would help me understand why I was born, but above all why I vanished, daughter, it's so sad, why I had to leave when you were so young, when I did not know you properly. I'd like to know why I abandoned you so soon, why I can't live with you any more. Maybe all that, the bitter separation, is due to the fact that you have to be ready, because the cameras are waiting for you, the stage is set, the dialogue is written, and the lights . . . look how brilliant the lights are . . . all for you, my beautiful daughter. And the faces watching you, staring at you: the director, the producer, the make-up artist . . . Come on, on to the set. I'm looking at you, watching over you, I'm not going to close my eyes. I have to look at you forever, daughter . . .'

Her father poked out his tongue and anxiously licked his top lip. The tongue was a tiny line darting in and out . . .

When Clara woke up she was on the verge of tears, or perhaps had already been crying: it is hard to tell if there are no actual tears to give the game away. She remembered her dream vividly, although she had no idea what it meant. She often dreamt of her father: he was a figure who was always part of her conscious-ness, someone who visited her with astonishing regularity. Uncle Pablo had once confessed he also dreamt of him. He put it down to the fact that his brother had died. 'Dead people always appear when we dream,' he used to tell her, adding that our only possi-bility of eternal life was to figure in other people's dreams.

She was lying on the bedroom mattress in the bleary light of dawn. As she stood up, she was struck by the white plaster on the wall in front of her, and the lines on the floorboards. She was still naked apart from her labels, but neither the fact that she had no clothes, sheets or blankets to cover her, nor the three labels attached to her body, had been able to disturb her blissful sleep. She sat on the edge of the mattress with her feet on the floor and wondered what she should do next.

It was then she heard voices.

The sound came from the living room. There were at least two people, and they were speaking Dutch. They were laughing, shouting, from time to time. Perhaps the noise they had made coming into the house was what had woken her.

She did not think they could be people from Conservation or Security. Perhaps they were workmen who had come to install something, or cleaners (how absurd). It could also be the first hyperdramatic rehearsal, an improvised scene they were putting on for her benefit. Or perhaps it was the artist himself, the painter who had contracted her, who had come with his group of assis-tants to examine the material for himself. Whoever it was, she needed to prepare herself.

She went into the bathroom, urinated (her bladder was full to bursting, but she only now realised this), then washed herself carefully with wet paper towels. She rinsed her face with water, smoothed her hair (none of this was necessary: her face was already shiny clean, her hair looked perfect); for a few moments her mind wandered to thoughts of dresses, colours, accessories, ways of presenting herself to strangers, what the best combina-tions might be, until she suddenly remembered she was not in her own apartment, but somewhere in Holland, and that anyway she was a primed and labelled canvas and that she should

174

appear exactly as she was to whoever had arrived at the house. She took a deep breath, walked across the bedroom, and opened the door.

Two men were walking to and fro between the front door and the living room.

The older of the two was struggling with a large canvas bag and did not see her as he went by. He had thinning hair, and wore a dirty T-shirt and jeans. He had long, hairy, almost ape-like arms. Behind thick glasses, his eyes looked like a pair of insects stuck in amber. But what caught Clara's attention was the turquoise-coloured label attached to a fold in his T-shirt. Someone from Art, she thought with a shudder. He was the first member of that select circle she had ever met. She held her breath like a believer in the presence of one of the great patriarchs of her faith. So they were from the Art department of the Van Tysch Foundation, no less: assistants of the Maestro and Jacob Stein. They were not as she had imagined, with their ordinary-looking faces and rather ragged appearance, but still the sight of the label set her heart racing.

The other man seemed very young. He had just left a bag on the carpet, and was now busy raising the blinds over the back windows, flooding the room with the dawn light. He said something in Dutch and turned round. As he did so, he discovered Clara standing in the doorway. He stood looking at her. She smiled faintly, but thought that to present herself would be inappropriate. At that moment, the older man also dropped his bag on the floor, and saw her too.

'Well, well, well,' the younger man said in Spanish, taking a few steps towards her.

He was tall and tanned, with a crewcut of black hair. Clara liked his face: thick but well-defined eyebrows, sideburns curled like commas, a moustache and beard straight out of a Three Musketeers film. He was wearing African necklaces, earrings, bracelets and leather wristbands. The badges on his jacket were a compendium of slogans in Dutch. Beside him, the older man looked like the hunchback servant of a diabolical professor. The contrast between them could not have been greater.

They said something in Dutch, pointing at Clara. She stood

quietly and calmly in the doorway, making no attempt to cover her naked body.

Once they had finished their brief dialogue, the younger one put his hand in his jeans pocket and took something out. It was a pair of pliers, with sharp, curved edges. He came over to Clara, smiling. Instinctively, she took a step backwards.

'The very first thing we do with anything we are going to prepare,' he said in a singsong Spanish with a South American accent, lifting the pliers to Clara's neck, 'is to get rid of the labels.'

Snip, snip, snip, and the three yellow pieces of cardboard fell at her feet.

She tensed her stomach muscles so that Gerardo could paint the eighth vertical line next to her navel. Gerardo wore rubber gloves and had a felt tip hanging round his neck which he used to write the number of the colour on her skin. She hardly felt him press as he wrote. Now he was using the felt-tip to draw an arabesque, a butterfly's wings under the eighth line: 8. Then he took off his gloves and started the timer.

The entire morning had been spent in the same routine. Clara was lying on her back on the chest of drawers, hands behind her neck and her legs dangling over the edge. She felt a little confused. She had always thought that the technique the Foundation's artists used must be more impulsive even than that of Bassan or Vicky, and yet here were the two men painstakingly testing colours all over her body. Gerardo was the one who painted her: he prised the lid off a tin, smeared some on his forefinger, drew a line on her stomach, then wrote the number under the line. After every three or four lines, he set up the timer and left her alone while he waited for the different colours – all of them shades of pink – to dry. Then he came back, opened another tin, and began the whole process all over again.

They had not told her their names: she had read them on their turquoise-coloured labels, next to their photos. The young one was Gerardo Williams. The older man, Justus Uhl. Clara supposed they were assistants of the main artist. Gerardo spoke Spanish very well, despite a certain Anglo-Saxon accent. She thought he could be Colombian, or maybe Peruvian. Uhl never

176

spoke directly to her, and his way of looking at her and dealing with her was considerably more curt than Gerardo's.

On the windowpane, between her body and the sun, an insect was buzzing against the glass: its shadow made a line, a trait, across her absolute nudity.

The timer went off, and Gerardo returned.

'Once we've decided on the exact tone, we'll make tests on your whole body,' he said, choosing another tin and lifting the lid. 'We'll use a porous body stocking, it's quicker. Have you ever used one before?'

'Yes.'

'Oh,' he said with a smile. 'I was forgetting you're an expert.'

'I'm no expert, but I've been working for several years as . . .'

'Don't talk . . . wait a moment. Stretch out more. With your hands held together above your head, as though you were an arrow. Like this.'

She could feel his cold finger sliding down her stomach. Then the timer again. If she closed her eyes, she could guess the number by the sensations on her skin: a curl, a line, a gap. As he was writing, his hand sometimes brushed her sex.

'You're from Madrid, aren't you?' Gerardo asked, busy prising open the lid of another tin of paint. She nodded. 'I've never been to Madrid, believe it or not. In Spain I only know Barcelona. Someday I must go to Madrid.'

'Where are you from?'

'Me? From here and there. I've lived in New York, Paris, and now Amsterdam . . .'

'You speak very good Spanish.'

From her stiff position on the chest of drawers she could see his eyebrow arch modestly. He loves being praised, she thought.

'I'm very good at everything, darling.'

To Clara, it did not sound like a joke.

'I can see that.'

'Well, the truth of the matter is that my father is Puerto Rican . . . this blasted tin won't open. It's shy.'

She smiled. Could there be any tin capable of resisting D'Artagnan? she thought. She watched him frown, flush with effort, grimace. His biceps were inflating like balloons.

177

'Uf, that's it.' As he was scraping out a sample with his finger (flesh pink like all the others, it was hard to tell the difference) he spoke to her again. 'Have you been to Amsterdam before?'

'Yes.' She recalled a trip she had made years earlier with Gabi Ponce, an adventure with rucksacks and worn-out trainers. 'I saw several works by Van Tysch in the Stedelijk.'

She could feel the cold line of paint: the first of a new row under her navel.

'Do you like Van Tysch?' Gerardo asked.

He still had his finger on her stomach. Was that an ironic gleam in his dark eyes? she wondered.

'He fascinates me. I think he's a genius.'

'Stay still for a minute. That's it . . . all done. I'll leave you for a bit while these dry, OK? . . . It's a beautiful day outside. Do you know where we are? In one of the cottages the Foundation uses for working on canvases. It's south of Amsterdam near a town called Woerden, not far from Gouda. Yes that's right, Gouda. Mmm . . . the cheese. Do you know this area?' – Clara shook her head. 'Further to the south there are some really pretty lakes.' He stared out of the window, then said something that really surprised her. 'Down there among the trees there's a fantastic landscape. You'd look wonderful posed there, among the trees, painted in flesh and light-pink tones.' He pointed to a spot Clara could not see from her horizontal position.

'Are you going to paint me?'

She liked his broad smile when she said that. His mouth was perhaps a little too big, but his smile showed how pleased he was.

'No darling, I'm only an assistant, as my label says. Justus is an assistant as well, but a senior one. We're only in the background of the photo. And we don't even appear with the important people at press conferences . . .'

'Is Van Tysch going to paint me?'

Gerardo stripped off the gloves and threw them into a bag. Clara could not see his face as he replied.

'All in good time, darling. Patience is a virtue in works of art.'

At that moment, something happened. Uhl arrived and started shouting furiously at Gerardo. His annoyance was clear.

The younger man flushed and stepped back. Clara could see it was Uhl who was in charge, and that perhaps he had criticised his assistant for talking too much to her – she was only a canvas, after all. Then Uhl turned round and stared at Clara's body stretched out on the chest. Clara gazed back at him uneasily. She hated the way those distant eyes scrutinised her from the far end of the tunnel of his glasses. She watched as he raised a finger like a knife and brought it down over her stomach. She told herself she would not move an inch unless they told her to. She tensed her muscles and waited. What's he going to do now?

She could feel Uhl's rough finger as it brushed her primed skin. He was not wearing gloves, and was the first person to touch her with his bare hands. The finger drew a line down her stomach. Clara was unsure whether this had any real purpose or was simply a way of distracting himself while he thought. She felt the finger travelling round her sex and could not avoid flinching. The finger was drawing invisible lines. The sensation did not so much excite her as *lay siege to* her excitement. She held in her stomach muscles and stayed as rigid as possible. The finger moved up her body, and drew a horizontal eight – or the symbol of infinity – around her breasts. Then it carried on up to her neck, her chin. She could hardly breathe. It reached her mouth, separated her lips. Clara helped by opening her jaw. The intruder felt for her tongue. And then, as if it had discovered all it needed, it withdrew.

They left her on her own. She could hear them chatting unconcernedly out on the porch.

What did Uhl's exploration of her body mean? Was it a way of judging the texture of her skin? She did not think so. She had felt quite uncomfortable during his examination.

When the timer went off, Gerardo appeared in her line of vision once more. He was wearing a fresh pair of gloves, and picked up another tin of paint.

'Justus is the boss,' he whispered. 'He's a bit special, but you'll get used to him. Which one is it now? Oh yes, shade 36.'

At midday they called her to eat. A plastic tray like an airline one was on the kitchen table. On it was a chicken and salad sandwich, a yogurt, an Aroxen juice, and half a litre of mineral water. She ate alone – the other two had their meal out on the porch. She was barefoot and naked, with a palisade of twenty-five, flesh-coloured and numbered lines painted on her stomach. After a rapid visit to the bathroom, the afternoon went on with no breaks. They painted another forty lines, this time on her back. The calendar of a shipwrecked sailor. The last of them climbed the curve of her buttocks. They left, came back to study the effect, occasionally took photos. Clara tried to convince herself that all this was a preamble, that the following day things would be different. She could not allow herself to admit that her first day of work for the Foundation was disappointing.

At a certain point, it began to grow dark. She still hadn't seen the landscape around the house.

'Don't have a shower tonight or put anything on over the lines,' Gerardo warned her. 'Lie down on your back on the mattress with the timer beside you. It will go off every two hours. Each time it does, turn over, just like a Spanish omelette.'

'Aha, OK.'

'We'll be back early tomorrow morning.'

'Aha.'

'Your dinner is in the kitchen. And remember: when you hear the timer, over you go.' He gestured with his hands.

'Like an omelette.'

'That's right.'

Gerardo's eyes shone as he smiled at her. Uhl's voice called to him, and he hastily left the room.

It happened in the middle of the night, the second time the alarm went off.

Face down on the mattress, Clara woke from her light sleep. As she turned over, her eyes still unfocused, she realised the colour of the darkness was changing.

It was very rapid, no more than the blinking of an eye. She turned her head to look out of the bedroom window on her left. All she could see were shadows, the outlines of trees and branches, yet she was sure that an instant before those shadows had been *different*. She leaned up, pressing her elbows into the mattress. Held her breath. Listened intently. Was that footsteps

180

she could hear, near the window? It was hard to know, because the wind was whipping the tree branches.

She searched the darkness with her gaze. She saw her naked legs, stretching out like two parallel lines. There were only three things in the bedroom: her, the timer, and the mattress. Behind her back, the timer was ticking off the seconds.

She stood up, and walked cautiously over to the window. It was completely dark outside. It's incredible how scary darkness like this can be in the middle of the countryside, she thought. Her skin wanted to pull on its body stocking of fear, but the primer made it impossible. The window was a world of black lines. She went up to it. For a fraction of a second, a monster with yellow features floated before her eyes – but she knew she was only seeing her own reflection, so was not startled.

There was nobody out there, or at least no one she could see. She listened. The wind rustled the branches.

She protected her body with her hands, and went back to the mattress. She lay down on her back. Her heart was pounding like a hammer in her ears.

She remembered the afternoon she had left her apartment to be primed. The feeling she had just had was like that earlier one, only much more intense.

She was sure someone had been looking in at her through the window just before the timer went off.

Someone who was outside the house, in the middle of the night, keeping watch on her.

3

The 'terrible' is in the circle.

Slowly, menacingly, the *Monsters* of the Haus der Kunst come back to life.

The girl floating in the glass swimming pool full of foul water is called Rita. She is the first to receive help, because she has to make a huge effort: spending six hours a day as organic waste with her hair caught up in plastic and excrement is no easy task. The work has been bought by a Swedish company, and the monthly rental has achieved the impossible: every day Rita dives into this amnion of shit and is happy to do so. In her time off she even manages to enjoy what might be called 'a social life' (although she complains that her hair smells). Now she is breathing deeply in the pool, waiting for the water level to go down. We cannot see her face, but we can see how her long legs wave in the water like pale white strands of seaweed.

And if she complains about her hair, she should spare a thought for Sylvie. Sylvie Gailor is *Medusa*, a painting valued at more than thirty million dollars, and with an astronomical monthly rent. This is because she has ten live snakes painted ultramarine-blue writhing around her head which have to be fed and replaced quite often. They are about the length of an adult hand, and are held in place by a delicate network of wires disguised as hair, which allows them to move their heads and tails. Snakes in general do not know much about art, so they get very nervous if we force them to put up with being clipped immobile for six hours a day. Some of them die on Sylvie's head; others thrash about despairingly. Ecological groups and animal protection societies have denounced the exhibit and protested outside the doors of the museums and galleries where it has been shown. All of them are well known to the organisers, and are a harmless minority compared to the people who protest against the other works in the collection. But nobody thinks of poor Sylvie. It's true she is well paid, but what can compensate for her insomnia, the strange repugnance she feels at combing her hair, the ghostly feeling she gets sometimes when she is talking, laughing, having dinner in a restaurant or making love, a feeling that someone is caressing her hair, pulling at her curls, scratching her head with nail-less fingers?

Ten metres behind Sylvie stands Hiro Nadei, an aged Japanese man painted in ochres, who holds a small jasmine flower in his right hand. Hiro is a real survivor of Hiroshima; he is sixty-six years old. When his city exploded in an atomic hell, he was five. He was in his back garden holding a jasmine in that same hand. Rescued almost unscathed from the ruins, the hardest thing was to get him to open his right hand, which was clenched like a fist. A month later, he let go: the flower was crushed beyond recognition. Two years ago, Van Tysch heard his story and called him to do a small painting. Mr Nadei was delighted: he is a widower, lives on his own, and wants to close the circle of his life dying as he should have done at that dreadful moment. The painting, entitled *The Closed Hand*, has been sold to an American. At the other end of the gallery, Kim, a young Filipino, is in the last stages of AIDS. He is on show lying in bed painted deathly grey, with an intravenous drip stuck like a skewer in his shrivelled arm. He has difficulty breathing, and occasionally has to be given oxygen. He is the sixteenth substitute for a work whose continuing existence makes it art: a painting which lasts as long as human tragedy. Of course, he is not doing it for the money. Like all his predecessors, Kim wants to die as a work of art. He wants his death to have a meaning. He wants to make the work last, precisely so that it will not last. Stein has found a brilliant phrase to describe it (he is very good at that kind of thing): *Terminal Phase* is the first painting in the history of art which will be beautiful only after it ceases to exist.

Near *Terminal Phase* is *The Doll*. Jennifer Halley, an eight-year-old work, is painted pink and stands wearing a black dress, cradling a doll in her arms. But the doll is alive, and looks like one of those starving embryos with a stomach like a black grape that sometimes raise their head out of the well that is the Third World. And what is apparently a child is, in fact, an adult – a dwarf and achondroplastic canvas by the name of Steve. Steve is naked, painted in dark colours, and cries and squirms in Jennifer's arms. A little further on is the hanged man, swinging on his scaffold. Next to him are the tortured girls. The pungent stench that brings tears to the eyes comes from *Hitler*, dressed in skins from dead animals sewn together. The mental retards in executive suits appear fascinated by the colours of their ties and the saliva dribbling down them like diamonds. Today Tuesday 27 June, four thousand people have visited this incredible exhibition. Because the screening process is so slow, it is impossible to accommodate all those waiting in a long human line down beyond the steps of the Haus der Kunst. Those who have not got in will have to come back tomorrow. The *Monsters* are finishing their day. Those paintings which have a brain, consciousness, limbs and faces, manage to feel happy about it, and say goodbye to their colleagues. It is time to rest. But none of them looks over at the circular podium in the centre of the room.

The 'terrible' is in the circle.

This is where the real *Monsters* are kept.

The rattle of lifting gear, and the protective glass surrounding them is removed. Five technicians and as many security guards were waiting at the foot of the high podium. The glass is heavy, hermetically sealed, and takes a minute to be lifted off completely. It is a fifteen-centimetre thick cylinder of transparent glass, with a similar top. For the first few months the exhibition was on tour, there was no such top. A bullet-proof glass wall three metres high was thought to be more than enough to protect them. Then when *Monsters* was on show in Paris, a visitor threw shit at the exhibit. It was his own excrement (as he later confessed), which he had been carrying in his pocket, and which had passed unnoticed through the metal detector, the X-ray screen, the body *doppler*, the image analysis programmes used on bulky clothing, pregnant women's stomachs, and pushchairs.

In the twenty-first century, as a journalist wrote about the incident, it is still possible to be a terrorist by throwing shit. Who knows, perhaps in the twenty-second century it will have become impossible. Tossed with an expert arm when the visitor reached the front row and was standing next to the security rope, the excrement flew in an arc through the air. Unfortunately, it missed: the faeces hit the top edge of the glass barrier and bounced back onto the public. Have you ever felt – asked the same journalist in his article – when you were visiting a modern art museum, that you were having shit thrown in your face?

Ever since then, the barrier protecting the Walden brothers had a top as well.

'How do you feel, Hubert?'

'Fine, Arnold, and you?'

'Not too bad, Hubert.'

The grey exhibition clothes the two brothers were wearing

184

came off easily thanks to hidden zips at the back. Stark naked, Hubertus and Arnoldus Walden looked like two huge sumo wrestlers fawned over by their attentive trainers. The technicians wrapped them in robes with their names on the back, and they tied them over their colossal stomachs, which overhung tiny genitals as bald as quails' eggs.

'One day you'll give us the wrong robe, and the price of the work will collapse.'

The technicians laughed as one at this shaft of wit – they had strict instructions not to get on the wrong side of the brothers.

'Pass me that cottonwool, Franz,' said Arnoldus. 'You're rubbing me as gently as though I were your mother.'

'Mr Roberston called again,' an assistant commented.

'He calls us every day,' Hubertus said mockingly. 'He's still thinking of making a film about us, written by that American Nobel prize winner.'

'He's part of the new *intelligentsia*,' Arnoldus said.

'He looks after us.'

'He wants us.'

'He wants to *buy* us, Arno.'

'That's what I said, Hubert. Could you spray some more solvent on my back, Franz? The paint is itching.'

'We only interest that old bastard because he wants to buy us.'

'Yes, but the Maestro wouldn't sell us to that asshole.'

'Or maybe he would: who knows? He's made interesting offers, hasn't he, Karl?'

'I think so.'

'He "thinks" so. Did you hear that, Arno? . . . Karl "thinks" so.'

'Be careful with the top step from the podium . . .'

'We know that, idiot. Are you new? Is this your first day in Conservation? . . . We're not new to this, you idiot.'

'We're old. We're eternal.'

Jennifer Halley's dress has been taken off. She was wearing only a pair of white socks with pompons (Steve, the achondroplastic model, was being wheeled away on a trolley). Several technicians were rubbing Jennifer's shiny body with cottonwool dipped in solvent. As the Walden brothers passed by her,

Hubertus tried to bow his head, although all he succeeded in doing was to lower it into his triple chin.

'Bye, my virginal fairytale princess! May angels fill your dreams!'

The girl turned towards him and gave him the finger.

Hubertus carried on smiling, but as he lumbered like a listing boat towards the exit, he screwed up his eyes until they were two dark hyphens.

'How uncouth our little whore is. I've a mind to teach her some manners.'

'Ask Robertson to buy her and put her in your house. Then both of us can teach her a lesson.'

'Don't talk nonsense, Arno. Besides, you know I prefer a good male lobster to a female oyster. Do you mind getting out of the way, miss, we're trying to leave.'

The girl from Conservation leapt out of their path, smiling and saying she was sorry. She was looking after the mental retards. The Walden brothers swept onwards, followed by a group of assistants. Hubertus' robe was purple; Arnoldus' carrot-coloured with green flecks. They had velvet hoods, with cords long enough to go round seven ordinary men.

'Hubert.'

'What is it, Arno?'

'I have to something to confess.'

'. . . ?'

'Yesterday I stole your Walkman. It's in my locker.'

'And I've got something to confess to you, Arno.'

'Tell me, Hubert.'

'My Walkman is completely fucked.'

Laughing their high-pitched laughs, the enormous twins left the gallery by an emergency exit.

The Haus der Kunst in Munich is a dull white oblong screened by columns, built next to the English Garden. Its detractors call it the 'Weisswurst'. It was inaugurated seventy years earlier with a triumphal procession by none other than Adolf Hitler, who wanted to use it as a symbol of the purity of German art. In the procession were young girls dressed as nymphs, who all moved like dolls and blinked their eyes at the same time as though being switched on and off. The Führer did not like that very much. Coinciding with this lavish opening, another small but no less important exhibition was taking place. This was of 'Degenerate Art', where works by painters banned by the Nazis, such as Paul Klee, were being shown. The Walden brothers knew the story, and they could not help wondering, as they plunged on majestically down the museum corridors towards the changing rooms, which of the two collections the great Nazi leader would have put them in. In the one symbolising the purity of the German race? Or with the 'Degenerate Art'?

Circles. Arno likes drawing circles. He draws himself as joined-up circles: at the top, his round head; then a big belly for body; and two legs sticking out of the sides.

'What's the matter with you, Hubert?'

'My skin is very sensitive since they changed the glue they put on, Arno. After the shower it stings.'

'That's strange, the same happens to me.'

They were in the labelling room, fully dressed, combing their hair with a neat parting. The technicians had just fixed on their labels and served them an abundant seafood dinner, which they had attacked with gusto.

The Waldens were two symmetrical beings, one of nature's rare exact photocopies. As usual in these cases, they wore identical clothes (made to measure by Italian tailors) and had identical haircuts. When one fell ill, the other did not take long to succumb as well. They had similar tastes, and were irritated by the same things. In childhood, they had been diagnosed with the same syndrome (obesity, sterility and antisocial behaviour), had gone to the same schools, performed the same jobs in the same firms, and been in the same prisons together, accused of the same offences. Their clinical and criminal records said the same: pederast, psychopath, and sadist. Van Tysch had called the two of them up one afternoon in the autumn of 2002, shortly after they had been declared innocent in the case of the dreadful murder of Helga Blanchard and her son. He had made them both works of art simultaneously.

Helga Blanchard was a German TV actress, a former lover of a Bayern Munich fullback. She had a boy of five from a previous

187

marriage, and was fortunate to have won substantial maintenance from the divorce. Nobody really knows what took place,
but early on the morning of 5 August, 2003, the outskirts of
Hamburg were very misty. When the mist cleared, Helga and
her son Oswald were found naked and nailed with tent pegs
half an inch thick to the floorboards of their country cottage. One
of the pegs joined the two corpses (her right hand and his left).
They also shared the fact that their tongues had been cut out,
they had been raped with a screwdriver, and their eyes had been
gouged out, or almost: Helga's right eye had been left untouched
so that she could get a good look at what was happening to her
son. The crime caused such a scandal that the authorities were
forced to make an immediate arrest, without any proof: so they
took in a lesbian couple who were Helga's closest neighbours,
and who around that time had been trying to get official permission to adopt a child. A mob of furious citizens tried to burn
down their chalet. Twenty-four hours later they were released
without charge. The younger of the two appeared on a TV programme, and the next day a lot of people were imitating the
stabbing gesture she made with her forefingers when she insisted
she had nothing to do with what had happened, and that neither
of them had seen or heard anything. The arrests continued: first
Helga's former husband (an impresario), then his current wife,
after that her ex-husband's brother, and finally, the footballer.
When the footballer was taken in, news of the case spread
beyond Germany and was talked about throughout Europe.

Then a surprise witness came forward: an old-fashioned
painter who still used canvas for his paintings, and had been
working that day on a countryside scene he was thinking of calling *Trees and Mist*. He was a doctor by profession, and a family
man. That quiet holiday morning he had been working on his
canvas when he saw two big circles rolling from tree to tree
through wisps of mist; they did not seem to him to have a naturally healthy colour. He looked more closely, and could make
out two naked, immensely fat men gliding through the woods
very near Helga Blanchard's cottage. So fascinated was he by
their anatomies that he abandoned all attempts to carry on with
his painting, and instead started to draw them in his sketchbook.

188

The sketch was published as an exclusive in *Der Spiegel*. After that, it was easy: the Walden brothers lived in Hamburg and had lengthy criminal records. They were arrested and put on trial. The young lawyer nominated to defend them was brilliant. The first thing he did was to cleverly destroy the evidence put forward by the doctor–painter. The trap he set for the witness is still remembered: 'If your painting is entitled *Trees and Mist*, and you, yourself, say you are inspired by the landscape around you, how could you be certain of seeing the defendants in a place filled with *trees* and *mist?*' Next he played on the jury's sentiments. 'Are they to be judged guilty simply because we don't like their appearance? Or because they have a criminal record? Are we to sacrifice them so our consciences can sleep soundly?' There was no way to prove that the Walden brothers had been at the scene of the crime, and the case quickly collapsed. As soon as they were released, the twins were visited by a very friendly dark-skinned, sharp-nosed man who reeked of money. When he pressed his fingers together, he showed elegantly manicured fingernails. He talked to the brothers about art, and the Bruno van Tysch Foundation. They were secretly primed and sent to Amsterdam and Edenburg. There, Van Tysch told them: 'I don't want you ever to tell anyone what you did, or what you think you did, not even yourselves. I don't want to paint with your guilt, but with the suspicion.' The work ended up being very simple. The Walden twins were posed standing face to face, dressed in grey prisoners' clothes and painted in diluted colours that emphasised the evil look on their faces. On their chests, like a row of medals, their criminal records were printed in small capitals. On their backs, a photo of Helga Blanchard hugging her son Oswald – standing out against a background of Venice, where they had had a holiday – with the obvious question: *Was it them?* Helga's family tried to stop Van Tysch using the image, but the matter was settled to the satisfaction of both parties thanks to a considerable sum of money. As far as hyperdramatic work went, there was no problem.

The Walden twins were born to be paintings. It was no accident that the only thing they had succeeded in doing in their lives was to stay still in a corner and allow humanity to heap abuse on them. They were two buddhas, two statues, two contented and unchanging beings. They were insured for an amount considerably greater than most of Van Gogh's creations. They had endured a lengthy calvary of being expelled from schools, sacked from jobs, of prison sentences and loneliness. The public, the same humanity as always, still looked on them scornfully, but the Waldens had finally understood that art can be born even from scorn.

There was still one question: *Was it them?* The killer of Helga Blanchard and her son had still not been found. Tell me, please: *Was it them?*

'When the answer to that question is known, our price will go down,' one of the brothers told a well-known German art critic.

So their stupid red-faced grins stay in place, their cheeks are like round bruised apples of rouge, and their eyes gleam with the memories of past orgies.

By now they had finished getting dressed and groomed, and put themselves in the hands of a larger than normal security team.

'That's Art for you, Miss Schimmel. Art with a capital "A" I mean . . . The request doesn't come from me, it comes from Art, and that means you have to fulfil it.' Hubertus winked at his brother, but Arnoldus was listening to music on his Walkman and didn't notice. 'Yes, a platinum blond . . . I don't care if that's hard for you to arrange for tonight . . . we want a platinum blond, Miss Schimmel . . . don't argue, silly woman . . . bzzz . . . bzzz . . . I'm afraid I can't hear you, Miss Schimmel, there's a problem on the line, I'll have to hang up.' Hubertus' tongue flicked in and out of his tiny lips with reptilian grace and speed. 'Bzzz . . . bzzz . . . I can't hear a word, Miss Schimmel! I hope you can find a platinum blond. If you can't, you'll have to come up yourself . . . wear a mac, but nothing else underneath . . . Bzzzz . . . I have to hang up! *Auf Wiedersehen!'*

'Who were you talking to?' asked Arnoldus, turning down his music.

'That stupid woman Schimmel. She's always causing problems.'

'We ought to complain to Mr Benoit. They should throw her out.'

'She should be begging on a street corner.'

'Or working as a whore.'

'Or they could chain her up, put a collar on her, give her an anti-rabies shot, and hand her over to us.'

'No, I don't like puppies. I don't like cleaning up dog poo. Tell me, Hubertus . . .'

'What, Arnoldus?'

'Do you think we're happy?'

For an instant, the two brothers stared up at the dark roof of their van, where the bright cyclorama of the Munich night was flashing by.

'It's hard to tell,' said Hubertus. 'Eternity is a huge tragedy.'

'And it lasts forever.'

Shimmering, quivering, the windows of the Wunderbar hotel were reflected in the van's shiny paintwork as it drew up at the front entrance. The four guards took up strategic positions. Saltzer, the leader of the squad, motioned to one of his men, who poked his head into the van's open back door and said something. Hubertus ceremoniously deposited his massive bulk on the pavement, in front of a row of tasselled porters. Arnoldus got his jacket pocket caught on the door handle. He pulled as hard as he could, and the pocket ripped. Too bad: he had about a hundred more made by the same tailor, and he could always wear one of his brother's if need be.

The security agent used a remote control to switch on the lights in the entrance hall to the suite. Background music emerged from dark corners like a sinuously elegant dark fish.

'All clear in the hall, over,' he said, talking into the miniature microphone beneath his mouth.

The living area contained a heated swimming pool, a bar and the painting by Gianfranco Gigli. A promising disciple of Ferrucioli, he had unfortunately died of a heroin overdose two years earlier. Thanks to his death, the few works he had completed (androgynous masked figures dressed in ballet dancer costumes) had soared in value. This Gigli work lay on the floor next to the swimming pool like a silky black panther. The mask had only the absolute minimum of features drawn on it. The entire work was embroidered by the shifting web of light made by the reflections on the surface of the pool. There was a smell of noble woods, and the temperature in this part was much more agreeable than in the rest of the suite.

'All clear in the living room, over.'

The agent's voice echoed from the labyrinth of rooms in the suite. Hubertus had walked over to the steel bar counter and was serving himself champagne. Arnoldus was trying unsuccessfully to reach down to his shoes. He wished one day he could touch his toes. His failure spoilt all his good humour.

'I'll never understand,' he began in a surprisingly quiet tone (he never raised his voice), 'why Mr Benoit doesn't provide us with appliances to help us when we're on tour. I've had an arseful of all this effort I have to make.'

'Arses are round,' Hubertus said, refilling his glass. 'In some people, they are two circles; in others, only one. Bernard's arse, for example . . . is it one or two?'

Luckily, Arnoldus could easily get his shoes off without needing to use his hands, and he did so. His trousers also came off after simply undoing a button.

'Hubert, do you mind lowering the lights on that wall? They're shining straight in my eyes.'

'If you moved, they wouldn't bother you, Arno.'

'Please . . .'

'OK. I don't want to argue about it.'

'All clear in the sauna, over' a distant voice moaned.

'Haven't you finished yet, Bernard? We're expecting someone, you asshole.'

'All clear in Bernard, over.'

'All clear in Bernard's little asshole, over.'

The security agent did not even look at them while he checked the living room once more. Their cruel jokes had long since ceased to have any effect on him. He knew why they were so impatient, but he preferred not to think about it. He did not want to have to imagine what would happen in that room when their visitor arrived.

The visitor was almost always accompanied by an adult. If he was a little older, he might come on his own, disguised as a bell-boy or a waiter so as not to arouse suspicion. But the normal thing was for him to be with an adult. Bernard did not know what happened afterwards, and did not want to know. Nor did he know when the visitor left, if he did leave, or how and where. That was not his responsibility. The problem . . . the problem comes from . . .

It's not that Bernard has moral scruples. It's not that he thinks he's doing something wrong by carrying out orders. He likes working for the Foundation. He earns more than he would any-where else, his job is not difficult (as long as there are no complications) and Miss Wood and Mr Bosch are ideal bosses. Bernard hopes to save enough to be able to leave work and the city, this and all other cities. He wants to go and live in peace in some remote spot with his wife and small daughter. He knows full well he will never do it, but he thinks about it all the time just the same.

The problem with works like the *Monsters*, thinks Bernard, is that they can never be substituted. If the Walden twins were not there, who could replace them? Their biographies were essential to the painting just as light and shade were to a Rembrandt. Without their past, *Monsters* would not be worth a cent: it would not have given rise to all the rivers of ink, all the tonnes of com-puter bytes; whole books, or encyclopedia entries would not have been written about it; there would have been no TV debates, or ferocious arguments among theologians, psycholo-gists, legal experts, educators, sociologists and anthropologists; no one would have tried to throw shit at them; there would not have been a whole legion of imitators; and nor would there be the astronomical profits generated by the exhibition loans the Van Tysch Foundation made to the world's most important museums and galleries. And that old Hollywood director, Robertson, would not be counting the days until Van Tysch made up his mind to sell the work.

Monsters was the goose that laid the golden eggs. The bad thing was, the goose knew it.

'All clear, over and out.'

'Leaving so soon, Bernard?'

'Don't you like us any more?'

'Of course he likes us, Arno. Bernard's little arse sighs for us.'

Whistling a show tune, Bernard shut the soundproof door between the living room and the hallway. He breathed a sigh of relief. His work was over for the night: *Monsters*, one of the most valuable works in the entire history of art, was safe and sound. And fortunately, he could no longer hear the twins.

As soon as art becomes divorced from moral considerations, it's on a slippery slope, thinks Bernard. Why can't the Maestro understand that? There are things which can't . . . which *should not* ever be turned into art, he thinks.

'I'm going to have a shower,' Arnoldus said. 'I'm still sticky with paint. I hope you haven't drunk all the champagne, Hubert.'

'Of course not, of course not. How could you think I'd be so fucking inconsiderate?'

'There's steam in the room: why don't you turn the temperature of the pool down a bit?'

'I like it hot, hot, hot. Mmm.'

Arno flapped his arm dismissively, and walked down the corridor to their luxurious bathroom. The shower taps were turned on, then came the sound of his *castrato* voice singing an aria.

Hubertus tested the water with his fingers. It was an enormous, circular pool. That is what they had demanded. The Walden brothers adored everything round. Everything that was geometrically in tune with their anatomies. Psychologically in tune with their preferences: the juvenile works from *The Circle*, for example. One of their favourite fan clubs (they had thousands of fans all over the world) was called *The Circle of Monsters*. They sent the brothers their round stickers with slogans defending artistic freedom of expression and attacking intolerance.

With Arnoldus' fight with the opera in the background, Hubertus bent forward into the water, and floated off like a buoy that has lost its moorings. His yellow neck label floated on the turquoise water, tugged along by the blubbery cylinder of flesh. In the centre of the pool, Hubertus Walden felt like the Primordial Egg, the solitary Ovule at the supreme moment of fecundation. The water was the same depth all round: if he stood up, it came to just above his belly. Grandpa Paul did not want there to be the slightest chance of them drowning. He half-closed his eyes, sunken in the rolls of fat like a pair of signet rings, as the shimmering light of the water dissolved into white stripes. It was fantastic to live surrounded by luxury, to be caressed by the waves of that immense tank heated to just the right temperature. He wondered if the head of naturally platinum blond hair would reflect up to the ceiling when the light from the walls fell directly on to it.

His brother was massacring another aria in the bathroom. As he listened, Hubertus thought what an abject, perverse, cowardly and vicious person Arnoldus was. He hated him profoundly, but could not live without him. He thought of him the way he did his own inner organs: as something intimate, unavoidable, repugnant. At primary school, it was Arno who was always getting into trouble, but both of them were punished. 'If one of you is to blame, the two of you will pay,' Miss Linz used to say, eyes shining. And that was how it had been all his life: with their father, the judges, the police. That fat, soft, sickly creature singing out of tune in the bathroom (although still without raising his voice) was the one who had led Hubertus astray. Wasn't it Arnoldus who had thought up the plan to amuse themselves with Helga Blanchard and her son?

A quell'amor . . . quell'amor che palpito . . .

He remembered it all only in fragments, as though wrapped in golden mists, almost like a fascinating sweet: the mother's eyes widening in terror, hmmm, the ear-splitting cries, the small agonising hands . . .

. . . Dell'universo . . . Dell'universo intero . . .

. . . flashes of fragile flesh, hmmm, mouths opening in perfect circles, a roundness drained of blood . . .

. . . Misterioso, misterioso altero . . .

At first it seemed as though they had messed up again. That amateur painter working with his easel near Helga Blanchard's house had seen them. But the defence lawyer with dandruff had been extraordinary. What had looked as though it could be the end of their lives had suddenly become a wonderful fresh start.

The serpent biting its own tail. The perfect circle. What a beautiful harmony the circle is, especially when it doesn't move, when it's dead or paralysed and a finger can slip easily all round it. And what a great man Bruno van Tysch was. Thanks to him they led the life they dreamed of, and beyond that a good chunk of immortality, too. How marvellous it was to be a work of art.

He turned round in the warm velvet.

It was then he noticed that the Gigli work had moved.

. . . *Croce e delizia . . . delizia al cooor . . .*

Drops of water in his eyes blurred his vision. He rubbed them. Looked again.

Croce, croce e delizia, croce e delizia . . . delizia al cooor . . .

The painting, a flexible shadow in a black mask with the silhouette of a fencing master in mourning, was walking slowly over to the bar. It moved so naturally that at first Hubertus thought it must simply want a drink. But it can't! he realised all of a sudden. It's a work of art! It's not allowed to move!

'What are you doing?' he asked. He raised his voice so high the question ended in a squawk.

The Gianfranco Gigli work did not reply as it walked round behind the bar, bent down and got something out. A small case. Then it came back round the bar, sat behind Hubertus' back, and snapped open the metal clips on the case. They sounded like gunshots in the almost completely silent room (*ah, aaah,ah-ah-aaaaaaahhh* came Arno's tremolo voice from the bathroom).

Hubertus thought about calling his brother, but hesitated. His curiosity kept him silent. He heaved his massive bulk to the edge of the pool. The Gigli was fiddling with something on the table. What could it be? Something it had taken out of the case. Now it was putting that to one side and picking up something else. It did everything in such a delicate, gentle, clean way that for a moment Hubertus approved. There was nothing he enjoyed more than the subtle delicacy of shapes: a ballet dancer; a young boy; an act of torture.

He concluded it must be an alteration Gigli had called for. Perhaps the artist had decided to make the work into a performance. At any rate, it must be something to do with art. Anything goes where art is concerned, nothing has its own intrinsic value.

Things are art just because, because artists say they are and the public agrees. Hubertus recalled a work by Donna Meltzer entitled *Clock*, which was attached to the wall and moved round by the hour, except that the artist had decided that it would lose ten minutes a day, and by the end of a fortnight would come to a complete stop. Paintings do not always have to do the same thing. Some evolve according to a pre-established plan their creator has devised. So this one? It had changed. It must have fresh instructions. What was the symbolism behind that? Our mechanised society (which would explain the strange appliances it was laying on the bar)? The symbol of authority (a pistol)? The mass media (a portable recorder and a miniature video camera)? Violence (a set of sharp instruments)? Maybe it was all of those. Whatever Gigli wanted. After all, he was the painter and the only one who . . .

Suddenly, he remembered that Gianfranco Gigli had been dead for over two years.

A heroin overdose – they had told him so in the hotel when they showed him the painting.

deliziaaa aaaal cooooooooor . . . ah-ah-ah-ah-aaaaaaaaahhhhh . . .

Hubertus stood quite still, hands on the marble edge of the pool and his body covered to the waist by water. Trails of it trickled like ants down his head and upper body. He looked like a wax mountain starting to melt. Could a work of art alter itself after the death of its creator? If so, was the result a posthumous work or a fake? Strange questions.

Then all at once Hubertus stopped worrying about what the Gigli figure was doing (Who cares what it's up to?) and felt a brutal rush of happiness. The sensation shot through three trillion molecules of body fat and produced a whirlwind in his mind similar to a powerful orgasm. He was overjoyed at being part of such a complex world, an existence that only rarely (if ever) could be explained or described in words, the secret, unending golden well-spring, the select circle they all belonged to – the Gigli painting, Van Tysch, the Foundation, the twins themselves and a few other chosen ones (well OK, let's leave the sad Gigli figure out of it, because it has to renew itself to stay up-to-date), the marvellous life which allowed them to indulge their fantasies

197

and to become the stuff of fantasies for others. Even the fact of being so enormously fat was an advantage in this world. To be as monstrous as a monster, Hubertus understood, could go beyond the limits of everyday reality and become a symbol, the *res* of art, an archetype, philosophy and meditation, theories and debates. Bless you, world. Bless you, world. Bless your power and possibilities. Bless all your secrets as well.

The Gigli painting appeared to have finally completed its preparations, whatever they were. It turned round calmly and headed off for another point, another destination inexorably chosen by a dead artist. Hubertus watched it expectantly. Where? Oh, to where are you directing your harmonic footsteps, divine, radiant creature? Hubertus Walden asked himself.

Overcome with planetary harmony, it took him a moment to realise that the work was heading for him.

When he was a child, Arnoldus was attacked by a tiger.

Infallible, precise, powerful, deadly. A black tiger with glinting eyes born of his dreams. It was his nightmare, his childhood terror. He would cry out and wake up Hubertus, and then inevitably the tiger would turn into his father's belt as it flew through the air and lashed his naked behind over and over again. ('I didn't mean to cry out, papa, please believe me, I couldn't help it.') The only thing their father hated was when they shouted. 'Do whatever you like, just don't shout,' he always told them: it was his constant obsession.

Unlike his brother, Arnoldus did not believe he had been compensated for his past. He thought that life was a commerce owned by someone different every day, which never pays you back if you have overpaid. It was true they were immensely rich now. They were considered a work of art of incalculable value. Mr Robertson, who might well become their new papa, loved them: Arno knew that Mr Robertson would never think of thrashing him with his belt if he heard him cry out in the middle of the night, while the bitter saliva of his worst nightmare slid down his chin. Now they were adored, respected and admired as great works of art. But could this new life give them the happy childhood they had not had? Was the worldwide reknown they now enjoyed retroactive? Could it transform their bad memories into good ones? No, it did not even change ways of behaviour. As an adult, Arnoldus still did not raise his voice. The tiger was dead, and so was his father, but life never gives anything back.

Listening to his brother splashing in the pool, Arnoldus wrapped a towel round his massive waist and began a belly dance in front of the mirror. Given the part of his anatomy involved, these dances were for Arno something more than a mere pastime: they became a kind of subtle attempt to understand the universe. The low, pseudo-Egyptian whistle that accompanied them came from his own lips, and he clicked his fingers as he gyrated. *Oh, dulce huri? me complaceras esta noche?* Looking at his porcelain fingers – he thinks as he sways his belly first one way, then the other – no one would suspect the presence of the huge bag of foul intestines hanging from its centre, that hungry anaconda curled up in a sack, that thick ship's rope covered in lard. How was it possible to be so fat? My God, what have you done to me? His mother told him she screamed (or was it his father?) when she saw them come into the world, when she saw their fantastic beauty, those creatures born with more flesh than her flesh. 'Aaagh!' Mrs Walden had cried. Their father (so she said) was equally horrified, and scolded her:

'Don't shout, Emma. Yes, they are monstrous, but don't shout, please. Above all, don't *shout* . . .'

Arnoldus Walden's vast pan-anatomy waddled its way down the lengthy corridor between bathroom and living room. He was still absorbed in his thoughts. He could no longer hear his brother's splashes. Did that mean that Platinum Blond had arrived? Had his brother broken his promise and started without him? Oh Hubertus, despicable being, the worst of all, vulgar, vile. Perverse mammoth, cruel bear. His brother loved to blame him for everything, and to claim he was responsible for all the good that happened to them. Arnoldus woke up every day trying to change. Trying to be more friendly, more human, more obedient (*seriously, please, believe me*) but, when he looked round at his brother, hatred oozed from his pores like flames from a ball soaked in alcohol. Having to stare at this reflection of himself disgusted him so much that he sometimes felt like smashing the mirror. Oh, yes: it was Hubertus who turned him into a *horrendous* being. Hubertus who pushed him down towards the abyss, forced him to dream of atrocities.

Take Helga Blanchard and her son, for example. Arnoldus had tried time and again to explain to Hubert that they had never done that family any harm. They had not even met Helga and her sweet son: it had all been a false memory planted in their minds by Van Tysch, a shadowy colour added to their bodies. 'Something like original sin,' was Arnoldus' way of explaining it. The shadow of an offence they had never committed, and which by that very token they would never be able to forget, because there is nothing more indestructible than things imagined. Perhaps they were not even guilty of the crimes they had done penance for in jail. After all, painting is itself deception: you think you can touch that fruit bowl, that bunch of grapes or the nymph's swelling breast, but when you stretch out your fingers you are brought up short, you realise that what looked like spheres are only circles, what looked like volume is a flat surface, the fingers' desperate desire to squeeze and fondle is left unassuaged. Arnoldus had a suspicion that the two of them were one of the Dutch painter's most successful illusions. Come to me, monstrous canvases, and I'll make you into an optical illusion.

The Maestro had been so clever in painting that terrible lie on their minds that his brother Hubertus had been completely taken in. Hubert really believed they had done it. Worse still: he believed that Arnoldus was the one deceived! 'You want to blindfold yourself with that explanation so you can forget what we did, Arno,' he used to tell him. And he added: 'But we *really* did what we did. Do you want me to refresh your memory? . . .' It was so unpleasant that Arnoldus no longer even tried to argue about it. What use was there trying to tell Hubert he was the one *mistaken*, that they had never committed such an atrocity, that it was all the product of Van Tysch's sublime art?

He looked down at the signature on his right ankle: BvT. A new worry had been preoccupying him for some time. Could Van Tysch be responsible for the hatred, the ferocious antipathy he felt towards Hubertus? Had he tried to awaken the Cain within him so that he could paint it? Be that as it may, the

Maestro was not very concerned about them any more. He had lost interest in them. It was said he was about to sell them.

Perhaps it was best to forget about Van Tysch and even about Hubertus, and to enjoy himself while he could.

He opened the door and entered the living room.

'Here I am, Hubert. I hope you haven't—'

He stopped in his tracks. There was no one in the pool. In fact, the whole room looked deserted.

'Tut, tut, this isn't very polite of you, Hubert.' Arnoldus looked all round him. The suite was like an endless basilica: columns, a domed ceiling; stone walls; indirect light; a long sacrificial altar in the shape of a bar counter . . .

It took him a second to spot the trail of liquid just to his right, a small trace of a darker colour on the fitted carpet, a trail of water from the pool, some god or other's zigzagging piss on the floor. Twisting his massive neck, Arnoldus followed it. At the end of the trail, belly in the air (a perfect sphere), lay his brother.

And standing next to his brother was a slight, masked creature: the black tiger of his infant terrors, his lithe, devouring nightmare.

When it leapt on him, Arnoldus – like an obedient child – did not cry out.

4

An isosceles triangle of light. Legs apart.

'Time for a break,' said Gerardo. 'Afterwards we'll try another effect.'

Clara closed her legs and the triangle disappeared. She was standing with her back to the two men, facing the window, her hair a flaming red, her body edged in rays of sunlight. She was painted in pink and ochre tones, with highlights of ivory and pearl. Her spine, the perfect 'V' of her lumbar region and the fleshy cross of her buttocks were a natural earth colour. Gerardo and Uhl had chosen these tints after careful study of the lines they had painted on her skin. They gave her a porous swimsuit and a colour cap, which she put on in the bathroom. Her primed skin and hair absorbed the colours perfectly, there was no need for varnish or fixing agents. Gerardo warned her that all the colours were provisional, and that they could all be modified over the next few days. So were the colour of her eyes – brilliant emerald green – that he had painted with a corneal spray, and the deeper pink lip outline he had drawn on her face. Finally, with gloved hands he swept her wet hair up into a small bun. When he threw the gloves into the wastepaper basket, they spattered the floor with drops of fake blood.

'You're done,' he said.

Clara left the bathroom and walked towards the living room, trailing the smell of oil paint in her wake. The first thing she did was to examine herself in the mirror. She could see the figure they were aiming at beyond the sketch: a young girl by Manet, tall, slender, red-headed, and with muscles clearly distinguishable from one another, but not violently so: as if drawn by an expert. In the sunlight, her hair was a shiny haemorrhage. She liked what they had done. She wished this was not just a sketch, that the unknown work they were painting with her would be exactly the same.

They had set up a video camera on a tripod and a powerful photographic studio spot, but to begin with they filmed her adopting different positions in natural light. It must be a beautiful day outside, Clara thought, as she stared at the open window in front of her, but in the room, with its cream walls and parallel lines of the floor, everything was bathed in a bright glow, as if she were inside a prism. She longed to have some free time to be able to explore outside.

'Your food is in the kitchen,' Gerardo told her.

She walked carefully back to the bathroom in order not to crack the paint on her body, and put on one of the robes hanging on the door. She usually liked to wear something when she had been painted so she would not spoil it while she ate or rested.

In the kitchen, a surprise was waiting for her. Her food tray was in the same place as the previous day, but this time Gerardo was sitting opposite her. He was taking the top off a pizza he had heated in the microwave. So it seemed they were going to eat together. She wondered where Uhl was, and why he had not joined them. She guessed there must be serious disagreements between the two men. Throughout the morning, this had been obvious from their raised voices, terse orders, and long periods of uncomfortable silence. It seemed obvious to her that Gerardo gave in to his older colleague, either because he admired him, or perhaps simply because Uhl was a rung higher on the Foundation ladder than he was. Clara decided it was best to be discreet.

She sat down and pulled the plastic cover off her tray. Her meal consisted of two triangles of sandwich with some kind of mayonnaise at the edges, grapes, wholemeal bread, margarine, cream cheese, a salad, a herb tea and an Aroxen juice with added vitamins. Before she picked up a sandwich, she took her prescribed pills with a sip of mineral water. Gerardo was busy devouring a slice of pizza.

They started to chat. He praised her quiescence, and asked who her teachers had been. She told him about Cuinet and Klaus Wedekind, and of the week she had spent in Florence working as a sketch for Ferrucioli. She could only eat very slowly, nibbling small pieces of sandwich, because the oil paint on her face pulled at her jaws, and she did not want to spoil it. As she was spreading a thick layer of margarine on the bread, she tried out a smile with her freshly drawn lips.

'Don't be mean. Tell me what you're doing with me.'

'Painting you,' replied Gerardo.

She stifled a laugh, but insisted.

'No, seriously. I'm going to be one of the works in the "Rembrandt" collection, aren't I?'

'I'm sorry, sweetheart, I can't tell you.'

'I don't want to know which figure I am, or the title of the painting. Just tell me if I'm going to be a "Rembrandt". '

'Listen, the less you know about what you're doing, the better, right?'

'OK. Sorry.'

Suddenly she felt embarrassed at having insisted. She did not want Gerardo to get the impression she thought he was more malleable than Uhl, easier to get artistic secrets out of.

They fell silent. Gerardo was playing with the top of a bottle of Coca-Cola he was drinking. He seemed out of sorts.

'Did my question upset you?' she asked concernedly.

His reply cost him a great effort, as though it was a difficult but unavoidable question.

'No. It's just that I'm a bit annoyed . . . not with you though, with Justus. The same old thing. I told you he has a very special character. I know him well by now of course, but sometimes I find it hard to take . . .'

'How long have you worked together?'

'Three years. He's a good painter – I've learnt a lot from him.' He looked towards the bright midday of the window. In profile, his face still seemed very attractive to Clara. 'But we have to do everything he says. Everything.'

He turned to look at her, as if those last words concerned her much more than him.

'He's in charge,' he added.

'He's your boss.'

'And yours, don't forget.'

Clara nodded, rather disconcerted. She did not know quite how to interpret what he had just said. Was it a warning? A piece of advice? She recalled the strange examination Uhl had given her the day before. When Gerardo said she had to do everything Uhl ordered, was he only talking about painting?

She finished the slice of wholemeal bread and picked up a grape in her shiny pink fingers. Seeing the curtains at the kitchen window, she remembered what had happened the night before. To change topics, she decided to mention it.

'Listen, there's something that . . .'

She stopped, and pushed the pips out of the grape. Gerardo stared inquisitively at her.

'Yes?'

'Oh, it's nothing really.'

'That doesn't matter, tell me anyway.'

He leaned towards her, elbows on the table. He seemed genuinely interested. Clara was touched by his apparent concern, and decided to tell him everything.

'Last night there was someone prowling outside the house.

Once when the timer went off I saw him looking in through the window. Then he vanished.'

Gerardo was staring at her.

'Don't tease.'

'I'm serious. It scared me to death. I went to the window and couldn't see anyone, but I'm sure I didn't dream it.'

'That's strange . . .' Gerardo stroked his moustache and chin in a way Clara had already noticed. 'There are no other people round here, only farms the Foundation owns.'

'But I'm sure I heard footsteps close to the window.'

'And you went over but didn't see anyone?'

'Aha.'

The young painter looked thoughtful. He pushed around some pizza crumbs. Under the shirtsleeve at the top of his left biceps, she caught sight of a tattoo.

'Maybe it was someone from Security. They sometimes patrol the farms to make sure the canvases are all right . . . Yes, I'm sure it was someone from Security.'

'Are there canvases in the other farms then?'

'You bet, sweetheart. We're full. Lots of canvases, lots of work.'

The thought that it might have been someone from Security reassured her, and did not seem at all unlikely. She was about to ask more when a shadow appeared between the light and them. Uhl had come into the kitchen. Clara realised something was wrong almost before she saw him. The painter was staring at her, face twisted with disgust, and muttering in unintelligible Dutch.

'What's he saying?' she asked.

Before Gerardo had the chance to reply, Uhl did something extraordinary. He took hold of the lapels of Clara's robe and tugged at them with all his might. His movement was so violent and unexpected that he pulled her to her feet, and she knocked the chair over. Uhl grabbed the robe belt and untied it. Clara's quivering breasts were exposed.

'Hey, what are you doing?' shouted Clara.

Gerardo had also stood up, and appeared to be arguing with Uhl. But it was obvious that the older man was winning. Stunned rather than angry, Clara closed the robe over her body. She could see that some of the paint on her stomach was smudged.

205

'No, no. Take it off,' Gerardo snapped.

'Take the robe off?'

'Yes, take it off. You're not supposed to be wearing anything, OK? The colours are very sensitive and could be damaged. I should have told you before. Justus is right. I . . .'

Uhl interrupted him, slapping the wall impatiently right next to Clara's head, as though to hurry her up.

'What's the matter?' she said indignantly. 'What kind of behaviour is this? I'm taking it off, dammit! See?'

Uhl snatched the robe from her and stormed out of the kitchen. Clara was fuming.

'What's his problem?' she asked.

'Go on eating and don't say a word. He has his ways, that's all.'

For a moment she caught Gerardo's gaze, and through her emerald-green corneas defied him to repeat that absurd phrase. 'He has his ways.' She did not know what most irritated her: Uhl's crazy behaviour or his assistant's submissive attitude. Then she decided to give in, reasoning that in any case she was only the canvas. She bent down, snatched up the chair and sat her sticky wet buttocks on the edge of the seat. She unscrewed the top of her Aroxen drink. Nothing has happened, she told herself. If the paint gets spoilt, that's their fault.

Gerardo did not say anything more. He finished his meal, and they went back to work.

The sun had moved round the window, so they lit the side-light and tested the shadows and effects in silhouette. Clara was still stunned. Her initial disgust had given way to a sense of astonishment at Uhl's weird attitude. She seriously wondered whether he was ill. Neither of the painters said a word to her. It seemed obvious that the incident had affected the play of forces in their unstable triangle: Uhl was still hard as flint, while Gerardo had apparently taken on the role of shock absorber between the two of them. Although he did not speak, every time he came close to change her position he tried to smile, as if saying: Just be patient. If we're on the same side, it'll be better. But this newly discovered sympathy was even more unbearable than Uhl's ridiculous conduct.

In mid-afternoon there was another break. Gerardo told her there was a juice and an infusion in the kitchen. She did not feel like either, but Gerardo insisted quite forcefully. She, of course, made no attempt to put the robe on again. She went into the kitchen and found the juice, but the sachet of herbs was on the edge of the saucer, and the cup was empty. She filled it with mineral water and put it in the microwave. She did not feel at all cold or uncomfortable standing there completely naked, only rather strange: she was used to wearing some protection when she had a break and her body was painted, so the order to remain nude still surprised her. While the microwave hummed in the background, she looked at the landscape she could see out of the triangular gap in the curtains: she caught sight of tree trunks, a hedge in the distance, a path. It looked as though they were very isolated.

The microwave pinged. Clara opened the door and reached for the steaming cup.

At that moment, a shadow flitted past her.

It was Uhl. He was wiping his hands on a rag, and did not even look at her as he came in. She turned the other way as well. She put the cup in its saucer and tore the sachet open. Uhl was moving around behind her. She had no idea what he was up to. She guessed he had come to get something out of the fridge, but did not hear the door. She became edgy as the silence continued. She was about to turn round to see what Uhl was doing, when all of a sudden she felt a hand between her thighs.

She started, and turned her head. She saw Uhl's eyes deep in his glasses only an inch from her face. Almost at once, his other hand gripped the back of her neck and forced her to go on looking to the front. She heard his hoarse Spanish:

'Don't move.'

She decided to obey without asking anything. The situation did not surprise her too much. In theory, she was a canvas. In theory, he was a painter. In theory, the painter could touch the canvas he was working on at any time and in any way he felt inclined to. She had no idea what kind of work they might be doing: perhaps even the fact of seizing her so brutally in the kitchen was part of it.

She breathed in to relax herself, and stayed with her hands on the edge of the sink. The fingers were feeling the inside of her left thigh very slowly, but because she was covered in oil paint, the sensation she got was not one of fingers touching her. She did not for example feel the warmth or cold of someone else's skin, or the extra sensations she might get from being stroked: it was simply the presence of two or three blunt objects moving over her flesh. They could just as well have been paint brushes.

The hand continued to climb; the other one was still gripping her left shoulder roughly. Clara tried to distance herself from those fingers which were not fingers or human flesh, but jointed rubber tubes climbing – still very calmly and gently – up the most sensitive part of her thigh. She wanted to believe it all had an artistic purpose. She knew the boundary was very difficult to establish: Vicky, for example, was constantly crossing it in both directions. The other humiliating possibility – that Uhl was abusing his position – would have led her to violently reject it. But so far she did not want to imagine this was the case.

So she stayed as still as she could, controlling her breathing, even though she knew what was the final and obvious destination of those fingers. The blue of the window, which she looked at steadily, hurt her eyes. *He's in charge. He's a very strange man, but he's in charge.* Could Gerardo have been preparing her for something he knew was going to happen?

The fingers spread out over her sex. Clara clenched her muscles. The fingers brushed lightly against the lips, but hesitated, as though waiting for some kind of reaction. But Clara had made up her mind not to move, to do nothing. She stood still, her legs slightly open (a triangle), her back to the painter. She held her breath, and all at once felt the fingers move away. The hand on her shoulder also disappeared. She turned her head, wondering what he would do next. Uhl was simply staring at her. His thick glasses and prominent forehead made him look like some monstrous insect. He was panting. His eyes were wild. A moment later, he left the kitchen. She heard him talking to Gerardo in the living room. She waited a few seconds, finished preparing her drink still looking towards the door, and drank it as though it were a bitter medicine. Then she did a few simple relaxation exercises.

When Gerardo called her back to work, she felt a lot more composed.

Nothing else happened that afternoon. Uhl did not touch her again, and Gerardo only gave her brusque orders. But while she was posing motionless and covered in paint, her mind was racing. Why did Uhl behave the way he did? Was he trying to abuse her, to frighten her, to stretch her the way Brentano did?

The only way for an artwork to behave in this confused, almost dreamlike world of body painting was to stay stretched and develop strategies for not surrendering, if things got any worse.

She was sure this was exactly what would happen, and soon.

She thought she would not sleep that night, but she immediately fell into an exhausted stupor.

She had no idea at what moment she felt once again that someone was watching her.

Lying naked, face down on the equally bare mattress, her mind slipped in and out of sleep. At a certain moment, the window, lit by the pale chalk of moonlight, suddenly darkened in shadow. But the shadow also made a noise in the grass.

She sat up as gracefully as a gazelle. There was no one outside the window.

Yet an instant before, a fraction of a second before there was no one, the rectangle had been filled with a silhouette.

She was sure it was a man.

She sat craning her neck in the darkness until a crazy wail made her shudder with fright. Her heart in her mouth, she recognised the sound as coming from the timer. She groped along the floor like a blind woman until she found it next to the mattress, and switched it off. She did not know why it had been on, because Gerardo had told her there was no need to use it that night. Her heart was pumping the blood through her veins. The beating felt like bubbles bursting in her temples. The house was one vast silence. Yet she experienced exactly the same feeling as she had the night before. And if she strained to listen, she thought she could hear the rustle of grass in the distance.

Whatever the truth, and even taking the best interpretation into account (that for example it was a Foundation security guard, as Gerardo had said), that mysterious presence disturbed her far more than anything else. She swung her legs off the mattress and took several deep breaths. After Uhl and Gerardo had left she had taken a shower to wash the paint from her hair and body. Without oil paint all over her, the terror felt more real, more immediate, less absorbing.

She waited a few moments, and could no longer hear the rustling of footsteps in the grass. Perhaps the man had left, or perhaps he wanted to be sure she had gone back to sleep. She was far too nervous to think at all calmly. But she knew several breathing exercises that would soothe her like a balm in only a few minutes. She began with the easiest, still trying to locate the exact source of her fear.

One of the things that had always terrified her most was the possibility that a stranger might come into her room at night. Jorge laughed whenever she woke him up in the early hours to tell him she had heard a noise.

Fine. Just face up to *your fear* and you'll conquer it.

She got up and walked across to the dark living room. Her breathing exercises had given her a false sense of calm that made her movements stiff. She had had an idea: she would call Conservation and ask for help, or at least advice. That was all she had to do. Just go over to the phone, dial the only number available to her, and talk to Conservation. After all, she was valuable material, and she was scared. She ran the risk of being damaged. Conservation had to help.

She remembered that the lights to the house were all in the entrance hall. She walked quickly out of the living room, into the dark hall and up the three steps to the front door. She flicked on and off the switches like someone firing rapid rounds against a hidden enemy. But she did not see anything strange. The full-length mirrors impassively reflected all the usual shapes. The tripod and the studio spot were exactly where Uhl and Gerardo had left them. The photograph of the man facing away from the camera was still there, and he still had his back to her (*It would have been very different if he were looking towards you now, wouldn't it?*). Beyond them, the three black windows in the living room and the back door looked exactly the same: they were shut and appeared protective.

She ran her primed tongue over her primed lips. She did not want to look at herself in the mirrors because she did not want to see a face with no eyebrows or lashes, only two eyes and a mouth (three dots opening into a terrifying triangle) beneath a cap of fine blonde hair. She was not in a sweat (there were no drops sliding down her skin or converting her brow into a gentle kind of *polder*, like those scattered throughout Holland), and she had no saliva to swallow, but both of those sensations were present, as punctual as stopwatches: the *effort* of her sweat, and the invisible agony of the lump in her throat. The sense of terror was still inside her, jagged and quivering. All the paint in the universe could do nothing to hide that.

Calm down. You're going to go over to the phone and dial. Afterwards you can close the blinds, one after the other. Then you'll be able to get back to sleep.

She edged like a sleepwalker towards a shrinking telephone, a telephone at the far end of a vanishing point. She did not want to look towards the windows as she was approaching it. For precisely that reason, she looked at them. All she could see were dark panes of glass that reflected her naked, yellow-hued body. The thought flashed through her that if she did see any kind of figure appear at one of those rectangles, she would go into a coma, become cataleptic, would turn into a vegetable and spend the rest of her days drooling in some asylum or other. It was as fleeting an instant as that of feeling giddy, a fraction of time no watch could measure. Horror had unbuttoned his mac in front of her and flashed his sex at her. There. The blinking of an eye. Then the feeling passed. And she had not seen anything at the window.

She reached the phone, picked up the navy-blue card and began very carefully to dial the number. Now she was standing directly in front of one of the windows. Beyond the wall of branches and wind, the trees and the night arched over everything. She must be completely visible to anyone watching from outside. Let him watch all he wants, thought Clara, just so long as he doesn't come any nearer.

'Good evening, Miss Reyes,' a young man's voice said into her earpiece. He spoke perfect Spanish. His voice was as reassuring as a Gouda cheese or a pair of clogs. 'How can we be of assistance?'

'There's someone prowling round the house,' she blurted out.

'Round the house?'

'Outside the house, I mean.'

A moment's silence.

'Are you sure?'

'Yes, I saw him. I've just . . . I've just seen him. Someone looking in at the bedroom window.'

'Is he still there?'

'No, no. I mean, I don't think . . .'

Another moment's silence.

'Miss Reyes, that's completely impossible.'

She heard a creaking sound behind her. She was so concerned about looking at the windows she had forgotten (*My God!*) about looking *behind her.*

'Miss Reyes . . . ?'

She turned round slowly as if in a dream. Or like a hanged man swinging round after being kicked in the side. She turned round in slow motion, on a carousel ride that presented her with distant images of the room (*the man facing the other way, and so on . . .*)

'Hello . . . are you still there . . . ?'

'Yes.'

Nothing there. The room was empty. But for that split second, she had filled it with nightmares.

'I thought you'd hung up,' the voice from Conservation said. 'I'll explain why what you said can't happen. All the farms around you belong to the Foundation, and access to them is limited. The entrances are guarded day and night by security staff, so that . . .'

'But I have just seen a man at the window,' Clara interrupted him.

Another silence. Her heart was beating wildly.

'Do you know what I think?' the man replied, his voice changing as if the explanation had just become crystal clear to him. 'That it's very likely you're right, and you did see someone. I'll explain. Sometimes, especially when there's new material, the guards do go up to the houses to make sure everything is all right. And Security has been a bit worried about the safety of our canvases recently. So don't worry: it's one of our men. Just to make sure, here's what I'll do. I'll call Security and ask them to confirm they're patrolling the area. They'll take all the necessary steps. And please, don't leave the telephone. I'll call you to tell you what they say.'

She found the silence that descended as she waited for him to phone her back much easier to bear. She was beginning to feel sleepy again when it began to ring. The voice was as reassuring as before.

'Miss Reyes? It's all sorted out. They've confirmed to me in Security that it is one of their men. They say they're sorry, and promise not to disturb you again . . .'

'Thank you.'

'In any case, I should tell you that all the Foundation's agents are properly identified with red badges in their lapels. If you see the man again and can make out his badge, there should be no problem. Now why don't you go back to bed and, if you like, leave a light on. That way, the agent will not have to approach your window to be sure everything is all right, and he won't frighten you.'

'Thanks a lot.'

'Don't mention it. And should you need anything else, don't hesitate to . . .'

Blah, blah. The usual polite phrases, but they had their effect. When she hung up, Clara felt much calmer. She drew the blinds of the three windows in the living room, the ones in the kitchen, and at the front of the house. She checked that the front and back door were secure. She only hesitated for a second before going into her bedroom. The window reflected the light from the empty room like a tank of black water. She went over to the window. *Here, just a few moments ago, there was someone looking in.*

213

It was someone from Security, she told herself. She could not remember having seen a red label on his lapel, but then of course she had not had much chance of seeing it. She closed the blind.

Despite what the man from Conservation had suggested, she did not want to leave any lights on. She went back to the front entrance and switched them all off. Then she walked back into the completely dark bedroom, lay on her back on the mattress, and stared up at the dense blackness of the ceiling. She did another breathing exercise and soon fell asleep. She did not dream of her father. She did not dream of the mysterious Uhl. She did not dream at all. Carried away by her exhaustion, she slipped pleasurably into unconsciousness.

The man hidden in the trees waited a while longer, and then crept towards the house once more.

He was not wearing any badge.

5

Susan is a Lamp.

The square label on her left wrist says: Susan Cabot, aged nineteen, Johannesburg South Africa, straw blonde hair, blue eyes, white skin, unprimed. Susan has been lighting meetings as a Marooder Lamp only for the past six months. Before that she had been another three decorations for the Foundation. She alternates this work with that of mediocre portrait painters (the contract she has with the Foundation is not exclusive) because when it comes down to it, a portrait simply means they cover your body with silicone and then mould you in whatever form the client wants. There is not much hyperdramatic work to it. Susan does not particularly like Hyperdramatism – that is why she abandoned her early career as a canvas and decided to become a decoration. She is aware she will never be an immortal work of art like the 'Flowers', but that does not bother her too much. The 'Flowers' have to keep up much more difficult positions for days on end, they are always on drugs and have become

real vegetables, roses, daffodils, irises, marigolds, tulips, perfumed and painted objects which no longer dream, enjoy
themselves, or live. Being a Lamp on the other hand allows you
to earn a bundle of money, retire young, and have kids. You don't
end your days like one of those sterile canvases condemned by
humanity to the hell of eternal beauty.

Early on the morning of 29 June 2006, Susan's bleeper went off
unexpectedly on her bedside table, and woke her from a deep
sleep. She dialled her code number on the hotel telephone, and
was instructed to proceed immediately to the airport. She was
sufficiently experienced to know this was no routine matter. For
the past three weeks she had been in Hanover, for six hours a
day – with intermediate breaks – lighting a small meeting room
where debates about biology, painting, and the relation between
art and genetics took place. Susan had not heard a word of them,
because she had been wearing ear protectors the whole time.
Sometimes she was also given a mask to put on, when she supposed that the guests were well-known faces who wanted to
remain anonymous. As a Lamp, she was more than used to
ignoring everything. But she had only rarely been called so
urgently in the middle of the night, and hardly given time to get
dressed, grab her bag with her equipment in it, and rush off to
the airport. There a ticket was waiting for her on a flight that left
for Munich half an hour later. In Munich she met up with other
colleagues (she did not know them, but that was common among
decorations). They were taken by private bus guarded by four
security men to the Obberlund building, a squat steel and glass
complex of offices and conference halls situated very close to the
Haus der Kunst, next to the English Garden. During the journey
she got a phone call from the decoration supervisor, a thoroughly
unpleasant young woman by the name of Kelly, who explained
briefly the position she was to occupy in the room she would be
working in.

Once they had arrived at the Obberlund, she had only twenty
minutes to get ready: she took all her clothes off, put on a porous
swimsuit and a colour cap for her hair, and then waited for the
paints to dry. After which she took off her suit and cap, checked
her body painted a rosewood pink and her dark teak hair, took

the lamp fittings out of her bag, clamped the base round her right ankle, and limped to the meeting room with cable in hand, trying hard not to stumble and fall. Her colleagues were also silently and efficiently occupying their positions. Susan lay on her back on the floor and took up her pose: hands on hips, backside in the air, the right leg lifted out straight and the left bent over her face. The lighting circle with four cold bulbs was attached to the ankle in the air. The cable was not wrapped round her leg, but curled off across to the plug. All Susan had to do was to stay still and let the lights shine. It was a difficult posture to maintain, but training and habit had turned her into a first-class object. Her operating time was four hours.

A short while later, someone – Kelly, in all likelihood – came and switched her on. The bulbs were lit, and Susan began to illuminate the room. Then a workman arrived to put on her ear protectors and the mask, then she was left in darkness and silence.

The meeting took place on the tenth floor.

The room the Obberlund managers had offered them was square, hermetic and soundproof. It had dark-tinted windows. There were only a few non-human pieces of furniture: metal and plastic chairs on a single leg were scattered around an enormous steel-grey-coloured carpet. All the other decorations were painted human bodies. There were Tables, Lamps, Ornaments by the window and, in the corners of the room, one stationary Trolley and eleven mobile Trolleys. Apart from the latter, which had to go from one side to another serving the guests and therefore had to see and hear clearly, the rest were wearing ear and eye protectors.

The working breakfast was served by the eleven Trolleys: freshly baked croissants, five kinds of bread, and three different butter substitutes, as well as coffee, coffee and tea substitutes – these last for Benoit, in particular, as he was very nervous. There was also a variety of fruit juices, pastas, cheese spreads and glasses of mineral water full of gleaming ice cubes. Finally, there was a selection of dried fruit in a bowl on one of the Tables (the guests had to go and get these, because the Table – a boy lying with his back on the ground, legs in the air, and a girl balancing

216

on his feet, both of them painted a fuchsia colour – could not move) and a dish of multi-coloured sweets between the breasts of a red Marooder Trolley, its body arched backwards with hands and feet on the ground, shiny copper hair brushing the floor.

One of the guests was eating these sweets non-stop: he would lean over, grab a handful of them and stuff them one by one under his moustache, as though they were peanuts. He was a young man with black hair and a high forehead. His eyebrows were as bushy as his moustache. His maroon suit was impeccable, and beautifully cut, although not as expensive as Benoit's. He looked like a cheerful, friendly, talkative sort: in other words, someone of little importance. But Bosch instinctively realised that *this* individual, this anonymous-looking young man with a moustache who was devouring all the sweets, was the *most important* of all the important people in the room. He was the Head Honcho.

Bosch had been appointed moderator. When he felt he had allowed them enough time, and caught a nod of approval from Miss Wood, he cleared his throat and said:

'Shall we begin, ladies and gentlemen?'

The mobile Trolleys, who were not wearing ear protectors, immediately left the room. Unavoidably curious, the eyes of the guests followed the procession of tall, varnished, naked bodies out of the room. For a minute, no one spoke. Finally, it was Paul Benoit who seemed to awaken out of a dream and opened the discusssion.

'Please, Lothar, how did he get in? Just tell me that. How did he get in? I don't want to get nervous, Lothar. Just tell me . . . I want you and April to explain to me . . . to us, *right now,* how on earth that bastard *got into* the suite, Lothar. How did he get into a hermetically sealed suite crammed with alarms, with five security men permanently on guard in the lifts, stairs and doorways of the hotel . . . How do you explain it?'

'If you'll give me a chance, Paul, I will explain,' Bosch replied calmly. 'He didn't have to get in: he was already inside. The Wunderbar hotel has hyperdramatic decorations. There was one in the suite: an oil painting by Gianfranco Gigli . . .'

'A worthless disciple of Ferrucioli,' Benoit spat. 'If he hadn't killed himself, his works would be sold by weight.'

'Paul, please.'

'Sorry. I'm nervous. Go on.'

'Four models take turns to be the Gigli work. Somehow, this guy managed to pass himself off as one of them – Marcus Weiss, forty-three years old, from Berlin. Weiss was the work on Tuesdays. When we discovered what had happened we went to the motel where he was staying. We found him bound hand and foot to his bed, and garrotted. The police calculate his death took place on Monday night. It was, therefore, not he who turned up the next day at the Wunderbar wearing the paint and the mask for the Gigli painting.'

'Have I understood correctly?' asked Rudolf Kobb, from the Foreign Office. 'We're looking for a guy who disguises himself as someone disguising himself as something else?'

'A guy who disguises himself as a model who is a work of art on show *inside* the suite,' Bosch corrected him.

'No. No. No, Lothar.' Benoit shifted in his seat, straightening the crease on his trouser leg. 'I'm sorry, but I'm not convinced. Who was the idiot who let him into the suite?'

'My men are not responsible, Paul. In any case, I have no problem assuming responsibility for them. On the dot of seven on Tuesday evening, a man who looked like Marcus Weiss, wearing the labels Marcus Weiss wears, and carrying Marcus Weiss' credentials, arrived at the Wunderbar. My men checked his papers, made sure everything was in order, and let him in. They had been doing exactly the same with Weiss for several weeks.'

'Why didn't they search his bag?'

'Paul, he was a work of art; he didn't belong to us. He was not from the Foundation. We cannot search the bag of a work that is not ours.'

'Who raised the alarm?'

'Saltzer. He phoned the suite at twelve as a matter of routine. No one replied, and perhaps that was when he made his only mistake. He chose to stay downstairs and call again later. According to him, sometimes the twins decided not to answer the phone. After ringing three times, he got worried and went up

218

to have a look. That allowed us to have more control over things than in Vienna, because we were the ones who discovered the bodies and informed the police when we were ready to do so. And I can forgive him his mistake, Paul. The guy was already *inside*.'

'OK, so he was inside,' Kurt Sorensen butted in, 'but how did he manage to get out?'

'That was the easy part. He went down the stairs to another floor. From there he took a different lift. And he probably used another disguise so as not to arouse any suspicions. Our men were trained to stop anyone *entering*, not anyone *going out*.'

'Do you get it now, Paul?' boomed Gert Warfell. 'This bastard is a real expert.'

There was an uncomfortable silence, after which the Head Honcho spoke with incongruous enthusiasm.

'Excuse me for changing the subject for a moment, but I wanted to say that I had the chance to visit the Haus der Kunst and the 'Monsters' exhibition yesterday. I wanted to congratulate you. It's incredible.' He appeared to be speaking to them all, although he was looking directly at Stein. 'There were some things I didn't understand, though. What's the point, for example, of putting a terminally ill AIDS patient on show?'

'It's art, *fuschus*' Stein replied in a level tone. 'The only reason for art is art itself.'

'I've also seen the exhibition,' the Europol representative, Albert Knopffer, said. 'What impressed me most was that eight- or nine-year-old girl carrying that African baby who turned out to be a dwarf male model. That gave me the shivers.'

'We could spend all day talking about the works,' said the Head Honcho as he reached for more sweets. 'I think they're even more profound than 'Flowers'. But let's be precise. They are different, the two shows can't be compared. However, they do seem more profound to me. Congratulations.'

'They are works by the Maestro,' said Stein.

'Yes, but you work with him. So congratulations are due to both of you.'

Stein nodded his acknowledgement.

'Lothar, why don't you tell us about the girl called Brenda?'

Sorensen asked. 'Just to fill in for our friends here,' he added, smiling at the Head Honcho.

Kurt Sorensen was the person who acted as the link between the Foundation and the insurance companies. He had learnt to get on with everyone, but Bosch did not like him. It was not just his pale face and vampire's brows that irritated him, but his character as well. He thought he knew everything, that he had all the latest and most accurate information.

'Fine, Kurt.' Bosch shuffled the papers on his lap. 'According to our information, the other days of the week Weiss was on show as another work, an oil painting by Kate Niemeyer at the Max Ernst gallery on Maximilianstrasse. On Monday after work, a girl was waiting for him outside the gallery. Weiss introduced her to a friend of his, another canvas. He told her she was called Brenda, and that she was an art dealer. Weiss' friend, whom we questioned yesterday, said that Brenda looked like a painting. I should point out that paintings can often recognise others of their kind. Apparently, Brenda looked very much like a young professional canvas: athletic body, smooth skin, striking beauty. Weiss and his friend Brenda, whom we don't know when or how he met, had dinner at a restaurant and then went to his motel. The following afternoon, Weiss left on his own. He said goodbye and handed his key in at reception. The receptionist knew Weiss very well, and says he saw nothing odd apart from the bag he was carrying. He didn't look too closely, but he swears it was not the bag Weiss usually carried – which, by the way, he had left in the restaurant the previous evening. Nobody saw the girl leave at any point that day, and I'm sure that whoever the receptionist was, they would have noticed someone like her. Nor did anyone go into Weiss' room. But, of course, the Weiss who left the motel *could not* have been the real one, because he was killed more than twelve hours earlier . . .'

'Therefore . . .' interjected Sorensen.

'Therefore we are led to believe that the false Weiss and the girl are the *same* person. In all likelihood what he was carrying under his arm was the disguise for Brenda.'

'Which allows us to link this to the girl who had no papers,'

Sorensen said, looking across at the Head Honcho. 'That's right, isn't it, Lothar?'

'Exactly. I think you all know about that already. In Vienna, Oscar Díaz met a girl with no residence papers, whom we can find no trace of. Later, a false Díaz turns up, and the body of the real one is found floating in the Danube, strangled with a wire cable. We must assume our man has repeated the same tactic.'

'If there is only *one* person involved,' Benoit said.

'That's true,' Gert Warfell agreed. He was the supervisor of the Foundation's Robbery Prevention and Alarms Section, an impetuous individual with the face of a bulldog. ' It could be several people, a complete team of silicone experts working together. It could be a man or a woman, or several men and women. It could be . . . Dammit, it could be anyone.'

The woman among the group of people Bosch had identified as *important* shifted in her seat, cleared her throat, and spoke for the first time. Her platinum blonde hair appeared chiselled. She was wearing a steel-grey suit with matching stockings. Her eyes were of exactly the same colour, too; and Bosch suspected her mind might be steely as well. He had been told her name was Roman. Her metallic eyes seemed to give off sparks.

'In short,' she said in a high-pitched voice with an American accent, 'if I have understood correctly, gentlemen, there is someone, or perhaps more than one person, who is dedicated to destroying Mr Bruno van Tysch's paintings. They have already succeeded twice, and apparently there is nothing to stop them from doing so a third time. How, therefore, can I offer my clients any reassurance? How can I persuade them to go on investing in the creation, upkeep and security of works which *anyone* could destroy *at any moment*?'

Various voices were raised, but it was Benoit who spoke for all of them.

'Miss Roman, our meeting here is aimed precisely at resolving that problem . . .' The collar of his splendid maroon shirt was stained with sweat. 'There have been failings in our security system which I am the first to recognise and regret, as you will have heard . . . but these gentlemen . . .' he gestured vaguely in the direction of Head Honcho, '. . . these gentlemen are not part of our security team. These gentlemen we have asked to help . . . do you know who these gentlemen are? . . .'

'Yes, I know who these gentlemen are,' Roman replied evenly. 'What I'd like to know is *how much* these gentlemen are going to *cost* us.'

Another hubbub, which immediately ceased when the Head Honcho began to speak.

'No, no, no. We won't cost the Van Tysch Foundation anything, Miss Roman. Let's be precise. Rip van Winkle is a European Union defence system. More precisely still, Rip van Winkle is a system paid for by the cohesion funds of all the member countries.' He paused to scoop up another handful of sweets from between the Tray's breasts. One of them fell and bounced off the taut naked stomach. 'Let's be precise. Neither Mr Harlbrunner, Mr Knopffer nor I are here because we will be paid more, nor because we have any economic interest in this affair. We are part of Rip van Winkle. Part of it, Miss Roman. Let's be precise. If we are here, it's simply because matters which affect our European cultural and artistic heritage affect all of us, as citizens of countries with long traditions. If a terrorist group threatened the Parthenon, Rip van Winkle would be called in. And if Bruno van Tysch's works are threatened by whatever group it may be, then Rip van Winkle will be involved. It's not about money, Miss Roman, it's about moral obligations.' Flinging his head back, he tipped the handful of sweets into his mouth.

'When people start making statements about morals, it always ends with bank statements,' Miss Roman declared, and nobody laughed. 'But if Rip van Winkle really means no extra costs for us, we have no objections.'

'By the way,' said a booming voice in English with a German accent, 'is it true what I heard? That the loss of those two fat monsters is the same as losing the *Mona Lisa*?'

He was a man with ruddy cheeks and a bushy white moustache. He looked like the typical Bavarian beer swiller of Hofbräuhaus posters. His name was Harlbrunner. His speciality (according to Head Honcho's introduction) was as the head of the Rip van Winkle SWAT teams. At that moment he was standing next to the Table with the dried fruits, scooping up almonds in his huge white hairy paw, while at the same time staring fascinated at the varnished open legs of the Table's top half.

For a moment there was a silence while the others looked surreptitiously at each other, as if weighing up whether or not it was worth answering his question. Then Benoit spoke:

'No one can . . . No one will ever be able to assess just what the loss of "Monsters" implies. The world we live in, the planet we inhabit, the society we have built . . . none of it will ever be the same again. "Monsters" offered the key to what we are, what we have been, what we . . .'

'Shit, he butchered them like pigs,' Knopffer from Europol growled, silencing Benoit. He had got up to look at the photos on the stomach of the other Table in the centre of the room, and was studying them closely. The Table's breathing had led to one of the photos falling off on to the carpet.

'Why these marks?' Rudolf Kobb from the Foreign Ministry wanted to know, as Knopffer passed him the photos.

'Ten cuts on each of them, eight of them crosses,' Bosch explained. 'They're the same as with *Deflowering*. He lays them on their backs with their legs open, but leaves the labels on. We don't know why he always makes these same cuts. He uses a portable canvas cutter, like the ones restorers use to saw wooden frames. And he always leaves a recording. We found this on the floor, between the two bodies. We can listen to it now, if you like.'

'Yes, we would,' said Head Honcho.

Bosch was about to get up, but Thea van Droon, sitting next to him, beat him to it. Thea was in charge of the Foundation's assault team. She had just returned from Paris after interrogating Briseida Canchares. As Thea stood up, Bosch could get a better view of Miss Wood, who sat hunched in a seat further away, chin on her chest, and her thin legs stretched out in front of her. She doesn't talk, she doesn't say a word, thought Bosch unhappily. She knows she's failed again, and she feels humiliated. He would have liked to comfort her, to reassure her everything would be all right. Perhaps he would get the chance later.

Thea made sure that the two naked young men who made up the Table had their ear protectors on properly. The portable recorder had amplifiers to improve the sound. It was on one of the youngsters' chest, while the speakers were balanced on the other's thighs. Thea pressed a button.

'*Art then became sacred,*' a nervous, panting voice said in English: a high falsetto voice, which the laboratories had identified as being Hubertus'. '*The figures were trying to . . . were trying to discover God and honour mystery . . .*' There was a pause of echoing sobs. Benoit grimaced as the noise filled the speakers. '*By representing death, man was striving to be immortal . . . All religious art involved . . . involved the same idea . . . torture and destruction were painted or sculpted with the aim of . . . with the aim of . . .*' by now, Hubertus was openly crying '*of affirming life even more . . . eter . . . eternal life . . . Pleeease . . . !*'

The recording broke down in a welter of hysterical sobbing, then picked up again in the calmer voice of Arnoldus.

'*The artist says: my art is death . . . The artist says: the only way I can love life is . . . by loving death . . . because the art which survives is the art which has died . . . if the figures die, the works survive.*'

'He must force them to read a prepared text,' Bosch said in the silence after Thea had switched the recording off.

'This guy is an insane bastard!' Warfell shouted. 'It couldn't be clearer! He may be very clever, but he's off his head!'

His features etched by the slender naked legs of a Marooder Lamp next to his seat, Benoit turned towards Warfell.

'It's all a bluff, Gert. They want us to think it's the work of a madman, but it's all a damned piece of make-believe that one of our competitors has dreamt up. I'm sure of it.'

'How is it possible for works to survive if the figures die?' Head Honcho wanted to know. 'What does that mean?'

Everyone was expecting Stein to answer. But it was Benoit who spoke.

'It doesn't mean a thing. As far as the figures for "Monsters" are concerned, their death means the work has vanished forever as well. There are no substitutes for them.'

Harlbrunner's grave cello boomed out again, from his post next to the dried fruit Table. As he talked, he carelessly stroked the shining surface of the thighs of the girl making the top half.

'Can anyone explain to those of us who are new to this what

on earth this ceru . . . cerublas . . . is?' Several voices completed the word 'cerublastyne' for Harlbrunner, but he did not seem able to finish the word himself. 'According to the reports, Weiss' face and hands were covered in it, weren't they?'

Now it was Jacob Stein's turn. He spoke very softly, but the sepulchral silence surrounding him made it seem louder.

'Ceru is a material similar to silicone, but much more advanced. It was developed in labs in France, England and Holland specifically for use in hyperdramatic art . . . *Galismus*, I think you, Mr Kobb,' he pointed at the man from the Foreign Ministry, 'have had your portrait done by Avendano, so you know what I'm talking about.'

Kobb smiled in agreement.

'Yes, it's identical to me. Sometimes it scares me, it's so real.'

Remembering the portrait of Hendrickje, Bosch also shuddered.

'In art, ceru is employed in many ways,' Stein went on, 'not just for models as portraits, but for official and fake copies, for complicated make-ups, and so on . . . a ceru expert can literally become *anybody*, man or woman. All you have to do is put a thin layer of it on the part you want to copy, let it dry, then remove it very carefully. It's the perfect disguise. Yet I must stress that you have to be a real expert to be able to handle the ceru moulds properly. They're even more fragile than the layer of skin you get on boiled milk.'

'From what I've heard so far,' said Head Honcho, 'our man *is* a real expert.'

There was a moment's silence. Then Stein, who seemed to be in a hurry, called on Benoit to sum up the conclusions from this preliminary meeting. Feeling the spotlight fall on him, Benoit sat up in his chair, put on a pair of reading glasses, and picked up the sheets of paper in front of him. He leaned slightly to his left so that the light from the Marooder Lamp would shine on the text.

'On 29 June 2006, in these offices kindly put at our disposal by the management of the Obberlund building, Munich, a crisis cabinet has been formed with the aim of . . .'

Their aims were clear enough. Conservation and Security had

drawn up an emergency twin-track strategy: defence and attack. There were three items under defence: withdrawal, identity and secrecy. The first consisted in withdrawing all the works by Bruno van Tysch on public display, first in Europe, then in the United States, and finally the rest of the world. 'Flowers' would be the first collection to return to Amsterdam, followed by 'Monsters', and then individual works like *Athene* in the Centre Pompidou. All the works would be kept in secure places. As for identity, this involved a system of checking all the employees who had any contact with the canvases using voice tests and fingerprint checks. Benoit suggested that all those who had been properly identified should then wear labels.

'But that would make us works of art as well,' Warfell objected.

'Is there really no other way to detect a ceru mask?' asked Head Honcho.

'*Fuschus*, no there isn't,' Stein replied. 'When ceru dries, it's like a second skin. It takes on the same temperature and consistency. You'd have to scratch the suspect to make sure who he was.'

The labels idea was left for further consideration. Then the secrecy angle was discussed. From now on, the anonymous criminal was to be known by the code name the 'Artist', as he called himself in the recordings.

'Only those of us in this crisis cabinet,' Benoit went on, 'will know everything about the Artist. All other experts or assistants will only be aware of part or even nothing at all of the information concerning the Artist, including details of the attacks and the progress of our investigations. Neither the insurance companies nor any investors who are not clients of Miss Roman here, nor it goes without saying the press or the public, will have access to any of this information. From this moment on, the very existence of the Artist is strictly confidential.'

The attack plan had a single heading: Rip van Winkle. Bosch had already heard of this European security system. It was controlled from a special department of Europol. Head Honcho defined it as 'self-defence and feedback'. Like the character in Washington Irving's story, the system could be 'sleeping' for years until a specific crisis 'woke it up'. Its chief characteristic was that once it had been awakened it could not be stopped until it had achieved its objectives. These objectives were an absolute priority. Each objective achieved became a 'result'. If necessary, Rip van Winkle could ignore all legal norms, all constitutions and ideas of sovereignty in order to obtain results. It was also self-correcting every week. If it was discovered that in that length of time no result had been achieved, all its agents were changed.

'Today it's us,' said Head Honcho. 'Tomorrow it could be others.'

Rip van Winkle would do everything necessary to get rid of the problem, and would use any means at its disposal. 'There are bound to be victims,' Head Honcho announced dolefully, 'and almost all of them will be innocent, though necessary. I repeat: necessary. The number of victims will grow exponentially in relation to the amount of time we need to achieve our objectives. It's like a secret war.'

In this instance, the main aim of Rip van Winkle was simple: to capture and eliminate the Artist, whoever he was, and whoever might be hiding behind that name.

Then it was Albert Knopffer from Europol's turn to speak.

'We won't spare any effort, I can assure you. You are all well aware of the great interest the Community has shown in the life and work of Bruno van Tysch and the Foundation you represent.'

'Absolutely,' said Head Honcho. 'It's a matter of pride for all Europe, and for us as European citizens, that Mr van Tysch has chosen to create his works here in the Old Continent, unlike so many artists who have emigrated. Not that I would like you to think that I am criticising those artists. I repeat . . .' here he grabbed the last remaining sweets from their bowl and swallowed them.

'. . . the Foundation is part of our European heritage, and we should therefore do all we can to protect it,' Knopffer finished his sentence for him.

While Benoit and Stein were returning the compliment, Bosch tried not to smile. He recalled that Gerhard Weyleb, who had been his boss before Miss Wood, had told him one day that the real masterpieces Van Tysch and Stein had created were the Europeans themselves. 'Don't you see: we're his finest hyper-dramatic work. That's the secret of his incredible success.'

Harlbrunner, who at that moment was resting his hand on one of the varnished knees of the girl who was the dried fruit Table, quickly intervened.

'Art is an absolute priority. You must forgive me if I don't know how to express this any better, but I'm convinced that art is Europe's number one priority.'

As he spoke, he tapped the girl's knee for emphasis like an orator.

A majestic dark-blue limousine glided like a giant fish along the Ludwig Leopold Avenue in Munich. The chauffeur, positioned several metres from the people sitting on the rear seat, wore a uniform and a peaked cap. On the left sat April Wood. She looked thoughtful, and was tapping the back of one hand with the forefinger of the other. Next to her, Stein's personal assistant was busy tapping at the keys of a laptop. Beyond her, head tilted back against the seat, Stein was putting drops into both eyes. His suit and the onyx medallion round his neck were the same shiny black.

Anyone who ever saw Jacob Stein immediately agreed on what he looked like: a faun. His eyebrows stood out above a deeply lined face; his eyes were hidden under dark protruding arches, his nose was prominent, and his thick, sensual lips pushed plumply through the curls of his greying beard. What was more difficult was to assess his real importance in the Foundation. Some people claimed the Maestro dominated him completely, others that he was the one who really reigned. Miss Wood did not dismiss either possibility. One thing was certain: this New York Jew with his faun's features and square head was the chief architect of HD art's success, the person who had turned hyper-dramatism into a world empire, a new form of culture. It was Stein who had designed the first human ornaments and objects, had organised the mass production of cheap copies of originals, and set up the pioneering academies for HD canvases. In spite of all this, he occasionally also found time to paint his own master-pieces.

'By a fortunate coincidence,' said Stein, screwing the top back on his eyedrops, 'it so happens that the excuse I used to get out of the meeting is strictly true, *fuschus*. The Maestro is expecting me in Amsterdam to supervise some of the sketches for the "Rembrandt" exhibition. And to top it all, those aerosols I've been using to prepare the figures for *Jacob Wrestling with the Angel* have given me conjunctivitis . . . Oh, thanks, Neve.'

Stein's secretary had leaned over and dried his eyes with a silk handkerchief. Then she folded the handkerchief, took the eye-drops from him, and put everything away in her bag. The whole operation took place in complete silence. Staring down at the swirls in the car's carpet, Wood caught a glimpse only of Neve's high-heeled shoes and tanned calves as she came and went.

'Which means I hope that what you have to say to me, Miss Wood, is really important, *galismus*,' concluded Stein.

Stein was jokingly nicknamed Mr *Fuschus-Galismus*. Nobody had any clear idea of what the two words Stein was always repeating actually meant, and Stein had never bothered to explain. They were part of the slang he used when talking to painters and canvases. His disciples had invariably picked up the habit.

'Postpone the opening of "Rembrandt", Mr Stein,' Miss Wood said directly.

Stein coughed, and his faun's features darkened.

'*Fuschus*, we turned the wife of the last investor who sug-gested that into a work of art, didn't we, Neve?' The secretary bared a perfect set of shiny white teeth and laughed a tinkling laugh that Miss Wood found faintly nauseating.

'I'm being serious. If the exhibition goes ahead, there's a strong probability that one of the works will be destroyed.'

'Why is that?' the painter asked with genuine curiosity. 'There are more than a hundred of the Maestro's works and sketches in collections and public exhibitions throughout the world. The Artist could choose any of—'

'I don't think so,' Miss Wood interrupted him. 'I'm convinced that, whether we're dealing with a lone madman or an organisation, the Artist is following a plan. Until now, Van Tysch has created two great collections, with the third due to be inaugurated in July. "Flowers", "Monsters", and "Rembrandt". Apart from that, the rest of his works are individual pieces. The Artist has destroyed *Deflowering*, from the first collection, and *Monsters*, from the second.' She paused, and raised her clear eyes to Stein. 'The third will come from "Rembrandt".'

'What proof do you have?'

'None at all. It's my intuition. But I don't think I'm wrong.'

The painter stared silently down at the fingernails on his right hand. He had designed five special brushes to fit into his nails, so that he could keep them as long and tapered as a classical guitarist's.

'I know I can catch him, Mr Stein,' Wood went on. 'But the Artist is not merely a psychopath: he is a real expert, who has planned everything beforehand and moves at incredible speed. Now I'm sure he has his sights on a work from the "Rembrandt" collection, and we have to defend ourselves.' All at once, Miss Wood's voice became husky. 'You know how I work. You know I will not accept mistakes. But when they do occur, my only consolation is to judge they were unforeseeable. So please don't force me to accept a mistake that is *avoidable*. Postpone the exhibition, I beg you.'

'I can't. Believe me, it's not possible. The "Rembrandt" collection is almost complete. The press showing is in a fortnight, and the public opening is on 15 July, the date of the four hundredth anniversary of Rembrandt's birth. The work to install the Tunnel in the Museumplein is already well advanced. And besides, the Maestro has spent too long working on it. He's obsessed by it, and I'm the guardian of the paradise of his obsessions. That is what I've always been, *galismus*, and it's what I intend to go on being . . .'

'And if we explain to the Maestro the danger his works are in?'

'Do you think that would worry him? Do you know any painter who would refuse to exhibit his works because they might be destroyed? *Galismus*, we painters always create for eternity, so we're not worried whether our works last twenty centuries, twenty years, or only twenty minutes.'

Miss Wood studied the patterns on the carpet in silence.

'I'm not going to say a word to the Maestro,' Stein went on. 'All my life I've acted as a buffer between him and reality. My own works are nothing compared to his, but I'm happy just to have helped him create them, by keeping him away from all the problems, by doing all the dirty work myself . . . My best work has been, and continues to be, the fact that the maestro can go on painting. He's a man ruled by the dictates of his own genius. An ineffable being, *galismus*, as strange as an astrophysical phenomenon – sometimes terrible, at others gentle. But if ever, at any moment, anywhere in the world, there has been a genius, then that person is Bruno van Tysch. The rest of us can only hope to obey and protect him. Your duty, Miss Wood, is to protect him. Mine is to obey him . . . ah! *galismus*, what a wonderful glow. Neve, look at the colour of the skin on your legs now, with the sunlight slanting in on them . . . it's lovely, isn't it? A touch of arilamide yellow dissolved in pale pink, varnish on top and you'd be perfect. *Fuschus*, I wonder why no one has thought of painting canvases for the interior of stretch limousines. We could use underage models. We've designed and sold all kinds of ornaments and objects for lots of places, but . . .'

'Postpone the exhibition, Mr Stein, or there'll be another work destroyed,' Miss Wood insisted, without raising her voice.

But all Stein did was study her in silence for a long moment. Then he smiled and shook his head, as if he had seen something unbelievable in her face.

'Find the man responsible,' he said, 'whoever he may be. Find the Artist, seize him, bring him back between your jaws, and everything will be all right. Or let Rip van Winkle do it for you. But don't try to put limits on art, *fuschus*. You're not an artist, April, you're just a hunting dog. Don't forget it.'

'Rip van Winkle won't be able to do a thing, Mr Stein,' Miss Wood said. 'There's something you don't know.'

She paused and looked round. Stein understood exactly what her attitude meant.

'You can say what you like in front of Neve. She's like my eyes and ears.'

'I'd prefer there not to be so many eyes and ears present, even if they are yours, Mr Stein.'

The limousine had pulled up at the airport entrance. Another car was waiting at the roadside to take Miss Wood back into the city. Stein waved his hand, and his secretary left the vehicle and shut the door. Wood looked up towards the chauffeur: the glass partition meant he could hear nothing.

'This is something no one else knows – neither the authorities in Munich, nor the members of the crisis cabinet, not even Lothar Bosch. But I want you to hear it. Perhaps it'll make you change your mind.' She fixed her cold blue gaze on Stein. 'Yesterday, as soon as we heard about *Monsters* being destroyed, I called Marthe Schimmel to see if she could tell me anything. She said the Walden twins had asked her to provide a young man for Tuesday night. You know that in Conservation they like to keep them happy. They were demanding a platinum blond. Schimmel was desperately trying to find a suitable candidate when she received a call cancelling their request. It was a voice she did not know, but he repeated the private number of Conservation in Amsterdam, and said he was one of Benoit's assistants. He told Marthe that the boy was no longer needed. Marthe thought of telling Benoit about this, but I told her not to. I called Benoit's assistants in Amsterdam one by one, and then his secretary. Finally I called Benoit himself. Neither Benoit nor any of his assistants ever gave that order, Mr Stein.'

Wood was staring Stein directly in the eye, without blinking. Stein stared back at her equally unmoved. There was a silence, then she went on:

'It *cannot* have been the criminal who made that call, because at that moment he was disguised as the Gigli work. That leaves only one possibility. *Someone* prepared things for him from *inside* so that there would be no problems destroying the work of art. It must have been someone high up, at least sufficiently senior to have access to Conservation's private codes. That's why I'm begging you to postpone the "Rembrandt" inauguration. If you don't, the Artist is bound to destroy another work.

A plane had just taken off, and was soaring through the blue sky like a mother-of-pearl eagle. Stein studied it, then turned to look at Miss Wood once more. A gleam of anxiety, almost fear, veiled the chilly depths of the Head of Security's eyes.

'However incredible it may seem, Mr Stein, *one of us* is helping that madman.'

6

When Clara awoke on that 28 June, Gerardo and Uhl had already arrived. She thought she could tell from their faces that this was going to be a very special session. They left their bags on the floor and Gerardo said:

'We're not going to try out colours on you today. We want to draw polygons.'

Polygons was the name for the posture exercises designed to test the canvas' physical capabilities. Clara ate a frugal breakfast and took the pills recommended by F&W to improve her muscle tone and reduce her bodily needs as much as possible. Gerardo warned her she had a difficult day ahead of her.

'Let's get on with it then,' she said.

They had brought a leather backless chair. Uhl carried it in from the van and put it in the living room. They moved the carpet and the sofa out of the way and began the exercises. They bent her over backwards, coccyx on the seat; they lifted one leg and then the other, stretched them both out, then bent them double. They chose a posture they liked and set the timer.

Staying immobile is above all a matter of not paying attention to anything. We always receive warnings, signals of increasing discomfort. The brain tightens the thongs on its own rack. Discomfort becomes pain, pain becomes an obsession. The way to resist (as is taught in art academies) is based on classifying all that copious information and keeping it at bay, without rejecting it, but without considering it as something that is *happening*. What, in fact, is happening is that the back is bent or the calf muscles are contracting. Beyond these events, there are only sensations: discomfort, cramps, a tangled rush of stimuli and thoughts, a flood of shards of broken glass. Given proper training, the canvas learns to control this enormous flow, to keep it at a distance, to watch it grow without having to change the pose.

Immersed in the effort of contortion, her head on the floor next to her hands, staring at the wall with her legs stretched upwards and her buttocks on the chair, Clara felt as though she were a nutshell about to crack and give way to something else. She knew of nothing better than an uncomfortable position like this to force her out of her own humanity. Her mind was stripped of memories, fears, complicated thoughts, and concentrated entirely on the masonry of her muscles. It was wonderful to cease to be Clara and become an object with scarcely any sense of pain.

It was so slight that at first she hardly noticed it.

As he was changing the position of her legs in the air, Uhl stroked her buttocks unnecessarily. He did it gently, avoiding any brusque or obvious fondling. He simply slid his hand down her tensed left thigh and cupped her rounded gluteus muscles. But hardly had he squeezed them than he took his hand away. Another confused length of time later, and Clara felt rough fingers on her right thigh. She blinked, raised her head and saw Uhl's hand descending towards her groin. Uhl was not looking at her as he touched her. She did not move, and once again Uhl moved his hand away almost immediately.

The incursion was more obvious the third time, when, after moving both her legs to a different position, Uhl felt clumsily for her sex. Startled, Clara doubled up and curled into a ball.

'Pose,' Uhl ordered, in an annoyed tone of voice.

Clara merely stared at him.

'Pose.'

From where she lay curled up, Uhl looked a threatening figure. But Clara was not really afraid. Something about the painter's attitude turned what had happened into something perfectly staged, gave it all the proper artistic touch. She decided to obey. Despite her protesting tendons (there is nothing harder than losing a difficult position and having to get back into it without any warming up), she got back on to the chair, lifted her legs in the air, and lay immobile with her head and arms on the floor. She thought Uhl was going to return to the attack, but all he did was stare at her for a while and then move away.

Clara knew that Uhl could be *pretending* to molest her for hyperdramatic reasons. The brushstrokes were so well done though, that despite all her experience as a canvas she found it impossible to tell where the real Uhl ended and the artist began. Besides, his pretence might equally well mean the molesting was *real* on the sidelines. Uhl could have received instructions from the main painter, but Clara had no idea how far he might be *abusing* his privileged situation. It was almost impossible to establish limits, because between a painter's gesture and a caress there are endless, unfathomable gradations.

The timer went off. The two assistants came back into the room and changed the sketch. They made her stand up, and took the leather chair away. Then they laid her out face down and tried different positions once more: head raised, right arm stretched out, left one pointing backwards, left leg in the air. The pose reminded her of someone swimming. They pulled on her extremities until her joints protested. It was obvious they wanted to sketch her stretched. A simple contraction was not enough: they wanted to emphasise the movements. When they were satisfied with the firm outline of her extended limbs, they set the timer again and left her on the floor.

It happened at some moment while she was in this new pose. She could hear his footsteps crossing the room and saw him kneeling beside her. Her position meant that her left breast and her sex were exposed: Uhl's hands took possession of both of them.

The gesture was so brutal Clara could not stop herself abandoning the pose and protecting her body. At that point something happened that took her breath away.

Uhl grasped her arms violently and spread them apart with unexpected, unnecessary force. She cried out in pain. It was the first time he had been violent towards her. In fact, it was the first time anyone had used violence against her since she had been primed. She was so surprised she could neither speak nor defend herself. The painter bent even closer, and buried his mouth in her neck, still pinioning her arms. She could feel his saliva, his tongue like a freshly caught octopus flung at her throat, his panting breath at her jugular.

'Are you crazy?' she groaned. 'Let go of me!'

Uhl did not seem to hear her. The frame of his glasses twisted under Clara's chin as his mouth slid down towards her breasts. She stopped struggling for a moment.

All at once, just as she had given up fighting him, Uhl came to a halt, sighed deeply, straightened up and released her wrists. He was breathing even more heavily than she was, and his face was all red. He pushed his glasses back on properly, and smoothed the hair at the nape of his neck. It was as if a sudden sense of shame had prevented him going any further. Clara was still on the floor, rubbing her wrists. For a few seconds they just looked at each other, getting their breath back. Then Uhl got up and left.

Clara thought she now had some idea what was going on: it had been her sudden *passivity* that had inhibited Uhl, as it had done on the previous occasions.

In itself, this did not change anything. It could have been a human rather than an artistic reaction: perhaps Uhl had not dared take things any further, or perhaps he was one of those men who only gets pleasure when they meet resistance. Yet Clara wanted to believe that the *brushstroke* meant he had to stop as soon as she no longer resisted. She filed the information away for use at a later date.

The new assault did not catch her unawares. They had sketched her as a table: face up, hands and feet on the floor, head thrown back and legs wide apart. At a certain moment, Uhl came towards her. She looked him in the eye and realised that it was all going to start again. This time she decided to resist. She abandoned her pose and stood up.

'Leave me alone, will you?'

Without warning, those long arms of his, as hairy as strands of hemp rope or brush bristles, grabbed her and forced her back towards the floor. Uhl's mouth opened and sought out hers. Disgusted, she turned her face aside and pushed against his chest with her elbows. Uhl resisted without much effort. Clara tried again, but met only a brick wall. It was true she had been

236

weakened by all the exercises she had been put through, but still it was obvious that Uhl was amazingly strong. The painter clamped her cheeks in one of his hairy paws and forced her mouth towards his, then slid his tongue over her primed, lipless mouth. Clara gathered her strength and struck out with both knees. This time she was more successful: she pushed Uhl aside and rolled over to protect herself.

'Stay still,' she heard.

The painter threw himself at her again, but Clara easily avoided him and kicked out a second time. She did not want to hurt him, but she was keen to see what would happen if she did not yield. By now she knew – or suspected – that Uhl was using a very simple method to paint her: he added a further degree of violence if her response was violent, but became gentler if her behaviour was submissive. When she *yielded*, he took the brush away. Clara wanted to find out exactly where this journey to absolute darkness that the painter was apparently proposing would lead them.

All at once everything took on the uncontrollable rhythm of a desperate struggle. Uhl seized her by both arms, she kicked out, Uhl's glasses clattered to the floor with a strangely disagreeable sound. He raised his hand as if about to hit her. Then she was really afraid. He could damage me, she thought. It was not the possibility of being hit that frightened her. She had been struck by the public or other canvases in some art-shocks, but that had always been planned by the artist, and agreed with her beforehand. What frightened her was the lack of control. He's getting more and more nervous, he could really hurt me and ruin my priming.

This thought led her to relax. Uhl threw himself on her, and started licking her chin and throat with his tongue.

But then he stopped once more.

Clara was still lying breathless on the floor, while Uhl struggled to his feet. They looked like two athletes at the end of some violent exercise. She stared him in the eye, but could make out nothing in his face apart from his weak gaze hidden deep behind the lenses of glasses that Uhl had just put back on with a neat gesture. A few moments later, the painter stepped back, and left the room, heading for the front porch.

237

Things had taken such a spectacular turn that when it was time for lunch, Clara scarcely wanted to eat. She did not want to have to break off from the sketches to immerse herself again in cold routine. She forced herself to do so, because she knew it was necessary to pause for a moment in this frenetic escalation. Before eating she went to the bathroom and washed, getting rid of all traces of Uhl from her mouth and neck. She stared at her reflection in the mirror. There were no marks apart from a slight redness on her wrists. Primed skin was much tougher than normal skin, so that Uhl would have had to paint her much more violently to leave lasting traces. She smiled, and her face took on the mischievous look that Bassan liked so much. I've found you out: you use force if I do. You want to sketch me as aggressive, she told herself. Her eyes were smarting, but she knew this was from having to keep them open all the time she was in the poses. She rinsed them with saline solution.

She ate lunch naked with Gerardo sitting opposite her. Uhl was somewhere unknown. Gerardo had already finished and observed her quietly.

'Did you see the man at the window again?' he asked.

For a moment she did not understand what he was talking about.

'Yes, but I called Conservation. They told me they were security guards, so I felt reassured. I slept very well for the rest of the night.'

'So it was as I said: guards.'

'Aha.'

They fell silent. She finished her sandwich and began to spread cheese on a slice of bread. All her muscles ached, but that did not bother her. She felt refreshingly angry, as effervescent as a fizzy drink shaken for hours. From time to time she glanced at the door to see if Uhl was coming in. She remembered his breath, and his violence. And also how everything came to a halt when she yielded. But what would have happened if she had not yielded? How far would his brushstrokes have gone, what remote shade of darkness might they have reached? That was what obsessed her. What would happen if next time she decided *not to surrender* at all, not to yield for anything? The possibilities were staggering.

'How did you get on this morning?'

Gerardo's question made her blink. The last thing she needed at that moment was banal conversation.

'Fine,' she said.

He put his elbows on the table, leaned over to her, and adopted a serious tone.

'Listen, there's something I have to tell you.'

They stared at each other in silence. Clara chewed her food quietly, waiting.

'Justus is annoyed.'

She said nothing. Her heart started beating faster.

'And it's not good if Justus gets annoyed, because if that happens, you and I are out on the street, right?'

'What do you mean?' she asked, innocently.

Gerardo appeared to be searching for the right words. He stared down at his hands on the tablecloth.

'We . . . we have some rules regarding young female canvases, if you follow me. And the canvases have to respect them. I don't like talking about this, but sometimes as in your case it becomes necessary – it seems you don't get it at all, do you?'

'What am I supposed to get?'

'That you are in a privileged position. You are a canvas contracted by the Van Tysch Foundation, which is quite something, believe me. But that could vanish at any moment. I already told you, Justus is a senior assistant. In other words, he's a painter of some importance here in the Foundation. You have to be aware of that. I'm not telling you this to scare you, but so that you understand . . . and do whatever is necessary, OK?'

'But I don't understand a thing.'

He puffed, and sat back in his seat.

'Then you really must be dumb. I'm warning you: Justus could throw you out on the spot if he wanted to.'

'And what am I supposed to do to prevent that?'

'You know perfectly well. Don't pretend to be stupid. He likes you a lot. You'll see.'

This fascinating exchange did not make sense to her. She

guessed this might be due to Gerardo's clumsiness, his rough, unconvincing way of doing things, the way he tried too hard to control his voice, his timid approach as if he were a kid playing at being the tough guy. For Clara, the most exciting thing was that Gerardo could be telling the truth. There was no way to be certain that all this was the farce it seemed on the surface.

'Are you threatening me?' Clara asked.

Gerardo raised an eyebrow.

'I'm simply trying to tell you that Justus is the boss, after him comes me, and that you are at our *complete and absolute disposition*. And that if you want to be painted by a maestro from the Foundation, the best thing is for you not to upset the assistants, got it?'

A vibration, a shudder of pure art ran through her body. For the first time she felt a certain *apprehension* at Gerardo's words, and she liked the feeling. She had been painted with another fine brushstroke, and the fact that she was completely naked added the appropriate dark tone. She crossed her ankles, stirred in her seat, and muttered as she looked away from him:

'All right.'

'I hope you'll be more friendly to Justus from now on, OK?'

She nodded.

'I didn't hear your reply,' he said.

This new pressure from the brush pleased her as well. She hastened to respond.

'Yes, all right.'

Gerardo rolled his eyes back and stared at her in a very odd way. Neither of them said anything more.

She tried 'being more friendly' during the afternoon session. They had posed her on tiptoe, like a ballet dancer. Time went by. As she was standing up, she could see herself in the mirrors. One of them only reflected half her anatomy, a split silhouette, a chaos of lines and volume. They left her like that for quite a while until Uhl suddenly came up behind her.

Right from the start, she returned his kiss, more ardently than he had begun it with. Her tongue darted in Uhl's dark mouth, she clasped him in her arms and pressed her naked body against his clothes.

It was like being stung by a bee. The painter tore himself from her and left the room. He did not approach her again all afternoon.

So, if I *yield,* everything stops, she reasoned. And if I *don't yield?'*

This second option scared her a lot.

She decided she would try it.

She was excited, but that night she collapsed into bed like a dead weight. She suspected it was because of all the pills she was taking. When she awoke, she presumed it was Thursday 29 June. She felt ready for a fresh assault. She could not remember anything that had happened during the night: it was as though she had passed out. She had gone to sleep with the blinds drawn again, and if any security guard had come near to the house, she had not been aware of it. And besides, she was beginning to forget her nocturnal fears, because the daytime ones were taking all her attention.

That morning they sketched her standing up, bending over backwards. They were difficult poses, and the timer settings seemed to her eternal. It was midday before she managed to really control her trembling limbs, and the pain in her vertebrae became nothing more than the passage of time. To her surprise, Uhl had not bothered her again. She wondered if the way she had given in to him the previous afternoon had brought things to a complete stop.

After lunch, Gerardo invited her for a walk. This surprised her a little, but she decided to accept because she wanted to get some fresh air. She put on a robe and a pair of padded plastic sandals, and the two of them walked down the gravel path to the front hedge. Then they went out on to the road.

As she had thought, the scenery was very pretty by daylight. To the right and left there were more gardens, hedges and red-roofed houses. In the distance there was a small wood, and before it the main road their van had travelled along. Clara was delighted to see the unmistakable outline of several windmills on the horizon. The scene was like a typical postcard from Holland.

'All these houses belong to the Foundation,' explained

241

Gerardo. 'It's here we make sketches of most of our models. We prefer these surroundings because we can be on our own. Before all the sketches were done in the Old Atelier, in the Plantage district of Amsterdam. Now though we make the sketches here, and if necessary we do the shading in the Atelier.'

Gerardo was behaving as though he felt *liberated*. He rested his hand gently on her shoulder whenever he wanted to point something out, and smiled wonderfully. It was as if the work atmosphere inside the house was even more exhausting for him than for her. They walked along the roadside listening to the soundtrack of a civilised countryside: birdsong mixed with the distant rumble of machinery. Every so often, a plane ploughed the sky with its brief roar. The muscles of Clara's back ached a little. She thought it was probably due to the difficult poses she had been put in that morning. She was worried, because she did not want anything to go wrong at the sketching stage. She was thinking all this when Gerardo spoke again.

'This is a rest period. An official rest, I mean. Do you understand?'

'Aha.'

'You can talk freely.'

'Fine.'

She understood perfectly. Some painters she had worked with used phrases like this to emphasise that the hyperdramatic work had been interrupted. Sometimes with human canvases it was necessary to make a clear distinction between reality and the blurred outlines of art. Gerardo was trying to tell her that from this moment on, he was he, and she was she. He was saying that he had left his brushwork behind and that he wanted to go for a walk and chat for a while. After that, everything would begin again.

But Clara was confused by the decision. Breaks were common practice in every HD painting session, but it was important to determine exactly when they were taking place, because otherwise the entire painterly construction could be destroyed in an instant. And this moment did not seem very suitable. The previous day, the same young man she was now out strolling with had told her threateningly that she should accept the sexual harassment of his colleague. That had been an especially intense piece of brushwork, but it was also extremely fragile, a subtle outline that could be ruined if it were not allowed to dry. She wanted to believe Gerardo knew what he was doing. And this rest period might well be make-believe, too.

After a short silence, Gerardo looked at her intently. They both smiled.

'You're a very good canvas, sweetheart. I'm talking from experience. First-class material!'

'Thanks, but I see myself as fairly ordinary,' lied Clara.

'No, no; you're very good. Justus thinks the same.'

'You two aren't so bad either.'

She was feeling increasingly uneasy. She would have preferred to go back to the house at once and resume the hyperdramatic tension. This idle conversation with one of the technical assistants frightened her. She refused to believe that Gerardo wanted to have the kind of boring exchange such as: What do you like doing, and what do you enjoy? She could only put up with Jorge talking that way, but Jorge was her everyday life, not art.

Stay cool, she told herself. Let him take the reins. He's a Foundation painter, a professional. He's not going to make any false moves with a canvas.

'Justus is better than me,' Gerardo went on. 'Seriously, sweetheart: he's an extraordinary painter. I've been an assistant for two years now. Before I was training to be a craftsman. Justus had just been made a senior. We became friends, and it was he who recommended me for this job. I've been very lucky, they don't take on just anybody. And I never liked painting ornaments. What I'm into are works of art.'

'Aha.'

'But what I'd like most of all is to become an independent professional painter. To have my own studio and canvases. Canvases like you: good, expensive ones.' Clara laughed out loud. 'I have lots of ideas, especially for outdoor works. I'd love to be able to devote myself to making outdoor works for collectors in hot countries.'

'So why don't you? It's a good market.'

'You need money to set up a studio like that, sweetheart. But one day I'll do it, believe me. For the moment, I'm happy. I'm earning lots of money. Not everyone gets to be a technical assistant in the Van Tysch Foundation.'

Clara was no longer irritated by Gerardo's smug tone. She saw it as part of his overall commonness. What she did find increasingly hard to take was this conversation. All she wanted to do was to get back to the house and go on with the sketching. Not even the delightful countryside and the fresh air could lift her spirits.

'What about you?' he asked.

He was smiling at her.

'Me?'

'Yes. What is it you want? What's your greatest aim in life?'

It did not take her a second to think of a reply.

'To have a great painter create a masterpiece with me.'

Gerardo smiled again.

'You're a beautiful work already – you don't need anyone to paint you.'

'Thanks, but I was talking about masterpieces, not simply something pretty. A work of genius.'

'You'd like someone to create a work of genius with you, even if it was ugly?'

'Aha.'

'I thought you liked being pretty.'

'I'm a canvas, not a catwalk model,' she said, more sharply than she had intended.

'Of course, nobody's denying that,' Gerardo said. The two of them fell silent, then he turned towards her again. 'Forgive me for asking, but might I know why? I mean, why are you so keen for someone to paint a great work with you?'

'I don't know,' she said sincerely. She had stopped to look at the roadside flowers. A comparison occurred to her. 'I guess a caterpillar has no idea why it wants to become a butterfly either.'

Gerardo thought about it.

'What you've just said is very pretty, but not strictly true. Because a caterpillar is destined to become a butterfly whether it wants to or not. But that's not true of works of art. We have to make believe.'

244

'That's true,' she admitted.

'Have you ever thought of leaving the profession? Of just being yourself?'

'I am myself.'

Gerardo turned to look at the trees along the roadside.

'Come on. I want to show you something.'

All this is a trick, thought Clara. A trap to darken my colour. Perhaps Uhl is hiding somewhere, and now . . .

They crossed the ditch and walked into the wood. He held her hand as they descended a steep slope. They reached a polygonal clearing hemmed in by trees with shiny leaves and dark chestnut trunks that looked as if they had been varnished. There was a strange, unexpected smell in the air, which somehow reminded Clara of that of newly made dolls. And then an odd noise: an artificial tinkling, like the breeze might make as it stirred the glass of a baroque chandelier. For a moment, Clara looked all round, trying to discover where this strange noise came from. Then she went closer to one of the trees and understood. She was fascinated.

'We call this part the *Plastic Bos*, the "plastic wood",' Gerardo explained. 'The trees, flowers and grass are all artificial. The sound you can hear is made by the leaves on the trees when the wind catches them: they're made of a very fragile material that makes them sound like slivers of glass. We use this place to sketch outdoor pieces the whole year round. It means we don't have to depend on nature. Winter and summer are exactly the same: the trees and the grass here are still green.'

'It's incredible.'

'I'd call it horrible,' he replied.

'Horrible?'

'Yes. These trees, this plastic grass . . . I can't bear it.'

Clara looked down at her feet: the carpet of thick, pointed artificial grass looked very soft. She took off a sandal and tested it with her bare foot. It was soft and springy.

'Can I sit down?' she asked.

'Of course, make yourself at home. Get comfortable.'

They sat down together. The grass was an army of tiny, elegant soldiers. Nothing in the clearing jarred. Clara stroked the

245

grass and closed her eyes: it was like sliding your hand through a fur coat. She felt happy. Gerardo on the other hand seemed increasingly sad.

'Nothing will make the birds settle here, you know. They realise at once that it's all a *trompe-l'oeil* and fly off at once to real trees. And they're right, dammit: trees should be trees, and people, people.'

'In real life, of course: but art is different.'

'Art is part of life, sweetheart, not the other way round,' Gerardo replied. 'Do you know what I'd like to do? To paint something in the natural–humanist style of the French school. But I don't, because hyperdramatism sells better and gives more money. And I want to earn lots of money.' He threw open his arms and exclaimed: 'Lots and lots of money so I can say to hell with all the plastic woods in the world!'

'I think this place is beautiful.'

'Are you serious?'

'Aha.'

He looked at her curiously.

'What an incredible woman you are. I've worked with a lot of canvases, sweetheart, but none of them was as formidable as you.'

'Formidable?'

'Yes. I mean . . . as *determined* to be a complete canvas, from head to toe. Tell me something. What do you do when you stop working? Do you have friends? Are you going out with someone?'

'Yes, I'm going out with someone. And I have male and female friends.'

'Anyone special?'

Clara was gently combing the grass. She merely smiled.

'Don't you like me asking you these things?' Gerardo wanted to know.

'No, it's all right. There is someone, but we don't live together, and he's not really my "boyfriend". He's a friend I feel attracted to.'

She smiled again, trying to imagine Jorge as her boyfriend. She had never thought of him that way. She went on to wonder exactly what Jorge was for her, what else they shared apart from

246

their night-time moments. All at once, she realised that she used him as a spectator. She liked Jorge to know every detail of what happened to her in the strange world of her profession. She tried not to hide anything from him, not even its most vulgar aspects, or what Jorge considered as vulgar: everything she did with the public during the art-shocks for example, or her work for *The Circle* or Brentano. Jorge was taken aback at this, and she enjoyed watching his face at those moments. Jorge was her public, her astonished spectator. She needed constantly to leave him with his mouth open.

'So when you're not a canvas, you lead a normal life,' Gerardo said.

'Yes, pretty normal. What about you?'

'I dedicate myself to work. I have a few friends here in Holland, but above all, I dedicate myself to work. And I'm not going out with anyone at the moment. I did have a Dutch girl-friend a while back, but we split up.'

After that there was a silence. She was still convinced Gerardo was a skilful painter, but now she was almost certain this was a real break. What did he mean by talking to her *sincerely*? There could be no sincerity between a painter and a canvas, and both of them knew that. In the case of artists such as Bassan or Chalboux, who were followers of the natural-humanist school, the sincerity was forced, another brushstroke, a sort of 'now we're going to be sincere', a technique along with all the others. Yet here was Gerardo apparently wanting to talk to her as if she was someone he had met on a train or bus. It was absurd.

'Look, I'm sorry, but isn't it getting rather late?' she said. 'Shouldn't we be getting back?'

Gerardo looked her up and down.

'You're right,' he finally admitted. 'Let's go back.'

Then suddenly as they were getting up, he spoke to her in a different, urgent whisper.

'Listen, I wanted . . . I wanted you to know something. You're doing very well, sweetheart. You've understood the response right from the start. But keep on doing the same thing, whatever happens, got it? Don't forget, the key is to *yield*.'

Clara listened to him in disbelief. It seemed incredible to her

247

that he was revealing the artist's secrets to her. She felt as though in the middle of a gripping drama one of the actors had turned to her, winked, and said: Don't worry, it's only a play. For a moment she thought it might have been a hidden brushstroke, but she could see from Gerardo's face that he was genuinely concerned. Concerned about her! The key is to yield. No doubt about it, he was referring to her reaction to Uhl: he was encouraging her to continue on the correct – or at least the safest – path. If you continue to yield the way you did yesterday afternoon, he was saying, Uhl will stop. Gerardo was not painting her: he was revealing secrets, the solution to the mysteries. He was the unfortunate friend who tells you the end of the film.

Clara felt as though he had deliberately tipped an inkpot over a sketch he had only just begun. Why on earth had he done it?

The poses continued all afternoon in complete silence. Uhl did not bother her again, but she had already forgotten him. She thought that Gerardo's slip was the worst mistake she had ever come across in her entire professional life: not even poor Gabi Ponce, who was not exactly subtle when it came to hyperdramatism, had been so crass. Even though she had suspected that Uhl's harassment was not for real, it was one thing to suspect it, another to *know* it for sure. With a single sweep of his brush, Gerardo had ruined the careful landscape of threats that Uhl and he had been painstakingly creating around her. Now any return to that make-believe was impossible: the hyperdramatism as such had disappeared. From now on there could only be theatre.

Later on, as she was going to bed, her anger subsided. She decided that Gerardo must be a novice. The refinements of pure hyperdramatism were obviously way beyond him. What most surprised her was that a painter like him had been given a position of such responsibility. Apprentices should not be allowed to sketch on originals, she thought. That should be reserved for experienced artists. Maybe all was not lost though. Perhaps Gerardo's clumsiness, the huge stain he had tipped over her, could be cleaned up thanks to Uhl's exquisite artwork. It could be that Uhl would find some way of increasing the pressure and making it part of the painting process again.

She was sure she would be frightened again.

As she fell asleep, this was her last wish.

When she woke up, everything was still incredibly dark. She had no way of knowing what time it was, even whether it was still night-time or not, because before she had gone to sleep she had closed the house shutters. She guessed it must still be night, because she could not hear any birdsong. She drew her hand across her face, then turned over, confident she could get back to sleep.

She was about to do so when she noticed it.

She sat bolt upright on the mattress, terrified.

The distinct sound of floorboards creaking. In the living room. It had possibly been something similar that had awakened her. Footsteps.

She was all ears, listening. All her tiredness and aching muscles disappeared as if by magic. She could hardly breathe. She quickly tried a relaxation exercise, but it did not work.

There was *someone* in the living room, by God.

She swung her feet on to the floor. Her brain was a whirling maelstrom of thoughts.

'Hello?' she called out in a quaking, horrified voice.

She waited without moving for several minutes, ready to confront the dreadful possibility that the intruder might burst in at any moment and fling himself on her. The silence all around her made her think she might have been mistaken. But her imagination – that strange diamond, that polygon with a thousand faces – sent fleeting sensations of terror to her mind, tiny inventions like slivers of pure ice. *It's the man facing the other way: he's stepped out of the photo and now he's coming for you. But he's walking backwards. You'll see him walk into the room backwards, heading straight for you, guided by your smell. It's your father, in his huge square glasses, coming to tell you that . . .'* She made a great effort to dismiss these recurring nightmares from her mind.

'Is there anybody there?' she heard herself say again.

She waited another prudent moment, her eyes fixed on the closed bedroom door. She remembered that all the light switches were in the hall. She had no way of lighting her room without leaving it and walking in the dark to the front wall. She did not have the courage to do it. Maybe it's a guard, she thought. But what was a security guard doing entering the farm at night and creeping about the living room?

The silence continued. Her heartbeats too. The silence and the heartbeats stubbornly measured their own rhythms. She decided she must have been wrong. There are many reasons wooden floorboards creak. In Alberca she had become accustomed to chance and its shocks: a sudden breeze bringing dead curtains back to life, the creaking sound of a rocking chair, a mirror suddenly disguised in darkness. All of this must be a false alarm raised by her weary brain. She could get up calmly, walk past the living room and switch the house lights on, just as she had done the night before.

She took a deep breath and put her hands on the mattress.

At that moment the door opened and her attacker swept into the room like a hurricane.

7

The New Atelier building in Amsterdam housed the head-quarters of Art, Conservation and Security for Bruno van Tysch's Foundation in Europe. It was a rather outrageous building, combining Dutch cheerfulness and Calvinist sobriety, with white-framed windows and seventeenth-century-style gables. To give it a cosmopolitan feel, the architect P. Viengsen had added twin columns à la Brunelleschi to the façade. It was on Willemsparksweg Avenue, near the Vondelpark in the Museum District, where all the artistic jewels of the city are to be found: the Rijkmuseum, the Van Gogh Museum, and the Stedelijk. The Atelier was eight storeys high, with three different blocks. Not unusual in Amsterdam, the entrance hall and first floor were below sea level. In his fifth-floor office, Bosch was probably safe from any threat of flood, although he didn't seem particularly aware of his good fortune.

His office – which included a V-shaped mahogany desk with four old-fashioned telephones on one end and three framed photographs on the other – looked out on to the Vondelpark. The photos were placed so that no one sitting opposite Bosch could see them.

The one closest to the wall was a portrait of his father Vincent Bosch. Vincent was a lawyer for a Dutch tobacco firm. The man in the portrait wore a moustache, had a penetrating gaze, and a huge head, which Lothar had inherited. He looked like a methodical, scrupulous character. The guiding maxim he tried to pass on to his children – achieve the best possible results with the means available – appeared to be chiselled into each and every one of his features. He would have been pleased with the results.

The photo in the middle was of Henrickje. She was pretty, with short blonde hair, a broad smile, and a certain horsiness about her jaw owing to over-prominent teeth. Bosch could vouch for the fact that her body was perfectly well proportioned: Hendrickje liked to show it off in attractive stripey dresses. She was twenty-nine, five years younger than Inspector Bosch, and was rich. They met at a party where an astrologer got them together because of their zodiac signs. Bosch was not attracted to her at first; they ended up getting married. The marriage worked perfectly. Hendrickje – tall, slender, wonderful, attractive, sterile (a problem diagnosed ten months after the wedding), ladylike and positive ('You have to think positively, Lothar', she used to tell him) enjoyed the privilege of having several lovers. Bosch, stubborn, serious, solitary, silent and conservative, only had Hendrickje, but felt that the mere fact of loving her did not mean he could hold her against her will, like the criminals he so detested. Respecting other people's wishes was part of the ideas of freedom that the young inspector had lived by during his troubled adolescence, when he was an *okupa* in a building on the Spui. It was almost perverse that the same Lothar Bosch who threw stones at the anti-riot squads from the Golfillo statue should a few years later join the city police. On the rare occasions when he still asks himself why he took that decision, he believes he can find the answer in the portrait of his father (back to him), and his sceptical Calvinist gaze. His father wanted him to study

Law, he wanted to be useful to society, his father wanted him to earn money, he did not want to work with his father. So why not become a policeman? A logical decision. One way 'to achieve the best possible results with the means available'.

To some extent, Hendrickje liked him being a policeman. This gave a certain security, or 'stability', to the image of their marriage. Their fights were as rare as were their moments of love, so that in this way, at least, their relationship was balanced. Then one foggy morning in November 1992, it had all come to a sudden end: Hendrickje Michelsen was returning by car from Utrecht when a lorry trailer guillotined her. The impact not only spilled her brains instantaneously, but took with them her head (her beautiful blonde-haired horsey head, the one we can see in the photo), and also her slender neck and part of her upper body. She had gone to Utrecht to visit a lover. Bosch heard the news while he was questioning a man suspected of several murders. He went numb, but chose to go on with the interrogation. Eventually the suspect proved to be terribly innocent. Then one evening in March, four months after the tragedy, a supernatural event took place in the house of the lonely, widowed inspector. The doorbell went, and when he opened it Bosch found himself face-to-face with a girl with straw-blonde hair who said her name was Emma Thorderberg. She was wearing a leather jacket and jeans, with a bag slung over her shoulder. She explained why she had come, and an astonished Bosch let her in. The girl went into the bathroom and an hour later it was Henrickje who came out, wearing her striped dress. She took several long, elegant strides with the bare, shiny legs of someone risen from the dead, and then took up a position in the dining room without so much as a glance at the open-mouthed Lothar. The painting was by Jan Carlsen. Like all artists, Carlsen had reserved the right to change the original: he had shortened the skirt and lowered the neckline to make her more seductive. Apart from that, the cerublastyne had created an exact equivalent: it was as if Hendrickje were alive.

Afterwards he found out who had sent him this surprise gift.

'It was Hannah's idea,' his brother Roland explained on the telephone. 'We weren't sure how you would take it, Lothar. If

252

you don't like it, send it back. Carlsen assured us we could sell it on.'

At first Bosch was tempted to get rid of the work of art. He felt so disturbed he could not eat in the same room but had to move elsewhere to avoid looking at it. He had no idea whether this feeling was due to the fact that Hendrickje was dead, or that he did not want to have to remember her, or for God knows what other obscure reason. Like the good policeman he was, he began by discounting the least likely reasons. If he kept photos and mementoes of his wife, why couldn't he bear *that*? This meant the first two possibilities could be dismissed. The final conclusion he reached was surprising: what disturbed him so much in the portrait had nothing to do with Hendrickje, and everything with Emma Thorderberg. What most intrigued him was not knowing who was hidden behind the mask. In order to free himself from this fascinating horror, he decided to approach the canvas. One night as she was leaving (the contract stipulated six hours on show at his house), he kept her back with a few banal questions about her profession. They both had a drink, and Emma turned out to be talkative and impetuous, not as educated as Hendrickje, with a less well-defined person-ality. She was more beautiful, more sympathetic, much less selfish. Bosch discovered something: Emma was not Hendrickje and never could be, but she was very worthwhile in her own right. Once he had discovered this (that Hendrickje was in fact Emma Thorderberg in disguise) the portrait became a carnival joke. He was no longer disturbed when he looked at it, or ate and read in its company. When he realised this, he decided to return it. After quickly compensating Carlsen, they succeeded in selling it to a collector his brother was treating for a throat infection. They even made a profit on the sale. So now Hendrickje is living with someone else. The only thing Lothar regrets is that Emma has gone, too. Because it's not art that is important, according to Bosch, but people.

Having met Emma Thorderberg led him to say yes when, a few years later, Jacob Stein called him to offer him the post of security supervisor at the Foundation. Bosch consoled himself thinking that it was not the hefty raise in salary that led him to quit the police force (not *just* that, at least). To Bosch, protecting works of art was the same as protecting *people*. In the end, as Hendrickje used to say – things tend to even out.

The third photo was a snapshot of his beloved niece Danielle, his brother's daughter. Roland Bosch, who was five years younger than Lothar, had studied medicine and become an ear, nose and throat specialist. He ran a prosperous private practice in The Hague, but was one of those people who only feels happy doing something out of the ordinary – risky sports, suddenly buying shares, impulse buying and selling, and so on. When looking for a wife he chose a famous and stunningly beautiful German TV actress who he had met in Berlin. He easily overcame the ugliness characteristic of the Bosch family, and was confident his only daughter would inherit her mother's looks. Danielle Bosch was pretty, it was true, but she was also a ten-year-old child, and Lothar felt she did not deserve such a family. Roland and Hannah had brought her up with a magic mirror that rendered her homage every day. The year before they had wanted their little goddess to go into cinema. They took her to various castings, but Danielle was a pretty poor actress, with rather too deep a voice. She was turned down, to her parents' disgust and her uncle's secret joy. Only two months ago, however, things had taken a new and unsuspected turn: Roland had decided to educate Danielle seriously and had sent her to a private school in The Hague. Bosch was surprised at the news, but he was also worried on Danielle's behalf. He wondered how the girl would get on in this atmosphere, so distant from her parents' uncritical adoration. Lothar loved Danielle with a passion only explicable in a childless widower of around fifty: not the Danielle that Roland and Hannah were creating, but the little girl who occasionally shared smiles and thoughts with him. Hendrickje had never met Danielle, but Bosch was sure they would have got on. Hendrickje and Roland were great friends.

According to Lothar Bosch, the world is divided into two categories of people: those who know how to live, and those who *protect* those who know. People like Hendrickje and his brother Roland belong to the first category; Bosch to the second.

254

He was staring intently at Danielle's photo, when Nikki Hartel came into his office.

'I think we've got something, Lothar.'

April Wood's office is on the sixth floor of the New Atelier. It is full of artworks. They are flesh-coloured nudes or near-nudes. No artifice, no fascinating colours, nothing complicated. Wood likes abstract body art, where the figures are shown as simple virgin anatomies in uniform colours: always white Caucasians, nearly always female, built like ballet dancers or acrobats. They are very expensive, but she can afford it. And the Foundation allows her to decorate her office as she likes. Almost all the works are by the new British school. By the door is a Jonathan Bergmann called *Body Cult* which Bosch particularly likes, perhaps because of its beautiful ballet posture. Standing at the far end of the room, legs apart and hands on hips, there is an Alec Storck painted with tanning lotions and sunscreens of different strengths. There are also three Morris Bird originals: a girl painted lunar blue standing on her head by the window, a boy balancing on one leg next to the desk – his yellow buttocks brushing against the telephone cable – and another ochre and fuchsia girl crouching on the floor like a frog about to leap.

Although he was used to this by now, Bosch was always taken aback when he went into the office.

'Yes?'

'April, good news.'

She was pacing up and down, hands behind her back, dressed in a silver-grey tubular dress. (Joan of Arc in her armour, he thought.) She looked like a queen surrounded by naked statues. Her face showed her concern.

'Let's go to the other room,' she said.

This small room was connected to her office by a short, mirror-lined corridor. It had no windows or human ornaments. Miss Wood closed the door so that the works could not hear them, and offered Bosch a seat. She sat opposite him. Bosch handed her the documents Nikki had brought him. There were several laser-printed photos.

'Look at this blonde woman. She was filmed on three different occasions by the video cameras in the entrance to the Vienna MuseumsQuartier in May. Now look at this man. He was filmed four times by the same cameras, on different days from the girl. And now the most incredible part.' He showed her a third sheet of paper with computer graphics. 'The morphometric analysis of their faces shows a high correlation. There's an eighty per cent probability that it is the same person.'

'What about Munich?'

'Here are the results. Three visits by her, two by him, on alternating days, during the second fortnight in May.'

'Perfect. We've got him. He had enough time to get back to Vienna and change into the girl without papers. But it would be even more perfect if we could compare him to the fake Díaz or the fake Weiss . . .'

'Surprise.'

Bosch handed her another sheet of paper. As he bent over Miss Wood, he could see how pale her face was beneath the shadow of her fringe. My God, she puts make-up on like a pharaoh, as if she were scared of anyone seeing her without protection, he thought. It was also true that she seemed different since their return from Munich. He guessed that the work did not help, but he wondered whether there was something else as well. His finger trembled as he pointed to the photo: it was of two men, one facing away, the other towards the camera. The one facing the camera was of athletic build, had long hair and wore sunglasses.

'This is taken by the video camera in the Wunderbar hotel. It shows the moment when the fake Weiss arrived at the hotel on Tuesday afternoon to do the Gigli work. The man with his back to the camera is one of our security agents checking his documents. We processed the image at once. The morphometric analyses coincide ninety-eight per cent with the man in Vienna and Munich, and ninety-five per cent with the woman. The possibility of false positives is around fourteen per cent. It's the same person, April, we're almost sure of it.'

'It's incredible.'

'I'm sorry, April, is something wrong?'

Bosch was alarmed that all of a sudden his colleague was sitting staring intently at a fixed point on the wall.

'I got a call from London,' said Miss Wood. 'My father is worse.'

'Oh, I'm so sorry. A lot worse?'

'Worse.'

Conversations about April Wood's private life tended to be monosyllabic, words uttered succinctly followed by prolonged silences. 'Good', 'bad', 'better' and 'worse' were the preferred options. As a result, all Bosch knew about her were rumours. He had heard that her father had influenced her significantly in a way he did not like to speculate on, and that he was now very ill in a private hospital in London. He also knew that Wood had never married, and that comments about her possible lesbianism were not infrequent. But the previous head of security, Gerhard Weyleb, had told him about her stormy relationship with Hirum Oslo, one of the most important and influential art critics in all Europe. Bosch admitted he only knew Oslo slightly, but even so could not see what possible attraction a woman like April could have found in that skinny, crippled, helpless creature.

Miss Wood was as passionate a mystery as the unexplored ocean bed. When they had first been introduced, Bosch had not liked her at all.

Judging by what had happened with Hendrickje, he surmised that he would end up falling in love with her.

'I'm really sorry about that, April,' he said.

She nodded briefly, then immediately changed her tone of voice.

'Great work, Lothar.'

'Thanks.'

Wood was not lavish with her praise, so these words made Lothar feel good. He did not believe he deserved them personally. It was his team who had done it all: the wonderful Nikki and the others. They had been busy with the task ever since Wood had suggested the possibility of comparing morphometric similarities in the images of all the people who had visited the exhibitions in Vienna and Munich. 'It's likely he came to explore the terrain before he went into action,' she had said, 'and most probably he did it in disguise.' The computers in the lower basement at the Atelier had not stopped their frantic activity since

Wednesday. Bosch had got the results that Friday morning, on his return from Munich. He was satisfied with his team's work, and pleased that she should acknowledge it.

'I'll tell you something,' Miss Wood said. 'My main doubt was whether it was *several* people or just one. In the first case, we would have been up against a well-structured organisation with people trained to carry out specific functions. The second possibility makes it more likely we're dealing with a *specialist*. That makes it more difficult, because we can't catch the small fry first and hope they lead us to the ringleader. We'll have to go shark fishing, Lothar. Are there any comparisons between the computer images of the girl with no papers and the supposed art dealer?'

'On the last page.'

Wood turned to it. On the left was a blow-up of the girl in Vienna and Munich; below them the face of the fake Weiss; at the top in the centre was the man spotted in Vienna and Munich; below that, a photo of Oscar Díaz; and on the right, the computer portraits of the girl without papers and the other girl called Brenda, drawn on the basis of information supplied by the barman in Vienna and Sieglinde Albrecht. They were six different people: it seemed incredible that a single person could have been all of them. Bosch could guess what Wood was thinking.

'What do you reckon?' he asked. 'Is it a man or a woman?'

'He or she is very slender,' replied Wood. 'I'm not sure about the sex, but they're very slender. When it's a woman, she's almost naked. When it's a man, he always wears suits and covers himself right up to the neck. But cerublastyne can't *take away*, it can only *add*. Look at those legs – the legs of the girl called Brenda. If it's a man, he must be of very slender build, and look very feminine, and have no body hair. Díaz and Weiss were of similar physical appearance, so probably he solved the problem by using a mould for the head and the thighs. Making the guy with the moustache's fat stomach was even easier: a theatrical prop, possibly. We haven't found any fingerprints anywhere, not even on the steering wheel of the van for *Deflowering*. That suggests our suspect uses cerublastyne moulds for the hands, which would also explain why *Deflowering*'s clothes were ripped to pieces, do

258

you remember? Díaz had big hands. If our man used them as moulds to make his cerublastyne hands it must have felt like he was using garden gloves. He couldn't do any delicate work. It would even have been difficult for him to unbutton his own jacket. The Artist has got very small hands, Lothar.'

Bosch shook his head as he studied the photos.

'It's incredible that this is only one person,' he said.

'I'm not so surprised,' replied Miss Wood. 'I've seen, guarded, and bought some transgender works which I'm afraid would completely destroy any convictions you might have about identity or gender. We live in a confused world, Lothar. A world which has become art, become simply the pleasure of concealing, of pretending to be something one is not, or that does not exist. Perhaps we never used to be like this, perhaps this has come about despite our true nature. Or perhaps we have been like this from the start, perhaps our *true* nature was always *concealment*, only now we have the means to make this possible.'

They fell silent. Bosch was taken aback by this philosophical outburst from a woman he considered the most practical person he had ever met. He wondered to what extent her father's illness was affecting her.

'I don't agree, ' he said. 'I'm convinced we're something more than mere appearance.'

'I'm not,' Wood replied in a strangely broken voice.

For a moment, they stared into each other's eyes. This was extremely painful for Bosch. She was so beautiful he could almost have cried. Looking at her gave him a stab of pleasure. In his youth he had smoked marijuana, and always had the same reaction on nights when he allowed himself certain excesses: a fitful sense of happiness that rolled down a dark slippery slope to end up in an equally tepid sadness. Somehow, his pleasures had always left behind a trail of tears.

'Be that as it may, the Artist is *art*,' she said after a further silence.

'What do you mean?'

'Until now we've thought he must be an expert, but now we can go further. You yourself said it: it's "incredible". Someone who's expert in cerublastyne knows how to use it, but that's all.

259

It would be like an ornament: the craftsman makes the disguise, and that's that. But what's the difference between an ornament and a work of art? A work of art is a *transformation*. Portraits are works of art because they transform themselves into the person they are representing.'

'A canvas . . .' Bosch murmured.

'Exactly. The Artist could be a former canvas who is expert in cerublastyne. There are bound to be several portraits in his curriculum.'

'A canvas who hates Van Tysch . . . a canvas who hates his painter. It sounds good.'

'It'll do as a working hypothesis. Do we have morphometric details of *all* the HD canvases in the world? Not just the ones on show now, but all the retired ones?'

'We could get them through the net. I'll talk to Nikki. But to study the details of all of them would take months, April. We need to narrow the field down.'

All of a sudden the atmosphere had changed. Now that he and Wood were thinking aloud, Bosch felt energetic and active. They both leaned forward studying the photos as they spoke.

'We can't narrow down the gender . . .'

'No, but we can be more precise about the professional experience: the use of cerublastyne for example. He or she has been more than an ornament or a marginal work of art. They may have done hypertragedy and art-shocks, but above all, lots of transgender art. We're up against a real expert in transgender work.'

'I agree, ' Bosch said.

'And we can assume he or she has worked for or otherwise been in contact with the Foundation: either as a sketch, an outline model, an original, whatever . . . How many do you reckon are left after that?'

'Several dozen.'

Wood sighed.

'Let's set the age limits as . . .' She thought for a second, then shook her head. 'Well, let's be logical about it. For example, we can eliminate kids and old people. It could be an adolescent or a young adult. We know the approximate morphometric details, so that will help. Talk to Nikki. Tell her she's looking for a model who's worked for us, young, of either sex, with experience in cerublastyne and transgender work, whose morphometric details fit. Once we've drawn up a list of possible suspects, we'll need to investigate where they are now, and cross off all those with a firm alibi. We need results by the middle of next week.'

'We can try.' Bosch felt euphoric. 'This is fantastic, April . . . We'll get there even before that Rip van Winkle outfit. It might even be us who captures him! I'd love to see Benoit's face if that happens . . .'

Miss Wood was staring at him. After a moment she said:

'There's one small problem, Lothar. After our meeting with the Rip van Winkle people in Munich yesterday, I went with Stein to the airport, if you remember.'

'Yes, but I don't know what you told him.'

'I think I might have put my foot in it. I told him things I shouldn't have. I can't trust anyone. No one, apart from the Maestro. But the Maestro is inaccessible.'

'Is that why you haven't told me? Because you don't trust me?' Bosch had asked the question as gently as possible. Nothing in his tone of voice or his expression could lead her to think he was offended.

Miss Wood gave no reply. She stared down at the floor. Bosch began to get anxious.

'Is it something that serious?'

Slowly, almost painfully, Wood told him about Marthe Schimmel and the platinum-blond boy. Bosch listened, disbelieving.

'That bastard has the advantage,' said Wood. 'Someone is passing him information from *inside*. Someone is helping him! I've had two sleepless nights just thinking about it . . . he must be someone senior: he knows the valid codes, has prior knowledge of our security measures . . . It could be . . . Who? . . . Paul Benoit. It could be Paul Benoit. Or Jacob Stein, even though I find it impossible to believe it could be him, which is why I told him my suspicions yesterday. I'm convinced Stein would never damage one of the Maestro's works: he admires him as much as I do, or even more . . . But in spite of everything, he's refused to postpone the "Rembrandt" exhibition . . . It could be Kurt Sorensen or Gert Warfell . . . Or Thea . . . Or it could be you, Lothar.' She fixed her blue eyes on him. Her face was a tense mask shiny with make-up. 'Or *me*. I know it's not me, of course, but I'd like *you* to think *it could be me* . . .'

'April . . .'

He had never seen Miss Wood in such a state. She had stood up and was almost trembling. She seemed on the verge of burst-ing into tears.

'I'm not used to having to work like this . . . I can't bear failing, and yet I know I'm going to fail . . .'

'For God's sake, April, calm down . . .'

Bosch stood up, too. He was thunderstruck. He wanted to embrace her, and despite the fact that he had never before done so, or even dared to try, he went up to her and put his arms round her. It felt as though he were enfolding such a fragile and ephemeral creature that he almost became frightened. Now that he was with her, now that he could *sense* her, April seemed like a small silver figurine, something tiny and tremulous perched on the edge of a table and about to fall off. This sensation led him to throw off all his remaining caution and to clasp her even more tightly. He joined his hands behind Wood's back and drew her to him. She was not crying, only trembling. She leaned her head on his shoulder and trembled. Unable to say a word, Bosch went on holding her.

Then all at once it was over. Her hands pushed him away gently but firmly. April Wood turned her back to him. When he could see her face again, Bosch immediately recognised the Head of Security. If she had noticed anything, if she had had some inkling of his affection, she apparently now dismissed it as unim-portant.

'Thanks, I feel better now, Lothar. The problem is . . . the thing is . . . someone in the Foundation wants to destroy works by the Maestro. That much is clear to me. The motive does not matter for now. Maybe he hates him. Or perhaps he's being paid to help. His antennae will go on passing information to the Artist, his damned antennae will go on doing that, and the Artist will work out his plan, or will change it (because I'm sure he *already* has a plan) on the basis of our decisions . . . In conclusion, I don't think we can catch him. Our only hope is to *anticipate* what he is going to do. We have to find out what his next target is and set him a trap *of our own.'*

She paused. She was as tough and hard as ever again. As she spoke, she frowned deeply.

'Let's start from the hypothesis that the Artist is going to try to destroy one of the "Rembrandt" paintings. Which one? There are thirteen of them. They are going to be on show in a five-hundred-metre-long tunnel specially built out of plastic curtain material in the Museumplein. The tunnel interior will be completely dark apart from the glow coming from the works themselves. We can't even use infra-red to protect them. Thirteen hyperdramatic works based on a similar number of works by Rembrandt: *The Anatomy Lesson, The Night Watch, Christ on the Cross, The Jewish Bride* . . . It's an amazing show, but it's very risky, too. If we only knew beforehand which work it might be, we could set a trap. But how can we find out? Some of the works aren't even finished yet. In fact, assistants from the Art section are still drawing sketches on our farms. How can we possibly know which painting the Artist will choose this time, if they aren't even completed?'

Bosch decided to be reassuring.

'I'm not so worried about the "Rembrandt" exhibition, April: there's almost an entire army guarding each painting inside and outside the tunnel, as well as the regional police and the KLPD. And in the hotel there'll be lots of security agents on guard inside the rooms. The paintings aren't going to be left alone for a second. We'll keep a constant check on the identity of our men by analysing their finger- and voiceprints. And they'll all be new guards, chosen at the last minute. What can go wrong?'

Wood stared at him, then asked:

'Have you been sent the list of the original models who will be the paintings?'

'Not yet. I know Kirsten Kirstenman and Gustavo Onfretti are two of them, but . . .' He saw April Wood's face cloud over with concern again. He could not bear it, and tried to encourage her. 'April, *nothing is going to happen*, you'll see. It's not just

simple-minded optimism, it's a logical calculation. We're going
to be able to rescue the "Rembrandt" collection, I'm—'

Wood interrupted him.

'You know one of the models intimately, Lothar.'

She paused. Bosch stared at her dumbfounded.

'Your niece Danielle will be one of the paintings.'

8

The arms flinging themselves at her in the darkness reminded
her of a drawing of night.

She screamed and tried to roll across the mattress, her brain
dissolving in an ocean of terror. Something clamped her wrists,
then a rough heavy weight fell across her stomach. She was flat
on her back, struggling and screaming. A spider controlled by a
higher intelligence felt for her lipless mouth, her mouth where
the lips had been stamped, and flattened itself against her. It was
a hand. She could not scream any more. Another hand was
crushing her right wrist. She fought to get a mouthful of air. The
gag left her nostrils free, but she needed to *swallow* oxygen. Her
breasts were crushed against some material. Two tiny mirrors
floated a few inches from her eyes: she could see them perfectly,
even in the darkness, and thought she caught sight of her own
gagged face in them.

'Be quiet . . . stay still . . . still . . .'

Now at last she knew who it was (that voice, those arms, there
could not be two people like that) and managed to *intuit* what
was going on. But the earlier impact had been too fierce, and she
was not prepared. She knew they wanted her *not to be* prepared.
Even so, she needed to be. If she was on the point of going
beyond the final barrier, she needed to gather strength. She struggled again. A hand clasped her hair.

'I'm going to tell you . . . to tell you . . . what will happen . . . if
you don't do as I wish . . . if you don't do as I wish . . .'

Each phrase poured into her ear was accompanied by a violent tug at her hair. Uhl made her see stars. But he had also made a mistake: he had allowed her to recuperate too much. Clara was mistress of her body and her emotions again. She was still very weak, but she could react. She slammed her feet on to the floor and flung her hips upwards in a move that took Uhl by surprise. She was expecting a more violent response, and it was not long in coming. He slapped her. Not very hard, but enough to stun her.

'Don't do that again . . . what are you playing at, eh . . . ?'

She lay still, panting, trying to work out what to do next. She knew that if she gave in, it would all come to a stop. She was *completely sure of that*. But she did not want to. If she took the risk, if she faced up to whatever Uhl was doing, he would increase the darkness of his brushstroke. If she went on fighting him, the stretching would cross the barrier and there would be a 'leap into the void'. She had never experienced this 'leap into the void' with any painter, because it was too dangerous a technique. It could end up badly: she could be damaged, perhaps seriously. And the damage could prove irreparable. Even though she was not working in an art-shock, it was clear that the sketch was very strong (*the toughest, most risky*). She was very frightened: she did not want to suffer or die, but nor did she want to halt the process. She no longer had any doubt that they were painting her, and she did not want to get in their way. She wanted to surrender to them just as she had to Vicky, Brentano, Hobber, or Gurnsich.

Still clasping her hair, Uhl stepped back as if he wanted to show her captured head to someone. The beam from a torch blinded her.

'Do as I wish, eh? . . . Are you going to be good? To give me what I want? . . .'

She responded by kicking out with her knee at the shadows. This caused her aggressor to fling himself on her again with renewed fury. She struggled to resist. She was terrified, and *precisely because of that*, precisely because of that, she wanted to go on. She was trembling, panting, expecting something terrible to happen, *hoping* that something *terrible* would happen, hoping that the black hand of art would finally lead her to that sovereign darkness from which there was no return, no possibility of salvation. She wanted Uhl to paint her with more intense, darker

shades: with Dutch colours. She fought like a wildcat, opened her mouth to bite him. She was expecting another slap, and prepared herself to receive it.

But instead, it all came to a halt. She heard shouts. Uhl let go of her. She found herself alone, face upwards on the mattress. She could hardly believe it. She recognised the youthful impetuousness of Gerardo's voice. The lights came on and made her blink.

In the kitchen, the silence was immense. Uhl had prepared coffee for Gerardo and Clara, and coffee substitute for himself. He explained in his rudimentary Spanish that he had high-blood pressure. Seeing what had happened in the bedroom half an hour earlier, this sounded like a joke, but none of them laughed.

'Sugar?' Uhl asked.

'No, thanks,' said Clara.

They were both still breathing heavily after their violent painting exercise. Clara had a few unimportant red marks that did not even hurt her. She had put her robe on. Uhl left the kitchen, and Clara and Gerardo sat in silence for a while, drinking their coffee. The morning was lightening outside the window. Against a background of distant traffic noise, the birds had begun their clear conversation. All at once, Gerardo looked directly at her. His eyes were red, as though he had been crying. His musketeer's chin and fine moustache looked less carefully groomed than usual, as if they were part of the general look of dismay on his face. But when a moment later he spoke, his tone was as bright and cheerful as ever.

'I've spoilt everything, sweetheart. But I swear to God I couldn't carry on. I simply couldn't. I couldn't care less if they throw me out. The Maestro might get rid of me, but it's all the same. I'm fed up with it.'

He looked at Clara and smiled. She remained cruelly silent.

'You were having a bad time, sweetheart. Very bad. Why didn't you yield? Didn't you know that the only way to lighten the tone was for you to give in? If you'd done that, we'd have stopped painting you . . .'

There was a silence.

'Come on, let's go for a walk,' said Gerardo, standing up.

'No, I'm not going.'
'Come on, don't be . . .'
'No.'
'Please.'
His tone of entreaty made her glance up.
'I've got something important to tell you,' he murmured.

It was early morning, and a cool northerly breeze rustled through the leaves, branches and the grass, raised clouds and dust, lifted the edges of clothing, the bottom of her robe, the fringe of her primed hair. The windmills were no more than ghostly shadows in the distance. Gerardo walked alongside her, hands in pockets. As they passed in front of hedges and houses, Clara wondered what other paintings were inside, and who was painting them. The small wood was off to her left. There was a scent of flowers and cut grass. The birds had started their special morning chorus.

'There are cameras,' was the first thing Gerardo said. 'That's why I didn't want to talk indoors. Cameras hidden in the room corners. You won't spot them if you don't know where to look. They're recording everything, even at night. Afterwards the Maestro views the recordings and rejects poses, gestures, some of the techniques.' He pulled a face wryly. 'And now he may reject me, too.'

'The . . . Maestro?'

She did not want to ask the most important question of all, but her heart was in her mouth as she stared at Gerardo.

'Yes. What does it matter if I tell you . . . I guess you knew right from the start. It's the Maestro Bruno van Tysch, himself, who is going to paint you. He's the one who has contracted you. You are to be one of the "Rembrandt" collection. Congratulations. That was what you wanted most of all, wasn't it?'

She did not reply. Yes, it was what she wanted most of all. And there it was. She'd got it. Her goal, her main objective. And yet she was hearing the news like this, walking along in a bathrobe in the midst of this stupid rural landscape, from the lips of this inept cretin, this bumpkin she could not even bother to hate.

'I've never seen Van Tysch in person,' she said, for the sake of saying something.

'You've been seeing him ever since you came to the house,' Gerardo said with a smile. 'The man in the photo with his back to the camera is him. It was taken by a famous photographer, Sterling I think his name is . . .'

Clara recalled the outline of the man facing away from the camera surrounded by darkness that had so impressed her since her arrival at the farm. That silent, tragic, black-haired figure . . . why hadn't she realised before now?

Van Tysch. The Maestro. The shadow.

'The Maestro will be giving you the final touches, sweetheart,' explained Gerardo. 'Doesn't that make you happy?'

'Yes,' she replied.

The sun had come out. The first rays climbed like a golden glow behind Clara's back. The trees, the wooden fences, the lane and her own body were bathed in light and started to throw shadows. Gerardo was still walking along, hands in pockets, staring down at the ground. He began to talk again, as if speaking to himself.

'Justus and I have been making sketches for the Maestro and Stein for some time now. For the "Rembrandt" collection for example we've already painted two figures besides you. With some of them we've managed the leap into the void, but they all pull back in time. They always pull back. Uhl and I could have reached the *limit* with you, but we were expecting you to pull back the way you did yesterday afternoon . . . If you had yielded again last night, it would all have come to a halt! Why on earth didn't you yield?'

'Why didn't you go on to the limit?'

Clara asked the question without raising her voice. Gerardo looked at her, but did not reply.

All of a sudden, Clara felt she could not contain her anger. She released it in slow bursts, not taking her eyes off him.

'From the start, all you've done is to try to ruin everything for me. During the break yesterday you told me things you should never have said . . . You revealed part of the technique Uhl was using! . . .'

'I know! I was only trying to help. I was worried we might hurt you!'

268

'Why didn't you just paint me, like Uhl did?'

'Uhl has an advantage.'

Clara was sure that if he had thought twice about it, Gerardo would have bitten his tongue before he said anything like that. All at once, his face had turned puce. He looked away from her.

'I mean I'm not like Justus . . . you could never . . . well, it's not relevant . . . what I'm trying to say is that with you he can pretend more easily, he can be cooler than I can. That's why he's taken the initiative right from the start.'

Clara stared at him in astonishment. It seemed incredible to her that Gerardo should refer to Uhl's tendencies like that just to excuse his own mistakes.

'We needed to create a climate of constant harassment around you,' said Gerardo. 'A sexual threat, but also the feeling you were being watched. Ever since they contracted you in Madrid, Art have been trying to convey that sensation. Justus and I took turns going round outside the farm at night and looking in at your window. We even made a noise so you would wake up and see us. Conservation had instructions to give you another, more reassuring explanation. This was to give us the surprise factor for whenever we decided, like today, to paint you with a more violent brushstroke. Then in the mornings we pretended to be getting on badly so you would believe Justus was an unpleasant character who abused female canvases. In fact, Justus is a wonderful person . . . all this is closely related to the work we're painting with you. It's a Rembrandt, but I can't tell you which one . . .'

'The instructions came directly from the Maestro, didn't they?' Clara would not take her yellow, primed brow and lashless eyes off Gerardo's face. 'And this morning's "leap into the void": Van Tysch was trying out an expression with me, wasn't he?' She was so desperately angry she almost choked. 'And you *messed up* the drawing. Completely. I was *nearly* drawn, nearly finished, and you . . . ! You got hold of me, you crumpled me up, you made me a paper ball and tossed me *in the shit*.'

She thought she was crying, but realised her eyes were still dry. Gerardo's face had become a pallid mask. Trembling with rage, Clara went on:

'Congratulations, sweetheart.'

She turned on her heel and walked off towards the house. Now the wind was blowing at her from the other side. She heard Gerardo's voice further and further off, increasingly shrill.

'Clara! . . . Clara, come back, please . . . Listen to me . . . !'

She speeded up without looking back, until finally she could no longer hear him. Polygonal clouds began to obscure the early sun. When she reached the house, Uhl was out on the porch. He waved to stop her, and asked where Gerardo was.

'He's coming,' she muttered.

It was then she noticed just how Uhl was looking at her. His tiny, dioptrical eyes were blinking in their glass prisons. Clara realised he was very nervous. The painter spoke in his hesitant Spanish.

'Van Tysch secretary call now . . . Van Tysch come here.'

She felt dreadfully cold. She rubbed her arms energetically, but the chill did not diminish. She knew it had nothing to do with the fact that all she was wearing was the short robe that barely covered her thighs: she had been primed with a protective layer of acrylic gesso and, like every other professional canvas, was accustomed to more extreme temperatures. This cold was inside her, and directly related to the news she had just heard.

Van Tysch. Coming there. His arrival expected at any moment.

A canvas' emotions faced with the presence of a great maestro are hard to explain. Clara tried to think of a comparison but could not: no actor would feel overwhelmed by the shadow of a great director; no student would get cold shakes like this in the presence of a professor they admired.

My God, she really was shaking. To prevent Uhl realising her teeth were chattering, she went inside the house and walked up and down the living room. Then she took off the robe and went into a simple sketch pose, almost reaching a state of quiescence.

Opposite her on the wall was the photo of the man with his back to the camera.

People only knew about Van Tysch's appearance from the changing images shown in magazines and reports. Nor did Clara know anything definite about his way of life. Painters and paintings talked about him a lot, but, in fact, their opinions had little basis in reality. Yet Clara could clearly recall the impressions of those who *had* seen him. Vicky for example, who had taken part in some master classes he had given, said she had felt as though she were in the presence of an automaton, a thing without life of its own, a Frankenstein's monster created by the monster itself. 'But its creator forgot to breathe life into him,' she added. Two years earlier in Bilbao, Clara had met Gustavo Onfretti, who was on show at the Basque Country Guggenheim as Ferrucioli's *Saint Sebastian*, and had been painted by Van Tysch as another saint: *Saint Stephen*. She had asked him about his experience with the great painter of Edenburg. The Argentine model had gazed at her darkly for a long while before saying only: 'Van Tysch is your shadow.'

Van Tysch. The Maestro. The shadow. *He was coming.*

She looked away from the photo and stared at the walls instead. She could see dull patches at the ceiling corners, and thought this must be where the cameras were hidden. She imagined Van Tysch studying his screen, pressing the keyboard, judging her expression and her worth as a canvas. She was annoyed with herself for not having thought of the possibility of hidden cameras before. A lot of painters used them: Brentano, Hobber, Ferrucioli . . . if she had known, or suspected it, she would have made a greater effort. Not that this would have been much use after the mess Gerardo had made of everything. What if Van Tysch was coming to sack her? What if he said to her (that is, if he spoke to her and not to his lackeys, because after all she was simply the *material*): 'I'm sorry, I've been thinking about it, and you're not the right person for this painting'?

'Calm down. Let it happen.'

Gerardo and Uhl had come into the room. They were storing paint pots in bags. Clara came out of her sketch position and looked at them.

'Are you leaving?' she asked in English. She did not much like the idea of having to face the Maestro on her own in the house.

'No, no we can't, we have to wait for him,' said Uhl. 'We're cleaning up a bit to create a good impression,' he added – or at least that's what Clara thought he said, because Uhl's English was very rapid. 'We have to wait to see if he wants us to continue in the same line or not. Perhaps he wants to do the sketching himself. Or perhaps . . .' This was followed by a rapid burst of words that Clara did not catch. 'It could be anything. We have to be prepared. Sometimes . . .' He raised his eyebrows, spread his hands and puffed, as if to demonstrate that Van Tysch was unpredictable and they could only expect the worst. She did not really understand what he was trying to say, and was too scared to ask him to explain. 'Understand?'

'Yes,' she said, lying in English.

'Keep calm,' Uhl replied in Spanish. 'Everything's all right.'

He's paying back my lie in Spanish, thought Clara.

The shadow.

Points, lines, polygons, bodies. And last of all, the shading that defines the outlines, adds volume to the definitive shape.

When we are waiting for someone we do not know, we see them as a silhouette rising up in front of us. So we start drawing them, filling in the details, *anticipating* them. We are aware the whole time that we are making mistakes, that the real person will not be exactly the same as our outline, but we cannot get it out of our mind. Then it becomes a fetish, a simple representation of the object, a doll we can practise on. We place ourselves in front of it and weigh up our possible reactions. What should I say or do? Will he like me as I am? Should I smile and be friendly, or should I be cold towards him, keep my distance? Clara had already drawn her Van Tysch silhouette: she imagined him to be tall and thin, silent, with a piercing gaze. Without knowing why (perhaps because she remembered a couple of photos from magazines) she had added glasses, with broad lenses that would increase the size of his pupils. She had given him some defects as well, naturally, because she was terrified she might be disappointed. Van Tysch would be ugly. Van Tysch would be selfish. Van Tysch would be rude. Van Tysch would be brutal. Clara soon discovered she could easily forgive 'defects' such as these in a genius like him. She tried adding others that were less pardonable: a Van Tysch who was stupid, clumsy or vulgar. The last of these, a *vulgar* Van Tysch, was the worst thing she could think of.

272

Even so, she tried to imagine it. A Van Tysch who talked and thought like Jorge (My God!), who would *calm her down,* and who she could *surprise.* A mature Van Tysch next to whom she, at twenty-four, could feel *superior.* Or a Van Tysch like Gerardo, wet behind the ears, unsophisticated. She chastised herself with all these Van Tysches, like wearing a hair shirt. She used them as a penitence for the pleasure that the real person was bound to bring her.

She decided the morning would be one long vigil. She set up her headquarters in the kitchen: she could see the front of the house from its window. She preferred to devote her time to *waiting* rather than to pretend, as Gerardo and Uhl were (they were outside on the porch, chatting) that nothing was going on. At noon she took a vitamin Aroxen drink from the fridge, perforated the top with a straw, and began to sip it. The robe was still half-open over her crossed thighs. For some time she had been thinking about *preparing herself* in some form or other. Perhaps it would be better if she were completely naked? What if she painted some features on her face, or at least coloured her eyes in or outlined her lips in the shape of a smile? But wasn't she a blank sheet? Shouldn't she go on being one? She concluded it would be best for her to be as passive as possible.

The sun began to cross the window, and brushed at her feet. As it climbed her shins, her primed skin sparkled. Occasionally she was startled by the noise of an engine or the fleeting passage of a vehicle on the lane outside. But calm soon returned.

A short while later, the kitchen door opened and Gerardo came in. He had taken his jacket off, and his sleeveless T-shirt with the Foundation logo showed off his biceps. He was fiddling nervously with the turquoise-coloured label with his name and photo on it. He opened the fridge, appeared to think better of it, closed it without taking anything out, and sat down opposite her at the far end of the table. Poor thing, thought Clara from her personal nirvana, infinitely compassionate.

'Listen, I'm really sorry for what happened out there, OK?' Gerardo said after a pause.

'No, no, on the contrary,' she hurriedly replied. 'I was silly. I'm sorry I got like that.'

They were sitting diagonally opposite each other, and had to turn their heads (Gerardo to the left, Clara to the right) to look at each other when they spoke. They listened to the reply staring at the window, the tiny rectangle of blue sky, the shadows of the clouds.

'Anyway, I wanted to tell you not to worry. If the Maestro has it in for anyone, it'll be me. You are the canvas and can't be blamed for anything, OK?'

'We'll let's be optimistic, shall we?' she replied. 'Perhaps Van Tysch is coming just to supervise the sketching. There's less than a fortnight to the opening.'

'Yes, perhaps you're right. Are you nervous?'

'A bit.'

They smiled at each other, then fell silent again.

'I've only seen him a couple of times,' said Gerardo after another pause. 'And then only at a distance.'

'You mean you've *never* spoken to him?'

'Never. Seriously, I'm not joking. The Maestro never talks to the assistants because he has no need to. The visible head of the Foundation is Mr *Fuschus-Galismus* . . . I mean Jacob Stein. He's the one who calls you, contracts you, talks to you, gives you orders . . . Van Tysch has ideas and writes them down. His assistants pass them on to us, and as technical assistants it's our job to carry them out, that's all. Van Tysch is a very odd person. I imagine all geniuses are. You know his life story, don't you?'

'Yes, I've read a few things.'

In fact, Clara had devoured every single one of the painter's biographies, and knew all the few confirmed details about him.

'His life is like a fairy story, isn't it?' said Gerardo. 'Out of the blue, a North American millionaire goes wild about him, and leaves him his entire fortune. It's incredible.' He leant back, head in hands and stared at the landscape outside the window. 'Do you know how many houses Van Tysch has now? Approximately six, except they're not houses, but palaces: a castle in Scotland, some kind of monastery in Corfu . . . but do you know, they say he never visits them?'

'What does he want them for then?'

'No idea. I suppose he likes having them. He lives in Edenburg, the castle where his father worked as a restorer. People who've been there tell so many stories it's hard to know what to believe. They claim, for example, that there's no furniture, and that Van Tysch eats and sleeps on the floor.'

'That seems a bit far-fetched.'

Gerardo was about to respond when they heard a noise. A van had pulled up by the front hedge. Clara's heart started pumping, her whole body became tense. But Gerardo reassured her.

'No, it's not him.'

But it must have been someone Gerardo and Uhl knew, because they both went out to the front to greet them. A black man with a cap and a black leather jacket got out of the van. After him appeared an older, bearded man and a girl with long black hair. The girl was very short, so the hair came down to the back of her legs. Both of them were barefoot, and their legs were stained with mud and red paint, or perhaps it was blood. They had orange labels round their necks, wrists and ankles, and they looked tired. Clara recalled that orange meant they were preparatory sketches, people who trained and prepared the final sketches. The black man was young and slim, with a beard like Gerardo's. His boots were caked in mud. A few moments later, they all said goodbye, and the black man and his tired, dirty models climbed back into the van and drove off.

'That was another assistant friend of ours,' Gerardo explained when he came back into the kitchen. 'He's working at a nearby farm with those preparatory sketches, but he had some news he wanted to tell us. It seems they've withdrawn the "Flowers" exhibition from the MuseumsQuartier in Vienna.'

'Why?'

'Nobody can understand it. Conservation says the canvases needed a rest, and they preferred to cut the length of time they were on show in the MuseumsQuartier in favour of elsewhere. But our friend says they're doing the same with "Monsters" in the Haus der Kunst at Munich. I've no idea what's going on. No, don't look sad like that. They're going ahead with "Rembrandt".'

By the afternoon there was still no sign of Van Tysch, and Clara could hardly bear it. Her anxiety was *humanising* her, stealing her

275

existence as an object from her and turning her back into a person, into a nervous young woman who wanted to bite her fingernails. She knew that to be so anxious was dangerous. She had to ward off this enemy, because the painter could arrive at any moment, and she had to be there waiting for him shiny and calm, ready for whatever Van Tysch might want to use her as.

She decided to do press-ups. She shut herself in the bedroom, took off her robe, and lay flat on the floor with her legs slightly apart. Pushing on her hands and toes, she began a series of rapid press-ups combined with deep breathing. At first, the effect was merely to make her heart beat faster, but as she continued, up down, up down, straining her arm and leg tendons, feeling the muscles in her limbs, she eventually managed to forget herself and the situation she was in, and surrendered to the exhausting sensation of being a body, a tool.

Time went by. She did not realise someone had come into the room until they were almost on top of her.

'Hey.'

She raised her head quickly. It was Gerardo.

'What is it?' she asked nervously.

'Calm down, there's nothing new. I just thought it might be better if we painted your hair so that the Maestro can tell us what he thinks of the colour.'

He did the painting in the bathroom. Clara sat astride a chair with her legs stretched out and a towel wrapped round her body. Gerardo used a cap soaked in a mahogany-red colour and a fixing spray.

'The butterfly emerging from its chrysalis,' he said, removing the cap gently. He began to put in the paint with his gloved hands. 'Isn't that what you said yesterday, when I asked you why you wanted to be a masterpiece? You said you didn't know, "but then a caterpillar doesn't know why it wants to be a butterfly". I told you it seemed to me a nice but false answer. You're no caterpillar, are you? You're a very attractive woman, even if at this very moment, with no features, primed, and your hair this red mahogany colour, you do look rather like a plastic doll who hasn't been painted yet. But underneath all the plastic, it's you who is the true work of art.'

276

Clara said nothing. She stared up at Gerardo's face over her shoulder.

'Shut your eyes . . . I'm going to use the spray . . . here goes . . .' She could feel the mist of liquid on her hair. Gerardo went on: ' I can understand you're upset with me, sweetheart. But do you know something? If last night's situation happened again, I'd do exactly the same all over again . . . I can only go so far. I am not, and never will be, a great master of painting people . . . . good, the colour's looking fine . . . wait, don't say anything . . . Justus could have made it, but he doesn't have the ambition. I'm incapable of scaring or hurting a girl I like, even for the sake of creating a great work of art. For me, all of hyperdrama becomes . . . you know what? . . . it becomes hypercomedy. I know I'm a bit of a clown, my mother always told me so. That's right . . . now we have to wait a few minutes . . .'

She listened to all of this in silence. When she opened her eyes again, Gerardo had disappeared from her field of vision. The strong smell of the hairspray filled her nostrils. Then Gerardo's hands reappeared. This time they were holding a small pot of ochre paint and a fine paintbrush.

'For me there's a frontier,' he said, dipping the brush in the paint and leaning over Clara's face. 'A frontier, sweetheart, that art will never be able to cross. The frontier of emotions. On one side there are people. On the other, art. Nothing in the world can cross that frontier.'

'He's painting eyebrows on me,' she thought. She stiffened, wondering whether she ought to tell him that perhaps the Maestro did not want her to have features, but in the end she said nothing. She could feel the cold curves of the brush on her forehead.

Gerardo's hand was steady as he drew the precise firm lines of the curves, and pointed the wet dip of the brush down towards her eyes. She shut them, and felt something like a bird's caress: tremulous beating, then the start of the delicate fringe of her eyelashes, the frame of her gaze.

'I believe in art, sweetheart, but I believe much more in emotions. I cannot betray myself. I prefer a thousand times a mediocre work of art to the contempt of someone I like . . .

Someone I have begun to . . . respect and to get to know . . . Don't move . . .'

Eyebrows. Small drops of brown lashes. The faintest of touches at the corner of her eyes. Clara was about to speak, but Gerardo stopped her with a gesture.

'Silence, please. The artist is about to put the final touches to his creation.'

A line curving neatly upwards from the left side of her mouth.

'I reckon the world wouldn't be so perverse if everyone thought the same as me . . . the lips are always really difficult . . . why have they got such a strange shape? It must be so they can tell lies.'

The line moved on downwards. To Clara it felt as though a bird were walking around the edge of her mouth.

'I like it,' said Gerardo, standing back to get a good look at her. 'Definitely, I like it. You've turned out very beautiful. Wait, then you can see yourself.'

He picked something up from the washstand. It was a small round mirror. He came back to her.

'Ready?'

Clara nodded. Gerardo was holding up the mirror as if he was a priest with a consecrated host, and put it in front of her face.

She looked at herself.

A face with features looked back at her.

Gentle waves beneath her forehead, elliptic waves, a symmetry of ochre curves. She raised her unexpected eyebrows, amazed at her newly born way of expressing astonishment. She blinked, and felt the caress of eyelashes darting like sparrows around the language of her eyes, eyes which had never been silenced, only deprived for some time of their appearance, but now once again shone full of light. She smiled and lifted the corners of her mouth to demonstrate that a slit cut into a face could never, ever be a smile; that a real smile was what Gerardo had painted on her: a mass of shapes relaxing, a distorted volume moving at the same moment as the eyes fulfil their mission and the eyelids close. It was wonderful to have features once again.

Gerardo held up the mirror with her face floating in it like a precious gift.

'At last I can see you smile,' he said, very serious. 'And hard work it was, sweetheart. But finally you're smiling at me.'

Clara was impressed by his seriousness. She thought that perhaps she had misjudged him from the start. It was like seeing him for the first time. As if there were something inside Gerardo that was much wiser, more mature than he himself or the words he spoke. For a moment she thought that Gerardo's face had also been painted, delineated like hers, but with more indistinct shadows. It was a fleeting vision, but for that split second she thought the secret of life consisted in getting beyond the features drawn, and reaching the people who lay behind them.

She had no idea how long she sat like that, in front of the mirror he was holding up for her, looking at it and at herself. All at once she heard his voice again. But the mirror was no longer there, and Gerardo was leaning over her. His face was taut and nervous.

'Clara . . . Clara, *he's here* . . . I heard his car . . . Listen to me . . . Do everything he asks you to . . . don't quarrel with his way of working, do you hear? . . . Above all, above *all*, don't argue with him . . . And don't be surprised *whatever* he asks . . . he's a very strange man . . . he likes to confuse his canvases . . . Be careful with him. Very careful.'

At that moment they heard Uhl's voice calling them. Words in frantic Dutch, the sound of doors. They ran to the living room, but there was no one there. The front door was open, and they could hear a conversation out on the porch. They went out together, then Clara came to an abrupt halt.

There was a man with his back to her, talking to Uhl. His silhouette stood out against the evening sky: an austere, black shadow.

Uhl saw Clara and gestured to her. He was very pale.

'Let me introduce you . . . to Mr Bruno van Tysch.'

Then the man turned slowly to face her.

Third Step

The Finishing Touches

Now we have to define the figures: to give them a look, an identity. Not until the figures have been fully delineated in this way can we say that the work is finished.

BRUNO VAN TYSCH *Treatise on Hyperdramatic Art*

'The question is,' said Alice, 'whether you can make words mean so many different things.'
'The question is,' said Humpty Dumpty, 'which is to be master – that's all.'

LEWIS CARROLL *Through the Looking Glass*

1

The figure seated behind the desk is a mature, thickset man. He is wearing an immaculate dark-blue suit with a red label attached to the top jacket pocket. He is sitting at the centre of a V-shaped desk, with three framed photos on one side of it. The light streaming in through two high windows behind him emphasises his bald patch, surrounded by tufts of white. There is a certain nobility to his features: blue eyes, aquiline nose, thin lips, and wrinkles that show the inevitable passage of time but give him a distinguished look. He appears to be listening closely to what he is being told, but if we observe him more closely, perhaps he is only *pretending* to concentrate. He is tired and worried, and cannot really take in what he is hearing, so he is barely following it. His head aches. And on top of all this, it's Monday. Monday 3 July, 2006.

'What's the matter, Lothar? You seem lost in space.'

Alfred van Hoore (the man speaking) and his colleague Rita van Dorn were studying him wide-eyed. At that moment (or until the moment Bosch went into his trance) they had been discussing the best distribution of security agents among the guests at the press viewing of the 'Rembrandt' collection on 13 July. Van Hoore thought extra protection was needed for *Jacob Wrestling with the Angel*, the only work from the collection due to be shown that day. The two agents on each side of the work were not enough – in Van Hoore's view – to prevent someone in the front row from leaping on to the plinth with a sharp instrument and damaging Paula Kircher or Johann van Allen, the two canvases who made up *Jacob*. He was arguing for another two agents to be placed in the centre, because an attack from there could not be repelled in time from the sides. And then there were the long-distance threats. He showed Bosch a computer simulation in which a supposed terrorist threw an object at the work from any point in the room. Van Hoore was young and loved simulations; he designed them himself. He had learned to programme them when he was coordinating security for exhibitions in the Middle East. Bosch thought Van Hoore would have liked to have been a film director: he moved the computer figures around as if they were actors, dressed them up and gave them human gestures. It was during the computer simulation that Bosch had got lost. He could not bear these silly cartoons.

'Perhaps it's because I'm tired,' he said as an excuse, drumming his fingers on the desk. 'But I do think you're making an interesting case, Alfred.'

Van Hoore's freckled face flushed.

'I'm glad,' he said. 'My reasoning is very simple: if we let Visual Security take care of the guests *nobody* will try anything. Any supposed terrorist would get away from them as quickly as possible. We need some of our people to form another group, which I have called Secret Visual Security. They would not wear uniforms or credentials, and would send alarm signals to the SWAT teams . . .'

Jacob Wrestling with the Angel was the first original from the 'Rembrandt' collection to be presented to the public. This meant there could not be too much protection. Nobody had seen the work as yet, but it was known that the figures were Paula Kircher (*Angel*) and Johann van Allen (*Jacob*) and that it was based on the Rembrandt painting of the same name. The models would be wearing few clothes, and their billionaire bodies – personally signed by Van Tysch – would be dangerously exposed during the four-hour presentation to the press. The Foundation's Security and Conservation departments were desperately concerned.

'I wonder,' said Rita, 'why we can't change half of Visual Security into a SWAT team in a crisis.'

Bosch was about to say something, but Van Hoore got in first.

'It's the same story as ever, Rita. Visual Security is not disguised and therefore forms part of the Foundation's official personnel. That in turn means it has to wear uniforms. But under the men's suits, specially designed by Nellie Siegel, there's scarcely enough room for a bullet-proof vest. And the women agents *couldn't* wear vests, or even electric stunners.'

284

'What the agents wear shouldn't affect their ability to protect the works,' Rita complained.

Bosch shut his eyes, wishing this also meant he would be unable to hear. The last thing he needed at this point was an argument between his assistants. His head was still throbbing.

'The Foundation is just as worried about *appearance* as security, Rita,' Van Hoore retorted. Unlike Bosch, he was quite happy to have an argument. 'There are no two ways about it. If there have to be ten people standing in a corner keeping an eye on everything, they ought to stand out. If possible, they should even all have the same colour hair. 'Symmetry, *fuschus*, symmetry,' he added, in a passable imitation of Stein's arrogant voice.

At that moment, Nikki came in. To Bosch, her arrival seemed like a breath of fresh air.

'Alfred, Rita: I think we'll have to call a halt to this interesting discussion for now. I need to talk to our search team.'

'As you wish,' Van Hoore said, disappointed. 'But we still need to talk about ID for the event.'

'Later, later,' said Bosch. 'I've got a lunch appointment with Benoit, but – listen everybody – before lunch I have a few minutes when *I have nothing scheduled*. Amazing, isn't it? I'll talk to you then.'

Rita and Alfred smiled as they stood up.

'Everything's under control, Lothar,' Rita said gently as she left. 'Don't worry.'

'I'll try to think positively,' Bosch replied, then suddenly realised this was the same reply he used to give to Hendrickje just to make her shut up.

When the door closed behind them, Bosch took his head in his hands and breathed out a great sigh. Sitting opposite him with the apex of the desk triangle pointing at her midriff, Nikki observed him calmly. That morning she was wearing a tight-fitting jacket and trousers, whose canary-yellow colour matched the lemon yellow of her hair. Her white earpiece sat on top like a diadem.

'I could have got here earlier,' said Nikki, 'but I had to repair the damage from spending all night in front of the computer screens with Chris and Anita. I didn't look much like a decent Foundation employee this morning.'

'I understand. Appearance is everything.' Bosch smiled in symmetry with Nikki's beaming smile. 'I hope it's good news you're bringing.'

She handed over several sheets of paper, explaining as she did so.

'Morphometric similarities, considerable experience with portraits, and in cerublastyne disguises. They have all taken part in transgender work with androgynous or either sex figures. And no one knows where any of them are: we haven't been able to contact them either through painters or previous owners.'

Bosch studied the sheets of paper spread out on the desk.

'There are about thirty of them here. Couldn't you reduce the field any further?'

Nikki shook her head.

'On Friday we started out with a list of more than four hundred thousand people, Lothar. By the end of the weekend we had cut it down to first of all five thousand, then two hundred and fifty . . . Anita jumped for joy when we managed to bring it down to forty-two. Early this morning we were able to sift out another fifteen. So this is the best we can do.'

'I'll tell you what we'll do now . . . what we'll do now . . .'

'What we'll do is take a couple of aspirins,' Nikki said with a smile.

'Yes, that's not a bad idea to start with.'

Lothar had to be careful. Nikki and her team were not part of the 'crisis cabinet' as the committee at Obberlund had been pompously baptised, and so were unaware of everything to do with the Artist and the destruction of the two paintings. All they knew was it was vital to find someone expert in the use of cerublastyne with particular morphometric facial characteristics. And yet it was absurd to keep them out of the investigation. Thea is not going to be able to follow up all the remaining twenty-seven leads on her own, thought Bosch.

'A person doesn't just disappear into thin air, not even a sexless ornament,' he said. 'I want you to leave no stone unturned: family, friends, their last owners . . .'

'That's exactly what we have been doing, Lothar. No results.'

'If need be, call on Romberg's team. They have the operational capacity to move around.'

'We could look for them for a year and still come up with nothing,' Nikki replied. Bosch realised her tiredness was making her irritable. 'They may be dead, or be in hospital under another name. Or perhaps they've quit the profession: who knows? We can't search for them all on our own. Why don't we inform Interpol? The police have more resources.'

Because then Rip van Winkle would find out, thought Bosch. And, after Rip van Winkle, the Artist. Miss Wood and he had decided not to rely on Rip van Winkle unless it was absolutely necessary. They guessed that the person helping the Artist was part of the crisis cabinet and therefore that anything Rip van Winkle did would have no effect on the criminal. Lothar tried to think of a plausible excuse.

'The police won't search for anyone unless they receive a complaint, Nikki. And even if a family member of one of the canvases has reported their disappearance, the police work at their own pace. It's got to be us.'

Nikki looked at him sceptically. Bosch realised she was too clever not to see this as a sham, because Interpol would have done a belly dance if the Foundation had asked it to, complaint or no complaint.

'All right,' Nikki agreed after a pause. 'I'll use Romberg and his team. We'll divide the work.'

'Thanks,' Bosch said sincerely. Nikki, you're much more intelligent than I gave you credit for, he thought admiringly.

The intercom buzzed, and the switchboard voice came on.

'Mr Bosch: you have Mr Benoit on line three, but he says that I can reply if you're too busy. And on line two, your brother.'

Roland, thought Lothar. He could not stop himself glancing across at the photo of Danielle. The girl was smiling mischievously at him. Thank God, Roland at last.

'Tell Benoit . . . what is it he wants to ask me?'

Benoit wanted to confirm they were having lunch together in his office at midday. Bosch said yes, impatiently.

'Tell my brother not to hang up,' he said, turning to Nikki. 'Find out where they all are now. We won't cross anyone off the

287

list until we're sure they're either dead, have been bought, or are up for auction.'

'OK, and don't forget the aspirins.'

'I couldn't forget them even if I wanted to. Thanks, Nikki.'

Bosch shut his eyes when Nikki smiled at him. He wanted to keep her smile as his last mental image of her before she left the room. Once he was on his own, he picked up one of the cordless phones and pushed line two.

'Roland?'

'Hello there, Lothar.'

Lothar pictured his brother speaking from his own office, beneath the ghastly hologram of a human throat he always had on the wall. Lothar still wondered what on earth had happened to the Bosch family. One of the great secrets of the universe would be solved when someone worked out why his father had been a lawyer for a tobacco firm, his mother a history teacher, he himself a policeman and then a security chief for a private art firm, and his brother an ear, nose and throat specialist. Without forgetting little Danielle, who wanted to be ... or rather, who already was ...

'Roland, I've been trying to get in touch with you for days ...'

'I know, I know.' He could hear his brother's nervous laugh. 'I was at a congress in Sweden, and Hannah went to Paris. I suppose you were ringing about Nielle. You've heard, haven't you? ... Well, we played a dirty trick on you, and we're both sorry about that. But you have to understand: Stein strictly forbade us to say anything to you. So to explain your niece's absence we made up the story about her becoming a boarder at school. Don't think you were the only one who was deceived though. I only found out about all this less than two months ago ... It was Hannah's idea to introduce Nielle to Mr Stein. And Van Tysch took her on as a figure for an original straightaway! It's all happened in complete secrecy. They even told us that if Danielle hadn't been underage, we need never have known about it.'

'I understand, Roland. Don't worry.'

'My God, it's incredible. Well, you'll know that better than me. They have ... what do they call it ... they've *primed* her, they've shaved her eyebrows off . . . At first we weren't even allowed to see her . . . then they took us to the Old Atelier and we could watch her through a two-way mirror. She had labels round her neck, her hand and her feet. I thought . . . we thought she looked like a beautiful creature. I think we should be proud, Lothar. But do you know what she's most proud about? The fact that it's her uncle who is protecting her!'

Again his laughter at the far end of the line. Bosch closed his eyes and held the earpiece away from him. He felt a strong urge to break something. But he did not dare cut Roland off.

'Make sure you protect her properly, Uncle Lothar. She's a very valuable work. Can you imagine . . . ? No, I don't think you could. Last week they told us what her starting price was. Do you know what I thought when I heard how much *our daughter* was worth? I thought: why on earth did I become a doctor and not a work of art as well? . . . We've been wasting our time Lothar, wasting our time. Can you believe it? She's only ten years old, but Nielle is going to make more money than you or I could dream of earning in *our whole lives*! I wonder what father would have made of all this. I think he would have understood. In the end, he always gave a lot of importance to the value of things, didn't he? What was it he used to say: "The best possible results from the means available . . ."'

A pause. Bosch was staring at Danielle's portrait on his desk.

'Lothar?' his brother asked.

'Yes, Roland.'

'Is anything the matter?'

Of course something's the matter, you idiot. The matter is that you've allowed your daughter to become a painting. The matter is that you've let her be part of this exhibition. The matter is I want to tear you to pieces.

'No, nothing in particular,' he replied. 'I wanted to know how you were.'

'We're very nervous. What's happening with Nielle has got Hannah climbing the walls. And that's logical. It's not every day that your ten-year-old daughter becomes an immortal work of art. I've heard that at the end of next week Van Tysch is going to sign her with a tattoo on her thigh. Does that hurt?'

'No more than your tonsil operations,' Bosch joked half-heartedly. Then he plucked up the courage to say what he had to say. 'Roland, I was wondering . . .'

He could see her. He could see her lying back in the garden at Scheveningen, with the shadows from the leaves of an apple tree making a jigsaw pattern on her skin. He saw her stretched out in the sun, or talking to him while she scratched the sole of her foot. He could see her at Christmas, wearing a turtle-neck jersey with her golden curls cascading down her back, her mouth stained with cake. She was a little girl. A ten-year-old girl. But the problem wasn't the almost impossible idea that she should become a painting. It wasn't the dreadful fantasy of finding her naked and immobile in some collector or other's house. Any of this would have been depressing enough, but Lothar would never have protested: after all, he was not her father.

The problem was the Artist.

Be careful. Don't let him suspect that Danielle might be in danger.

'Roland, I was wondering . . .' he tried to sound as casual as possible. 'This is between just you and me . . . But I was wondering whether it might not be better to show a copy rather than Nielle.'

'A copy?'

'Yes; let me explain. When a model is underage, the parents or legal guardians always have the last say . . .'

'We signed a contract, Lothar.'

'I know, but that doesn't matter. Let me finish. To all intents and purposes, Nielle will still be the original model of the work, but for a short period another girl will replace her. That's what we mean by a copy.'

'Another girl?'

'Expensive works always have substitutes, Roland. They don't even have to look the same: there are products to disguise them, you know. Nielle would still be the original, and when someone buys her we would make sure it was her who was on show in the buyer's house. But if we substitute her we can avoid her having to be in this exhibition. They are always very difficult. There'll be lots of visitors, and the hours are very tough . . .'

290

Lothar was amazed at himself, at his ability to be so revolt-
ingly hypocritical. Above all, he was astonished to realise how
little he was concerned about the girl who would stand in for
Danielle. He himself recognised how desperate this plan was,
but it was a choice between his niece and an unknown girl.
People like Hendrickje would have opted for being sincere, and
openly revealing what was going on, or accepting that Danielle
would have to run the risks, but he was not as perfect as
Hendrickje. He was vulgar. And vulgar people, as Bosch saw it,
behaved in exactly this way: meanly, in a convoluted fashion.
All his life he had preferred silence to words, and now was going
to be no exception.

'You mean that as parents we have the authority to withdraw
Danielle from the work and get them to use a substitute in her
place?' Roland asked after a pause.

'That's right.'

'And why would we want to do that?'

'I've already explained. The exhibition will be tough for her.'

'But she's been preparing for it for three months, Lothar. She's
been painted in secret at some farm or other south of Amsterdam, and I . . .'

'I'm telling you from experience. This kind of exhibition is
very hard . . .'

'Oh come on, Lothar.' His brother's voice had taken on a
mocking tone. 'There's nothing *bad* about what Nielle is doing. If
it appeases your Calvinist conscience, Nielle isn't even going to
be on show naked. We don't yet know the title of the work or
what the figure will be like, but in the contract we signed it stip-
ulates quite clearly that she won't be naked in public. Of course,
for all the sketches they made of her she was completely in the
nude, but that was in the contract, too . . .'

'Listen, Roland.' Bosch was trying to stay cool. He was holding the phone in one hand, while he briskly rubbed his temple
with the other. 'It's not a question of how Nielle will be on show
or how prepared she is for it. It's simply that the exhibition will
be *very tough*. If you agree, a substitute can take her place in the
Tunnel. Showing a copy rather than the original is quite common
in a lot of exhibitions . . .'

There was a silence. Bosch felt almost like praying. When Roland spoke again, his tone of voice had altered: it was more serious, harsher.

'I could never play a trick like that on Nielle, Lothar. She's very excited. I go hot and cold just thinking about her and the amazing opportunity she's got. Do you know what Stein told us? That he had never seen such a young and yet so professional canvas. That's what he called her: a canvas . . . And he also said that with time, our daughter might even become a new Annek Hollech! . . . Can you imagine our own Nielle being the *Annek Hollech of the future*? Just think of that!'

The outside world disappeared for Bosch. All that was left was this excited voice scratching at his eardrums.

'I have to admit it cost me a lot to imagine my daughter this way, but now I'm fully behind it, and Hannah agrees with me. We want Nielle to be on show and admired. I think that's the secret dream of all fathers. I can understand that the experience may be tough, but it can't be any worse than being in a film or play, can it? You'd be surprised how many children are famous works of art nowadays . . . Lothar? . . . are you still there? . . .'

'Yes,' said Bosch, 'I'm still here.'

For the first time, Roland's voice sounded hesitant.

'Lothar, is there some problem you're not telling me about?'

Ten cuts, eight of them in crosses. The bones were splintered and the inner organs reduced to dust, to cigarette ash. How about that for a problem, Roland? How about me telling you the story of a madman called the Artist?

'No, Roland, there's no problem. I think the exhibition will be fine, and Danielle magnificent. Bye.'

After he hung up, he got to his feet and went over to the window. A golden sun hung heavily over the small buildings and the green space of Vondelpark. He recalled that a weather forecast had said there would be rain in the week of the opening. Perhaps God would bring down a flood on those damned curtains and 'Rembrandt' would be postponed.

But Bosch knew he would have no such luck: history showed that God protected the arts.

*

Benoit occasionally liked to give the impression he hid nothing from the works of art. In his velvety office on the seventh floor of the New Atelier there were eight of them, and two at least were sufficiently expensive for the Conservation director to show as often as he could that he treated them with more respect than human beings. This of course included holding conversations with his guests in front of them without getting them to put on ear protectors.

His office was tranquil and comfortable, cushioned in blue. The light sparkled intensely on the shoulders of the painting by Philip Brennan, who was only fourteen years old, and was situated behind Benoit. Bosch noticed him blink from time to time. Hanging from the ceiling in a glass cage with breathing holes was an authorised copy of *Claustrophilia 17* by Buncher. Behind Bosch, an Ashtray by Jan Mann was bent over holding its ankles, with the tray on its rump. In the window, the splendid anatomy of a blonde Curtain by Schobber stood in a ballet pose awaiting the order to be drawn. The food was served by two utensils created by Lockhead: a boy and a girl who moved with gentle, perfumed, catlike gestures. The Table was by Patrice Flemard: a rectangular board perched on the back of a shaven figure painted manganese blue, which in turn was balanced on the back of another similar figure. They were tied to each other by their hands and ankles. The bottom one was a girl. Bosch suspected the top one might be as well, but it was impossible to tell for sure.

The lunch was in fact a small feast. Benoit had not missed a trick: eel and dill soup with strands of seaweed, hock of venison done in nutmeg with vine leaves and a herb and chicory salad, followed by a dessert that looked like the clues from a recent crime: a bilberry and raspberry *mousse* in a buttermilk sauce, all of it prepared by a catering company that supplied the Atelier daily. Before and after the meal, Benoit carried out the ritual of his medicines. In total he took six red-and-white capsules and four emerald-coloured pills. He complained about his ulcer, claimed he could not eat anything at all, and that when he did he had to take all the medicines as a precaution. Despite this, he also tried the Chablis and the Lafitte that the Lockhead figures elegantly placed before him on the Table. As it breathed gently, the

Table made the wine bottles sway. Bosch ate little and hardly touched the wine. He found the atmosphere in the office stifling.

They talked of all they could mention out loud in a room full of a dozen people besides themselves (even though the silence made it seem there were just the two of them): about 'Rembrandt' and the discussion with the mayor of Amsterdam about installing the curtain structure in the Museumplein; about the guest list for the opening; about the increasingly likely possibility that the Dutch royal family would visit the Tunnel before the official opening.

When the conversation languished, Benoit stretched out his hand to the Ashtray's inverted backside and took a pack of cigarettes and a lighter from the big golden dish balanced between the buttocks. The Ashtray was obviously masculine and was painted a matt turquoise colour, with black stripes running down his shaven legs.

'Let's go to the other room,' Benoit said. 'Smoke isn't good for paintings or ornaments.'

You're a master of hypocrisy, Grandad Paul, thought Bosch. He knew Benoit had decided from the outset they would have a further talk in private, but wanted his works of art to think he was doing it so as not to bother them while he smoked.

They went into the next room. As Benoit shut the heavy oak door, he began to speak almost without a pause.

'Lothar, it's chaos out there. This morning I met Saskia Stoffels and Jacob Stein. The North Americans want to suspend things. Financing for the new season is at a halt. They're worried about the Artist, and they don't like the massive withdrawal of Van Tysch works. We've been trying to sell them the idea that the Artist is a European problem, a local question. We've explained that the Artist is not for export. He operates in Europe and only in Europe. But they reply: "Yes, yes that's fine, but have you caught him yet?"'

He stubbed out the cigarette in a metal ashtray. It was a perfectly normal cheap ashtray: Benoit only spent money on flesh and blood ornaments. While he was talking, he took a small aerosol out of the inside pocket of his immaculate Savile Row jacket.

'Do you have any idea what it costs to run this company, Lothar? Every time I have a finance meeting with Stoffels the same thing happens: I get vertigo. Our profits are huge, but the gap is even more enormous. And as Stein was saying only this morning, before we were the pioneers. But now . . . My God.' He opened his mouth, pointed the aerosol at his throat, and squirted a couple of times. He shook the spray violently, then squirted another dose. 'When Art Enterprises started up in 1998, we said it wouldn't last two years, do you remember? Now it's the sales leader in America, and has a monopoly in the choice sector of California collectors. And this morning Stoffels told us the Japanese are doing even better. Believe it or not, but Suke's turnover in 2005 was almost half a billion dollars more than the Foundation and Art Enterprises combined. Want to know how?'

'Ornaments,' replied Bosch.

Benoit nodded.

'They've hit us hard, even in Europe. Nowadays there is nothing, absolutely *nothing* as good as Japanese human artefacts. The worst of it is that European craftsmen are relying on the Japanese to sell their work. That wonderful Curtain in my office, for example: have you seen how perfect it is? . . . Well, it's by Schobber, an Austrian craftsman, but it's distributed by Suke. Yes, that's right . . . It may sound odd, but I just wish that the Artist were part of Suke. If we could link that crazy psychopath to Suke, it'd be the perfect way to stop them . . . but we won't be that lucky.'

He put away the aerosol and held a hand in front of his mouth. He breathed out and sniffed. He did not seem happy with the result, or perhaps his ulcer was playing up again. Bosch could not be sure. Benoit sat down and remained silent for a while.

'These are difficult times for art, Lothar, difficult times. The figure of the solitary artistic genius still sells, but *independently* of the artist. Van Tysch has become a myth, like Picasso, and myths are dead even when they're still alive because they no longer have to create to sell; all they have to do is sign the ankle, thigh or backside of their works. Yet their works are still those which sell *the best*, and consequently are the *most* important. Which means the death of the artist. And that is the destiny of art today, its inevitable goal: the death of the artist. We've gone back to Pre-Renaissance days, when painters and sculptors were regarded as little more than skilled craftsmen. So the question becomes . . . If artists are no longer needed for art, but are still essential for business, what are we to do with them?'

Benoit had the habit of asking questions without expecting any specific answer. Bosch knew this and waited for him to go on.

'This morning Stein suggested something odd: that when Van Tysch goes, we'll have to *paint* another one. Art will have to create its own artists, Lothar: not in order to *be* art, because it doesn't need them, but to make money. Nowadays anything can be a work of art, but only a *name* will have the value of a Van Tysch. So we'll be forced to *paint another Van Tysch*, to create him out of nothing, endow him with the proper colours and let him shine in the world. How did Stein put it? . . . Let me remember the exact words he used . . . I learned them by heart because they seemed to me . . . Ah, yes. "We have to create another genius to guide humanity's blind footsteps, someone at whose feet the powerful can continue to lay their treasures" . . . *Fuschus*, that was wonderful.' He paused for a minute and frowned. 'But it's some task, isn't it? Creating the Sistine Chapel will always be easier than creating Michelangelo, won't it?'

Bosch nodded vaguely.

'And how is your investigation going, Lothar?' Benoit asked, suddenly changing the subject.

Bosch knew the moment had come when Benoit would *demand* replies to his questions.

'It's not. We're waiting for the reports from Rip van Winkle.'

Don't trust anyone, April Wood had warned him. Tell them we're at a standstill. From now on, it's up to the two of us.

'What about April? Where is she?'

'She had to go urgently to London. Her father's worse.'

It was true that Wood had been obliged to return to London at the weekend because of her father's state of health. But she had told Bosch she would be working from there. Not even he knew what sort of work she meant, but it seemed obvious to him that she had already worked out her plan for a counterattack. Bosch put his trust in her plan.

He said goodbye to Benoit as quickly as he could. He needed a few moments' rest. At the door, the Conservation director stopped him, as he squirted his throat again with the halitosis spray.

'If you can, stir up the BAH people a bit. They're putting on a carnival for the week of the opening. The police say there may be five thousand of them from several countries. That would be good for us.'

The BAH was one of the international organisations most bitterly opposed to hyperdramatic art. Its founder and leader, the journalist Pamela O' Connor, accused artists such as Van Tysch or Stein of human rights abuses, of child pornography, white slave trading, and degrading women. Her accusations were listened to, and her diatribes sold well, but no law court would uphold her claims.

'I don't think they'll let off any fireworks, Paul,' Bosch said. 'Pamela O'Connor's people seem to have got tired even of writing pamphlets.'

'I know, but I'd like you to irritate them a bit, Lothar. We need a whiff of scandal. Everything is against us for this opening, even the title. Who on earth thinks Rembrandt is important nowadays, apart from four or five cretins who specialise in ancient art? Who is going to pay to come and see a homage to Rembrandt? The public will come to find out *what Van Tysch has done with Rembrandt*, but that's different. We're expecting lots of people, but we need to at least double the numbers. The queues have to reach the Leidesplein. A fight between members of the BAH and our security people would be ideal . . . We put journalists in the right place, there'll be photos, news reports . . . the fact is, groups like BAH are very useful. Would you believe it, but Stein has even suggested that we secretly finance them?

Bosch could believe it.

'Do whatever you can to raise the temperature,' Benoit said with a wink.

'I'll try to think positively,' Bosch replied.

He left without even mentioning to Benoit the topic that most worried him: the presence of Danielle in the exhibition.

2

The young woman standing next to the tree is wearing only a short white robe tied at the waist, hardly enough protection to go out into the street in or remain still in the open air. But other things about her appearance are more fascinating. For example, someone has drawn eyebrows, lashes and lips on her face with a paintbrush, and her hair is a shiny mahogany and smells of oil paint. The skin visible to us – her face, neck, hands and feet – has an artificial sheen, as if it has been covered in plastic. Yet, however strange her appearance, there is something in her gaze – something which has nothing to do with the mask of paint or her absurd clothing, a deep-seated trait that was there before she became a drawing, a figure, and is still there for us to see in the depth of her eyes – which would perhaps lead us to pause and try to get to know her better. A child would be fascinated by her body's marvellous colours. An adult would be more intrigued by her gaze.

The man standing opposite her is one of this century's best artists; in the future he will come to be regarded as one of the greatest of all time. Knowing this, we might expect his features to be touched by his celebrity. He is a tall, slender man of around fifty. He is dressed entirely in black, and has a pair of glasses dangling round his neck. His face is long and narrow, topped by a shock of jet-black hair that is going white at the sides. He has a deep forehead, furrowed with lines. Two darker lines, as if reinforced by pencil, make up his eyebrows. His eyes are large and dark too, but are slightly hooded, giving the impression his gaze is half-hidden, and could always see more. He has a prominent, straight nose. The curve of his lips is defined by a fine moustache and neat chin. His cheeks are completely clean-shaven. If we try to subtract his features from our memories of his photos and interviews, from what we know about the man they reflect, and think about it carefully, we will come to the conclusion that no, there is nothing extraordinary about his face, it is we who add whatever may be special from what we know about him. He could easily be the doctor I visit, the murderer once seen fleetingly on TV, the mechanic who hands me back my car after a service.

He has not spoken to her directly as yet. He gave some instructions to Uhl in Dutch which Gerardo had quickly translated. She was to put on her robe and go with him: the Maestro liked painting in the open air. They left the house in silence, with Van Tysch walking in front of her. The temperature that Friday afternoon was excellent, perhaps a little cool, but Clara did not mind. Nor was she worried about having forgotten her sandals. She was far too nervous to bother about such details. Anyway, although the gravel stuck to her feet, she was used to going barefoot. Van Tysch opened the gate, and Clara rushed to get through before it closed behind him. They crossed the lane and walked across the grass until they came to the *Plastic Bos* Gerardo had shown her the day before. Rays of sunlight filtered beneath the low branches, like golden brushstrokes from a drawing pen. Van Tysch came to a halt and she did the same. They stood looking at each other for a few moments.

The *Plastic Bos* spread like a puddle of water in the midst of the small pine wood. Twenty metres long and six metres wide, it was marked out by eleven fake trees which differed from the real ones because they were prettier and because their leaves made a sound like hail when the wind rose. Clara did not object to the plastic wood. To her it seemed to go with the rest of Holland, the country of landscapes by Vermeer and Rembrandt; of towns for elves like Madurodam, with tiny houses, canals, churches and monuments all built to scale; of dykes and *polders* where land has been created by the human will in its eternal struggle with the sea. She stood on the soft silicone grass carpet, next to one of the trees. The sun shone straight into her eyes, but she tried not to blink.

She wanted to have her eyes wide open, because Van Tysch was only three metres away from her.

'Do you like Rembrandt?' was the first thing he said, in fluent Spanish.

His voice was deep, majestic. In the theatre of ancient Greece, voices like his represented Zeus.

'I don't know his painting very well,' Clara replied. It was hard to get her yellow, primed tongue around the words.

Van Tysch repeated the question. It was obvious her reply had

299

not satisfied him. Clara looked inside herself, and spoke with complete sincerity.

'No,' she said. 'The truth is, I don't like him.'

'Why?'

'I don't know. But I don't like him.'

'Nor do I,' the painter unexpectedly said. 'That's why I never get tired of looking at his paintings. We have to confront what we don't like time and again. His painting is like a trusted friend: it offends us because it tells us the truth.'

His voice sounded weak and tired. Clara thought he must be an immensely sad man.

'I'd never thought of it like that,' she murmured. 'That's a very interesting way of looking at it.'

Then she thought Van Tysch had no need of any praise from her, and bit her lip.

'Is your father dead?' he asked all of a sudden.

'Pardon?'

He repeated the question. At first it seemed strange to Clara that Van Tysch should change the subject so abruptly. But she was not in the least surprised that he knew details of her life. She imagined the Maestro must investigate all the canvases he took on.

'Yes,' she replied.

'Why do you get so frightened at night?'

'What?'

'When my assistants woke you up by making a noise outside your window. Why did you look so terrified?'

'I don't know. I was frightened.'

'Of what?'

'I don't know. I've always been afraid of someone breaking into my house at night.'

Van Tysch came up to her, took hold of her chin, and tilted it as if he were examining a jewel in the light. Then he stepped back again, leaving her head leaning over to the right. The sun's rays were garlanding the tree branches. The atmosphere in the plastic wood was damp, like a prism, so that the sunlight refracted in drops of pure colour.

She thought he was studying her pose, but she could not be sure.

300

'My mother was Spanish,' was his next comment.

These brusque changes of topic were apparently normal in any dialogue with him. They did not bother Clara.

'Yes, I know,' she said. 'And you speak very good Spanish.'

Once again she realised how stupid her praise must sound. But Van Tysch went on as if he had not heard her:

'I never knew her. When she died, my father tore up all her photos, so I never even saw her. Or rather, I only saw her in the drawings he made of her. They were watercolours. My father was a good painter. So I saw my mother for the first time thanks to his paintings, which means I'm not sure he didn't make her more beautiful than in real life. And to me she looked very, very, very beautiful.' He had pronounced the three 'verys' slowly, making a different sound each time, as if trying to discover hidden meanings in the word by pronouncing it differently each time. 'But perhaps it was all due to my father's art. I've no idea whether the watercolours were better or worse than the original, I've never known or had any wish to know. I did not know my mother, and that's that. Later on I came to understand that is normal. I mean it's normal *not to know*.'

He paused and came up to her again. He moved Clara's head in the opposite direction, but then appeared to change his mind and pushed it back to the original position. He stepped away, then drew near again. He put a hand on the back of her head and bent it forwards. He put on the reading glasses hanging round his neck and studied something. Then he took off his glasses and walked away once more.

'Your father must have died young, too,' he said.

'My father?'

'Yes, your father.'

'He died at the age of forty-two of a brain tumour. I was nine at the time.'

'So you didn't know him either. You've seen images of him, but you never really knew him.'

'Yes, I did a little. By the age of nine I already had some idea about him.'

'We always have some idea about things we don't know,' Van Tysch replied, 'but that doesn't mean we know them any better.

301

You and I don't know each other, but we have already formed an idea of one another. And you don't know yourself, but you've already formed an idea about yourself.'

Clara nodded. Van Tysch went on.

'Nothing around us, nothing we know or do not know, is either completely known or unknown. It's so easy to invent extremes. It's the same with light. Did you know there's no such thing as *total* darkness, even for a blind person? Darkness is full of presences: shapes, smells, thoughts . . . And take a look at this summer evening light. Would you say it was pure? Take a good look. I'm not just talking about the shadows. Look *between the cracks* of the light. Can you see the tiny specks of darkness? Light is embroidered on a very dark canvas, but that's hard to see. We have to mature. As we do so, we come to understand that truth is an intermediate point. It's as if our eyes accustomed us to life. We understand that day and night, and life and death, too, perhaps, are merely different points in the play of light and shade. We discover that truth, the only truth worthy of the name, is shade.'

After a pause, as though he had been thinking about what he had just said, he repeated:

'The only truth is shade. That's why everything is so terrible. That's why life is so unbearable and terrible. That's why everything is so dreadful.'

Clara could not hear any emotion in his words. It was as if he were talking aloud as he worked. Van Tysch's mind was spinning in a void.

'Take off your robe.'

'Yes.'

As she was doing so, he asked her:

'What did you feel when your father died?'

Clara was folding her robe over a tree branch. The air enfolded her naked, primed body like a caress of pure water. The question brought her to a halt. She looked at Van Tysch:

'What did I feel when my father died?'

'Yes. What did you feel?'

'Not a lot. I mean . . . I don't think I felt it as badly as my mother and brother. They knew him better, so it was worse for them.'

'Did you see him die?'

'No. He died in hospital. He was at home when he had a crisis, a fit. He was taken to hospital, and I wasn't allowed to see him.'

Van Tysch went on staring at her. The sun had moved round and lit part of his face.

'Have you dreamed of him since?'

'Occasionally.'

'What sort of dreams?'

'I dream of . . . of his face. His face appears, he says strange things to me, then he disappears.'

A bird sang and then fell silent. Van Tysch screwed up his eyes to look at her.

'Walk over there,' he said. He pointed towards the shade under a fake tree.

The plastic grass bent docilely under her bare feet. Van Tysch raised his right arm.

'There is fine.'

She stopped. Van Tysch had put his glasses on again, and was coming over. He had not touched her: all he had done was to *out-line* her with his curt orders, but already she felt changed, as if her body were different, better *drawn* than ever before. She was convinced her body would do whatever he asked of it without waiting for her brain to agree. And she was determined she would lay her mind at his feet as well. All of it. Completely. Whatever he said, whatever he wished. Without limit.

'What happened?' Van Tysch asked.

'When?'

'Just now.'

'Now?'

'Yes, now. Tell me what you're thinking. Tell me *exactly* what you're thinking right now.'

She started to speak, almost without the words needing to pass through her brain.

'I am thinking that I've never felt this way with any painter before. That I have surrendered to you. That my body does what you tell it to almost before you even say it. And I'm thinking my mind has to surrender, too. That's what I was thinking when you asked me what had happened.'

303

When she finished it was as though a weight had been lifted. She thought about it. She found she had nothing more to confess. She remained silent like a soldier waiting for orders.

Van Tysch took off his glasses. He looked bored. He muttered a few words in Dutch, then took a handkerchief and a small bottle out of his pocket. Somewhere in the heavens a plane roared by. The sun was in its dying moments.

'Let's get rid of those features,' he said, wetting a corner of the handkerchief in the liquid and approaching her once more.

She did not move a muscle. Van Tysch's finger inside the handkerchief rubbed roughly at her face. As it came down towards her eyes, Clara forced herself to keep them open, because he had not told her she could close them. Distant images of Gerardo reached her like remote echoes. She had felt good when he painted her face, but now she was pleased Van Tysch was going to rub it all out. It had been yet another act of clumsiness by Gerardo, like a child scribbling in the corner of a canvas Rembrandt was considering using. She was amazed Van Tysch had not protested.

When he had finished, Van Tysch put his glasses back on. For a moment, she thought he was not satisfied. Then she saw him put away the bottle and the handkerchief.

'Why are you scared someone might break into your house at night?'

'I don't know. It's true, I've no idea. I don't think anything like that has ever happened to me.'

'I saw the night-time footage we took of you, and I was surprised at the terror on your face when my assistants came near the window. I thought we might be able to fix an expression like that. To paint it, I mean. And perhaps I will. But I'm after something better than that . . .'

Clara did not say a word. She just went on staring at him. Behind his head, the sky was going dark.

'What did you feel when your father died?'

'I felt pretty bad. It was just before Christmas. I remember it was a very sad Christmas. Over the next year I gradually began to feel better.'

'Why did you blink?'

'I don't know. Maybe it was your breath. When you speak, you breathe on my face. Do you want me to try not to blink?'

'What did you feel when your father died?'

'Very sad. I cried a lot.'

'Why do you get so excited if someone breaks into your house at night?'

'Because . . . excited? No, it doesn't excite me. It frightens me.'

'You're not being sincere.'

This took her by surprise. She responded with the first thing that came into her head.

'No. Yes.'

'Why are you not being sincere?'

'I don't know. I'm frightened.'

'Of me?'

'I don't know. Of me.'

'Are you excited now?'

'No. A little, perhaps.'

'Why do you always reply in two contradictory ways?'

'Because I want to be sincere. To say everything that occurs to me.'

Van Tysch seemed vaguely annoyed. He took some paper out of his jacket pocket, unfolded it and did something extraordinary. He flung it in her face.

It struck her and floated to the plastic ground. As it fell, Clara could see it was a crumpled catalogue of *Girl in Front of a Looking Glass* by Alex Bassan. The catalogue contained a close-up photo of her face.

'I saw that photo when I was looking for a canvas for one of my "Rembrandts". I was immediately taken with the luminous quality of your gaze,' Van Tysch said. 'I gave orders for you to be given a contract, I had you stretched and primed and paid a fortune for you to be brought from Madrid as artistic material. I thought that shining light would be ideal for my work, and that I could paint you a lot better than that fellow. So why can't I? I haven't found it in any of the footage we took of you in the farm. I thought it must be related to your night-time fears, and ordered my assistants to make the leap into the void with you in the early hours of this morning. But I don't think it has anything to do with the tension of a moment, so I decided to come here personally. Just now when I was approaching you I thought I could catch a glimpse of it for a tenth of a second. I asked you what had happened. But I don't think that it has anything to do with you. I think it exists independently of you. It appears and disappears like some shy animal. Why? Why do your eyes suddenly light up like that?'

Before she could reply, Van Tysch started speaking in a very different voice. It was an icy whisper, a galvanic current.

'I've grown tired of asking you questions to make it appear and try to fix it in your gaze, all you do is give idiotic replies so I can't find what I want anywhere. You behave like a pretty little girl with an eye on her opportunity. A beautiful body asking to be painted. You think you're very beautiful and you want to be noticed. You want to be made into something wonderful. You think you're a professional canvas, but you've no idea what it means to be a canvas, and you'll die without ever finding out. The video tapes from the farm have shown me that as a canvas, you're absolutely mediocre. The only thing that interests me in you is what you have in your eyes. There are things within us that are greater than we are, but even so are still minute. For example, your father's tumour. Tiny things that are more important than our lives. Frightening things. They are what art is made from. Occasionally, they come out: that's what we call "purging" them. It's as though we were vomiting. To me, you are less than your vomit. It's *your vomit* I want. Do you know why?'

She said nothing. She was pleased somehow that she had no tears, because above all she wanted to cry.

'Tell me. Do you know why I want it?' Van Tysch repeated the question in an offhand way.

'No,' she murmured.

'Because it's *mine*. It's inside you, but it's mine.' He jabbed at his chest with his forefinger. 'That glow that sometimes appears in your eyes *belongs to me*. I was the one who first saw it, and so it's mine.'

He stepped back, turned round, walked away a few paces. Clara could hear him fiddling with something. When he came back, she saw he was holding a pipe he had just filled.

306

'So here we'll stay, just the two of us, until I see it appear.'

He brought a match flame down over the pipe bowl. The darkness around them grew deeper and deeper. He tossed the match to the ground and put it out with his foot.

'One of the advantages of a non-flammable plastic wood,' he said.

It was this strange joke, *precisely* this wretched joke inserted into his frozen monologue, which seemed to her the worst insult of all. She had to use all her strength to avoid saying or doing anything, to keep looking at him evenly.

'I'm going to chase that little shining animal in your eyes out of its hiding place,' said Van Tysch. 'And when I see it come out, I'll catch it. The rest is of no interest to me.'

Then after another moment, he added:

'The rest is only you.'

Clara did not know how many hours she had been standing immobile on the plastic grass, with the night air on her smooth naked body. A cold north wind had sprung up. The sky was completely overcast. A slow, deep-rooted chill that seemed to come from within her body, was boring into her willpower like a drill. But she suspected that her suffering did not come from her physical discomfort but from *him*.

Van Tysch came and went. Occasionally he walked up to her and studied her face in the growing darkness. Then he would scowl and move away again. Once he left the wood altogether. He was away for some time, and when he came back he was carrying what looked like fruit. He leaned back against a plastic tree and began to eat, ignoring her completely. Standing there without moving, she saw him in the distance as a dark stain with long legs, a huge, skinny spider. Then she saw him lie down on the grass and fold his arms. It looked as if he were having a nap. Clara felt hungry, cold, and had a tremendous desire to relax her pose, but none of that mattered to her at that moment. She was trying above all to hold on to her willpower.

Then all of a sudden Van Tysch approached her again. He came stumbling towards her, snorting like a furious beast.

'Tell me,' he roared.

She did not understand. He gave a kind of furious groan. His voice broke in the middle of a word, like that of a veteran smoker.

'Tell me *something*!'

But she did not know what to say. She had been silent for hours, and found it hard to break free of her inertia. But she obeyed him. The words poured out as if it were just a question of opening her mouth.

'I feel bad. I want to do the best I can, but I feel bad because you look down on me. I think you're mad or a sad bastard, or perhaps both at the same time. I hate you, and I think that's what you wanted. I can't bear you looking down on me. Before you excited me. I swear, I got excited feeling I was in your hands. But not now. Now I couldn't give a shit about you. And here I am.'

When she finished, she realised Van Tysch had scarcely been listening to her. He was still staring at her eyes.

'What did you feel when your father died?' he asked.

'Relief,' Clara said straightaway. 'His illness was terrible. He lay on the sofa all the time and dribbled. He farted in front of me and grinned like an animal. One day he vomited in the dining room, then bent down and started searching for something in the vomit. He was ill, but I couldn't understand that. My father had always been such an open, cultured man. He loved classical painting. That *thing* was not my father. That was why I was relieved when he died. But now I know that . . .'

'That's enough,' Van Tysch said without raising his voice. 'Why are you so frightened that someone might get into your room at night?'

'I'm frightened they might hurt me. I'm frightened someone might hurt me. I'm telling you all I know!'

The wind had risen. Her robe shifted on the branch of the nearby tree, then fell off. Clara was unaware of this.

'It's hard to be sincere, isn't it?' growled Van Tysch. 'We're always taught that it's the opposite of telling lies. But let me tell you something. For many people, sincerity is nothing more than the *duty* not to tell lies. So it's a pretence, too.'

'I'm trying to be sincere.'

'That's why you're failing.'

The wind whipped at the hem of Van Tysch's jacket. He turned up the lapels to protect his neck from the wind, and started rubbing his hands. All of a sudden he pointed at Clara's head with his forefinger.

'Something in there is moving, turning round, hiding. It wants to get out. Why are you so harsh with yourself? Why do you take all this as though it were a military exercise? Why don't you do something silly? Don't you need to empty your bladder?'

'No,' said Clara.

'But try. Pee right here.'

She tried. Not a drop.

'I can't,' she said.

'You see? You said: "I can't". Everything with you is being able to do something or not. "I can do this, I can't do that" . . . Forget about yourself for a moment. What I want is for you to understand . . . No, not to understand . . . What I want is to tell you that you *do not matter* . . . But what's the point of talking if you don't believe me.' He paused, as if he were trying to think of a simpler way to put it. Then he went on, speaking slowly and emphasising his words with his hands. 'You are simply the carrier of something I need for my work. Look, I'm the one being sincere now, I know it's hard to do, but think of yourself as a nutshell; I want to crack you open, not because I hate you or *look down* on you. Not even because I think you're special, but because I am looking for what you have inside. I'll throw the rest away. Let me do it.'

Clara said nothing.

'At least tell me you don't want me to do it,' Van Tysch said calmly, almost begging her. 'Fight me.'

'I want to give you what you're asking for,' she stammered, 'but I can't.'

'There you go again: "I can't." I set you a trap. Of course you can't. But see how you're making an effort? You won't accept that you're simply a vehicle. It's as if the nutshell could split itself open, without any kind of pressure from outside.' He raised his hand and placed it gently on her naked shoulder. 'You're freezing. And look how you're trembling. See how right I am? Even now you're *making an effort. Making an effort!* I think the best thing is to leave it.'

He walked away again. When he came back he was carrying her robe.

'Get dressed.'

'No please.'

'Come on, get dressed.'

'Please no please.'

Clara was perfectly aware that Van Tysch was using a fairly crude painting technique: false compassion. But his brushstroke had been masterly. Something within her had given way. She felt it as she might have felt the approach of death. That almost unbearable idea – putting her robe back on and ending everything at a stroke – had shattered something very hard inside her. Her shoulders began to shake. She realised she was crying without tears.

He studied her for a moment.

'That expression is good,' he said, 'quite good, but I still can't see anything special in your eyes. We'll have to try something else.'

He fell silent. Clara shut her eyes tight. Van Tysch was still studying her.

'It's incredible,' he muttered. 'You have enormous willpower, but you can't get rid of yourself. You're pulling at your face muscles, keeping the reins tight. Come on, come on . . . Do you want to be a great work? Is that why you agreed to be painted? Do you want to be a masterpiece? . . . How wrong can you be. Look . . . Even now while you're listening to me, you're getting tense . . . your will is whispering to you: "I have to resist!"'

He raised his hand and touched her breast. He did it without any emotion, as if he were touching a gadget to see how it worked. Clara moaned: her breasts were cold and sensitive.

'If I touch you, if I *use* you, you become a *body* again, do you see? Your expression changes, and I like the way your mouth falls open, but that's not what I'm after exactly . . . No, it's not what I'm after . . .' He took his hand away. 'A lot of painters have created works with you, and very beautiful they were too. You are very attractive. You've done art-shocks. You like challenges.

310

As an adolescent you were part of *The Circle.* You went off to Venice last year to be painted by Brentano. So much experience,' Van Tysch said ironically. 'You've become an icon of desire. You've been used to excite people's pockets. You were trying to be a *work*, and they've turned you into a *body*.' He pushed her hair out of her eyes. Clara could sense his pipe tobacco breath on her face. 'I've never liked a canvas that's been in the hands of lots of other painters. That way it gets to believe *it* is the painting. But a canvas never, ever is the painting: it is *only the painting's support*.'

'I know perfectly well what I am!' Clara exploded. 'And now I know what you are, too!'

'Wrong. You don't know what you are.'

'Leave me in peace!'

Van Tysch was still staring at her.

'That expression is better. Wounded pride. Self-pity. The way your lips tremble is interesting. If only your eyes would shine, it would be perfect! . . .'

There was a long pause. Then Van Tysch leaned over her and put his elbow on her left shoulder. His jacket brushed against her naked body, and the weight of his arm on her shoulder forced Clara to remain tense. She sensed he was looking at her simply as an interesting problem of painting, a drawing difficult to pull off which he still did not feel satisfied with. She looked away from his eyes. An eternity went by until she heard his voice again.

'What miserable wretches we human beings are. Whoever said we could perhaps be works of art? My "Flowers" have backache. My "Monsters" are cretinous criminals. And "Rembrandt" is like a joke version of real paintings by a real painter. I'll tell you a story. Hyperdramatic art was invented by Vasili Tanagorsky. One day he went to a gallery where they were holding the opening of a show of his. He got up on the platform and said: "I am the painting." What a joke. But Max Kalima and I were very young in those days, and we took him seriously. We went to visit him. By then he had senile dementia and was in hospital. From his window you could see a beautiful English sunset. Tanagorsky was staring at it from his armchair. When he saw me, he waved

311

towards the horizon and said: 'Bruno, what do you make of my last painting?' Kalima and I laughed, thinking this time it was a joke. But no, this *was serious*. Taken as a whole, nature is a much more admirable painting than man.'

As he talked, he drew his finger over Clara's features: her forehead, nose, cheeks. His elbow was still resting on her shoulder.

'What terror . . . what immense terror there will be the day a painter succeeds in making a *true* work of art of a human being. Do you know what I think that work will be like? Something the whole world will *detest*. My dream is one day to create a work for which I will be insulted, looked down on, cursed . . . that day for the first time in my life I will have created art.' He stood back and handed her the robe. 'I'm tired. I'll go on painting you tomorrow.'

He turned his back on her and walked off. Despite the almost total darkness he seemed to know exactly where he was heading. Hands in the pockets of her robe, Clara followed him. She stumbled along, teeth chattering with cold, her body cramped because of the length of time she had stood without moving. Gerardo and Uhl were waiting on the porch. The outdoor lights gave them a golden halo. It was as though nothing had happened: to Clara it seemed as if they were in exactly the same position as before. Gerardo stood with hands on hips. The silent shadow of Murnika de Verne, the Maestro's secretary, loomed in the darkness, in the Mercedes parked outside the house.

Suddenly, as if a thought had just struck him, Van Tysch halted and came back towards them. Clara came to a halt as well.

'Come closer to the car,' Van Tysch said. 'Not too close. Stop there.'

She walked over to the spot he was indicating. The top half of her body was reflected in the dark car door window.

'Look towards the car window.'

She did. All she could see was her own body wrapped in the robe, and her short red hair glowing dully in the darkness. All of a sudden, Van Tysch's wavering shadow appeared alongside her. His voice had an edge of despair to it.

'There! I've seen it again! . . . In the catalogue photo you are with a *mirror*! It's mirrors that do it! It's mirrors which produce *that* in your eyes! I've been a fool! A real fool!'

He grabbed Clara by the arm and dragged her towards the house. He shouted instructions to his assistants, who disappeared inside at full tilt. By the time Van Tysch and Clara reached the living room, Gerardo and Uhl had placed one of the full-length mirrors in the centre of the room. The painter placed Clara in front of it.

'Was that it? . . . Was it something so simple I was looking for? . . . No, don't look at me! Look at *yourself*! . . .'

Clara stared at her own face in the glass.

'You look at yourself and you *catch fire*!' Van Tysch exclaimed. 'You can't avoid it! You look at yourself and you . . . you become something else! . . . Why are you so fascinated by your own image?'

'I don't know,' she said after a pause. 'Once when I was a child I went into the attic . . . There was a mirror in there, but I didn't know that . . . I saw it and got scared . . .'

'Move back.'

'What?'

'Move back to the wall, then look at the mirror from there . . . That's right . . . perfect, when you look at yourself from a distance, your expression changes . . . It becomes *more intense*. When you came too close to the car, it disappeared . . . Why? . . . because you need to see yourself from a distance . . . your distant image . . . or perhaps it needs to be *smaller*? . . . But I also caught a glimpse of that expression when I came up to you in the *Plastic Bos*! But then there were no mirrors around . . . !' He stopped and raised his forefinger. 'I was wearing glasses! Glasses! . . . What do they mean to you?'

Clara did not think she had jumped at the mention of this word, but Van Tysch had noticed it. He came up to her with his glasses on, took her face in his hands. When he spoke, his voice was almost gentle.

'Tell me, come on, tell me. We all have things inside us – tiny, fragile, domesticated things, like children. They are minute details, but they're more important than all the rest of our lives. I know you're struggling to remember something like that.'

A tiny Clara was staring back at Clara from the lenses of Van

Tysch's glasses. The words came obediently from her mouth, infinitely removed from her obliterated consciousness.

'Yes, there is something,' she whispered. 'But I never gave it much importance.'

'That is exactly what makes it so important,' said Van Tysch. 'Tell me.'

'One night, my father came into my room . . . He was already ill by then . . .'

'Go on. But don't stop looking at yourself in my glasses while you're talking.'

'He woke me up. He woke me up and frightened me. But he was already ill . . .'

'Go on.'

'He brought his face right up to mine . . .'

'Did he put a light on?'

'A bedside lamp.'

'Go on. Then what did he do?'

'He brought his face next to mine,' Clara repeated. 'That was all he did. He was wearing glasses. His glasses were very large. Or so they always seemed to me. Very large.'

'And you saw yourself reflected in them.'

'Yes, I think so . . . Now I remember that . . . I could see my face in the lenses. For a moment I thought it was a painting: the glasses had a thick frame like a picture frame . . . and I was inside the glass . . .'

'Go on! What happened then?'

'My father said some things I didn't understand. "Is something wrong, daddy?" I asked him. But all he did was move his lips. All of a sudden, I don't know why, but I thought it wasn't my father but someone else who was with me. "Daddy, is that you?" I asked him, but he didn't reply. And that scared me even more. I asked again: "Daddy! Please, tell me it's you!" But he didn't respond. I started sobbing as he left the room, and . . .'

'That's perfect,' said Van Tysch. 'You can stop now. That's perfect.' He signalled to Gerardo and Uhl to come over. 'Look at the expression on her face now . . . A mixture of terror and pity, love and dread. It's perfect. It's come to the surface. I've painted it. It's mine.'

He turned to them and began to give instructions in Dutch. Clara realised he must be talking about the painting. His attitude had completely changed. He was not angry or emotional any more. It was as though he were thinking aloud, absorbed in mere technical problems. Then he fell silent and looked back at Clara. Still fraught by her memories, she could only manage a weak smile.

'I never thought that something that happened to me as a little girl could mark me especially . . . I . . . My father was very sick and . . . that was how he behaved. He didn't mean me any harm . . . In time I came to understand that . . .'

'I'm not concerned whether the experience marked you or not,' Van Tysch replied harshly. 'I'm a painter of people, not a psychoanalyst. Anyway, as I've already told you, you don't matter to me in the least, so spare me your crass observations. I've got what I was looking for. We'll put a mirror in front of you, one the public can't see but where you'll be reflected. And that will be it.'

He said nothing more to Clara. He gave a few final instructions to Gerardo and Uhl, and left the house. The Mercedes started up. Then there was silence.

She returned from the bathroom wrapped in a towel, her hair blonde again, with no eyebrows, her skin primed. Gerardo was sitting on the floor of the living room, leaning against the wall. When he saw her come in, he got up and handed her a folded piece of paper. It was a colour photocopy of a classical painting.

'I suppose there's no harm you knowing now. It's *Susanna Surprised by the Elders*. Rembrandt painted it in about 1647. Do you know the story? It's from the Bible . . .'

He told her it. Susanna was a virtuous young woman married to an equally virtuous young man. Two elderly judges spied on her when she was bathing in the garden of her house. She refused to submit to their demands, and they accused her of adultery. She was condemned to death until Daniel, the wise judge, saved her at the last moment by proving the accusation against her was false.

'In Rembrandt's painting, Susanna, with dark red hair, has

315

just taken all her clothes off apart from a sheet . . . The two old men can be seen behind her . . . They are about to fling themselves on her . . . One of her feet is in the water, as if she had been pushed by one of the old men . . .'

That had been the idea behind all the sketches they had made of her, Gerardo explained: her mahogany hair, her nakedness, the spying on her at night, the way the two of them had preyed on her and insulted her. That was the basis of the hyperdramatism.

'The sketch is finished,' said Gerardo. 'Now we have to put the finishing touches to the painting. From now on we'll delineate your pose and the colour of your body, and fix your hyperdramatic expressions. The work will still be hard, I warn you, but the worst is over.' He sounded very relieved. 'Then we'll place lamps to illuminate you with light and shade, and put you in the spot the work has been allotted in the Tunnel.' He paused, then asked with a smile, 'How do you feel after the storm?'

'Fine,' she said. And burst into tears.

She felt a thin, strange wetness course down her cheeks. It was such a strange sensation that at first she did not realise what it was. As she moved into Gerardo's arms for protection, she discovered that, for the first time since she had been primed, she was crying real tears.

3

The woman striding purposefully towards the house has short hair, is very slender and is wearing expensive casual clothes: jerkin, blouse, tight jeans and boots; she has sunglasses on, and is carrying a small bag in her left hand. Her determined manner seems out of place in this peaceful scene. On both sides of the gravel path she is walking along, there is a perfectly trimmed lawn, the precise shadow of a line of trees and a hedge separating the garden from a meadow where several skewbald ponies can be seen. Further off, the landscape is one of gentle hills, carpets of tufted grass, with darker clumps of bushes and woods, the end-

316

less luxuriant reaches of Dartmoor in the southwest of England. The afternoon is drawing to a close, and the sun is dipping to the horizon to the left of the woman. The house she is headed towards has two wings: the main part is long, with two chimneys and eight windows; the second, perpendicular to the first, is not as grand. A maid in impeccable uniform is waiting at the front door. She is plump and has waxy white skin. She smiles as the woman approaches, but her smile is not reciprocated. A virtuoso bird, of a kind that would no doubt intrigue an ornithologist, is singing somewhere.

'Good evening, miss. Please, come in.'

The pleasant, ruddy-cheeked maid had a Welsh accent. Although Miss Wood did not reply, this did not seem to perturb her in the slightest. The house was comfortable and spacious, with a smell of noble woods.

'Be so kind as to wait here, miss. The master will attend you immediately.'

She was in an immense living room; three semicircular stone steps led down into it. Wood stepped down them very slowly, as though she were taking part in a spectacle. Her Ferragamo boots resounded on the stone. At first she considered taking off her sunglasses, but then the glinting glass wall at the far end of the room made her change her mind. Her Dior glasses matched her short hair with its cinnamon highlights. Her beauty adviser in the New Bond Street salon had suggested she wear sports clothes in brown and cream. Wood chose a fine cotton jerkin, a collarless blouse with ribbons and tight jeans. To go with this, she had a small, light, many-sided bag: it was as if the fingers of her left hand were holding nothing.

She cast a quick glance around her while she stood waiting. Sober, spacious, comfortable and rustic was her verdict. 'He has more money, but his tastes haven't changed,' she thought. Big native rugs, a three-piece suite in neutral colours, a huge chimney-piece and a glass wall at the far end, with a double door leading out into a kind of magnificent garden of paradise. There were only two works of art in the room: one next to the far doors, the other close to the right-hand wall, beyond the enormous rug. The latter was a blond young man of around twenty. He was naked, and shielded his genitals with both hands. He had not been painted, only lightly primed. He was openly breathing, blinked frequently, and followed Miss Wood's movements closely. It was as though he was not a painting, but a perfectly normal and attractive boy, standing naked in the room. He was called *Portrait of Joe*, and was by Gabriel Moritz. Moritz was one of the French natural-humanist school.

Wood knew all about them. Natural-humanism rejected any attempt to turn a person into art, and so was utterly opposed to pure hyperdramatism. To the humanists, works of art were first and foremost human beings. Their models did not have their bodies painted and were put on show exactly as they were in daily life, naked or dressed, posing almost without taking up quiescence.

The natural-humanists were also determined not to hide any of the body's blemishes: Wood could see the scar from what must have been a childhood scrape on *Portrait of Joe*'s right knee, and the curl of a distant appendix operation. The boy seemed a little bored with being on show. While Miss Wood was looking at him, he cleared his throat, puffed out his chest, and ran his tongue over his lips.

The other work was better, but was from the same tendency. Wood already knew it, and had no need to go closer and read its title: *Girl in the Shade* by Georges Chalboux. The body of *Girl in the Shade* was less appealing than the Moritz. It looked like a university student who had decided to play a joke on its friends by taking all its clothes off and standing still.

The stands by the side of the two works displayed all the accoutrements for maintaining humanist paintings: small trays with bottles of water and wafer biscuits that the works were allowed to turn to whenever they liked, signs they could hang on the wall to say that the painting had gone for a rest or was absent for a while, even one which said: 'These people are working as a work of art. Please respect them.'

Miss Wood finished studying the works and swung her tiny bag from side to side as she walked round the room. She detested French humanist art in all its forms: from Corbett's 'sincerism' to the 'democratism' of Gerard Garcet and the 'absolute liberalism' of

318

Jacqueline Treviso. Works that asked permission to go to the bathroom or simply went without asking, outdoor pieces which ran for cover when it started raining, paintings which haggled over how many hours they should work, and even the poses they should adopt, who butted in to your conversations with other people, who had the right to complain if they were upset about something or to share your food if they saw you eating something they fancied. April Wood definitely preferred pure hyperdramatism.

She heard a noise and turned round. Hirum Oslo was coming up the garden path, limping and leaning on his stick. He was wearing cream-coloured trousers and jersey, with a red Arrows shirt. He was a tall, good-looking man. His dark skin seemed at odds with pronounced Anglo-Saxon features inherited from his father. He had short black hair, brushed back off his forehead, where his eyebrows were thick and expressive. Wood found him the same as ever, perhaps a little thinner, with large sad eyes that he got from his Indian mother. She knew he was forty-five, but he looked more like fifty. He was a concerned man, alert to everything going on around him, anxious to find someone with problems to whom he could lend a helping hand. Miss Wood thought it was this outpouring of solidarity that aged him: it was as if part of his good looks had been rubbed off on others.

She walked to the glass doors to greet him. Oslo smiled at her, but first of all stopped to have a word with the Chalboux work.

'Cristine, you can take a rest whenever you like,' he said to her in French.

'Thank you,' the painting smiled, nodding her head.

It was only then that Oslo turned to greet Miss Wood.

'Good afternoon, April.'

'Good afternoon, Hirum. Could we talk without the works of art?'

'Of course, let's go to my office.'

His office was not in the house but at the bottom of the garden. Oslo liked to work surrounded by nature. April Wood could see he was still a keen gardener: he grew rare plants and identified each of them with labels as though they were works of art. As he let Miss Wood pass in front of him in a narrow part flanked by tall cactuses, Oslo said to her:

319

'You look very attractive.'

She smiled without replying. Perhaps to avoid the silence, he went on quickly:

'The withdrawal of Van Tysch's works in Europe has nothing to do with Restoration, does it? But if I'm not mistaken, it has to do with your presence here today?'

'You're not mistaken.'

Because of his limp, Oslo made slow progress, but Miss Wood had no problem keeping in step with him. She seemed to have all the time in the world. The shadows deepened as they reached the coolness of a clump of oaks. A murmur of water could be heard somewhere in the distance.

'How was your journey? Was it easy to find my lair?'

'Yes, I took a plane to Plymouth and rented a car there. Your directions were spot on.'

'That depends on the person,' Oslo said with a smile. 'Some dolts manage to get lost coming out of Two Bridges. Recently I had a visit from one of those artists who want to put music in their works. The poor man was going round and round in circles for two hours.'

'I see you've finally found the perfect refuge: a lonely spot in the middle of nature.'

Oslo was not sure whether or not April Wood's comment was entirely well meant, but he smiled all the same.

'It's much pleasanter than London, of course. And the weather is good. Today though it's been cloudy since dawn. If it rains, I'll put the outdoor pieces inside. I never leave them out in the rain. Oh, and by the way,' – Wood noticed an odd change in his voice – 'You're going to get a surprise . . .'

They had reached the spot where the sound of water was coming from. It was an artificial pond. In the centre stood an outdoor work of art.

After a pause during which Oslo tried in vain to guess what Miss Wood was feeling, he said:

'It's by Debbie Richards. I really think she is a great portraitist. She used a photo of you. Does it bother you?'

The girl was standing on a small platform. The bobbed hair was exactly right, and the Ray-Ban glasses were very similar to

320

the ones she wore, as was the green suit and miniskirt. There was one important difference (Wood could not help noticing it): the naked legs had been corrected and lengthened. They were long and shapely, much more attractive than hers. But it's obvious, painters always make you look more beautiful, she thought, cynically.

The portrait stood motionless in the pose it had been placed in. Behind it was a wall of natural stone, and on its right a small waterfall cascaded. Who could the girl be who looked so like her? Or was it all thanks to cerublastyne?

'I thought you didn't like portraits that used ceru,' she commented after a while.

Oslo laughed briefly.

'You're right, I don't. But in this case it was essential for the portrait to look like the original. I've had it for a year now. Are you annoyed I commissioned a portrait of you?' He asked, looking at her anxiously.

'No.'

'Then we won't mention it any more. I don't want to make you waste time.'

His office was in a glass summerhouse. Unlike the living room up at the house, it was a jumble of magazines, computers and books piled in unsteady columns. Oslo insisted on clearing his desk a little, and Miss Wood let him do so without a word. Without knowing why exactly, she felt ill at ease. Nothing about her revealed this fact, except that the knuckles on the hand gripping her bag were white.

It had been a low blow, a real low blow. She would never have thought that Oslo still wanted to remember her, least of all in this romantic way. It was absurd, meaningless. She and Hirum had not been seeing each other for years. Of course, they heard news of each other, particularly her of him. Ever since Hirum Oslo had abandoned the Foundation and become the guru of the natural-humanist movement, almost every art magazine mentioned him, either to praise or denigrate him. At that very moment, Oslo was putting away a well-worn copy of his latest book, *Humanism in HD Art*, which Wood had read. During her plane journey she had planned out their meeting, and had decided to comment on some passages from the book – that way they could avoid talking about the past, she thought. But the past was there, in every inch of the office, and no conversation could avoid it. And as if that were not enough, there was that unexpected portrait by Debbie Richards. April Wood turned her head to look out across the garden. She caught sight of it immediately. 'He's placed it so he can see it from his chair while he's working.'

Oslo finished tidying up, and turned to face the pale, slender figure in dark glasses. Is she annoyed? he wondered. She never shows her feelings. You never know what's really going on inside. He decided he could not care less if she were annoyed. She was the last person to reproach him for his memories.

'Sit down. Would you like a drink?'

'No, thanks.'

'I'm preparing my little talk for next week. There's going to be a big retrospective of the French open-air school. There are papers, round tables. I'm also responsible for the conservation of thirty of the works, among them ten underage ones. I'm trying to arrange for the minors to be on show for less time and to have more substitutes. And I still haven't received the site inspection reports. It's in the Bois de Boulogne, but I need to know exactly where. Well . . .'

He gestured as though to excuse himself for talking about his own problems. There was a pause. Oslo, who was trying to avoid an embarrassing silence, was relieved when Miss Wood began to speak.

'You're doing well as Chalboux's adviser, I see.'

'I can't complain. French natural-humanism started modestly, but now it's fashionable all over Europe. Here in England we're still reluctant to import it, because of Rayback's influence. And because we tend not to worry so much about other people. But some English artists are already changing their attitude, and have joined the humanist tendency. They've suddenly discovered they can produce great works of art and still respect human beings. In general though it's very difficult here.'

Oslo talked in his usual even tone, but April Wood could detect the emotion behind it. She knew it was something close to his heart.

A moment later, his features relaxed.

'Well, I suppose you haven't come all the way from London to learn about my menial responsibilities. Tell me about you, April.'

April Wood began reluctantly, but eventually spoke much more than she had intended. She began with a few details about her private life. Her father was in his final hours, she told him, and they had phoned her urgently from the hospital to tell her death could come at any moment. She was very busy in Amsterdam but had felt obliged – that was the word she used, 'obliged' – to come to London for a few days, in case anything happened. Yet she was not wasting her time. From her London home she had been able to send faxes and emails, and held lengthy talks with specialists all over the world, as well as with her own team. And she had decided finally to ask Oslo for his help. But she preferred to come and see me, he thought with a sudden rush of emotion.

'We're in crisis, Hirum,' Miss Wood said. 'And time is running out.'

'I'll do whatever I can to help you. Tell me what's happening.'

In less than five minutes, Miss Wood explained the situation to him. She did not go into all the details, but left them to his imagination. Nor did she tell him the titles of the works that had been destroyed. Oslo listened in silence. When she had finished, he asked anxiously:

'What works were they, April?'

Wood looked at him for a while before replying.

'Hirum, what I'm going to tell you is absolutely confidential, as I'm sure you understand. Apart from a small group we've called the "crisis cabinet", nobody knows anything, not even the insurance companies. We're preparing our ground.'

Oslo nodded, his black, sad eyes wide with concern. Miss Wood told him the title of the two works, and there was silence again. The muffled sound of the waterfall in the garden could be heard through the glass windows. Oslo was staring down at the floor. Eventually he said:

'My God . . . that poor child . . . that little girl . . . I'm not so sorry for those two criminals, but that poor little girl . . .'

Monsters was just as valuable, if not more so, than *Deflowering*, but Miss Wood was well aware of Oslo's ideas. She had not come to discuss them.

'Annek Hollech . . .' Oslo said. 'I last talked to her a couple of years ago. She was charming, but she felt completely lost in that terrible world of human works of art. It wasn't just that lunatic who killed her. We all contributed to her murder.' He turned to face Wood. 'Who? Who can be doing this? And why?'

'That's what I want you to help me find out. You're considered one of the most important specialists in the life and work of Bruno van Tysch. I want you to tell me names and motives. Who could it be, Hirum? I don't mean the person destroying the canvases, but the one who is paying for their destruction. Think of a machine. A machine programmed to annihilate the Maestro's most important creations. Who would have the motive to programme a machine like that?'

'Who do you think it could be?'

'Someone who hates him enough to want to do him as much harm as possible.'

Hirum Oslo leaned back in his chair, blinking.

'Everyone who has ever met Van Tysch both loves and loathes him. Van Tysch succeeds in producing masterpieces precisely because he creates that kind of contradiction in people. You know the main reason why I left him was because I found out how cruel his working methods were. "Hirum," he used to say, "if I treat the canvases as people, I'll never make works of art out of them."'

Who am I telling this to, Oslo thought. Look at her sitting there, her face sculpted in marble. My God, I reckon the only person who has ever managed to really move her has been Bruno van Tysch.

'It's true that life hasn't helped him to be any different. His father, Maurits van Tysch, was probably even worse. Did you know he collaborated with the Nazis in Amsterdam? . . .'

'I heard something to that effect.'

'He sold his fellow countrymen, Dutch Jews; he handed them over to the Gestapo. But he was clever about it; he made sure there were hardly any witnesses left. So nothing could ever be proved against him. He knew how to swim with the current.

324

Even today there are some people who question whether Maurits was a collaborator. But I think that was the reason why, immediately after the war, he emigrated to the tiny, peaceful town of Edenburg. It was there he met that Spanish woman, a child of Spanish Republican exiles, and they got married. She was almost thirty years younger than him, and I've no idea what attracted her to Maurits. I suspect he had the gift his son inherited twice over: the ability to dominate other people and turn them into marionettes for him to use for his own ends. A year after Bruno was born, his mother died of leukemia. It's easy to imagine how this embittered Maurits still further. And he took it out on his son . . .'

'As I understand it, he was a painting restorer.'

'He was a frustrated painter,' Oslo said with a wave of his arm. 'He took on the job of restoring pictures in Edenburg castle, but his dream was to be an artist. He was not much good at either task. Do you know, he used to thrash Bruno with his paint-brushes?'

'I don't know anything about my boss' life,' April Wood responded, smiling briefly.

'Maurits used long-handled brushes to reach some of the paintings hanging high up on the castle walls. Apparently, he never threw away the worn-out brushes. I don't think he kept them specially to thrash Bruno with, but that's what he did.'

'Did Van Tysch tell you this?'

'Van Tysch never told me anything. He's as silent as the grave. It was Victor Zericky who told me. He was Bruno's childhood friend – perhaps his only friend, because Jacob Stein is nothing more than a worshipper. Zericky is a historian who still lives in Edenburg. He gave me a couple of interviews, and I managed to get a few facts from him.'

'Go on, please.'

'Everything could have ended there: a child mistreated by his parents who later perhaps might have become another restorer and frustrated artist . . . worse even than Maurits, because Bruno couldn't even draw properly,' Oslo giggled nervously. 'Whereas we know his father could . . . Zericky showed me some water-colours Maurits did that Van Tysch had given him: they're very

325

good ... But then the miracle happened, the "fairytale" as the Foundation's history calls it: Richard Tysch, the North American millionaire, crossed his path. And everything was changed forever.'

Wood was writing some of this down in a notebook she had taken out of her bag. Oslo paused, and gazed out of the window at the encroaching dusk in the garden.

'Richard Tysch was the person who made it possible for the Maestro to become the boss of an empire. He was a madman, a useless and eccentric millionaire who inherited a fortune that he threw away and several steel firms he sold as soon as his father died. He was born in Pittsburgh, but he saw himself as the direct descendant of the Pilgrim Fathers, those Puritan pioneers to the United States. He was obsessed with finding out about his family. He investigated where his name came from. Apparently, the Van Tyschs of Rotterdam split into two branches during the heyday of the Dutch West India Company. One ancestor went to North America, and founded the line that became steel and business barons. Richard Tysch wanted to find out about the "other branch", the European side of his family. At that time, the only two people of that name were Bruno's father and his Aunt Dina, who lived in The Hague. In 1968, Tysch went to Holland and paid a surprise visit to Maurits. He had been planning just a short, uneventful visit. He wanted to talk to Maurits about art (he had learnt he was a restorer), pick up some mementoes, and return to the United States loaded down with photos and historic "roots". But then he met Bruno van Tysch.'

Oslo was staring down at the filigree inlay on the knob of his cane. He caressed it absent-mindedly as he went on with his story.

'Have you seen photos of Bruno as a child? He was incredibly attractive, with his thick black hair, pale face and dark eyes, that mixture of Latin and Anglo-Saxon he has. A real young faun. His eyes had a strange fire to them. Victor Zericky says, and I believe him, that he could hypnotise people. All the girls in the village were crazy about him, even the older ones. And quite a few men felt the same, I can tell you. He was thirteen at the time.

Richard Tysch met him and fell for him. He invited him to go and spend the summer in his Californian mansion, and Bruno accepted. I suppose Maurits saw nothing wrong with it, especially considering how generous this god from the other side of the Atlantic had been. From then on, the two of them saw each other every summer, and kept up an extensive correspondence while Bruno was at school. Van Tysch later destroyed the letters. Some people say they had a Socrates–Alcibiades kind of relationship, others put it more crudely. All we can be sure of is that six years later, Richard Tysch left Bruno his entire fortune, and shot himself in the mouth with his shotgun. They found him propped on the trunk of a column in his *palazzo* on the outskirts of Rome. His brain was decorating the wall mosaics. Now the *palazzo* belongs to Van Tysch, as do all his other European properties. His will came as quite a surprise, as you can imagine. Of course, what relatives he had, all of whom had quarrelled with him, challenged it, but without success. Add to this the fact that Maurits had died two years earlier, and we can conclude that all of a sudden Bruno found himself with all the money and freedom in the world.'

Oslo's attention was caught by something that brought him to a halt: two workmen were out in the garden helping the model portraying Miss Wood out of the tank. Her hours on show were over. Oslo continued watching the removal of the portrait as he carried on speaking.

'I have to admit that Bruno made the most of both. He travelled all over Europe and America, and set himself up for a time in New York, where he met Jacob Stein. Before that he had been in London and Paris, where he had been in touch with Tanagorsky, Kalima and Buncher. It's hardly strange that he should have been so enthusiastic about hyperdramatic art: he was born to tell other people what they should do. He had always been a painter of people, even before Kalima started to build a theory around the new movement. Bruno used his fortune to make HD the most important art of this century. The truth is, we owe a lot to Van Tysch,' Oslo ended, perhaps more cynically than he had intended.

'This is getting us nowhere,' said Miss Wood, tapping her

notebook with her pen. 'From what you tell me, Van Tysch could have as many enemies as he does admirers.'

'Exactly.'

'We'll have to approach it differently.'

Out in the garden, the Debbie Richards model was now completely naked, and one of the workmen was carefully folding up the painted clothing while the other helped her into her robe. Miss Wood studied the girl's physique (even barefoot, she was several centimetres taller) and vaguely wondered if Oslo thought she was equally attractive. The cerublastyne joins around the neck were clearly visible. What could her real face be like? Miss Wood did not know and did not want to know.

As she was thinking this, she took off her sunglasses and rubbed her eyes. Oslo thought: My God, she's so thin, so skinny. He guessed that April Wood's nervous problems about eating must have increased in recent years. The 'guard-dog' was all skin and bone.

He had known her as a puppy.

It was in Rome in 2001, during a series of courses Oslo was giving on the conservation of outdoor pieces. He had never worked out what it was about this slender girl of only twenty-three that had attracted him so much. At first sight, it seemed easy enough: April Wood was beautiful, she dressed with striking elegance, and her culture and intelligence were obvious. Yet there was something within her that led people to immediately reject her. In those days she was working as the security chief for Ferrucioli, and despite the fact that she was already wealthy, she lived on her own and had no close friends. Oslo thought he had discovered what kept her isolated: a deep, slowburning hatred that was like a hidden poison. April Wood emanated hate through every pore.

With the infinite patience he had always shown when it came to helping others, Oslo took it on himself to find the antidote. He managed to find out something about her life. He learnt that her father, an English art dealer living in Rome, had put pressure on April as an adolescent to become a canvas. He also learnt that she was being treated for a problem of nervous anorexia that dated from the time when her father wanted at all costs to make her into a work of art. 'He would call second-rate painters to sketch me in the nude,' April confessed to him one day. 'Then he took photos of me and sent them to the great masters. But I discovered just in time I didn't have the patience to be a canvas. So I devoted myself to protecting them instead.' But to her, 'protecting canvases' meant exactly that. It was as though she did not see them as human beings. The two of them often had arguments about it. Finally Oslo understood that Miss Wood's worst poison was *Miss Wood*. An antidote to that poison would only have done her more harm.

When April Wood joined the Foundation as its new security director, the distance between them grew. In 2002 they saw each other still less, and by 2003 absence threw its chilly mantle over them both. The word 'end' had never been pronounced. They were still friends, but knew that anything there might have been between the two of them had finished.

Oslo thought he was still in love with her.

Wood put her glasses on the desk and looked at him.

'Hirum, I'll be straight with you: the person destroying the canvases has the advantage over me.'

'Has the advantage?'

'One of our own people is helping him. Someone from the Foundation.'

'My God,' murmured Oslo.

For a tiny instant, a split second, he thought she had become a little girl once more. Oslo knew that behind her indomitable will there was concealed a poor, lonely and frightened creature which occasionally surfaced in her gaze, but which he was astounded to see at this very moment. But that moment soon passed. Wood took control of her facial expression once more. Not even an expert in cerublastyne could mould a mask as perfect as April Wood's *real* features, thought Hirum Oslo.

'I have no idea who it is,' she went on. 'It could be someone in the pay of our competitors. Someone anyway who is in a position to pass on *restricted* information about when our security people are working, the places where we have our models for safe-keeping, and lots more. We're being *sold*, Hirum, from inside and outside the Foundation.'

'Does Stein know?'

'He was the first person I told. But he refused to help. He's not even going to try to get the next exhibition postponed. Neither Stein nor the Maestro wants to get mixed up in this. The problem when you work for great artists is that you have to sort your life out for yourself. They're on another plane. They see me as a guard dog – they even call me that – and I don't blame them: that is exactly what they employ me to be. And until now they've been happy with what I've done. But now I'm on my own. And I need help.'

'You've always had me, April. And I'm here for you now.'

They heard laughter out in the garden. It came from young people of both sexes. They were talking and laughing like students on a picnic as they came up to the summerhouse. They were wearing sports clothes and carrying bags on their shoulders, but their skin looked as shiny as polished mirrors in the light from the electric bulbs that had just come on among the trees. They had an almost supernatural appearance, like angels with well-defined bodies, beings from a far-off universe that Hirum Oslo and Miss Wood felt exiled from. They found it hard to look on them without regret. Oslo muttered an apology to Miss Wood, and went to the door.

Wood understood at once that this must be a daily ritual: Oslo's paintings were saying goodbye to him. He talked to them, smiled and joked. She thought of her own house back in London. She had more than forty artworks, almost half of them human ornaments. Some of them were so expensive they carried on in their poses even when she was not there, even if she was away for several weeks. But Miss Wood never said a word to any of them. She crushed out her cigarettes in Ashtrays that were naked men, lit Lamps that were adolescents with depilated, virgin sexual organs, slept next to a painting of three youngsters painted blue who were in perpetual balance, washed alongside two kneeling girls who held gold soap dishes in their mouths, but at no time, not even when they finally left her house at the end of a long day's work, did it ever occur to her to talk to them. But here was Oslo, relating to his paintings like an affectionate father.

330

After saying goodbye to them, Hirum Oslo sat down again, and lit the desk lamp. The light flamed in Miss Wood's cold blue eyes.

'What time do you have to leave?' he asked.

'It doesn't matter. I've got a private plane waiting for me in Plymouth. And if I don't feel like driving, I can call a chauffeur to come and pick me up. Don't worry.'

Oslo put the tips of his finger together. His face showed he was worried about something.

'I suppose you've thought of going to the police.'

Miss Wood's smile was heavy with tiredness.

'This guy has all the police forces of Europe on his trail, Hirum. We're getting help from organisations and defence departments that only swing into action in very special cases, when the security or the cultural heritage of one of their member states is threatened. Globalisation has made the methods of a Sherlock Holmes seem very old-fashioned, I suppose, but I'm one of those who prefer old-fashioned methods. Besides, their reports end up with the crisis cabinet, and I'm convinced one of the members of that cabinet is the person who is helping our suspect. But worst of all, I have no time.' She paused, and then added: 'We suspect that he's going to try to destroy one of the paintings in the new exhibition, and that he's going to do it *now*, during the exhibition. Perhaps in a week or two, perhaps earlier. He might even attack on the day of the opening. I can't wait much longer. Today is Tuesday 11 July, Hirum. There are four days left. I am des-per-ate. My people are working on it day and night. We've devised some very complex protection plans, but this guy has a plan of his own, and he'll dodge us just as he has until now. He's going to destroy another painting. And I have to stop him.'

Oslo thought for a minute.

'Tell me a bit about his *modus operandi*.'

Wood told him about the state the paintings had been found in, and the use of the canvas cutter. She added:

'He records the voices of the canvases saying weird things which we reckon he must force them to read. I've brought you written copies of both recordings.'

She pulled some sheets of paper out of her bag and passed them to him. By the time Oslo had finished reading them, the garden was dark and silent.

'The art that survives is the art that has died,' he read aloud. 'That is odd. It sounds like a declaration of principles of hyper-dramatic art. Tanagorsky always said that HD art would not survive because it's *live* art. It may sound like a paradox, but that's the way it is: it's made from real flesh-and-blood people, and so is ephemeral.'

Miss Wood had abandoned her notebook, and was leaning forward, elbows on the edge of the desk.

'Hirum, do you think that the recorded phrases reveal a deep artistic knowledge?'

Oslo raised his eyebrows and thought before he responded.

'It's hard to say, but I think so. "Art is also destruction," it says further on. "Before it used to be just that." And it names cave artists, and the Egyptians. I see it this way: until the Renaissance, broadly speaking, artists worked for "destruction" or death: bison on cave walls, figures on tombs, statues of terri-fying gods, medieval descriptions of hell ... But from the Renaissance onwards, art began to work for life. And that went on until the Second World War, believe it or not. After that con-flict, there was a shrinking of awareness. Painters lost their virginity, became pessimistic, no longer believed in their own craft. Even today, well into the twenty-first century, we're still suffering the consequences. All of us are the inheritors of that dreadful war. This is our Nazi inheritance, April. This is what the Nazis have achieved ...'

Oslo's voice had diminished to almost a whisper. It was as dark as the nightfall closing in around them. He was speaking without looking at Miss Wood, staring instead at his desk.

'We've always thought humanity was a mammal which could lick its own wounds. But in fact we're as fragile as a huge paint-ing, a beautiful but terrifying mural painting which has been creating itself over the centuries. That's what makes us so fragile: slashes on the canvas of humanity are hard to repair. And the Nazis slashed the canvas to ribbons. Our convictions were smashed, and their fragments scattered throughout history.

There was nothing we could do with beauty, except to grieve over it. There was no way we could get back to Leonardo, Raphael, Velázquez, or Renoir. Humanity became a mutilated survivor whose eyes are wide open to horror. And that's the Nazis' real victory. Artists still suffer from that inheritance, April. In that sense, in only that sense, it's true to say that Hitler won the war forever.'

He raised his sad eyes to look at Miss Wood, who sat listening to him silently.

'Just like in the university, I'm talking too much,' he said with a smile.

'No, go on, please.'

Oslo stared down at the elaborate knob of his cane while he went on.

'Art has always been very sensitive to the currents of history. After the war, painting fell apart; canvases became daubs of bright colours, a sort of crazy revolution of amorphous shapes. Art movements and tendencies lasted less and less time. One painter even said, quite rightly, that the avantgardes existed simply to provide material for the following day's tradition. There were *action paintings*, *live art*, *performances*, *pop art* and art that defied classification. Schools were born and died in a day. Each painter became his own school, and the only acceptable rule was that there were no rules. Then hyperdramatism came on the scene: and that in many ways is closer to destruction than any other artistic movement.'

'How's that?' Miss Wood asked.

'According to Kalima, the great theorist of HD art, humanity is not only contrary to art, it *cancels it out*. That's what he says in his books, I'm not inventing it. To put it simply: an HD work is more artistic the less *human* it is. That is what hyperdramatic exercises are aimed at: stripping the model of their condition as a person, getting rid of their convictions, their emotional stability, their willpower, undermining their dignity in order to transform them into a *thing* they can make art out of. "We have to destroy the human being in order to create the work," say the hyperdrama-tists. That's what the art of *our time* has become, April. That is the art of our world, of this new century of ours. And not only have they dispensed with human beings: they've also dispensed with all the other arts. We live in a hyperdramatic world.'

Oslo paused. Miss Wood could not help thinking yet again of the Debbie Richards portrait. That woman who was more attractive than she was, whom Hirum had on show in his house to remember *her*.

'As is usually the case,' Oslo went on, 'this savage tendency has given rise to opposite reactions. On the one hand, people who believe you have to go to the absolute extreme and degrade the human being to an unbelievable extent: that was how art-shocks, hypertragedies, *animarts* and so on were born, and human artefacts . . . and the corollary, the ultimate degradation of *stained art* . . . But on the other, there are those who believe you can create works of art with human beings without having to degrade or humiliate them. And that's how natural-humanism came about.' He raised his hands in the air, and smiled. 'But I'm not trying to convert you.'

'You mean,' Miss Wood said, 'that whoever wrote those texts was thinking in hyperdramatic terms?'

'Yes, but there are strange phrases. For example, the one at the end of both texts: "If the figures die, the works persist." I can't see how an HD work can persist if its figures die. That's taking Tanagorsky's paradox to the extreme. They are confused texts, and I'd like more time to be able to analyse them at greater leisure. At any rate, I don't think we should take them literally. I remember that in *Alice*, Humpty Dumpty reckoned he could make words mean whatever he wanted. Something similar is going on here. Only the person who wrote them can tell us what he meant.'

'Hirum,' Miss Wood said after another short pause, 'I've read that *Deflowering* and *Monsters* were considered very special in Van Tysch's output. Why is that?'

'It's true, they are very different from the rest of his production. In his *Treatise on Hyperdramatic Art*, Van Tysch says that *Deflowering* is based on a vision he had as a child, when he was going to Edenburg castle with his father. Maurits wanted Bruno to observe him at work so that he could learn the skills of the trade. Bruno used to go with him every summer in his school

334

holidays, and they would walk together along a path bordered with flowers. In one part, there was a bank of wild narcissi, and one day Van Tysch thought he saw a young girl standing among the flowers. He might really have seen her, but he thinks it must have been a dream. The fact is that *Deflowering* became for him a symbol of his childhood. The smell of wet wood that the work gives off . . . that the work *gave off* . . . is a reference to the summer storm that broke over Edenburg on the day he saw the vision.' Oslo twisted his lips. 'I met Annek when Van Tysch was painting that work with her. The poor child thought he cared for her. And he used her feelings in his work.'

There was another pause. Miss Wood was staring at him out of the shadows.

'In *Monsters* his aim was to represent Richard Tysch, and perhaps Maurits as well. Of course, the Walden brothers did not look anything like them, but it was a *caricature*, a sort of artistic revenge against people who had been influential in his life. He chose a couple of psychopaths and hung a criminal record round their necks which has still not been properly confirmed. The Walden brothers were capable of a lot of things, but Van Tysch probably made them seem even more perverse than they were by using the notoriety of the case in which they were accused of murdering Helga Blanchard and her son. So the comparison between the two figures in the work of art and those in his past is perhaps concealing something else. Maybe Van Tysch is trying to tell us that neither Richard Tysch nor Maurits were as evil and perverse in reality, as they are when he remembered and painted them: deformed, grotesque, pederasts, criminals, just like one another. The only link between *Monsters* and *Deflowering* then is the past. No other painting he has done is so directly related to his own life.'

'What about "Rembrandt"?' Miss Wood leaned forward in her seat. 'Do you know the description of the works in his new collection?'

'I've heard something about it, like all the critics.'

'I've brought you a catalogue with the most up-to-date information,' she said, pulling a black pamphlet out of her bag. She opened it out on the desk. 'There's a short description of each

335

work. There are thirteen of them. I need you to tell me which of them, in your opinion, could be specially related to Van Tysch's past like those other two.'

'April, it's impossible for me to tell that on the basis of a description in a catalogue . . .'

'Hirum: in London all the past week I've been sending this catalogue to the four corners of the earth. I've talked to dozens of art critics on all five continents, and I've drawn up a list. All of them told me exactly the same as you, and I've had to insist with all of them, although you're the only one to whom I've told the whole truth. They protested, but eventually all of them gave me their opinion. I need you to do the same.'

Oslo stared at her, feeling sorry for the desperate gleam in her eyes. He thought it over for a moment before replying.

'It's very hard to say whether there'll be any work like those two in "Rembrandt". I think it's a very different collection to "Monsters", just as that was different to "Flowers". On one level, it's a homage to Rembrandt on the four hundredth anniversary of his birth. But we also have to remember that Rembrandt was Maurits' favourite painter, and perhaps for that very reason, because he was his father's favourite, the collection has some very odd things in it. In *The Anatomy Lesson*, for example, instead of a body there's a naked, smiling woman, and the students look as though they're just about to throw themselves on her. *The Syndics* shows Van Tysch's teachers and colleagues: Tanagorsky, Kalima and Buncher . . . *The Jewish Bride* could hide references to his father's collaboration during the war; it's even been said that he has disguised the female model as Anne Frank . . . the *Christ on the Cross* is a kind of self-portrait . . . Gustavo Onfretti, the model, is painted to look like Van Tysch and is hanging from a cross . . . in other words, in "Rembrandt" nearly all the works are directly related to Van Tysch and his world, in one grotesque way or another . . .'

'But this guy is only going to destroy one of them,' Miss Wood snapped. 'And I need to know which one.'

Oslo could not bear to meet her imploring eyes.

'And what will you do if I say a probability among the thirteen? You'll give that one more protection, won't you? What if

336

I'm wrong? Will that make me responsible for a death? Or more than one, perhaps?'

'You won't be responsible for anything. I've already told you, I'm collecting the opinion of experts all round the world, and I'll choose the work that gets most votes.'

'Why not ask Van Tysch?'

'He didn't want to see me,' replied Wood. 'The Maestro is inaccessible. And besides, he hasn't even been told that *Deflowering* and *Monsters* have been destroyed. He is on top of his private summit, Hirum. I can't reach him.'

'What if the majority of experts are wrong?'

'Even if that's the case, nothing will happen. I'm not going to put the original work at risk.'

All of a sudden it was Hirum Oslo who felt nervous. As he stared at Miss Wood's face lit by the desk lamp, he realised what she was proposing. His whole body went tense.

'Hang on a minute. Now I understand. You're going to . . . you're going to put a *copy* as *bait* for this madman . . . A copy of the work that gets most votes . . .'

There was another pause. Oslo was convinced he had hit the nail on the head.

'That's your idea, isn't it? And what will happen to the copy? You know very well we're talking about human beings . . .'

'We'll protect the copy,' she said.

Oslo was quick to realise she was being insincere.

'No, you won't. It wouldn't be of any use to you if you protected it . . . you want to use it as *bait*. You want to set a *trap*. You're going to hand over one, or more, innocent people to this psychopath, in order to save the others!'

'A copy of a Van Tysch work is only worth fifteen thousand dollars on the market, Hirum.'

Oslo could feel the old fury gripping him.

'But they are *people*, April! The copies are people, too, just like the original!'

'But they're not worth anything as art.'

'And art isn't worth anything compared to people, April!'

'I don't want an argument, Hirum.'

'All the art in the world, all the damned art in the world, from

337

the Parthenon to the *Mona Lisa,* from the statue of David to Beethoven's symphonies, is *rubbish* compared to even the most insignificant of people! Can't you understand that?'

'I don't want an argument, Hirum.'

There she was, thought Oslo, there she was, unmoving, and the world would go on turning. We are defending the world's heritage, she always said, we are defending the great human creations, pyramids, sculptures, canvases, museums, all of them built on dead bodies, bones on bones. We are protecting the heritage of injustice. We buy slaves to haul blocks of granite. We buy slaves to paint their bodies. To make Ashtrays, Lamps, and Chairs. To disguise them as animals and men. To destroy them according to their price on the market. Welcome to the twenty-first century: life is disappearing. but art survives. Some consolation.

'I'm not going to have anything to do with an act of injustice,' said Oslo.

Unexpectedly, Miss Wood smiled at him.

'Hirum: you've seen lots of works by Van Tysch in your life, and you know a copy can't compare, artistically, with an original by the Maestro, can it?' – Oslo agreed – 'You say that both of them are human beings, and I agree with you. It's precisely because the material is the same that the value is different. And when one has to make hard choices, one has to choose the more precious thing. I've already told you I don't want to argue, but I'll give you an example. Your house is on fire and you can only save *one work of art.* Would you save *Bust* by Van Tysch or a copy of *Bust?* In both cases we're talking about an eleven- or twelve-year-old girl. But which of the two would you save, Hirum? *Which of the two?*'

This time there was a long silence. Oslo wiped the sweat from his forehead. Miss Wood continued, with another smile:

'That's the kind of "act of injustice" I'm asking you to commit.'

'You haven't changed,' Oslo replied. 'You haven't changed a bit, April. What is it you're really trying to prevent? The loss of a painting, or of confidence in yourself?'

'Hirum.'

That electric whisper of hers. That frozen murmur which

338

paralysed you the way the bifid taunt of a snake paralyses its tiny victim. Wood leaned over forwards as though her body had lost its centre of gravity. She spoke very slowly, in a tone that made Hirum squirm in his seat.

'Hirum, if you want to help me, tell me your damn opinion once and for all.'

Another pause and then, in the same tone of voice and with her blue quartz eyes fixed on him, she added:

'Forgive me for such a rapid visit, Hirum. In fact, you've helped me a lot already. You don't have to do any more.'

'No, wait, pass me the catalogue again. I'll study it and give you a call tomorrow. If I see one painting that looks more likely than the others, I'll tell you.'

He hesitated a moment before he went on, as if wondering whether it was worth obtaining any kind of promise from someone who looked at you the way she did, and who could talk in such a terrible whisper.

'Promise me you'll do all you can to make sure no one is injured, April.'

She agreed, and handed him the catalogue. Then she stood up, and Oslo walked back to the house with her.

Night was falling on the world.

4

The landscape is one of hands opening in the darkness as though trying to catch something. They are hanging from streetlamps, are stuck on walls and the ironclad sides of trams, they flutter beneath the arches of the canal bridges. This is the image chosen to publicise 'Rembrandt': the hand of the Angel from *Jacob Wrestling with the Angel,* the work being shown to the press in the Old Atelier this very day, Thursday 13 July, the work which will fire the first salvo in the most amazing show of the decade.

Bosch shuddered to think that they could not have found a more appropriate symbol. He knew there was another *hand* stretched out in the darkness, trying to catch something. As the days went by, Miss Wood's fears seemed to him more and more reasonable. If before he had doubted that the Artist was going to attack 'Rembrandt', now he was sure of it. He was convinced the criminal was there, in Amsterdam, and had already laid his plans. He would destroy one of the canvases unless they could find some way of stopping him. Or of protecting the work he was targeting. Or setting him a trap.

The sky was lined with heavy clouds as Bosch arrived at the New Atelier that Thursday morning. Above the Stedelijk roof could be seen the black tops of the curtains that made up the 'Rembrandt Tunnel', as the press had baptised the exhibition tent erected on the Museumplein. It was a cool day even though it was midsummer. Bosch recalled that the weather forecast had spoken of rain for Saturday, the day of the opening. Rain, yes, and thunder and lightning, too, he thought. When he entered his office, he saw that all his phones had unanswered messages, but he could not deal with any of them because Alfred van Hoore and Rita van Dorn were waiting for him with a CD-ROM and a burning desire to tell him things and, in the case of van Hoore, to show him his new computer simulations. Both of them had stickers for the exhibition on their jacket lapels: a tiny Angel's hand above the word 'Rembrandt'. Bosch found the stickers absurd, but was careful not to say anything. His two colleagues were smiling with satisfaction at the progress of their security measures, which Stein had complimented them on. They both seemed pleased with themselves. Bosch felt rather sorry for them.

'I'd like you to see this model, Lothar,' Van Hoore was saying, pointing to the three-dimensional skeleton of the Tunnel on his computer screen. 'Does anything attract your attention?'

'Those red dots.'

'Exactly. Do you know what they are?'

Bosch stirred in his seat.

'I imagine they're the public emergency exits.'

'Exactly. And what do you think of them?'

'Please, Alfred, you tell me. I've got a dreadful morning ahead of me. I'm not up to facing an exam.'

340

Rita smiled silently. Van Hoore looked offended.

'There are *too few* exits for the paintings, Lothar. We've thought more about the public, but let's take an extreme case. A fire.'

He pressed a key, and the spectacle began. To Bosch's mind, Van Hoore was staring at the screen with the same fascination that Nero must have observed Rome burning. In a few seconds, the three-dimensional tunnel was consumed by flames.

'I know the curtains aren't flammable, and Popotkin has assured us that the chiaroscuro lighting does not short-circuit like ordinary lights. But let's just imagine that in spite of everything, there is a fire . . .'

Igor Popotkin was the physicist who had designed the lighting to produce the effects of light and shade. He was also, like many Russian scientists who had received their training during the period of *glasnost* and *perestroika*, a poet and a pacifist. Stein used to say that in a year or two they would award him a Nobel prize, although he was never quite sure what for. Bosch had seen Popotkin a couple of times during his visits to Amsterdam. He was a little old man with bovine features. He loved smoking dope, and had frequented all the coffee shops in the red-light district to get little bags of the stuff.

'What do you think would happen if there were a fire, Lothar?'

'That the public rushing for the exits would get in the way of the paintings,' Bosch replied, submitting finally to the grilling.

'Exactly. So what is the solution?'

'To make more exits.'

Van Hoore's face was a picture of fake compassion, like a quiz show host who has detected a wrong answer.

'We don't have time for that. But I've had an idea. One of the security teams will be dedicated to getting out the artworks if there is a disaster. Look.'

Tiny figures in white shirts and trousers wearing green jackets appeared on the screen.

'I call them the Artistic Emergency Personnel,' Van Hoore explained. 'They'll be at collection points in the centre of the Tunnel horseshoe, with special vans ready and waiting to whisk away the paintings if need be.'

341

'Fantastic, Alfred,' Bosch cut in. 'Really. I like it. It's the perfect solution.'

When Van Hoore's fire was extinguished, it was Rita's turn. She simply went over what had already been decided. The works would be picked up by the same identified security men. Inside the Tunnel there would be a security team every hundred metres. They would be armed and have torches, but were not to shine any light unless there was an emergency. There would be three controls at the entry point, with the usual machines: X-rays, magnetic checkers and instant imaging screens. Cases and parcels would have to be left at the entrance. Baby pushchairs would be prohibited. Nothing could be done about handbags, except for random searches of any suspicious-looking persons, but the possibility of anyone being able to bring in a dangerous object in a bag that was not detected by any of the security screens was less than 0.8 per cent. In the hotel where the works were to be kept (the name of which would not, of course, be revealed to the public) there would be round-the-clock guards of three people per painting. The guards who were on duty inside the rooms would have to undergo strict fingerprint and voice tests each morning. They would wear tags that could only be used once, with codes that would change every day. They would carry guns, and electric batons.

'By the way,' Rita asked, 'Why has there been this last-minute change in the list of security guards, Lothar?'

'That was my decision, Rita,' Bosch replied. 'We're going to bring a new team in from our headquarters in New York. They'll be here tomorrow.'

Alfred and Rita looked at each other, puzzled.

'It's an extra security measure,' Bosch said to settle it. He was trying to seem as natural as possible, so they would not think he was hiding anything from them. Neither Van Hoore nor Rita knew anything about the Artist, or about the plans he and April had been hatching together.

'It'll be the best protected exhibition in the history of art,' Rita said with a smile. 'I don't think we need to worry so much.'

At that instant, Kurt Sorensen's spiky head appeared round the door. He was with Gert Warfell.

'Do you have a moment, Lothar?'

Of course, come right in, thought Bosch. Alfred and Rita gathered up their things, to be replaced in the blink of an eye by the newcomers. There followed a giddying discussion about the security of all the important guests to the Tunnel. None of them brought up the question that was most worrying Bosch until the very end. It was then that Sorensen said:

'Will he attack or won't he?'

Warfell and Bosch looked at each other, as if weighing up each other's anxiety. Bosch concluded that Warfell seemed much calmer and relaxed than he did.

'No, he won't attack,' Warfell said. 'He'll stay hidden in his lair for some time. Rip van Winkle has got him by the balls.'

No, he's got us in his grasp, thought Bosch, observing him coolly. And perhaps it's one of *you two* who's helping him.

Bosch had lost what little confidence he had in Rip van Winkle after reading their first reports. They offered three sorts of 'result': a psychological profile of the Artist, an operational profile, and what in the strange terminology of the organisation was known as a 'pruning' – that is, the elimination of access routes. The psychological profile had been drawn up by twenty experts working independently. They agreed only on one thing: the Artist had the classic traits of a psychopath. He was undoubtedly a cold, calculating individual who refused to submit to authority. The messages he forced his victims to read could mean that he was a frustrated painter. Beyond this, their opinions differed: there was no agreement on what sex the Artist was, or his sexual preferences; for some experts he was one person, for others, several people. The operational profile was even more ambiguous. The border systems of the member countries had still not been coordinated satisfactorily. Every case of fake documents that had been discovered by the police in recent weeks was being studied, but some countries seemed reluctant to provide all the information. Descriptions of Brenda and the woman with no papers had been circulated to all the customs officials, but it was impossible to arrest someone simply because they looked like a computer-generated image. All the factories that produced cerublastyne were being investigated. All large movements of money between accounts in European banks were being traced, because it was thought the Artist must be extremely wealthy. Suppliers and manufacturers of cassettes were also being questioned.

Last but not least was the 'pruning'. This was the most depressing part of all. Some of the questioning of cerublastyne experts had been 'special'. Bosch had no idea what went on during these 'special' sessions, but the people who had been questioned never appeared again. Head Honcho had warned them: there would be victims, 'innocent but necessary' ones. Rip van Winkle moved forward blindly, like a crazed leviathan, but at the same time, it tried to cover up the tracks it left in its advance: the 'special' interrogations could not under any circumstances become public knowledge.

Bosch knew it was a race against time, with only one possible winner. Either art or the Artist would triumph. Europe was doing what it always did in these cases: protecting humanity's creations, the inheritance humanity passed on to itself down the generations. In comparison to this inheritance, humanity itself was disposable. A consecrated work of art was worth far more than a few miserable individuals, even if they happened to be a majority. Bosch was well aware of this from his days as a *provo*: what was sacred, even if only for a minority, was always more *numerous* than the majority, precisely because it was accepted by everyone.

Or almost everyone. Perhaps the people interrogated by Rip van Winkle had different views, thought Bosch.

But nobody had listened to them.

'By the way,' Sorensen said, 'tomorrow we have a meeting with Rip. In The Hague. Did you two know about it?'

Bosch and Warfell knew about it. The meeting had been announced in the latest report. Apparently, Rip van Winkle had produced some fresh results, and wanted to discuss them face to face. Sorensen and Warfell were of the opinion this meant the Artist had already been caught. Bosch was not so optimistic.

At midday, close to lunchtime, Nikki appeared in Bosch's office. She was holding up her hand and making a 'V' sign. Bosch almost leapt from his seat, until he realised this did not mean 'victory', but 'two'. Well, that's a kind of victory anyway, he thought enthusiastically. Yesterday there were four.

'We've managed to eliminate another two suspects,' Nikki announced. 'Do you remember I told you Laviatov spent time in jail for theft? Well, he's given up being a canvas now and is trying to establish himself with a hyperdramatic gallery in Kiev. I've talked to him and some of his employees, and they confirmed his alibi. He hasn't been out of the city in weeks. And we've had confirmation that Fourier committed suicide six months ago after a failed relationship with one of his previous owners. The company that sold him kept it quiet so as not to scare the other canvases. So we're left with only two without alibis.'

She spread out her sheets of paper on the desk. Two photos, two people, two names. One face framed by long chestnut curls, with a piercing blue gaze. The other almost child-like, featureless, shaven-headed.

'The first is called Lije,' Nikki explained. 'He or she is about twenty, but we're not sure which sex. He's worked mostly in Japan with artists such as Higashi, but he's not Japanese. He specialises in transgender works and art-shocks. We know more about the other one. His name is Postumo Baldi, he was born in Naples in 1986, so he is twenty as well, and male. He's the son of a failed painter and a former ornament, who are now divorced. There is evidence that the mother took part in marginal art-shocks, and that she used her son with her from a very early age. Baldi also specialised in transgender work. In 2000, Van Tysch chose him as the original for *Figure XIII*, one of the few transgender pieces the Maestro has done. Since then, he's been in art-shocks and portraits.'

Bosch stared at the two photographs as though hypnotised. If Miss Wood's intuition was correct, and if the computer screening process had not let anything slip through, one of these two was the Artist.

'Just think,' Nikki said with a smile, 'Lije could be in Holland as we speak. In fact, he might even be in Amsterdam.'

'What?'

'That's right. His trail disappears after he took part clandestinely in two art-shocks at Extreme, a place for illegal works in the red-light district. That was in December last year.'

'I've heard of Extreme,' said Bosch.

'The owners haven't been very forthcoming. They say they have no idea what became of Lije after that, and they refused to give any information to the team of interviewers we sent to talk to them. I'm thinking of sending Romberg's people to pull their teeth out, if you authorise it.'

Bosch was staring at Lije's expressionless features, unable to make up his mind whether they belonged to a man or a woman.

'What about Baldi?'

'We lost trace of him in France. The last work he definitely took part in was a transgender piece by Jan van Obber for the dealer Jenny Thoreau, but he didn't even fulfil his contract. He walked out and vanished off the map.'

Bosch thought for a moment.

'It's up to you,' Nikki said, raising her blonde eyebrows.

'Van Obber lives in Delft, doesn't he? Call him and fix an appointment for tomorrow afternoon. I have to go to The Hague in the morning, so I could visit Delft on the way back. Tell him no more than that we're looking for Postumo Baldi. And send Romberg's men to Extreme.'

After Nikki left his office, Bosch still sat contemplating the two faces, these two anonymous youths whose smooth features stared back at him from the photos. 'One of these two is the Artist,' he thought. 'If April is right – and she always is – one of them is him.'

5

Light is the very last touch. Gerardo and Uhl are installing it in the farm living room. They have been at it since early in the morning, because the equipment is very delicate. The chiaroscuro lamps have been specially created for the exhibition by a Russian physicist. Clara stares at the strange fittings: metal bars from which protrude arms with bulbs on the end. They look to her like steel racks.

'You're going to see something incredible,' said Gerardo.

They closed the blinds. In the dense darkness, Uhl flicked a switch and the lamps gave off a golden glow. It was light, but it did not illuminate. It seemed to paint the air a golden colour rather than to reveal objects. Thanks to the flashing speed of electricity, the entire room had become a seventeenth-century oil painting. A minimalist still life by Franz Hals; *prêt-à-porter* Rubens; postmodern Vermeer. Standing opposite her, the only figure in this domestic tenebrist canvas, Gerardo was smiling.

'It's as if we were inside a Rembrandt picture, isn't it? Come on, you're the protagonist.'

Barefoot and naked, Clara walked towards the light. It was a friendly, tempting light, the dream of a suicidal moth: she could stare at it endlessly without it harming her eyes. There were gasps of admiration.

'You're a perfect work of art,' Gerardo praised her. 'You don't even need painting. Do you want to see yourself? Look.'

There was the sound of wood scraping along the floor, and she could see one of the mirrors being brought over.

She caught her breath.

Somehow, in some way, she knew this was what she had been searching for all her life.

Her silhouette stood out from the darkness of a classical painting as if painted with golden brushstrokes. Her face and half the curtain of her hair were incrusted with amber. Clara blinked at her gleaming breasts, the lavish crown of her sex, the outline of her legs. As she moved, she sparkled like a diamond under the light, and became a different kind of work. Each of her gestures painted a thousand different canvases of herself.

'I wouldn't mind having you at home under these lights,' she heard Gerardo say in the darkness. *'Naked Woman on a Black Background.'*

She could hardly hear him. It seemed to her that everything she had dreamt of ever since she had discovered Eliseo Sandoval's artwork in her friend Talia's house, everything she had scarcely dared say or admit to herself when she decided to become a canvas, was here now in the reflection of her body under the chiaroscuro lights.

She understood she had always been her own dream.

*

That morning the poses were easier. It was what Gerardo called 'filling in'. They had already chosen the exact colours: a deep red for her hair, drawn up in a bun; mother-of-pearl mixed with pink and yellow for the skin; a fine ochre line for the eyebrows; chestnut eyes with a tinge of crystal; her lips outlined in flesh tints; the areolas of her breasts a matt brown colour. After she had showered, washed and returned to her original primed colours, Clara felt better. She was exhausted, but she had reached the end of a long journey. The previous fortnight had been full of harsh poses, colour experiments, efforts to concentrate, and then the masterly brushstrokes Van Tysch had used to define her expression as she stared into the mirror, the slow passage of time. Only the final detail was left.

'The signature,' Gerardo said. 'The Maestro will sign the works in the rehearsal room at the Old Atelier this afternoon. And you will all pass into eternity,' he added with a smile.

Uhl drove the van. They turned on to the motorway and soon saw Amsterdam in the distance. The sight of that city, which had always seemed to Clara like a pretty doll's house, lifted her hypnotised spirits. They crossed several bridges and headed for the Museumsplein along narrow, tidy streets, accompanied by never-ending streams of bicycles and the clanking procession of trams. They spied the impressive bulk of the Rijksmuseum. Beyond it, in the pearly-grey midday light, they could see a huge mass of dense shadows. The sun's rays filtering through the clouds gave the massive structure an opalescent sheen. It was as though a tidal wave of oil were sweeping over Amsterdam.

'Rembrandt's Tunnel.'

They had decided to have a look at it before they went to the Old Atelier for the signature session. Clara was excited about discovering the mysterious place where she would be exhibited. They parked close to the Rijksmuseum. It was not exactly a hot summer's day, but she did not feel at all cold beneath the padded light sleeveless dress she was wearing. She also had on a pair of lined plastic slippers as well as the three labels that identified her as one of the original figures for *Susanna Surprised by the Elders*.

They walked into Museumstraat and found themselves face to

348

face with the Tunnel almost unintentionally. It looked like the mouth of a huge mine covered with curtains. It was a horseshoe shape, with the U open towards the rear of the Rijksmuseum. The main entrance was protected by two rows of fences, flashing lights and white and orange vehicles with the word *Politie* written on the side. Men and women in dark-blue uniforms were on guard at the fences. Some tourists were taking photos of the colossal structure.

While Gerardo and Uhl went to talk to the policemen, Clara stopped to get a good look at the Tunnel. From the entrance, which was easily as tall as any of the great classical buildings in Amsterdam, the curtains rose and fell, dipping down or rising up to the clouds in the sky like a majestic circus tent, snaking in among the trees and enveloping them, blocking streets and cutting off the horizon. In between the two wings of the horseshoe was the central area of the Museumplein, with its artificial pond and monument. There was something strange and grotesque about this vast black shape squatting like a dead spider on Amsterdam's delicate cityscape, something Clara found hard to define. It was as though painting had become something else. As though it was not an art exhibition that was involved, but something infinitely more challenging. The entrance was covered by one of Rembrandt's famous last self-portraits. His face beneath the cap – his bulbous nose, the scrawny moustache and the wispy Dutch goatee beard – peered sceptically out at the world. He looked like a God weary of creating. The curtain over the exit was a blow-up of the photo of Van Tysch facing away from the camera. We go in through Rembrandt's chest, and come out through Van Tysch's back, Clara thought. The past and present of Dutch art. But which of the two geniuses was more enigmatic? The one who showed his painted face, or the one who hides his real identity? She could not decide.

Gerardo came up to her.

'They're checking our documents so we can go in,' he said, pointing to the Tunnel. 'What do you make of it?'

'It's fantastic.'

'It's almost five hundred metres long, but it's bent in the shape of a horseshoe so it will fit into the park. You go in this end, and

349

come out over there near the Van Gogh museum. Some parts of it are forty metres high. Van Tysch wanted it erected near the Rembrandthuis, cutting off streets and even emptying buildings, but of course they wouldn't let him. The curtains are made of a special material: it blocks out all exterior light and keeps the inside as black as a well, so the works will only be lit by the chiaroscuro lights. We can walk through it. But keep close to us.'

'Why? What could happen to me?' Clara asked with a smile.

'Well, tramps spend the night in there. And drug addicts slip in under cover of dark. And then there are the protest groups, the BAH and the others ... yes, the BAH, the *Bothered About Hyperdrama*. You must have heard of them, haven't you? ... They're our most faithful followers,' Gerardo smiled. 'Tomorrow they're holding a protest outside the Tunnel, but there are always a couple of trouble-makers who try to get in to put up posters. The police are on patrol inside the Tunnel, and arrest one or two of them every day. Come on, let's go.'

Clara was pleased at Gerardo's concern for her. In other circumstances she might have thought he was worried about *Susanna*, but this time she was sure it wasn't that. It was *her*, Clara Reyes, that he was afraid of losing.

Uhl was waiting for them beside a small gap in the entrance curtain. It's as though we were going in under Rembrandt's head, thought Clara. Dim lights from bulbs fixed in the curtain showed them the way. But as soon as they were properly inside they were enveloped in an unknown darkness. The street noises had disappeared, too: all that could be heard were distant echoes. Clara could scarcely make out Gerardo's shape in front of her.

'Wait a moment; your eyes will get used to it.'

'I'm starting to see something.'

'Don't worry, there's nothing in the way. The path to follow is a gentle narrow ramp, indicated by the lights. All you have to do is walk forward. And once the works have been installed and are lit by the chiaroscuro lighting, they'll be reference points. Can you feel the guide rope? Stay close to it.'

Gerardo went ahead. Clara was in the middle. They went forward slowly over the smooth ground, groping like blind people for the rope at the edge of the track. All she could see of Gerardo were his feet and part of his trouser legs. The rest of his silhouette was swallowed up in the darkness. It seemed to her as though she was walking through the night of the world.

'Is everything all right back there?' she heard Gerardo say.

'More or less.'

Uhl said something in Dutch, Gerardo replied, and the two men laughed. Gerardo translated for her:

'Some of the works say this place gives them the creeps.'

'I like it,' Clara said firmly.

'This darkness?'

'Yes, absolutely.'

She could hear Gerardo and Uhl's footsteps and the flapping of the labels on her wrist and ankle. All of a sudden the atmosphere changed. It was as if the space had suddenly got bigger. The sound of their footsteps was different. Clara stopped and looked up. It was like peering into an abyss. She felt a kind of upside-down giddiness, as if she was in danger of leaving the ground and plunging up into the heights of the tent curtains. Whole choirs of silence converged in the pitch-black air above her head. She suddenly remembered Van Tysch's pronouncement that absolute darkness did not exist, and wondered whether the Maestro had not been trying to contradict himself with the design of the Tunnel.

'They call this part the "basilica".' Gerardo's voice floated in front of her. 'It's the first dome. Almost thirty metres high. There's another even higher one in the other wing of the U. In the centre of this one they're going to put *The Anatomy Lesson*, and further on *The Syndics* and *The Slaughtered Ox*, which has several figures hanging from the roof by their ankles. You can't see the background now because there's no lighting.'

'It smells of paint,' Clara murmured.

'Oil paint,' Gerardo said. 'We're inside a Rembrandt painting, after all. Had you forgotten? But come on, don't get left behind.'

'How do you know I'm being left behind?'

'Your yellow labels give the game away.'

Clara's legs were shaking as she walked. She thought it must be that her muscles were unused to this perfectly normal exercise

351

after all the tough days of holding poses, but she suspected as well that it was because of the emotion this infinite darkness aroused in her.

'We've still a way to go before we reach the spot where *Susanna* will be exhibited,' Gerardo said. 'But look, can you make out those dark struts in the distance?'

Clara thought she could see something, but perhaps it wasn't what Gerardo meant. She could barely make out his hand pointing into the darkness.

'We've almost reached the bend in the horseshoe. That's where *The Night Watch* will be: it's an incredible mural, with more than twenty figures. Beyond that, *Young Girl Leaning on a Window Sill* and the small portrait of *Titus,* Rembrandt's son. On this side there'll be *The Jewish Bride* . . . and now we're coming to the spot where they'll show *The Feast of Belshazzar.*'

As they edged forward, Clara suddenly saw something amazing in the depths of the darkness: will-o'-the-wisps, glow-worms moving in straight lines.

'The police,' Uhl explained behind her.

It must have been one of the patrols Gerardo had told her were on duty in the Tunnel. They passed by them. Ghostly forms with berets and light flashing off their badges. Clara made out smiles and words in Dutch.

Then they continued on into the bowels of an abandoned universe.

'Do you believe in God, Clara?' Gerardo asked all of a sudden.

'No,' she replied simply. 'What about you?'

'I believe in something. And things like this Tunnel prove to me that I'm right. There is *something more*, don't you agree? Otherwise, what led Van Tysch to build all this? He himself is the tool of something higher, even though he doesn't know it.'

'Yes, he's Rembrandt's tool.'

'Don't try to be funny. There's something above and beyond Rembrandt, too.'

But what? Clara wondered. What was there above and beyond Rembrandt? Unintentionally, almost unconsciously, she looked up. She saw darkness curled around a shadowy light, a light so dim she was not sure if her eyes were inventing it, as

352

weak as the light from a remembered image, or a dream. A shapeless mass of shadow.

Uhl interrupted her thoughts with a sentence behind her back. Gerardo laughed and answered him.

'Justus says he'd love to know Spanish so he could understand what we're talking about. I told him we're talking about God and Rembrandt. Ah, look . . . on that wall is where they're going to put *Christ on the Cross*, and further on . . .'

Clara could feel fingers touching her own. She let herself be led to the guide rope. The feeble glow from the lights helped her make out the contours of a fabulous garden.

'This is where *Susanna* will be. Can you see the steps at the edge of the water in the pool? The water won't be real, it'll be painted, like everything else. The lighting will be from above, and the main colours will be ochre and gold. What do you reckon?'

'That it's going to be incredible.'

She heard Gerardo laugh, and felt his arm going round her shoulders.

'You're the incredible one,' he murmured. 'You're the most beautiful canvas I've ever worked on . . .'

She did not want to pause to consider what he might mean by that. Over the past few days she had hardly spoken to him in her breaks and yet, however strange it might seem, she had felt closer to him than ever. She remembered the evening a fortnight earlier when Van Tysch had appeared, and Gerardo had painted her features, and the way he had looked at her while he was holding up the mirror. In some unfathomable way, she thought, both of them had helped recreate her, give her new life. But whereas Van Tysch had solely painted *Susanna*, Gerardo had also helped define *Clara*, to sketch a new, still diffuse Clara, still dark and undefined. At that moment, she did not feel she had the strength to consider all that this discovery implied.

They emerged from the far end of the horseshoe, out through Van Tysch's dark back, and stood blinking in the daylight. It was not a sunny day, far from it: the sun was having difficulty breaking through a grey veil of clouds covering the sky. But compared to the sublime pitch-black darkness they had just left, Clara felt

she was looking at a blindingly hot summer's day. The temperature was perfect, despite an unsettling wind.

'It's almost noon,' said Gerardo. 'We should go to the Atelier
in the Plantage district to get you ready and have the Maestro
sign you.' As he gazed at her, an inscrutable smile stretched his
cheeks. 'Are you ready for eternity?'

She said she was.

Tomorrow. Tomorrow was the day.

She could feel the sheets rub against her labels, and the signature like a child's hand on her ankle: something that neither hurt
nor pleased her, but was simply there.

'Tomorrow *I'll begin eternal life.*'

After the signing session, she had been taken to her hotel.
There was a security guard keeping watch on her, even in her
room, because now she was an immortal work of art. And they
have to prevent at all costs any immortal work dying, she
thought, smiling to herself.

It had happened around five in the afternoon. Gerardo and
Uhl had taken her to the Old Atelier, the sprawling complex of
buildings the Foundation used in the Plantage district. There
they had painted her in one of the cabins with two-way mirrors
in the basement. They had let her dry, then put on a padded
dress and led her to the signing room. Nearly all the 'Rembrandt'
works were there. Clara saw some incredible sights: two models
hanging by their ankles next to a constructed ox carcass, a regiment of bloody riders; a wonderful dream mixing Dutch Puritan
clothes and the nakedness of mythological flesh. She saw
Gustavo Onfretti nailed to a cross, and Kirsten Kirstenman
stretched out on an operating table. She met for the first time the
two old men of *Susanna*; one of them gaunt, with a penetrating
gaze, the other as solid as a wardrobe. She recognised the first of
them immediately, despite the paint obscuring his face: he was
the old man she had seen being checked in the room next to hers
at Schiphol airport. Both of them were wearing flowing robes,
and the tones of their faces denoted lasciviousness and liver
problems. She hardly had time to speak to them, because she
had to be placed in position on the podium: naked, crouching at

the feet of the First Elder, completely *Susanna*, completely defenceless.

A long time went by before Van Tysch and his assistants appeared. Clara thought Gerardo and Uhl were among them. Perhaps also there was the black assistant she had seen getting out of a van a fortnight earlier. Curled up on the ground, she saw a procession of women's calves, and barefoot men and women go past: probably sketch models. Then the dark tubes of Van Tysch's black trousers. Phrases in Dutch. Van Tysch's voice. Other voices. The sound of implements. Someone had switched on a bright light and was shining it on her. Then the buzz of the electric tattoo needle.

Clara had been signed on many occasions. She was well aware of the physical sensation when a painter signed part of her body with any kind of delicate instrument. But this was completely different. It was like the first time. To be a Van Tysch original *was* different. She felt as though she had reached an end, had been finished. At twenty-four, she was complete. But beyond this ecstatic feeling of being finished, who would understand her? Who could go with her in her journey into darkness? Who would help make her transition to the sublime an easy, quick one? All at once, in the split second before the tattoo needle touched her, she stopped thinking and wishing. She felt a kind of empty dark sensation inside herself, as if she had stepped outside her body and had switched off the light. Now I'm thinking like an insect: she remembered Marisa Monfort's advice when she was priming her memories. Now I'm a *real* work of art.

Something was tickling her left ankle. She could feel the needle circling round as it drew 'BvT' on her bone. Of course she did not even look at Van Tysch while he was doing this. She knew he wasn't looking at *her* either.

And now in the hotel, on that first night, she was waiting.

Tomorrow was the day. Tomorrow she would be on show for the first time.

When at last she fell asleep, she dreamt that she was once again outside the door to the attic in the Alberca house, except that she wasn't an eight-year-old girl, but a twenty-four-year-old woman who had been signed on the ankle by Van Tysch.

Even so, she was desperate to get into the attic. 'Because I haven't seen the horrible yet. I'm a Van Tysch painting, but I still haven't seen the *horrible*.' She went up to the door and yanked it open. Someone stopped her with a hand on her arm. She turned, and saw her father. He looked terrified. He was shouting something as he tried to prevent her going into the room. Gerardo was standing next to him, shouting as well. It was as though they wanted to save her from a mortal danger.

But she struggled free from all the hands keeping her back, and ran towards the dark depths.

6

Because in the depths there is only darkness.

April Wood opened her eyes. At first she could not remember where she was or what she was doing there. She raised her head and saw she was in a broad bed in the middle of a darkened room. She slowly realised this must be the Vermeer Hotel, and that she had arrived in Amsterdam to watch the Maestro signing his works at the Old Atelier. In theory, the session was private, but Foundation staff could attend if they so wished. Wood wanted to see the finished works in their poses, to get to know them as well as the Artist doubtless did. As soon as the signing was over, she had come back to the hotel and gone to bed, so doped up with sleeping pills she had not even taken off her clothes. She was still wearing the tight black suit with a silver thread she had gone to the Atelier in. She glanced at her watch: 20.05 on Friday 14 July, 2006. Less than twenty-four hours to the opening of 'Rembrandt'.

There was a big mirror on the far wall of the room. She got up and considered herself in it. She looked dreadful. She remembered she had almost fallen unconscious. The imprint of her head still hollowed the pillow.

She unzipped her suit, stepped out of it and threw her clothes on the floor. The bathroom was wall-to-wall marble. She pressed the light switch and turned on the shower. As a warm jet of water sprayed over her body, she mentally went over what she knew. What did it amount to? A lot of opinions, and thirteen terrible possibilities.

After talking to Hirum Oslo on Tuesday, she had called several other critics from London. She had given them all the same excuse, except for Oslo (why did you tell *him* the truth, she wondered): that she had to draw up a list with the most valuable, intimate and personal works by Van Tysch in order to place the security people properly. So far, none of the critics had refused to give their opinion. The Maestro, on the other hand, had refused to see her. April could not object: he was her boss, and his only obligation was to pay her. 'He's very tired,' said Stein, to whom she had spoken the previous afternoon in the Atelier. 'After Saturday, he's going to shut himself away in Edenburg. He doesn't want anyone to see him.' Stein himself seemed exhausted. 'We've reached the end,' he had told Miss Wood. 'The end of a creative act is always sad.'

Miss Wood stepped nimbly out of the shower. The huge hotel towels were like bearskins. As she wrapped herself in one, she glanced down at the electronic weighing scales at her feet. She forced herself to avoid the temptation. It was not too much effort: the temptation was there like a dull ache, an uncomfortable sensation lodged somewhere in her brain. But Miss Wood knew that if she gave in over small things like that, she would immediately be defeated by much bigger ones. *She did not want* to know what she weighed: or rather, *she did*, but she was not going to find out. She knew she had put on weight, she could feel it in the outline of her hips and waist, but she had decided to diet and only have fruit juice with vitamins. And to concentrate even harder on her work.

She took a deep breath, left the bathroom, sat down on the bed still draped in the towel, and breathed in deeply one, two, three more times. So long as she was wrapped in the towel, there was no need for her to look at herself in the mirror. She was fat as a pig, a real sight, but the towel preserved her dignity. Of course, she could always get dressed, that is, to *try* to reach the wardrobe where her clothes were, and disguise the revolting mass of blubber in a blouse and trousers. She preferred not to think of what might happen if she could not fit into her trousers, if the zip could not overcome the rolls of fat.

Several minutes went by before she could feel her anxiety subsiding. She went over to the chest of drawers, opened her briefcase, and took out the file she had printed out the day before with the list of critics and the photos Bosch had sent her from Amsterdam detailing the exact position of each of the works in the Tunnel. Her hands were trembling as she laid them out on the bed, and sat in front of them like a Red Indian outside his wigwam, still enveloped in her towel.

The list was very striking. Some critics had voted for more than one painting. She had added up the total score in points. It was like a competition, she thought, but the prize for the winning work would be ten slashes from a portable canvas cutter.

1	*Christ on the Cross*	19
2	*The Syndics*	17
3	*The Anatomy Lesson*	14
4	*Bethsabe*	12
5	*The Night Watch*	11
6	*The Jewish Bride*	10
7	*The Feast of Belshazzar*	7
8	*The Slaughtered Ox*	2
9	*Young Girl Leaning on a Windowsill*	1
10	*Titus*	1
11	*Jacob Wrestling with the Angel*	1
12	*Susanna Surprised by the Elders*	1
13	*Danae*	0

For the moment, it was the *Christ* in the lead. But *The Syndics*, with the figures of Tanagorsky, Kalima and Buncher, was close behind. Hirum Oslo had called her on Wednesday with his vote: *Christ on the Cross*.

The *Christ* and *The Syndics*. One of them was in danger. Usually the great art critics did not make mistakes. Or did they? Could art be made into an objective science? Wasn't it the same as trying to determine what a poet might have meant by a strophe written in the distant past? What if she took the risk and prepared a trap with the *Christ* and *The Syndics*, only to find that the Artist destroyed *Titus* or *Jacob Wrestling with the Angel*? What if *Danae*, the only painting no expert had linked to Van Tysch's life, was the chosen one? How far can any critic know what lies hidden in the soul of an artist he has studied and admires? How far can the painter himself know? What about the Artist? How much did he know about Van Tysch? Miss Wood knew straightaway that if the Artist knew the painter *better than anyone else*, then her plan would fail.

If you let yourself be defeated by small things, you'll immediately lose out in big ones. She had no intention of letting that happen.

She put the papers back in her briefcase, crossed in front of the mirror with eyes closed, unwrapped the towel next to the wardrobe, and chose her clothes carefully. Everything must be perfect, and it will be perfect.

She had said the magic words. Would she need the magic oath as well? As a little girl, these rituals had been very effective. Whenever her father posed her against a wall, with flowers in her hair, her mouth and nipples painted, and a piece of cloth covering her pubis, so that he could take photos of her, Miss Wood swore the magic oath. It had a specific aim; it was like an offering to the iron god of her willpower. And often the oath had worked. I swear I'm going to keep up this pose, to stand still like this and stay here in the sun without moving a muscle.

She could not put the blame on her father for all she had suffered. When it came down to it, he had only wanted life to be better for both of them. How can someone be guilty for wanting what everybody in the world wants? Now her father was dying in a London hospital. She had gone to see him for the last time a few hours before she took the plane to Amsterdam. Of course, sunk as he was in the layers of his illness, he had not recognised her. April Wood had stood there observing him through her dark glasses. She had wanted to share with him this tiny slice of his death. You're not guilty of anything, Poppy, she had decided. Nobody is guilty, thought Miss Wood, the small portion of guilt that is ours is more than paid for in this life, which is hell enough.

The existence of heaven might be a question of faith, but there was no possible discussion about hell. No one could be an atheist about hell, because hell existed, it was here, this was it. There's nothing more, Poppy, and you've paid all your debts. That was her prayer at his bedside. Then she left.

Robert Wood had been an ambitious person, but to April Wood the difference between 'ambitious' and 'successful' lay entirely in the fact that the former had failed. Her father had been a failure. Nobody could have foreseen this failure when he left England and set himself up in Rome, first of all as an assistant at an international art dealer's, and then as a private dealer himself. For several years, things had gone very well for him, thanks to the growing boom in Italian hyperdramatism. My God, artists like Ferrucioli, Brentano, Mazzini or Savro owed everything to him. *Signor* Wood had spotted the importance of works such as *Genevieve* and *Jessica* painted by the young Ferrucioli, and had earned him huge sums of money. He had sensed that human artefacts would be a force to be reckoned with long before his less perceptive colleagues. And unlike other hypocrites, he had not closed his eyes and pretended to be scandalised by child or adolescent art. He had even defended Brentano's early work, his most extreme, toughest creations, and dismissed as 'whitened sepulchres' those who protested at the real scenes of girls whipped and imprisoned in iron cages, because he knew those very same people were the ones who bought 'stained' art clandestinely. Italian art owed a great deal to Robert Wood, but none of the artists had returned him the favour. That was something April Wood could not forgive.

For a few years, everything had gone well: her father had grown rich, had bought a wonderful villa near Tivoli, he had a wife who loved him, and a daughter who was growing more fascinatingly beautiful every day in front of his eyes.

When exactly had things started to go wrong? When had her father started to nose-dive, and to take his family with him? It was hard to tell. She had still been a little girl. Her mother had been the first to leave. April preferred to stay – among other reasons, because her mother hated her. It was as if she also blamed her for her husband's failure. Following the divorce, Robert Wood had found himself on his own. Who now remembered the *signor* who had stirred the awareness and the wallets of the Italian collectors? But his beautiful only child did not abandon him. Could she possibly blame him for trying to convert her into art?

It's true though, there was one small detail you didn't take into account, Poppy: I was very young, and didn't understand. I was only twelve or thirteen. You should have explained things better. Told me, for example, that you wanted to do it for my sake, not just so you could sell me to a great painter, but for my own sake, to make me into something great, something eternal, something that in some way would immortalise you.

One day a second-rate artist visited them. She had been told she must obey this painter's instructions so that the photos he took would be attractive, and then important painters would want to use her. The man took her into the garden and began to sketch her while her father was photographing her from the porch. Over the next six hours, April was put into more than thirty different poses. Her father forbade her from eating or drinking anything during sessions like these: maybe he was right, because works of art were not allowed to eat or drink when they were posing, but it was very hard on her. She was exhausted, and perhaps for that reason could not quite get it right, or perhaps the painter wanted her to make even more effort: the fact is, they started an argument and her father came out. 'I'm doing it properly!' she shouted at him. Then she saw him take his belt off. April can still remember he did not hit her with all his strength, but she was naked, and was only twelve, so the blow was ferocious. She ran off wailing. Her father called her back: 'Come here.' Trembling, she came back to him, only to receive another blow. All this took place while the painter looked on calmly.

'And now, listen to me,' Robert Wood had said, in a cool, level voice. 'You must never do things *properly*. You must do them *perfectly*. Don't forget, April. To do something *properly* is to do it *badly*. Because if you let yourself be defeated by little things, you'll immediately lose out in the big ones.'

You were right, and I should have understood that earlier.

She began the lengthy process of getting dressed.

You also used to say: 'Perhaps you think I like making you suffer, April, but all I want to do is make you understand you have to give *everything* to art. A little sacrifice is not enough. You have to give everything. Art is voracious.'

As an adolescent, she had not been able to understand this. It was only later she realised it was true. Art demanded everything because, in return, it offered you eternal pleasures. What were physical bodies compared to that? Bodies die a lingering death in hospitals, punctured by rubber tubes, or are beaten to the point of tears with leather belts, but art survives in the remote regions of the untouchable. April had eventually understood and accepted this. Until now, everything had gone well. Now though she was confronting a fearful problem, a gigantic imperfection. But she would emerge triumphant.

You're very clever whoever you are, Artist or model. You're good, I'll give you that. But I am better. I swear that I'm going to stop you destroying another canvas by Van Tysch. I swear I'm going to protect Van Tysch's works with all my strength. I swear I won't allow another of the Maestro's works to be destroyed. I swear I'm not going to make any more mistakes . . .

Blouse, trousers, her inseparable sunglasses, her short hair with a neat parting on the right. She had managed to get dressed.

She thought about what she was going to do next.

The critics were no use, that was obvious. Had critics ever been any use for anything? A good question, but not the right moment to try to answer it, Miss Wood told herself. The Maestro himself was no help. Yet she did not think it wise to reject the plan out of hand. They *had* to choose one of the works. And they could not take too many risks: the painting they chose had to be the one the Artist was most likely to target.

There was only one thing in her favour: she knew that the two works destroyed up to now had been *directly* related to Van Tysch's life, to his *past*. There was no reason to think it would not be the same with the third. It could well be the *Christ*, but she needed proof. Something to tell her her choice was not wrong.

She had to find out more about Van Tysch's past. Perhaps

there was something in it which could provide the link to one of the 'Rembrandt' works.

She picked up the phone and dialled a number.

She had already made her mind up. She would use the only means open to her to delve into the Maestro's past.

7

The worst thing about being a luxury ornament – thinks Susan Cabot – is that you have to be constantly available. Paintings generally have a strict timetable. That is a definite advantage, even though a lot of them have to work more than ten or twelve hours a day. But ornaments and artefacts have to be ready to go anywhere at any time, whether it is day or night, whether or not it is raining, or whether they feel like it or not. And when you've been shut up for a fortnight, it's worse still.

She had got the call early that morning. She was not asleep: she was lying in bed with the light on (not *her* light, but the bed-side lamp, an ordinary, non-human lamp) and smoking. She did not usually smoke a lot, but recently she had been overdoing it, perhaps because she felt so nervous. In fact, she had good reason to do so. She had been shut up in rooms like this one for more than two weeks now, cut off from the outside world. They were in small hostels used as store houses for ornaments, run by trusted Foundation employees. Food and everything else they might need was brought to them. Susan had a TV, books and magazines (curiously, there were never any newspapers – she wondered why, and guessed that those in charge thought news-papers might be dangerous). And, of course, she had all the accessories she needed for her work, including a ton of cosmetic and hygienic products, boxfuls of them almost every day. They included revitalisers, exfoliants, moisturisers, firming lotions, conditioners and polishers. Not forgetting the hypothermics, the hyperthermics, skin protectors, retexturisers and desensitisers. And the spare bulbs, too.

Susan was a Lamp designed by Piet Marooder. She needed bulbs.

She had imagined the phone call so often that when it finally came, she could hardly believe it. It was early on Friday morning. Bells from a nearby square lent the long-awaited moment a strange solemnity.

'Oh, shit.'

She leapt out of bed, stared at herself in the bathroom mirror, and after she had washed her face decided she would do. She chose a blouse and a pair of jeans, but of course did not put on any underwear. She checked she had all she needed in her bag. She still had a few minutes to spare.

The woman who had come to fetch her was small, and spoke with a French accent. As Susan climbed into the back of the passenger vehicle, she recognised several of the women she had worked with in the Obberlund.

It took so little time to reach their destination that she suspected they must be in The Hague or another city close by. It was still before dawn when they clambered out into the cool morning air and made their way into a beautiful big classical building (*running, running everywhere, like an army*). They assembled in the big main room, where they were given instructions. They would be wearing ear and eye protectors. At least it's better than being shut up any longer, Susan consoled herself.

An hour later, and she was ready. She stood in a corner of the room in her usual position: right leg raised, with the luminous sphere attached to her ankle; left leg bent at a right angle, her backside in the air. The pose meant her genitals were in full view of everyone, but the first thing a Lamp learns – inevitably – is not to feel ashamed. She was switched on at half-past nine. Out of the corner of her eye she could make out Opphuls Chairs, and a huge Lamp by Dominique de Perrin made up of a man and a woman which had just been installed on the ceiling. This must be a very important meeting.

Susan's pose meant she was staring at her own thighs. She was thinking of her boyfriend. His name was Ralph, and he was a Mordaieff Chair. At that very moment, Ralph might be somewhere in Europe having to put up with the weight of someone important enough to sit on him. Because of their work obligations, Ralph and Susan only rarely saw each other, even when they were in the same room. She did not envy him: she had been a Chair as well, and she preferred to be a Lamp and hold up a light rather than a person. Her father, a South African engineer who worked in Pretoria, had wanted Susan to study and have a brilliant career. How about four hundred watts, Daddy? Is that brilliant enough for you?

Shortly before half past eleven, a young woman came up to her. It was not the small woman with the French accent or, fortunately, the stupid klutz who had been in charge of them at Obberlund. This one bent down and placed the protectors on her. The world of senses was closed to Susan.

The only non-human thing in the room (which was not very large) were the heavy pair of red curtains, beyond which the twin skyscrapers of The Hague were visible in the distance. Bosch was the last to arrive. He sat on a free Opphuls Chair, and leaned his elbows on its sweaty hands and tense arms. The Chair was breathing under his backside. It was a strange feeling, like sitting on a barrel floating in a calm sea. The piece of furniture was naked, and bent like a hinge on the floor, arms and buttocks raised. A small leather top was placed on them. The Chair's raised legs provided the backrest. The models who were Chairs were strong, and athletically built. They were painted brown, and were perfectly trained. They could be of either sex. Judging by the shape and size of its upper body, Bosch's Chair appeared to be male. Bosch tried not to move too much or to make any sudden gestures: he had sat quite frequently on Chairs of different ages and sexes, but had always been polite and respectful.

A select naked silver service was circulating around the room. They were Silverware by Droessner. They were aged between fifteen and eighteen, and at first sight were all female, unless they were transgender pieces – which Bosch did not rule out. They had been covered from head to foot in a layer of liquid mother-of-pearl, on which Droessner had traced a subtle filigree of bluebirds perched on branches or settled in nests. There were birds on breasts, backs, on buttocks and on abdomens. All the Silverware was wearing ear and eye protectors, which left them deaf and blind, but even so their work was faultless. They moved round the room in a never-ending circle, like an Escher drawing, carrying small trays with food and drink. After a certain number of predetermined steps, they came to a halt in front of each guest and bent over with their tray. The guest was free to accept the offer or not. The only thing he or she was not allowed to do was to touch them. Precious silverware is not to be touched, thought Bosch, not even here.

A Silverware leaned over in front of him, and Bosch chose what looked like a martini. As the ornament was moving on, another one arrived from the opposite direction. Their trays bumped into each other, and the two of them immediately moved apart, continuing on their blind way like ants whose antennae clash in the long file back to their nest. There was a bisexual De Perrin Lamp on the ceiling, and other Lamps, almost all of them female, shone in the corners of the room. There were Tables and Trolleys, too. Bosch wondered who was paying for all this expensive decor. Cohesion funds again?

Jacob Stein and April Wood were the most notable absentees. Apart from them, the whole of the 'crisis cabinet' was there. Head Honcho, still apparently fascinated by the sweets Tray, quickly summed up why they were there, with a spectacular announcement:

'Rip van Winkle has captured the Artist with a margin of error of less than 0.05 per cent. To be precise: 0.05.'

'Could you translate that for those of us who have studied humanities?' Gert Warfell asked.

Head Honcho launched into a complicated explanation. Fifteen suspects had been arrested, five of whom had passed to a higher level of suspicion. According to the information Rip van Winkle had, one of these was almost certainly the Artist. The other ten had been eliminated. Once they had determined which of the five was the one they were looking for, they would eliminate the others. The Artist would be interrogated thoroughly until they were certain he was not withholding anything at all. After that they would discover all the ramifications and eliminate them. Then they would eliminate the Artist. And finally, Rip van Winkle would eliminate itself.

'We will be the last to be eliminated. Let's be precise. We will eliminate ourselves, because once all this is over, the crisis cabinet will be disbanded, Rip van Winkle will go back to sleep, and we will never meet again. Besides, to all intents and purposes, we have never met,' he finished. And stuffed another handful of caramels into his mouth.

'That's good news,' said Miss Roman. Bosch could not tell whether she was talking about the elimination of the Artist or of Head Honcho. Miss Roman's Chair was masculine: the strong, tight dun-coloured buttocks bearing her weight were clearly visible from where Bosch was sitting.

'Have any of them confessed?' Gert Warfell asked, leaning forward. He was constantly fidgeting, and Bosch could see his varnished seat tensing his muscles as Warfell shifted around. 'I mean, any of the five suspects.'

'Three of them have said they were guilty. That doesn't mean anything of course, but it's more than we had a fortnight ago.'

'That's amazing news,' Benoit said enthusiastically. 'Don't you think so, Lothar?'

'What information have the five suspects given?' Bosch asked, ignoring Benoit.

Head Honcho had stretched out his hand to take a glass of whisky. The Ornament paused for just the right length of time, then continued on its cautious, blind way. Light from the Lamps was reflected on its nacreous buttocks, making them look like some fabulous bird's eggs.

'For the moment that's confidential,' Head Honcho replied. 'It will be provided in subsequent reports, once we've assessed it.'

'Let me put it another way. Have any of the suspects said anything they could only know if they were the Artist?'

'Lothar is trying to say he doesn't trust Rip van Winkle,' observed Sorensen.

Bosch protested, but Head Honcho did not seem to attach any importance whatsoever to Sorensen's comment.

'The interviews are taking place in various European cities, and I don't have all the information to hand. But we are not torturers, if that is what is being suggested: was ask questions before we shoot. No information has been obtained by force.'

Bosch was far from convinced that this assertion was true, but he preferred not to challenge it.

'So we can say the problem has been dealt with,' Warfell exclaimed.

'Only just in time,' said Sorensen. 'The opening is tomorrow.'

'Mr Stein will be very pleased, I'm sure,' Benoit said, eyes shining, as though congratulating the whole of humanity.

'I was hoping to sort this out as soon as possible, so I could go off on vacation,' Harlbrunner's booming voice roared. The Chair squashed beneath his tonnage was, as far as Bosch could tell, a girl.

The meeting was adjourned. As the crisis cabinet members used the hands of their Chairs to stand up, Benoit turned to Bosch and asked whether he would mind having a few words when they got outside. Bosch minded a lot, not only because of his appointment with Van Obber that afternoon, but because the last thing he needed at that moment was to talk to the Head of Conservation – but he knew that he could not refuse. Benoit suggested they talk in the Clingendael park. He said he really liked the Japanese garden there. They went in his car.

Neither of them spoke during the journey. An architectural kaleidoscope of The Hague flashed in through the tinted glass of the car windows. This was where Bosch had been born, although he had lived in Amsterdam from early childhood. He briefly wondered if anything of The Hague was still in him. He thought that perhaps there was something of The Hague everywhere in the modern world. Just as in M.C. Escher's etchings, his native city contained another one inside itself, which in turn contained another, and so on to infinity. The Madurodam was a scale model of Holland, 'the smallest biggest city in Europe', as his father used to say. The Mesdag Panorama showed a painting 120 metres in diameter, also to scale. In the Mauritshuis you could get a glimpse of the past thanks to the Holland the great masters had painted. And if it was HD art you were looking for, any collector would find ten official galleries, and four times as many private ones, as well as the Gemeentemuseum and the brand-new Kunstsaal. There were legal adolescent art galleries like Nabokovian or Puberkunst; the clandestine utensils in Menselijk;

the public art-shocks offered by Harder and the Tower; the ani-marts in the Artzoo. And if you felt like taking photos, where better than in the garden of *Het Meisje* in Clingendael? Fake cities and real human beings disguised as works of art. If you spent a day in The Hague you could end up confusing appearance and reality. Maybe it was because he had been born there – thought Bosch – that his mind seemed always shrouded in mist, as if he could not distinguish any boundaries.

Clingendael park was full of tourists, even though the increas-ingly heavy clouds threatened an unpleasant surprise before the evening was out. Benoit and Bosch began to stroll down the avenues, hands behind their backs. A slightly chill breeze lifted the ends of their ties.

'I read recently in *Quietness*,' Benoit said, 'that an exhibition of retired canvases is being organised in New York. There have already been several successful sales in the United States. It's Enterprises that is financing them, of course. And the writer said it was a stroke of genius, because what else could an old-age pensioner do but sit in some corner or other looking at people and having them look at him? Stein doesn't like the idea much though, because he's not really interested in old canvases, but I'm sure it will soon catch on in Europe. Just imagine all the old folk who can hardly live on their pensions all of a sudden finding they are multi-million dollar works of art. The world is spinning round, Lothar, and it's calling on us to spin with it. The question is: do you accept the invitation, or do you step off and watch it go by?'

This was not a real question, so Bosch gave no reply. When they came to a small clearing, they saw several girls rehearsing postures in front of *Nonsense* by Rut Malondi. Bosch guessed they must be students learning to be canvases. Of course, unlike the original, none of them was naked or painted: that would have been illegal. The law allowed the work of art to be exhibited with no clothes on in public places, but the students were only ordinary people, and were not allowed to do so. Bosch could see how they longed one day to leave being a person behind. He thought that perhaps Danielle felt the same.

Benoit stood for a long while in silence staring at the motionless bodies of the apprentice canvases posing on the grass in their jeans and blouses, folders and jerseys at their feet.

'Do you think they really have caught him, Lothar?' he asked all of a sudden.

This time it was a real question.

'No. I don't think so, Paul. But it's possible.'

'I don't believe it either,' said Benoit. 'Rip van Winkle has the same problem as Europe: disunited union. Do you know what our problem is as Europeans? We want to go on being ourselves while at the same time we're part of the whole. We're trying to globalise our individuality. But the world needs fewer and fewer individuals, fewer races, fewer nations, fewer languages. What the world needs is for us all to know English and, if possible, for us all to be a bit liberal. In Babel let everyone speak English and bring on the tower, says the world. That's what globalisation demands, and we Europeans aspire to that without giving up on our individuality. But what is an individual nowadays? What does it mean to be French, English or Italian? Take a look at us: you're Dutch with German ancestors, I'm French but I work in Holland, April is English, but she lived in Italy, Jacob is North American and lives in Europe. Before, our artistic traditions used to differentiate us, but now things have changed. A Dutchman can create a work of art with a Spaniard, a Romanian with a Peruvian, a Chinaman with a Belgian. Immigration has found an easy job market: it can become art. Nothing separates us from anyone else any more, Lothar. At home, I've got a cerublastyne portrait of myself by Avendano. It's exactly like me, as exact as a mirror image, but the model substituting the original this year is a Ugandan. He's in my office, where I see him every day. In him I can see my features, my body, my own appearance, and I think: My God, inside me there's a black man. I've never been racist, Lothar, I swear, but it seems to me unbelievable to look at myself and to know that underneath, under my skin, is hidden a black man, that if I scratch hard enough at one of my cheeks I'll see the Ugandan appear, immobile, that Ugandan I have inside me who I can't get rid of even if I wanted to . . . among other reasons, because the portrait is by Avendano and costs an arm and a leg.'

'I understand,' said Bosch.

'I wonder what we would see appear under the skin of Europe if we scratched it, Lothar?'

'We'd have to scratch a lot, Paul.'

'Right. But there's one consoling thought. There's something that links me to the Ugandan, something I share with him which makes me think that deep down we're not that different after all.'

After a pause, Benoit continued his walk. Then he said:

'We both want money.'

At the end of the walk, mirrored by a pond and crouching on some rocks, was *Het Meisje*, the best-known work in Clingendael park, and perhaps in the entire city. *Het Meisje*, 'The Young Woman', was a delicate Rut Malondi piece. Some people called it the *'Little HD Mermaid'* of The Hague. Her body was half-hidden by a loose-fitting shirt painted snow-white, which flapped in the breeze. Her face, perfectly detailed in cerublastyne, and the gentle hyperdramatism of her blue gaze filled the leisure hours of the passers-by. She was a permanent outdoor piece, but in the harsh Dutch winter the city council protected her under a thermostatically-controlled plastic dome. The canvas can not have been more than fourteen years old. She was the sixteenth substitute, and was painted to look exactly the same as the earlier ones. A whole regiment of tourists surrounded her, snapping away. It had become a tradition to offer her flowers or throw her scraps of paper with poems written on them.

Benoit came to a halt opposite her, by the pool's edge.

'You must have heard that there'll soon be a change at the top,' he said. 'Van Tysch is going into a decline, Lothar. Or rather, he's completely wrecked. That's what happens when someone becomes immortal: they die. The only reason we don't see them rot is that it's hidden under layers of pure gold. The search for a replacement has already started. I was wondering who will take over.'

'Dave Rayback,' said Bosch without a moment's hesitation.

'No. It won't be him. He's an artistic genius – I've got several of his originals in Normandy, and I've paid a fortune to have them permanently on show there. They're so good I don't want them to leave even for a pee. As an artist, Rayback has more than enough qualities to take over. But his great defect is that he's too

371

clever, don't you think? A genius should always be a bit of a dummy. People tend to look at geniuses and smile, thinking: Look at them, poor things, so busy creating their sacred works, but as lost as ever. That's the image of genius that people buy. So a genius who is intelligent as well makes people uncomfortable. It's as if we thought intelligence was only for mediocre people. Or as though being a genius was incompatible with wanting to amass a fortune, lead a country or command an army. We expect the leader of a government to be "intelligent". We might even say he has been a "good" president. But however good he may be at his job, he'll never be a "genius". Do you see the difference?'

'So if it's not Rayback,' said Bosch, 'who is it going to be? Stein?'

'Not likely. Stein is one of those people who need a boss to approve of their work. I can remember a phrase by Rayback that I liked a lot: "Stein is the best of all those who aren't artists." It's true. Forget about Stein. The only role he has in this is as a voter: he and others like him will choose the new genius. And I can assure you that the chosen one will be an unknown, one of the general run of the mill. The Foundation can not fail now. We've become a huge business, Lothar. The future stakes are enormous. Mummy and Daddy will give every child a beginner's guide to HD painting. We'll create part-time models that will cost the amateur painter a hundred euros. We'll get human artefacts and ornaments legalised, and when that happens we will place an eighteen-year-old Receptacle, Tray or Ashtray in your home for a thousand or two thousand euros. We can expand our cerublastyne portraits and our mass-production workshops. And once we can include violence in completely legal and cheap art-shocks, we'll have taken another step forward similar to legalising drugs. HD art is going to change the history of human-ity, I promise you. We're becoming the most successful business in the world. Therefore we need someone pretty stupid to repre-sent us. If we were represented by an intelligent person, we would fail. Good business needs a fool out front, and a lot of clever people behind him.'

All at once Bosch began to understand why Benoit wanted to talk to him. Sly old fox. When you're expecting a mutiny, you try to find people on your side, don't you? But then a second, more disturbing explanation flashed through his mind: what if Benoit was the person helping the Artist? Perhaps he wanted to finish off Van Tysch and speed up the transfer. While he was thinking this over, Bosch pushed the tip of his tie back inside his jacket. *Het Meisje*'s white shirt was fluttering in the breeze. A Japanese girl threw her a rose. Bosch looked more closely and saw it was plastic. It bounced off *Het Meisje*'s bare knee and fell into the pond.

Then Benoit said something unexpected.

'I'm really sorry about your niece, Lothar. And I understand you. It must be very worrying, especially with the way things are. I wanted you to know it was nothing to do with me. It was Stein who chose her as a model, and the Maestro agreed.'

'I know.'

'I called her first thing this morning to see how she was getting on. She's fine, but a bit nervous, because Van Tysch is going to sign her today. I have to tell you I phoned her because she's your niece, although you know it's against the rules to have any contact with the canvases before Van Tysch has signed them.'

'Thanks, Paul.'

Benoit went on talking quickly, as if he had not yet got to the point he was trying to make.

'I'll always be beside you, Lothar. I'm with you. And I'd like you to feel the same. I mean that whatever happens, whoever might come *after* Van Tysch, we will continue to support each other, won't we?'

A clump of pansies was growing near Benoit's feet. He bent down, picked one, and threw it into the air. But his aim was bad, and the pansy flew over *Het Meisje*'s painted head. Benoit looked as crestfallen as a footballer who has missed a decisive penalty.

'I've got a copy of that wonder in Normandy,' he confessed to Bosch, pointing at *Het Meisje*. 'A cheap, tawdry copy of the kind they sell you in art shops with the words "Souvenir of The Hague" inscribed on its buttocks. The model is over twenty years old now, of course. But I still like it. I'm sorry, I've kept you a long time. Did you have to go somewhere?'

'Unfortunately, yes. But I'll be there on time.'

'See you tomorrow, Lothar.'

'Yes, tomorrow at the opening.'

'I must say, I wish this was all over.'

Bosch left him without replying.

On his way to Delft, he called Van Obber to say he would be late. The painter's hoarse voice came on the line. 'No problem,' he said. 'I've nowhere to go.' Bosch hung up and tried to have a nap. The meeting with Benoit flashed into his mind. It was obvious the Artist was still at large, and Benoit had realised it. Rip van Winkle was a way for Europe to make a good impression with a company that brought the biggest number of tourists to the Old World, but that was all. The Artist was still free. And he was ready.

He was just dozing off when the call came. It was Nikki.

'Lije suffered first-degree burns over half his body and was interned for life in a psychiatric clinic in northern France, Lothar – we've checked. Apparently, it happened during the December art-shocks, but Extreme covered it up to avoid upsetting the other artists and canvases.'

'How did it happen?'

'In one of the paintings they were using candles to spill different-coloured hot wax on to Lije's body. Someone was clumsy, there was a fire: Lije was tied up, and no one bothered to help him get out.'

'My God,' muttered Bosch.

'That leaves Postumo Baldi. He's the only one without an alibi.'

'I'm just on my way to Delft to see Van Obber,' Bosch explained. 'I want you to get me all the information you can about Baldi: any tapes on him, the recordings and interviews Support made when he was *Figure XIII*. Send them to my home.'

'OK.'

As the car entered Delft, Bosch felt rather strange. What could Van Obber tell him? What did he want out of him? All at once he understood that he wanted Van Obber to *paint him a face*. Some features. Knowing Baldi *might be* the Artist was not, in theory, going to have any immediate consequences. The security measures for the exhibition were not going to be changed in any way. But perhaps Van Obber would be able to paint a picture of Baldi, which would help Bosch add some details to the misty, androgynous outline he had in his head.

In Delft, grey-bellied clouds were gathering on the far horizon. Bosch got out of the car in Markt square, next to the New Church, and told the driver to wait for him there. He wanted to walk. A moment later, and he found himself surrounded by pure beauty.

Delft. This was where the painter Vermeer, that expert in subtle detail, had been born. Those were different times though, thought Bosch, times when it was still possible to feel and think, times when beauty had still not been completely discovered. He reached Oude Delft with its ancient canal, and gazed at its tranquil waters, the mouth-wateringly green lime trees, and the indented skyline of roofs, all of it gleaming despite the sky's refusal to collaborate with the light, all of it shining and pure like the pottery Delft had made famous. Bosch felt moved. Once upon a time then, things *had been clear*. When had everything been overtaken by shade? When did Van Tysch come down from the skies, and dark shadows fill every corner? Of course, it wasn't Van Tysch's fault. Not even Rembrandt's. But seeing Delft like this was to understand that in the past, at least, there was a *meaning* to things, they were diaphanous, full of sweet details that artists liked to note and reproduce skilfully. Bosch thought that in some way humanity had grown, too. There was no room any more for a naive humanity. Was that a good or bad thing? At school, one of his teachers used to say there was one good thing about hell: at least the condemned *knew* where they were. There could not be the slightest doubt about it. And now Bosch conceded he was right. The worst thing about hell was not the roasting heat, the eternity of torment, the fact of having lost God's love or of being tortured by devils.

The worst thing about hell is not knowing whether you are already in it or not.

Van Obber lived in a pretty brick house by the canal, topped off with white gables. It was plain that the roof was in need of repair, and that the window frames could do with a new coat of paint. The painter himself opened the door. He was a man with straw blond hair *en brosse*. He was agonisingly thin, with dark circles round his eyes and bruises everywhere. His face was beaded with sweat. Bosch knew he was no older than forty, but he looked at least fifty. Van Obber registered his surprise. His face contorted in a grimace that might have been his way of smiling.

'I'm in urgent need of repair,' he said.

He led Bosch to a creaking staircase. The upper floor was a single, large room that smelt of paint and solvents. Van Obber offered him an armchair, sat in another one, and began breathing heavily. For a while, that was all he did.

'I'm sorry for this sudden visit,' Bosch said. 'I didn't mean to put you out.'

'Don't worry.' The painter wrinkled the dark lines round his eyes. 'My whole life is routine . . . I mean I always do the same . . . that makes things difficult, because things never stop changing . . . At least I don't really have too many money problems . . . forty per cent of my works are still alive . . . there's not many independent painters who could say as much . . . and I still get some rent from my paintings . . . I don't paint adolescents any more . . . you can't get the material, because it's expensive and soon gets frightened . . . I used to do everything before: even ornaments and *pubermobilair*, which are prohibited . . .'

'I know,' Bosch said, interrupting the slow but inexorable flow of words. 'I think, in fact, that in one of your last works you used Postumo Baldi, didn't you? For the portrait you did for Jenny Thoureau in 2004.'

'Postumo Baldi . . .' Van Obber lowered his head and put his hands together as if he was praying. His red nose shone in the light from the window.

'Postumo is fresh clay,' he said. 'You touch him and stand him somewhere, and he adapts to it . . . You can poke or pull his flesh . . . do anything you want with him: animarts of a snake, dog or horse; a Catholic virgin; an executioner for stained art; bare carpets; transgender dancers . . . he's extraordinary material. To say he's "first class" comes nowhere near it . . .'

'When did you get to know him?'

'I didn't get to know him . . . I met him and used him . . . That was in the year 2000, in a gallery for stained art in Germany. I'm not going to tell you where it is, because I don't even know: guests are always taken to it blindfolded. The art-shock was an anonymous triptych called *The Dance of Death*. It was a good piece. The stained material was exceptional: a coachful of young students of both sexes. You know, the classic way of getting material for stained art: the coach falls into water in an accident, the bodies never reappear, it's a national tragedy . . . and the students, who have been forced to leave the bus beforehand, are secretly taken to the painter's workshop. In those days, Baldi must have been fourteen, and he was painted as one of the figures of Death who had to sacrifice the stained material. When I saw him he was flaying two of the students, a boy and a girl, and painting skulls on their skinless flesh. Although they were in a very bad way, the students were still alive, but Baldi seemed so beautiful to me I wanted to contract him for my own paintings. He was very expensive, but I had the money. I told him: "I'm going to paint something out of this world with you" . . . All I used was a little cerublastyne . . . a very restricted palette: a few dull pinks and some watery blues. I added a jet-black hair implant down to his feet. I made the sex imprecise, which wasn't difficult. I demanded a lot of him, but Postumo was up to everything. I used him as a man and as a woman. I tortured him with my own hands. I treated him like an animal, like something I could use and then throw into the rubbish . . . I'm not saying that Postumo was good at everything. He was a human body, and had the limits of one. But there was *something* in him, *something* that was . . . *his way of negating himself.* That was how I painted my work *Succubus*. That was the first painting I did with him. Do you know what Postumo's next work was, Mr Bosch? . . . A *Virgin Mary* by Ferrucioli . . .'

Van Obber opened his mouth to laugh, and Bosch could see his stained teeth. 'People might ask: "How can the *same* canvas be painted as a *Succubus* by Van Obber and a *Virgin* by Ferrucioli?" The answer is a simple one: that's art, ladies and gentlemen. That is precisely what art is, ladies and gentlemen.'

He fell silent, then after a while added:

'Postumo is not mad, but he's not sane either. He's neither evil nor good, man or woman. Do you want to know what Postumo is? *He's whatever the painter paints on him.* Postumo's eyes are *empty.* I asked them for emotion, and they gave it me: anger, fear, rancour, jealousy ... but then, once work was over, their light went out, they *emptied* ... Postumo's eyes are as empty and colourless as mirrors ... Empty, colourless, as beautiful as ...'

His words broke off in dreadful sobbing. In the ensuing silence, several thunderclaps could be heard. It was starting to rain over Delft.

Bosch felt sorry for Van Obber and his shattered nerves. He supposed solitude and failure made for poor companions.

'Where do you think Baldi might be now?' he asked gently.

'I don't know,' Van Obber shook his head. 'I don't know.'

'As far as I know, he abandoned a portrait you made of him for a French art dealer, Jenny Thoureau, in 2004. Was that typical of Baldi? To leave a work in the lurch before the date stipulated in the contract?'

'No. Baldi fulfilled all his contracts.'

'Why do you think it was different this time?'

Van Obber raised his head to look at him. His eyes were still glistening, but he had regained his calm.

'I'll tell you why,' he murmured. 'He got a *more interesting* offer. That's all there is to it.'

'Are you sure of that?'

'No. It's just a suspicion. I haven't seen him again, or heard any more about him. But I repeat – the only thing that interested Baldi was money. If he quit one work, it was because they offered him a better one. I'm sure of that.'

'An offer to be another painting?'

'Yes. That's why he left. Naturally, I wasn't surprised: I was a loser, and Baldi was too good for me. He was destined for something much better than to be a Van Obber painting.'

Bosch thought this over for a minute.

'That happened two years ago,' he said eventually. 'If Baldi walked out to become another work, as you say, where is that painting now? Since the Jenny Thoureau portrait his name hasn't been seen anywhere. . .'

Van Obber said nothing. This time it did not seem his mind had strayed off into distant recesses: it was more as if he were considering what to say.

'He's not finished,' he said all of a sudden.

'What?'

'If he hasn't appeared, it's because he's not finished. It's logical.'

Bosch thought about what Van Obber had said. An *unfinished* painting. That was a possibility neither he nor Miss Wood had thought of. They were following two trails in their search for the Artist: either he was still working, or he had left the profession. But until now neither of them had even considered he might be working in a painting *that was not yet finished.* That would explain his disappearance and his silence. A painter never shows his work until it is complete. But who could be devoting so much time to painting Baldi? And what kind of artwork were they trying to create?

As Bosch was leaving, he heard Van Obber's voice again from the armchair.

'Why do they want to find Postumo?'

'I don't know,' Bosch lied. 'My job is just to find him.'

'Believe me, it's better for everyone that Postumo has got lost. Postumo is more than a simple work of art: he is *art*, Mr Bosch. Art. Pure and simple.'

He stared up at Bosch with his exorbitant, sick eyes and added:

'Which means that, if you find him, be careful. Art is more terrible than man.'

When Bosch left Van Obber's house, a grey, ceaseless rain covered the city. Delft's beauty was melting in front of his eyes. He wished with all his heart that Rip van Winkle had really arrested the Artist, but he knew they had not. He was convinced that, whether or not it was Postumo, the criminal was still on the loose and was ready to spring into action during the exhibition.

8

The Artist went out into the street at night.

It was raining in Amsterdam, and the weather was on the cold side. Summer had been put into abeyance. All the better, he thought. Hands in pockets, he walked under the distant light from the streetlamps, letting the rain cover him with a fine spray like a flower. He crossed the Singelgracht bridge, where the lights were making garlands in the water and the drops of rain were tracing concentric circles, and walked on until he reached the Museumplein. He strolled past the area containing the silent Rembrandt Tunnel. The police guarding the entrance glanced at him without paying any particular attention. He looked like a perfectly ordinary individual, and that was how he acted. He could be a man or a woman. In Munich he had been Brenda and Weiss; in Vienna, Ludmila and Díaz. Only on the inside was he a single person. He reached the far end of the horseshoe and continued on his way. He reached Concertgebouw square, where the most important concert hall in Amsterdam stood. But now the music had finished, and everything lay silent. The Artist did not cross Van Baerlestraat. Instead, he turned right towards the Stedelijk, and began his return journey towards the Rijksmuseum. He wanted to explore and check everything. His progress was blocked by metal fences marking out an area reserved for van parking. He leaned on one of the fences and stared into the night.

A small 'Rembrandt' poster was tied to a lamppost a little further on. The Artist stared at it through the drizzle. The Angel's hand was opening in the darkness.

He read the date on it: 15 July 2006. The next day.

The fifteenth of July. Exactly. *Tomorrow will be the day.*

He moved away from the fence, turned down Van de Veldestraat and walked on. The rain eased off as he made his way back to the Singel.

Tomorrow, in the exhibition.

Everything around him was dark and unlovely.

Only the Artist looked like pure beauty.

Fourth Step

The Exhibition

I am not concerned about exhibition.

BRUNO VAN TYSCH *Treatise on Hyperdramatic Art*

'I should win easy', said the Lion.
. . .
The Eighth Square, at last!

LEWIS CARROLL *Through the Looking Glass*

09.15.

When Lothar Bosch awoke, Postumo Baldi was in his bedroom.

He was standing three metres from his bed, looking at him. The first thing Bosch thought was that he did not seem particularly dangerous. He's not dangerous, he told himself. The second thing he realised, with precise, terrible intuition, was that this was not a dream: he was wide awake, it was daytime, it was his house on Van Eeghenstraat, and Baldi was in his bedroom, naked, staring at him thoughtfully. His appearance was that of a skinny adolescent with protruding bones, but his gaze was full of beauty. Despite everything, Bosch was not afraid of him. I can overcome him, he thought.

At that point, Baldi began a graceful, silent dance, a whirlwind of light. His thin body danced all round the room, then returned to its initial position, and the world seemed to come to a halt with him. Then he started to move again. And stopped a second time. Fascinated, it took Bosch some time to realise what was going on: he had fallen asleep with the virtual reality visor on while watching the 3-D images the Foundation had taken of Baldi when he was fifteen years old.

Bosch swore, switched off the machine and took off the visor. The bedroom looked empty, but Baldi's iridescent after-image still floated in the air. The brightness outside the window was that of a rainy day: the day the 'Rembrandt' exhibition was to open.

The images had not helped Bosch clarify things a lot. Van Obber had not been exaggerating when he had said Postumo was 'fresh clay': a hairless, smooth creature, a beginning, a human point of departure, the start of all shapes.

Bosch got up, refreshed himself in the shower, and chose a sober dark suit from his wardrobe. At half-past ten he would have to be with the vehicles parked round the Tunnel to supervise the launch of the security operation. Now he was in front of

383

his mirror struggling to fix his tie properly. He had got the silk folds wrong yet again. He could not remember having been as nervous as this since Hendrickje's death.

He's never attacked at an opening. You ought to calm down. Perhaps he isn't even in Amsterdam. Who says April Wood is right? Perhaps he's already handed himself over at some Munich police station or other. Or maybe . . . stupid knot . . . Maybe Rip van Winkle really have caught him . . . Get a hold of yourself. Think positively. For once in your life, think positively.

All at once he heard the pitter-patter of rain. He went out onto the terrace: the Vermeer landscape had started to change into a Monet. The raindrops had begun to meld together greens, ochres, the reds and whites.

OK, so the rain's here.

As he finished dressing, he allowed himself a last thought for Danielle. He did not want to pray, even though he knew that, contrary to what religion teaches, not only the Devil but God himself can create temptation. Nevertheless, he improvised a short prayer. He did not aim it at anyone in particular, beyond looking up at the lowering clouds. She's the only one who has nothing to do with any of this. Protect her. Please, protect her.

After that, he went downstairs. It was going to be an exhausting day, and he knew it.

He had at least succeeded in throttling himself properly. His tie was correctly knotted.

09.19.

Gerardo took a pinch of burnt yellow colour and brushed it onto Clara's cheek.

'The Maestro is going to check all the paintings this afternoon before the opening.'

'I thought he wasn't going to come again.'

'He always likes to have a last look before he leaves. Stay still now.'

He chose a very fine brush and painted her lips with a layer of weak vermilion. She saw him smiling only a few centimetres from her face. He looked like a miniaturist bending over a book of prints.

384

'Are you happy?' he asked her as he dipped his brush in the paint again.

'Yes.'

The assistant took off Clara's haircap, uncovering a shock of mahogany red curls. Gerardo dipped his brush again, and returned to her lips.

'I'd like to go on seeing you after all this is over. I mean, after you've been bought.' He paused, dipped a finger in some kind of solvent, and scraped at the corner of her mouth. 'Because you must know you've already been bought. You'll be sent to the home of some millionaire collector or other. But I'd like to go on seeing you. No, don't talk. You mustn't talk now.'

His words were as gentle as the brushstrokes he was using to outline her. She felt as though he were kissing her all over.

'You know what they say. That there can't be any relationship between a painting and a painter, because hyperdramatism doesn't allow it. Well, that's the theory anyway.' He lifted off the brush, dipped it in the paint, came back to her, wiped with a rag, painted another line. 'But with me things will be different, because I'm a *very bad painter*, sweetheart. That will compensate for you being such a good painting.'

The assistant interrupted Gerardo and spoke to him in English. They talked briefly about the exact tone of the shading on the sides of Clara's body, and consulted the Maestro's written instructions. Then Gerardo bent towards her lips, and stood observing them closely for a while. He did not seem satisfied. He disappeared from her field of vision, then almost immediately reappeared, his brush dripping red.

Clara was lying on her back on a small bed in one of the rehearsal rooms in the basement of the Old Atelier. She had been brought there early that morning to be finished and placed in the Tunnel.

'We have to be careful,' said Gerardo; 'thousands of people are going to see you today.'

He brushed gently twice against her upper lip. It was like the touch of a butterfly's wings.

'I don't want to hurt you,' he went on. 'I would never hurt you. But I thought that . . . keeping my feelings to myself would

385

not help me do things any better. I'm more serious than you give me credit for, sweetheart. No, don't talk.' He lifted the brush off as Clara opened her lips. 'You are the work. I'm the only one who can talk. You are in the painting.'

He dipped the brush, and caressed her again with a lighter shade of red.

'I've also heard that a painter often falls in love with his work. I think that's true. But in my case there's something strange: I think I have painted myself as well to some extent. I mean to say that I've been pretending. Sometimes I even think I'm not who I think I am. Every day I get up, look at myself in the mirror, and thank my lucky stars. But things aren't that simple. Look at this moustache and beard.' He plucked them as he spoke. 'Are they a painter's, or are they paint? I've believed it for a long while now, without wanting to look any further, without wanting to see. What is there beyond all this? someone might ask. Well beyond it, there are people. I don't look on you as a painting. I can't see you as a painting.'

He dabbed at her lips to remove a blot. They looked at each other for a moment. As she stared into his huge, twinkling eyes, a strange thought that had already occurred to her several times flashed through her mind once more: maybe Gerardo was not such a poor painter after all; maybe he simply did not want to paint *Susanna*. The figure did not appeal to him. What he wanted to capture in her face was not the sorrowful gleam or the horrified sense of shame, not that 'canvas of horror and pity' described by Van Tysch. Gerardo wanted to capture her for what she was. Clara Reyes. To regain her, cleanse her, give her light. He was the first artist she had met for whom she was more important than his own work.

Uhl came in. He said they were being too slow, and that they should start painting her back. The three of them helped her to stand, and she lay down on her front.

The process went on, but this time in silence.

10.30.
'Edenburg, miss,' the driver said.

The scenery in the background to the River Geul, in southern

386

Limbourg in Holland, was out of this world. Woods and valleys glittered in the splendid summer sun, interspersed with rectangular wooden farmhouses. Edenburg appeared almost out of the blue as they came round a bend, at the end of the highway: a mound of steep-roofed houses dominated by the majestic presence of the castle where once upon a time Maurits van Tysch had worked as an art restorer. Miss Wood knew Edenburg. The interviews the painter had conceded her had been brief and tense. Van Tysch had never been concerned about the security of his works: his only duty was to create them.

Miss Wood knew it was raining in Amsterdam, but here in Edenburg there was nothing but sun, warmth, and groups of tourists bearing cameras and road maps. The car advanced slowly along the narrow cobbled streets, which retained all their old-world charm. A few curious passers-by stared at the luxury vehicle. The driver spoke again to Miss Wood.

'Are you going straight to the castle? If that's the case, we'll have to leave the centre of town and take the Kasteelstraat.'

'No, I'm not going to the castle.' She handed him an address. The chauffeur (a polite, attentive southerner who was anxious to keep the 'lady' happy, and who wore a fixed smile despite having to wait almost half an hour for her plane in Maastricht) decided to stop and ask a local the way.

The idea had occurred to her the night before. She had suddenly remembered the name of the man Oslo thought of as 'Bruno van Tysch's best childhood friend': Victor Zericky. She thought it would be a good idea to begin her visit to Edenburg by calling on him. She had called Oslo that same night, and he had been quick to supply her with the historian's address and telephone number. Zericky was not at home when she called to set up an appointment. Perhaps he was away. But she was confident she would see him.

The driver was having an animated conversation with an assistant from a tourist shop. Then he turned to Miss Wood.

'It crosses Kasteelstraat.'

11.30.

Gustavo Onfretti made his way into the Tunnel surrounded by security guards and personnel from Art. He was wearing a padded suit and the usual yellow labels. His body had been painted in ochre and flesh tints. Thin layers of cerublastyne lent his face a certain similarity to the Maestro, but also to Rembrandt's Jesus Christ. I'm both of them, he thought. He was one of the last paintings to arrive, and he knew it was going to be hard to get into position.

He was to be crucified six hours a day.

Wrapped in a winding sheet that smelt of oil, Onfretti walked along the ramp in the darkness to reach the part of the Tunnel where the cross had been set up. It was an artistic cross rather than a real one: it had several devices designed to make his pose less painful. Even so, Onfretti was sure that no device could spare him all the suffering, and this intimidated him a little.

But he had accepted his chalice. He was a masterpiece, and as such was prepared to suffer. Van Tysch had worked on him for a long while in Edenburg so there would be no mistakes. Of any kind. Everything had to be perfect. As he was signing him the previous day, the Maestro had looked him straight in the eye. 'Don't forget, you are one of my most intimate and personal creations.'

This sincere declaration gave Onfretti the strength to bear all he knew awaited him.

13.05.

Jacob Stein had finished his lunch and sat facing the neat lines of the coffee cup. The Table was solid, one of his own designs. It was made up of a glass top held up by harnesses on the shoulders of four kneeling adolescents bathed in silver. A frieze encircled the entire table, creating swirls between the different figures. The adolescents were *almost* exactly the same height, but the one on the far left corner was a little taller, which meant the surface of the dark, steaming coffee in the cup was slightly askew. Of course, like all the other decorations in the room, the Table was an illegal piece of furniture worth billions. Stein was absent-mindedly leaning his foot on a silver thigh.

He knew that, unlike his room, Van Tysch's 'zone' in the New Atelier was empty. Stein liked to live surrounded by luxury, and had decorated his dining room according to his own tastes with paintings, ornaments and utensils by Loek, Van der Gaar, Marooder and himself. More than twenty adolescents, some of them motionless, others following choreographed steps, were breathing in the room, and yet the silence was immense.

Only Stein appeared alive.

He was going over all he had to do in his mind. By now, all the paintings should be in position inside the Tunnel, waiting for the Maestro. The opening was scheduled for six, but Stein would not be there: Benoit would take his place and look after all the dignitaries. His own presence was needed elsewhere, where he also had to look after an extremely important person.

Fuschus, power was another kind of art, he thought. Or perhaps a handicraft, showing the ability to control everything. He had been a real master at it. Now he had to surpass himself. It was a very delicate moment, perhaps the most delicate in the Foundation's entire history, and he had to be up to it.

All at once his secretary Neve appeared at the far end of the room.

Even though he was well aware that the expected moment might happen at any time, the announcement that it had truly arrived made his faun's features relax into a happy grin. He stood up leaning on the Table, producing nothing more than a slight quiver from the four silvery girls – and a blink from the one on whose thigh he had been resting his foot – and made for the door.

His visitor stood fascinated for a moment in the doorway, staring wide-eyed at all the warm bodies decorating the room. This was soon followed by a beaming smile and a shake of Stein's hand.

'I'd like to welcome you to the Van Tysch Foundation,' Stein said quickly in fluent English. 'I know you understand English perfectly. I wish I could say the same of my Spanish.'

'Don't worry about that,' replied Vicky Lledó with a smile.

14.16.

Miss Wood had been sitting on the lawn for more than three hours. She had opened one of the fruit juices she kept in her bag and was taking slow slips and staring up at the clouds. It was a tranquil spot, just made to shut one's eyes and rest in. Somehow it reminded her of her house in Tivoli: the same summer sound-track, with birds singing and dogs barking in the distance. Victor Zericky's house was small, and its apple-green fence showed signs of having been repaired by an expert hand. The garden was full of flowers: an ordered arrangement of plants trained by human hand. The house was shut. It seemed there was no one in.

The old man in the house next door had told her Zericky was divorced and lived on his own. Miss Wood suspected this was his way of telling her he had no fixed timetable, but came and went as he pleased. Apparently, Zericky was in the habit of going away for days on trips to Maastricht or The Hague to collect information for his work as a historian or simply because he felt like stretching his legs and finding new paths along the banks of the Geul.

'I'm not saying it to put you off, 'added the old man, who had hair like marble and cheeks as pink as if he had just been slapped, but if he doesn't know you're here, I'd advise you not to wait. As I told you, it could be days before he returns.'

Miss Wood thanked him, went over to her car, and leaned in at the driver's window.

'You can go wherever you like, but be back here at eight.'

The car pulled away. Miss Wood looked for a suitable spot, sat down on the grass, and leaned her back against a tree. She could feel the rough grooves of the trunk through her thin jerkin; she devoted herself to the difficult task of letting time pass by.

She had nothing else to do anyway, and she had never minded waiting if it was essential to her work. In fact, she rather enjoyed this parenthesis of birdsong and perfumed breeze. She finished her drink, put the empty carton in her bag, took out another one. She only had two left, but she needed to drink liquid. She felt increasingly weary: her eyes were drooping behind the dark barrier of her glasses, and from time to time she almost nodded off. She could not remember how long it was since she had eaten anything solid – two days perhaps, or even longer – and yet she did not feel at all hungry. Yet she would have paid a fortune to have a full thermos of coffee with her. She was hot. She took off her jerkin and left it on the grass. But then in her sleeveless dress she felt chilly.

390

It did not occur to her to wonder whether Zericky might not come at all. The fact was, she had let her mind go blank. All she knew was that she would wait there until she could wait no longer. Then she would go back to Amsterdam.

She sat drinking more juice while the breeze ruffled her hair.

16.20.

'Nothing to report, sector two.'

'Situation normal, sector three.'

'Nothing, sector four.'

As he listened to this litany from the guards through the loudspeakers, Bosch was not even thinking of the Artist. Instead, he had been reflecting on circuses. As a child he had seen very few, because his father Victor did not like them. Going to the circus was not the best way to make use of the means available. But willy-nilly, all children visit a circus, and Bosch had eventually got to see one, too. When he was there, he did not enjoy it: from the dangerous acrobatics to the wretchedness of the caged tigers, from the meringue-faced clowns to the magicians' packaged tricks, it had all seemed to him a sorry and sad affair.

Now here he was in another circus. The attractions were different, but there was an audience, tents, magic tricks and wild beasts. And it all seemed to him just as sad.

He was sitting inside one of the two Portakabins taken over by Security. There were six trucks on either side of the Tunnel, parked in places that allowed them free access to the recovery and rescue vehicles. Each pair of these trucks was occupied by a different department: Art, Conservation and Security. They had set up closed-circuit TV monitors in the Portakabins to supervise the parts of the Tunnel where works were being exhibited, as well as the entrance, exit and the central square where the paintings were to be picked up. Portakabin A covered the first six works in the first arm of the horseshoe. Portakabin B was in charge of the other seven; it was parked near the Van Gogh museum, and this was the one Bosch was seated in.

The cameras trained on the Museumplein showed a spectacle that would doubtless have Paul Benoit rubbing his hands with delight, thought Bosch. There was still an hour and a half to go to the opening, and the line of shiny umbrellas already reached round the Rijksmuseum and as far as the Singelgracht. Some people had been waiting in the same place since dawn or the previous night, standing in front of the first security barrier, ticket in hand. The police had set up a barricade all along Museumstraat and Paulus Potterstraat to prevent trouble. Despite this – and once again, to Benoit's delight – *there was* trouble in both places: members of BAH and other groups opposed to HD art were waving banners and shouting slogans against the Foundation. Adjacent to the Tunnel, in the area occupied by the television crews, several presenters were unfurling their microphones.

In violent contrast, the Tunnel monitors were filming in silence. Some works had already been installed, but in the case of others like *Christ* the process had not yet been completed. Bosch watched the play of light and shade as Gustavo Onfretti was crucified. They had spent more than four hours attaching him to the rectangles of painted wood by means of something like transparent hoops. Onfretti had to stay in the exact position Van Tysch had painted, which was very demanding. By comparison, the 'descent' would be easy. Flashes from his near-naked body glinted on the TV screens as it was caught in the torch beams.

'Who would want to spend six hours a day like that?' commented Ronald, who was watching the *Christ* monitor. Ronald was overweight and at times like these stuffed himself with doughnuts. An open box of them lay near his screen, and he was busy biting into one. Part of the sugar frosting had fallen on to his red card.

Sitting in front of *The Feast of Belshazzar* monitor, Nikki smiled.
'It's modern art, Ronald. We don't understand it.'

'But this is meant to be classical art,' protested Osterbrock, the man looking after *Danae*, as he pressed various switches in the seat opposite Bosch. 'After all, they're Rembrandt paintings, aren't they?'

The Portakabin's narrow central aisle was full of Foundation personnel coming and going. Bosch could not help observing them. He looked at all of them, those he had known for some time and those he did not know at all; at Nikki, Martin, Ronald the doughnut-eater, at Michelsen, at Osterbrock. He studied their smiles, their routine gestures, their voices. All of them had been through identity checks before they joined the team, but Bosch watched them as though he were watching a shadow moving in the midst of motionless shadows. Then he turned to look again at the monitor showing the front of the long queue outside.

'Where are you? Where are you?'

That same morning Europol had received a description of Postumo Baldi. Bosch had sent it to them through the proper channels, to some extent using members of Rip van Winkle. Soon afterwards, he had begun to get information.

The Naples police did not know of his whereabouts. Those in Vienna and Munich had not found any trace or sample of body fluid or hairs at the scenes of the crime which compared with their data. All the clues they had found were from disguises or artificial substances. There was not a single organic residue, only plastic and cerublastyne. As though the Artist were a doll. Or perhaps a canvas. Europol was going on with its tireless search on computers all over the world. They were looking for clues that might link Baldi to some place or event. They were checking hospitals and cemeteries, reports of minor offences, crimes committed by others, unsolved cases. The Missing Persons Bureau had tracked him from Naples to Van Obber and Jenny Thoureau, from the house he was born in (since demolished) and his parents – mother's current whereabouts unknown – to the last hotels he had stayed in during 2004. But that was where all tracks ended. At the end of that year Baldi had abandoned his job as a portrait in the house of Mademoiselle Thoureau without explanation, and from that moment on, the earth had swallowed him up. A lot of people thought he must be dead.

In spite of the air conditioning which filled the interior of the Portakabin with a throbbing, unending supply of cool air, Bosch could feel the sweat coursing down his back. Postumo could be one of the faces he was looking at. Baldi could be any of them, he was infinitely interchangeable. In himself he was nothing more than the air a knife slices through as it strikes its blow: invisible, but vital. *His eyes were mirrors. His body, fresh clay.*

The *Young Girl Leaning on a Windowsill* seemed to be staring back at him from her distant pedestal shown on monitor number nine. It was his niece Danielle whom Van Tysch had chosen to recreate that particular Rembrandt painting. The chiaroscuro lighting had not yet been switched on, so Danielle did not stand out from the darkness of the Tunnel. Bosch could not even see her face.

'There he is,' someone said behind his back, startling him.

The speaker was Osterbrock. He was pointing to the monitor that showed the people entering the Tunnel from Museumstraat. A dark stretch limousine was gliding towards the entrance. Its image disappeared as it passed through the first police barrier.

'It's Van Tysch,' said Nikki. 'He's come to give the finishing touches to the paintings.'

'And to switch on the chiaroscuro,' added Osterbrock.

Bosch wondered where Miss Wood might be. Why on earth had she decided to leave all of a sudden? Did she want to keep well out of the way?

He did not think that was the reason. He trusted her. He could not trust anyone else.

He wished the exhibition was already over. Or at least that this day (this interminable day when the hours dragged by as though drenched in oil) would end as soon as possible.

16.45.
Clara wished the day would never end.

She was crouching by the side of a pond of still waters, surrounded by trees and shadowy scenery. Everything smelled of paint, everything was rigid. This was the background to *Susanna Surprised by the Elders*. Clara was completely naked, painted in dense tones of rose, ochre and cadmium red, with streaks of deep mahogany. Her face was reflected in a mirror placed in the base of the plinth, invisible to the public. This was all she could see clearly, but even though she could not see them, she could *sense* the presence of the Elders behind her back, petrified, monstrous chimeras, mountains tilting towards her body, cliffs of oil paint.

She had just been put into place and had still not reached quiescence. Time passed like the people flowing round her (technicians and workmen, security agents): something that went by without touching her. Yet she could tell that the exhibition had not yet opened because the chiaroscuro lighting had not been switched on.

At a certain moment, a silhouette moved out of the public gangway, leapt over the security rope, and walked towards the plinth. Behind it came an entourage of legs. Something important was going on. Two dark shoes came to a halt beside her colour-stiffened thighs. She heard again that distant, grave voice, the fluent Spanish like a tolling bell.

'Keep looking at yourself in the mirror.'

It was like an electric shock. She obeyed, of course.

So it was true the Maestro gave all the works a final check, just as Gerardo had told her. The shadow flitted from figure to figure, giving instructions to the Elders as well in words she could not make out. Then the shoes came back, like strange patent leather animals, mysterious sharks with polished snouts sniffing at her body. A moment's pause, then they turned away. All that was left were echoes. Then the enchanted silence.

Clara went on contemplating the distant cameo with its painted features.

17.30.

The darkness was complete.

'What now?' Bosch asked nervously, staring at his screen. 'Why don't they light the stupid lamps?'

'They're waiting for Van Tysch to give the order,' Nikki replied.

'It won't be long now,' said Osterbrock.

They turned back to the monitors. A silhouette stood out from all the others, motionless, back to the camera. Torch beams picked it out fleetingly.

'The great panjandrum,' Ronald moaned, devouring the image with the same eager hunger as he polished off his doughnuts.

Every moment needs its setting, thought Bosch. This was a world in which valuable things had become solemn. And all solemnity requires a setting, a ritual, and lofty personages up on podiums admired by fascinated, open-mouthed people. Nothing can be done naturally: artifice, some degree of *art* is always nec-essary. Why not light the lights? Why not let the public in? After all, it was only a question of pressing a few buttons. But no. This is a solemn moment. It has to be registered, collected, recorded, made eternal. It has to be long-drawn-out.

'They're taking photos of him,' Nikki commented, chin in hands. Bosch noted a dreamy tone to her words.

Van Tysch had been illuminated by a slanting spotlight: he was an island of light in five hundred metres of twisting darkness. He had his back to the camera. His kingdom was not of this or any other world, thought Bosch. His kingdom was himself, all alone, in the middle of that glittering lake. Shadowy sorcerers blessed him with their magic rays.

The painter raised his right arm. Everyone held their breath.

'Moses parting the waters.' Ronald displayed his sarcasm once again.

'Well, something's not working,' Osterbrock said, 'because the Tunnel is still dark.'

'No,' Martine cut in, leaning over his shoulder. 'The signal is when he lowers his arm.'

Bosch looked across at all the screens: they were dark. He was worried that the Tunnel was in darkness for so long. The 'great panjandrum' had demanded it. Before the start of this sabbath, the witches had to honour him with their will-o'-the-wisps. Then when the photo and filming session was over, Satan would lower his paw and his very own inferno would start, his abominable, fearful inferno, the most terrible of all because no one knew it for what it was. Because the worst thing about hell is not knowing if you are already in it.

The arm descended.

The three hundred and sixty filaments designed by Igor Popotkin lit as one, their light-filled mouths yawning. For a moment, Bosch thought the paintings had disappeared. But they were still there, only transformed. As though a majestic brush had endowed them with just the touch of gold they needed. The paintings were burning in an ill-defined bonfire. Framed by the TV screens, they looked like classical canvases, but with figures that had depth and volume, had been given a life of dimensions. The backgrounds stood out, the mist took on the air of a landscape.

396

'My God,' said Nikki. 'It's more beautiful than I could have imagined.'

Nobody replied, but the silence seemed to contain tacit approval of her words. Bosch did not agree.

It was not beautiful. It was grotesque, terrifying. The sight of Rembrandt's works transformed into living beings did arouse an emotion, but to Bosch this was not the product of beauty. It was obvious that Van Tysch had reached the limit: no one could go any further in human painting. But the path he had chosen was not that of aesthetics.

There was nothing beautiful in the crucified man, in the young girl leaning on a windowsill, face as pale as death, in the feast in which the dishes were people, in the naked woman with her red-painted hair spied on by two grotesque individuals, in the silhouette of the girl with phosphorescent eyes, the boy wrapped in painted furs, the angel strangling the kneeling man. There was nothing beautiful in them, but nothing *human* either. And the worst of it was that it all seemed to accuse Rembrandt as much as Van Tysch. It was a sin shared by both men. Here before you is the negation of humanity, the two artists seemed to be saying. Condemned for being what they were. In a night of horror, mankind invented art.

This is our condemnation, thought Bosch.

'Hats off to him, no doubt about that,' a voice said after an endless silence. It was Ronald.

On the screen, Stein raised his hands and applauded. Violently, almost furiously. But there was no sound, which made the clapping on the screen look like a silent convulsion. Hoffmann, Benoit and the physicist Popotkin joined in. Soon all the figures around Van Tysch were clapping their hands like frenzied dolls.

The first to follow suit inside the Portakabin was Martine. As they beat together, her slender, flexible palms sounded like gunshots. Osterbrock and Nikki added their excited burst of clapping. Ronald's applause though was muffled, as if bubbles were escaping from his pudgy hands. All this noise in the confined space of the Portakabin deafened Bosch. He could see Nikki's cheeks were on fire.

What were they applauding? Good God, what were they applauding, and why?

Welcome to madness. Welcome to humanity.

He did not want to be the exception, to be the odd one out: he hated drawing attention to himself. He told himself he had to stay within the picture frame.

He beat his hands together and produced sounds.

17.35.

In Portakabin A, Alfred van Hoore was sitting in front of the monitor focused outside the Tunnel, observing the deployment of what Rita had baptised the 'parrot brigade'. His Artistic Emergency Team was waiting in Museumplein. They were green-and-white phantoms with yellow oilskins standing beside the evacuation vehicles. Van Hoore knew it was highly unlikely they would be needed, but at least his idea had won the approval of Benoit, and even of Stein himself. You had to start somewhere. In firms like the Foundation you had to come up with new proposals.

'Paul?' Van Hoore spoke into the microphone.

'Yes, Alfred,' he heard Spaalze's voice boom in his headphones.

Paul Spaalze was the captain of this improvised team. Van Hoore had put complete trust in him. They had previously worked together on coordinating security for exhibitions in the Middle East, and Van Hoore knew Spaalze was one of those who 'act first and worry about it afterwards'. This meant he was not someone for making long-term plans, but who was indispensable at moments of crisis.

'Less than half an hour before the flock troops in,' Van Hoore said, through a storm of interference. 'How is everything going out there, Paul?'

It was a rather useless question, because Van Hoore could see from the monitor that 'out there' everything was fine, but he wanted Spaalze to know he was watching things closely. He had spent many long hours designing emergency evacuation procedures on his computer, and he did not want his captain to lose heart from having nothing to do.

'Well, you know,' Spaalze roared. 'The worst catastrophe I'm facing at the moment is the possibility of a mutiny. Did you know they made us sing like sopranos for the voice identity checks, and to touch the screens as though we were paintings before they would let us into the blasted central square? My men didn't like that at all.'

'Orders from above,' said Van Hoore. 'If it's any consolation to you, Rita and I had to undergo the same torture.'

In fact, Van Hoore himself had wondered what the exact reason was for all the additional security measures: this was the first time he had been asked to go through these physical tests before getting in. Rita had not liked it any more than he had, and had even got annoyed with the agents who were blocking the way. Why hadn't Miss Wood told them anything about it? What did the change in the shifts for the recovery and supervision personnel mean? Van Hoore had a suspicion that the withdrawal of the Maestro's works in Europe had something to do with all this, but did not dare speculate what exactly it meant. Above all, he was hurt that he was not yet important enough to be let into the secret.

'They don't trust us,' he said.

Rita van Dorn, feet up on the desk while she stirred a cup of steaming coffee in a plastic cup, looked over at him in an offhand manner, then went on staring at the screens.

17.50.

A technician from the Art division held the umbrella aloft as Van Tysch climbed into the limousine. Stein was sitting waiting for him. Van Tysch's secretary, Murnika de Verne, was in front beside the driver. Journalists and cameramen thronged behind the security barrier, but the Maestro had not answered any of their questions. 'He's tired and does not want to make any statement,' his entourage said. Benoit, Nellie Siegel and Franz Hoffmann would be delighted to become prophets for a few minutes, and reveal the words of God for the microphones, but the Maestro had to leave. The car door closed. The driver – smart, blond-haired, wearing sunglasses – aimed for one of the exits the police had cleared. An agent allowed them out. His oilskin was gleaming in the rain.

Van Tysch looked back one last time at the Tunnel, then turned to the front. Stein put a hand on his shoulder. He knew Van Tysch detested any show of affection, but he was doing it for himself rather than the Maestro: he needed the other man to understand to what extent he had obeyed him, all the sacrifices he had made.

And how many he still had to make, *galismus*.

'It's finished, Bruno. Finished.'

'Not yet, Jacob. There's still something to be done.'

'*Fuschus*, I swear that . . . you could say it's already done.'

'You might say it, but it's not.'

Stein thought of a possible reply. This was how it had always been: Van Tysch was the eternal question, and he had to find the replies. He leaned back in his seat and tried to relax. Impossible. The great painter was as distant and inscrutable as the works of art he created. Next to him, Stein always felt a bit like Adam in the Garden of Eden after he had disobeyed God, with a certain transparent sense of shame. Any silence before Van Tysch contained an implicit recognition of guilt. It was a really unpleasant feeling. But what did that matter? Stein had spent twenty years of his life watching the Maestro transform human bodies into impossible things, and changing the world. He had enough material to write a book, and one day he would. But he still felt he did not know him any better than the rest of the world. If Van Tysch was a dark ocean, he had simply been a dyke to dam it, an electric power station which could change the extraordinary torrent into gleams of gold. The Maestro needed him, would go on needing him. Up to a point.

Just then, a phantom reared up in the front seat.

Murnika de Verne had turned her head and was regarding Stein through the tousled curtain of her jet-black hair. Stein looked away from the empty, lifeless eyes. He knew very well that it was not Murnika staring at him, but *the Maestro*. Murnika de Verne *was* Van Tysch to an extent that no one, except Stein, could suspect. The Maestro had painted her like this, with that wild look of hers.

Murnika kept staring at him, her anxious mouth hanging open like a starving dog's. She seemed to reproach him for something, but also to want to alert him.

400

The car glided on through the darting rain.

Her fixed stare disturbed him.

'*Fuschus*, Bruno, don't you believe me?' he said to defend himself. 'I swear I'll take care of everything. Trust me. Everything will be fine.'

He was talking to Murnika, but his words were intended for Van Tysch. He was making the same mistake a spectator sometimes makes when he believes the eyes of a painting are following him, or when a ventriloquist's dummy addresses him in the middle of an act. But in this case, it was Van Tysch who seemed like the dummy. Murnika de Verne appeared horribly alive and painted. She stared at him for a moment longer, then the life went out of her and she turned back to face the front of the car.

Stein drew a deep breath.

The windscreen wipers tussled with the rain. The only noise Stein could hear was this ticking like a clock (or a pendulum, or a paintbrush) as the limousine sped along the motorway towards Schiphol.

'Everything will be fine, Bruno,' Stein repeated.

18.35.

'We met at school in Edenburg,' Victor Zericky explained. 'My family is from here. Bruno only had his father, who was born in Rotterdam and who probably told him, among many other things, that there was nothing to be done here.'

Zericky was a tall, strong-looking man with blond hair going white. He looked like a well-intentioned man for whom things had not always gone as he had wished. Yet there was something about the way he screwed up his eyes when he talked that suggested there might be some hidden secret, some forbidden room, some distant family curse on him. His house was as cramped as it appeared from outside, and smelt of books and solitude. Half an hour earlier, when he returned after his long walk along the Geul with his dog and was showing Miss Wood in, he had confessed that his wife had left him because she could not bear either of these things. 'Neither books nor solitude,' he said with a laugh. But that did not mean he lived like a hermit, far from it: he went out a lot, was sociable, and had his friends. And he loved to discover nature on walks with his dog.

Miss Wood explained who she was, and gave a partial account of why she was there. She said she wanted to know more about the man whose works she was protecting, which was reasonable, and Zericky nodded, seeming to accept the excuse. Miss Wood launched into an entertaining monologue about the 'tremendous difficulty in finding the real Van Tysch' in the numerous books written about him, which had made her determined to get to the bottom of the problem and interview his great childhood friend. 'Tell me everything you remember,' she asked him, 'even if you don't think it's important.'

Zericky narrowed his eyes. Perhaps he suspected a deeper reason behind Miss Wood's visit, but he did not seem to want to discover what that might be. In fact, he was flattered by her request. It was obvious he liked to talk, and he did not often have the opportunity. He spoke first about himself: he gave classes in a school in Maastricht, although the previous year he had asked for leave in order to catch up on all his unfinished projects. He had published several books on the history of south Limburg, and at present was gathering material for a definitive study on Edenburg. Then he began to tell her about Van Tysch. He had got up to fetch a grimy folder from his bookshelves. In it were a pile of photographs. He passed some of them to Miss Wood.

'At school he was incredible. Look.'

It was a typical school form photograph. The children's heads shone white and round like so many pinheads. Zericky leaned over Miss Wood's shoulder.

'That one's me. And this is Bruno. He was very beautiful. It took your breath away just to look at him, whether you were a boy or a girl. His eyes shone with an inexhaustible gleam. His jet-black hair, inherited from his Spanish mother, his plump lips and thick black eyebrows that looked as if they had been drawn on with ink, gave him the harmonious look of an ancient god . . . That's how I remember him. But it was more than just beauty . . . how can I explain it? . . . He was like one of his paintings . . . there was something that went beyond what you can see. There was nothing for it but to bow at his feet. And he loved that. He enjoyed directing us, giving us orders. He was born to create things with others.'

For a split second, Zericky's eyes opened wide, as though they were inviting Miss Wood inside to see all that they had seen.

'He invented a game, which he sometimes played with me in the woods. I stood stock still, and Bruno placed my arms, head, or feet in the position he wanted. He used to say I was his statue. The rules were that I couldn't move until he gave me permission, although I must say that he made up the rules as well. Does that mean Bruno could do whatever he liked? Yes and no. I think he was more of a victim.'

Zericky paused as he put the photo back in the folder.

'I've thought a lot about Bruno over the years. I've come to the conclusion that he never cared about anyone or anything, but not because he was really uninterested in them so much as in order to survive. He was used to suffering. I remember one of his typical gestures: when anything hurt him, he would look up to the skies as though imploring aid. I used to say it made him look like Jesus, and he liked the comparison. Bruno always saw himself as a new Redeemer.'

'A new Christ?' Miss Wood repeated.

'Yes. I think that's how he sees himself. A misunderstood god. A god made man whom all of us have tortured.'

19.30.

He was out there somewhere.

All of a sudden Bosch had been filled with that terrible conviction.

He was out there somewhere. The Artist. Waiting.

Hendrickje, who had put her superstitious faith in his old bloodhound's sense of smell, would have bet anything that he was right. 'If *that* is what you *feel*, Lothar, don't think twice about it: go with it.' He stood up so brusquely that Nikki turned towards him, intrigued.

'Is something wrong, Lothar?'

'No. I just feel like stretching my legs. I've been sitting down for hours. I might walk over to the other control post.'

In fact, one of his legs had gone numb. He tapped his shoe on the floor to help the blood flow.

'Take an umbrella: it's not raining hard, but you could get soaked,' said Nikki.

Bosch nodded, but left the Portakabin without taking an umbrella.

It was raining outside – not heavily, but with a steady persistence – although it was quite warm. Bosch blinked, and walked a few paces away from the Portakabin to savour the atmosphere.

The huge tent of the Tunnel was less than thirty metres from him. It shone like petrol in the rain, and looked like a mountain shrouded in mourning clothes. The vehicles parked round it left narrow corridors that were thronged with personnel: workmen, police, plainclothes agents, the sanitary team. The sight inspired confidence and security.

But there was something *more*, a thread he could perceive although it was almost invisible, a *background* colour, a deep note playing beneath the surface fanfare of noise.

'He's *here.*'

Two of his men passed by him and said hello, without receiving any reply from Bosch apart from a brief nod. He swung his head from side to side, studying shapes and faces. He would not have been able to say how, but he was sure he was going to recognise Postumo Baldi when he saw him, whatever his disguise. *His eyes are mirrors.* But he could not rid himself of his sense of unease, even though he knew it was unlikely Baldi was there at that very moment. *His body is like fresh clay.* Maybe I'm just nervous because today is the opening, he told himself. That was easy to understand, and with the understanding came a sense of calm.

'Don't try to understand, Lothar. Listen to your spirit, not your mind,' was what Hendrickje used to tell him. But then, Hendrickje read her tarot cards like others read the morning papers, and saw her horoscope as set in stone just like events that had already taken place. Despite this, you didn't see that lorry waiting for you on your way back from Utrecht, did you Hendri? You didn't foresee the astrological confluence of your head and

404

the back end of that trailer. All your intuition suddenly converted into stardust, eh, Hendri?'

He walked over to the barriers. Why would he be here *today*? That's absurd. The only reason would be for him to explore the terrain. That's the way he operates. First he gets to know the surroundings, then he attacks. He's not going to try anything today.

He flashed his ID card and an agent let him through. He found himself caught up in the crowd coming out of the long night of the Tunnel – their eyes wide, fascination still shining in their faces, and swam against the current of this tide of humanity. Further on, beyond another row of barriers, was the central square from which all the paintings would be picked up. There were fewer people in there. Bosch could see the green and white uniforms of Van Hoore's team. They all seemed to be like him: nervous but at the same time calm. It was understandable. Never before had such astronomically valuable works of art been exhibited in a place like this. Outdoor pieces were much easier to guard; still simpler the ones in museums. 'Rembrandt' though was a huge challenge for the Foundation personnel.

He made for the Tunnel entrance. To his left, near the Rijksmuseum, was concentrated a small but vociferous group of BAH members waving banners in Dutch and English. The rain did not appear to dampen their enthusiasm. Bosch considered them for a moment. The main banner showed an eye-catching illustration (a blown-up photo) of a Stein original called *The Stepladder*, with the fourteen-year-old adolescent Janet Clergue. Her buttocks, breasts and genitals had been scribbled over and censored. Other placards displayed texts hastily written in capitals: HYPERDRAMATIC ART EXHIBITS NAKED CHILDREN. WANT TO BUY A NUDE EIGHT-YEAR-OLD GIRL? ASK AT THE VAN TYSCH FOUNDATION. VAN TYSCH'S *FLOWERS*: LEGALISED PHYSICAL AND MENTAL TORTURE. PROSTITUTION AND SALE OF HUMAN BEINGS . . . IS THAT ART? VAN TYSCH *DEGRADES* REMBRANDT IN HIS NEW COLLECTION. Another long, unfurled banner went into greater detail, in smaller lettering: 'How many models are there in the world *over* forty? How many grown men compared to young *girls*? How many HD works are *clothed* people in *normal* poses? How many are *naked* young women in *suggestive* poses?'

405

'What scum,' one of the security guards at the entrance muttered to Bosch. 'They're the same sort who wanted to prohibit Michelangelo's nudes in the Sistine Chapel.'

Bosch agreed half-heartedly and walked on.

He is *here*.

It was easier to get across the crowd of people at the entrance than at the exit, because they were slowed down by the three security filters at the mouth of the Tunnel. Bosch crossed through the queue. He was still intending to call on the other team in Portakabin A. But he came to a halt once more.

He's *here*.

He looked at the street musicians, the vendors, the people handing out catalogues and flyers.

Somewhere.

Further on, near the Rijksmuseum gardens, a large group of young artists were taking advantage of the presence of so many people to show their works. Models with painted bodies posed naked in the rain. There were more than thirty of them. The prices were real bargains; you could snap up a painting for less than five hundred euros. Not that they were very good: they trembled, lost their balance, sneezed, could be seen to scratch their heads furtively. Bosch knew that many of them were relatives or friends of the painters rather than real professionals. Buying one of them was a real risk, because you never knew who you were inviting into your home. You could wake up one morning and find the painting gone, along with your credit cards.

The rain was like a cold sweat on Bosch's forehead. Why could he not rid himself of this oppressive sense of menace?

All at once he changed his mind, turned round, and headed for the Tunnel.

20.00.

The driver had reappeared at five minutes to eight, but Miss Wood told him to carry on waiting.

'It's true he suffered a lot, and he compensated with his excessive passion for art,' Zericky went on. 'First there was his father, who treated him badly. Then that pederast sorcerer, Richard Tysch, who he spent those summers with in California. They all wanted to have their way with him, but he ended up having his way with every one of them . . .'

'Have you seen him again? Van Tysch, I mean.'

Zericky raised his eyebrows.

'Bruno? Never. He left me behind as well, along with all his other memories. I know we're neighbours now, but I've never felt like going to ask to borrow a cup of milk.' Miss Wood copied his weary smile. 'Some time ago I got a few phone calls from Jacob Stein. And also from that . . . that secretary of his, the odd one . . .'

'Murnika de Verne.'

'Exactly. They would ask me if I needed anything, as if they wanted to show me that he never really forgot his friends. But I never spoke to Bruno again, and I never wanted to. How a friendship ends is as mysterious as how it begins,' Victor Zericky said: 'it simply happens.'

Miss Wood nodded. Hirum Oslo's tranquil shadow had suddenly flitted through her mind. Yes, the end is as mysterious as the beginning. And as mysterious, too, as the part in the middle. It simply happens.

'Am I boring you?' Zericky asked affably.

'No, on the contrary.'

As he was talking, Zericky was absentmindedly pulling some sheets of paper out of another folder. Miss Wood asked:

'What are those drawings?'

'They're old watercolours, pastels, carbon sketches and ink drawings his father did. I thought you might like to see them. Maurits thought he was a painter, did you know that? One of his great frustrations was that Bruno could not draw,' he said, with a brief laugh.

'From what I can see, the father could, though,' said Miss Wood as she looked at the drawings one by one. She recognised some landscapes of the village with the castle in the background.

'He wasn't bad at all, was he?' Zericky agreed. 'One day I must sort out the collection properly. Perhaps I'll write a biography of the Van Tysch family and use them to illustrate . . . What's the matter?'

Zericky had seen the sudden change in April Wood's expression.

407

20.05.

Bosch decided to get into the Tunnel through one of the emergency exits, at the far end. He walked down the whole length of the first side. The rain had eased to a fine drizzle. Even so, he seemed to have got drenched. Why on earth had he not picked up a blasted umbrella? When he reached the area close to the Stedelijk gardens he waved his magic card once more, and passed through the barriers. In front of him was the impressive black curtain. The way in was a labyrinth of folds to help prevent any light penetrating inside. Two guards were on duty. Although they recognised him at once, he still had to go through the rigorous checks he himself had set up. He placed his left hand on the plasma screen that analysed his fingerprints, and spoke into the microphone. He was so nervous he had to repeat the voice test twice. They finally let him through. Bosch was pleased that the security measures were working so well.

When he got inside the Tunnel his eyes closed without any need for lids.

20.10.

'What's this?' asked Miss Wood.

Zericky looked at the drawing she was holding up, and smiled.

'Oh, that was how Maurits crossed out the drawings he didn't like. He never tore them up. He scribbled on them with a red pen, and always in the same way. He was a violent man, but he liked his routines.'

It was a China ink drawing of a human figure, probably a villager from Edenburg. It was scrubbed out with big red crosses. Zericky saw something had attracted the woman's attention, because he saw her place her forefinger on the paper and mutter something. It was as though she were counting the crosses.

'He always crossed them out like that?' she said, in a very odd voice. Zericky wondered what had so intrigued her, but the years and loneliness had made him discreet.

'Yes, as I said.'

Miss Wood counted them again. Four crosses and two vertical lines. Eight lines in crosses and two parallel lines. Ten lines altogether. *My God.* She counted them again: she didn't want to make a mistake. Four crosses and two separate lines. Eight plus two. Ten in total. She picked up the remaining drawings and flicked through them. She stopped when she came to another crossed out one. It was the rough sketch of a face, traced in pencil. The crosses and vertical lines again. Four plus two. Eight and two. Ten altogether.

She turned to the historian, trying to stay calm as she spoke.

'Mr Zericky. Do you have any more drawings?'

'Yes. In the cellar.'

'Could I see them all?'

'All of them? There must be hundreds of them. Nobody has seen them all.'

'It doesn't matter. I've got time.'

'I'll get the folders.'

20.15.

When he found himself inside the Tunnel, Bosch realised immediately it was very different from seeing it on the monitors. It smelt of paint and there was a strange warmth about it: all his senses told him he was in a different universe. The feeling was similar to contemplating a lake at night and then plunging headfirst into its dark waves. The silence was awe-inspiring, and yet there were sounds: the echoes of footsteps and coughs, whispered comments. There were also the grave harmonies of a majestic music that came from the great dome of the Tunnel. Bosch recognised it: *The Funeral Music for Queen Mary*, by Purcell, with its drumbeats from beyond the grave.

In among these baroque shadows, Bosch could make out the first painting. The tumultuous crowd forming *The Night Watch* took up a large part of the bend in the horsehoe, and gleamed in the chiaroscuro lighting. Twenty painted, motionless human beings. What meaning could there possibly be to that absurd army? Like all Dutchmen, Bosch knew the original on show in the Rijksmuseum: it was a typical portrait of a military company, in this case commanded by Captain Frans Banning Cocq, but Rembrandt's stroke of genius had been to paint them at work, as though he had photographed them as they were patrolling the street. Van Tysch on the other hand had *petrified* them. And the figures were full of grotesque details. The Captain, for example, was a woman, and the red sash of his uniform was painted on her stomach. His lieutenant was a yellow monster in ruffs and a wide-brimmed hat. The golden girl with a hen dangling from her waist was completely naked here. The soldiers still bore lances and muskets, but their faces were covered in blood. Torn to shreds, their banner lashed the darkness of the canvas. The background was filled with huge structures like a Piranesi invention. A woman dressed in leather was weeping. A shadowy shape on four legs wearing a hangman's cap was crawling at the lieutenant's feet.

By comparison, the modest, solitary figure of *Titus* on show a few metres away on a small plinth seemed to lack interest: it was a young boy – Rembrandt's son in the original – dressed in furs and wearing a cap. But the play of lights and paint lent him a constantly changing look. The optical effect was similar to the shifting gleams of a diamond's facets. Bosch screwed up his eyes and thought he could see by turns the head of an unknown animal, the luminous face of an angel, a porcelain doll, and a caricature of Van Tysch's features.

'The guy is completely crazy,' he heard a visitor say in a clear Dutch voice as like him he filed past in the darkness, 'but he fascinates me.'

Bosch could not make up his mind whether he agreed with this anonymous declaration. He went on, without stopping in front of *The Feast of Belshazzar*, with its banquet of human beings. What most interested him was further on, floating in a lake of glittering browns.

When he reached her, Bosch tried to swallow, but discovered his mouth was completely dry.

Danielle was standing still, quietly beautiful in the midst of all the ochre tones. The *Young Girl Leaning on a Windowsill* was a truly magnificent work, and Bosch could not help but feel proud. She was leaning against a chestnut-brown sill, staring into space with eyes that looked like jewels set in a face the colour of alabaster. The white paint was so dense it seemed almost obscene to Bosch. He could not understand why Van Tysch had wanted to shroud Danielle's pretty features in this snow. But what most amazed him was to realise it was *her*. He would not have been able to tell how he knew, but he would have recognised her from a thousand similar figures. Nielle was there, inside that bloodless mask, and there was something in the position of her hands or the tilt of her shoulders that gave the game away. Bosch lost himself in contemplation of her for several moments. Then he continued on his way.

Like a powerful condor, Purcell's music was soaring up into the far reaches of the darkness.

Bosch still did not understand. What had the painter been trying to say with this timeless, black world, this mystery of lights and music pouring down from the heights? What kind of message was he trying to convey?

20.45.

It was unbelievable. There they were. A girl standing on some flowers. Two fat, misshapen men. There were two drawings: the first in pastel, the second in China ink. They were not crossed out. She had come across them while she was looking for more examples of Maurits' crossing out.

Deflowering and *Monsters*, Miss Wood thought, scarcely able to believe her eyes, Van Tysch's most *personal* works: they are *based* on *his father's old drawings*, and no one knows it, not even Hirum Oslo. Nobody has taken the trouble to look at Maurits' legacy closely enough. Perhaps not even Van Tysch himself suspects it. Maurits wanted him to draw, to become the successful artist he never managed to be. But little Bruno did not know how to draw. So what he did was adopt some of his father's drawings for his own art. It was a kind of compensation . . .

She had separated these drawings from the pile, and went on looking. Zericky returned after a few minutes with yet more folders. He put them down on the table, raising clouds of dust, and began to undo the ribbons.

'These are the last,' he said. 'That's all I have.'

'Van Tysch saw these drawings as a child, didn't he?' said Miss Wood.

'Possibly. He never talked to me about it. Why do you ask?'

Instead of replying, she asked another question.

'Who else has seen them?'

Rather confused, Zericky smiled.

'As thoroughly as you, nobody. A few researchers have glanced at a folder or two here and there . . . but what is it you're looking for exactly?'

'Another one.'

'What?'

'Another one. The third.'

There's one missing. *The third most important work*. It must be here somewhere. It's not an *exact* copy of one of the 'Rembrandt' paintings. In fact, neither of the other two is an *exact* copy of Van Tysch's work . . . the adolescent for example is not naked, and there aren't any narcissi at her feet either . . . but her pose is *identical* to Annek's . . . there has to be *something linking it to* one of the works: a character, or a group of characters . . . or perhaps . . .

She tried to remember the paintings as she had seen them during the signing session the previous day: the characters; their poses; the clothes they wore; the colours. If I could identify *Deflowering* and *Monsters,* I must be able to spot the third one.

'Hey, calm down,' Zericky begged her. 'You're throwing all the drawings on the floor..'

Swear that you're going to find it . . . Swear you're going to do it . . . Swear you're not going to fail this time . . .

Every so often she came across a crossed-out drawing: always four crosses and two vertical lines. But it was not the moment to try to unravel the meaning of this other incredible coincidence. Nor could she worry about the most troubling mystery of all: how had the Artist managed to see the drawings? Could it have been one of the 'researchers' Zericky had mentioned? And if he hadn't seen them, how else had he chosen the third work to destroy?

One thing at a time, please.

The last drawing in the folder was of a flower. Miss Wood threw it down so violently that Zericky got annoyed.

'Look, you're going to tear them if you treat them like that!' the historian exclaimed, reaching out to take them from her.

'Don't touch me,' whispered Miss Wood. In reality it was not so much a whisper as a rattle in her throat that froze the blood in Zericky's veins. 'Don't even try it. I'll soon be finished, I swear.'

'Don't worry,' Zericky said haltingly. 'Take your time . . . make yourself at home . . .'

She must be ill, he thought. Zericky was not a conventional sort, but solitude had made it hard for him to accept any shocks. Anything unexpected (a crazy person in his house going through all the drawings, for example) horrified him. He started to think of a plan to get close to the telephone and call the police without this psychopath noticing.

Miss Wood opened another folder and put aside two landscape studies. Then a carbon drawing with a night-time wood. Drawings of birds. Still lives, but no slaughtered ox. A young girl standing arms akimbo, but she did not resemble the *Girl Leaning on a Windowsill*.

20.50.

As he advanced along the Tunnel, Bosch spotted one of the guards. His red badge shone dully in the light from the plinths. His face was a blur of shadows.

'Mr Bosch?' the man said when he had identified himself. 'It's Jan Wuyters, sir.'

'How is everything going, Jan?'

'All quiet so far.'

Beyond Wuyters the sharp linear splendour of the crucified *Christ* loomed in the distance. A trick of perspective made it look as though it were floating above Wuyters head, as if he were being offered special divine protection.

'I'd be happier if there was more light and we could see the face and hands of people properly,' Wuyters added. 'This is a slum, Mr Bosch.'

'You're right. But it's Art that's giving the orders.'

'I guess so.'

All at once, Bosch decided Wuyters was a very convincing Wuyters in the darkness. He was *almost* sure it was him, but as in a nightmare, tiny details confused him. He would have liked to have seen the man's eyes outside in the daylight.

413

'To tell you the truth, sir, I wish today's opening was over,' Wuyters' silhouette whispered.

'I share your feelings entirely, Jan.'

'And the horrible smell of paint . . . isn't your throat burning?'

Bosch was just about to reply when all hell broke loose.

20.55.

Miss Wood was staring at the watercolour, without moving a muscle. Seeing the change in her attitude, Zericky leaned over her shoulder.

'It's lovely, isn't it? It's one of the watercolours Maurits did of her.'

Miss Wood looked round at him uncomprehendingly.

'It's his wife,' Zericky explained. 'The young Spanish woman.'

'You mean this woman was Van Tysch's *mother*?'

'Well,' said Zericky with a smile, 'I think she was. Bruno never knew her, and Maurits destroyed almost all the photos of her after she died, so Bruno only had these drawings by Maurits to know what she looked like. But it is her. My parents knew her, and according to them they are a very good likeness.'

First, the remembrance of his childhood. Then his father and Richard Tysch. Now his mother. The third most personal work. Miss Wood no longer had the slightest doubt. She did not even need to look in the remaining folders. She knew exactly which painting the drawing related to. Her hand was trembling as she consulted her watch.

There's still time. I'm sure there's still time. Today's exhibition hasn't even finished yet.

She left the watercolour on the table, picked up her bag and took out her mobile phone.

All at once, something like a sudden presentiment, the shudder of a sixth sense, paralysed her.

No, there's no time left. It's too late.

She dialled a number.

What a shame you could not do it perfectly, April. Doing things well is doing them badly.

She put the phone to her ear and heard the distant screech of the call.

414

Because if you let yourself be defeated in small things, you'll lose out in the big ones too.

The telephone voice sounded in the minute darkness of her ear.

20.57.

Lothar Bosch had faced up to a crowd on several occasions in his life.

Sometimes he had been part of it (but even then he had needed to *protect himself* from it); at others, he had been part of those trying to disperse it. Whatever the case, he had known the phenomenon since his youth. He had never been able to draw any useful lesson from his experiences: he thought he must have survived by pure luck. A terrified crowd is not something a person can learn to resist, just as you can never learn to walk in the eye of a hurricane.

It all happened very quickly. First there was a shout. Then many more. A few moments later, and Bosch realised the full extent of the horror.

The Tunnel was roaring.

It was the deep roar of underground bells, as if the earth he was standing on had a life of its own and had decided to prove it by rearing up.

The darkness prevented him from comprehending exactly what was going on, but he could hear a ringing sound from the roof's metallic structure and from the curtain walls nearest to him. My God, the whole thing's coming down, he thought.

That was when the panic started.

Wuyters, the guard who had been talking to him just a few moments earlier, was swept away by a surge of shouts, gaping mouths and hands clawing for the open air. A thrusting piston of bodies flung Bosch against the guide rope. For one atrocious instant he saw himself crushed by the stampede, but fortunately the torrent of humanity was not headed in his direction: it was just forcing its way past. Fear made the crowd run blindly towards the far end of the Tunnel. The stanchions securing the rope held, so Bosch clung on and avoided falling off the ramp.

415

The worst of it, he thought, was not being able to see anything, plus this obscene carnival darkness, in which only a minimum of movement was possible. It was like being shoved under a woollen blanket with a lion.

A woman was screaming next to him, trying to get out. The fact that her breath smelt of tobacco was a stupid detail that seized hold of Bosch's terrified brain. He thought he understood that she was holding a child by the hand, and was begging the monster to respect her, at least not to devour her tiny charge. Then Bosch saw her swept under (had she bent down? been swept away?) then reappear further on, waving a tremulous, wailing little creature above her head like a banner. Go on, go on, get him out of here, Bosch wanted to shout, get your child out of here. He was trying to help her when he was struck by another blow, and fell over the edge of the ramp.

He felt he has falling through space. The darkness outside the ramp was so intense his eyes could not calculate the distance separating him from harm. Even so, he managed to put his hands out and parry his fall. For a second or two he could not even work out what had happened, why he was in this strange position of floating along horizontally. Then he understood that all the chiaroscuro lighting must have gone off.

That must be it, because in the entire length of the Tunnel he could not see a single light, not even a speck. The paintings had been swallowed up in the shadows. And he was in the belly of the darkness.

He tried to get to his knees, but was knocked flat again. Something, or some mass of things, swept over him. Somebody had thought that beyond the ramp there might be another exit, and now everyone was running towards this remote possibility. Perhaps it was true that the emergency exits for the paintings could also be used by the public: even though they were further off, they were much easier to get to. The problem was finding them.

Bosch finally managed to stand up and check he had no broken bones. All around him, dumbfounded shadows heaved. He tried to guide them because he knew where the exits were. He started shouting at people who were like stampeding elephants in the black centre of a storm.

416

'The far end! The far end!'

But: the far end of what? They started running towards the lights. But the lights were getting closer, too. A magical brush painted a sudden majestic white stripe on the sweating, terrified face in front of Bosch. Then the darkness added black, and the face disappeared. Another brush sketched an outstretched hand, then a summery shirt, a fleeting silhouette. In the midst of the Guernica panic, Bosch waved his arms like a drowning man.

'Stay calm, stay calm,' he heard a voice say.

Just hearing words that made sense reassured him a lot. It was a shred of coherence that might lead to some communication. Then there were the lights, which must be torches. He ran towards them as though the darkness engulfing him were flames, and his body needed to douse itself in light. He struggled to push away another person desperate to reach the privilege of light. Darkness is cruel, he thought. Darkness is inhuman, he thought.

'It's Lothar Bosch here!' he shouted. He felt his jacket lapel, but his ID badge had been torn off.

'Calm, stay calm,' the voice offering the gift of light repeated.

A beam struck his face, blinding him. It did not matter: he preferred to *be* blinded rather than to be *blind*. He raised his hands, begging for light.

'Stay calm, nothing has happened,' the voice said in English.

Bosch wanted to laugh. So nothing had happened?

It was then he realised that it was true that whatever had happened was over. He could no longer hear the sinister creaking of the Tunnel's metallic structure.

The torch painted another face: a woman from the crowd who was weeping as she tried to speak. Bosch contemplated this mask of tragedy as carefully as he had studied the paintings only a few minutes earlier.

He staggered out of the Tunnel inferno, guided by the rescuing torches, but feeling as lost as everyone else around him. Night had not yet fallen, and it had even stopped raining, but the dense ceiling of grey clouds made the sunset even more impressive. Under this colourless sky, the central square was a riot of

417

colour. It was as if the Rijksmuseum had burst open and peopled the streets with Rembrandt's dreams.

The Table and Maid from *The Feast of Belshazzar* were being helped into their robes by people from Conservation. King Belshazzar, swathed in a heavy painted turban, was panting loudly. The soldiers from *The Night Watch* were still holding aloft their lances and muskets, and looked for all the world like an army of dead men, astonishment filling their bloody faces. The girl with the chicken at her waist, naked and gold-painted, was a flickering flame at the foot of the recovery vehicle. At the opposite end of the horseshoe, *The Syndics* were climbing into more vehicles, while the students from *The Anatomy Lesson* ran about in their white ruffs. Kirsten Kirstenman's pale blue body was being carried on a stretcher. The paintings were all jumbled up with ordinary people. Out in the open, Van Tysch's masterpieces looked like the final nightmare of a painter on the point of death. Where could Danielle be? Where exactly had *Young Girl Leaning on a Windowsill* been on display? Bosch could not remember. He was completely disorientated.

Suddenly he recalled that the painting had been on show beyond *The Feast*. He remembered he had decided not to spend much time on that one so he could get to her as soon as possible.

He saw a man from Conservation whom he recognised. He was nervously attaching a label round the neck of Paula Kircher, the Angel from *Jacob Wrestling with the Angel*. Paula was wearing a huge pair of wings in a gleaming pearl-grey colour, fixed on her back like a monstrous, useless parachute. Another assistant had run over to protect her priceless ochre nakedness in a robe, but it was impossible to put on without removing her wings, so Paula just wrapped herself in it like a towel. People milling round her knocked against her feathers with their heads or shoulders: a fireman tore one out with his helmet. It was Paula who replied to Bosch's desperate question: she seemed a good deal calmer than the man trying to put her labels on.

'She's with the *Christ*.'

She pointed towards a side exit. But there was no vehicle there. 'My God, where is she? Has she already been evacuated?' He ran wildly over to the exit. A female security agent from the

418

inside team was consoling a woman who, probably, was a person rather than a painting. Bosch decided this because she was not painted. Next to him was a figure who *was* a painting: maroon clothing and a face like a cardinal by Velázquez: perhaps one of the characters from *The Night Watch*. Bosch interrupted the agent with his hasty question.

'I don't know, Mr Bosch. She might have been evacuated already, but I can't be sure. Why don't you call up control on your radio?'

'I haven't got one.'

'Use mine.'

The girl unhooked the microphone and passed it to him. As he was putting the headpiece on, Bosch realised there was a piano tune coming from his chest. It was his mobile phone ringing in his inside pocket. Bosch had no idea when it had started. Then all at once it fell silent. He decided not to worry about the call for now. He would track it down later.

Calm, stay calm. First things first.

The radio operator sounded in his ear with a marvellously clear voice. Like the voice of an angel in the midst of disaster, thought Bosch. He asked to speak to Nikki Hartel, in Portakabin A. The operator seemed more than happy to comply, but first she needed the code that Bosch himself, on Miss Wood's instructions, had insisted everyone must have in order to talk by phone or radio to the people in charge. Shit! He closed his eyes and concentrated, while the operator hung on. For security reasons he had not written it down anywhere: he had learnt it by heart, but that was in another century, in another era, in a time when the universe and its laws were different, before order was abolished by chaos and Rembrandt and his works had taken Amsterdam by storm. But he usually had a good memory. He remembered the code. The operator confirmed it.

When he heard Nikki's voice, he almost felt like crying.

Nikki sounded even worse.

'Where did you get to?' he heard her energetic, youthful voice in his earpiece. 'Everyone here was . . .'

'Listen, Nikki . . .' Bosch interrupted her. Then he paused for a second before going on.

Above all, it's important to speak calmly.

'I guess you've got a lot to tell me,' he said. 'But first of all, there's something I need to know . . . Where is Nielle? Where is my niece?'

Nikki's reply was immediate, as if she had been expecting his question right from the start. Yet again, Bosch was thankful for her immense efficiency.

'She's safe, in an evacuation vehicle. Don't worry. Everything's under control. The thing is, *Young Girl Leaning on a Windowsill* is a painting with only one free-standing figure, like *Titus* and *Bethsabe*, and so Van Hoore's team evacuated her before the other more complicated works.'

Bosch understood her explanation perfectly, and for a second the relief he felt kept him from saying anything else. But then he realised something.

'But most of the works are still here. They're even getting out of the vans again. I don't understand.'

'The evacuation was suspended five minutes ago, Lothar.'

'What? That's absurd! . . . The earthquake could happen again at any moment . . . And perhaps the curtains wouldn't withstand . . .'

Nikki butted in.

'It wasn't an earthquake. And it wasn't a fault in the Tunnel construction, as we thought at first. Hoffmann has just phoned. It was something Art dreamed up without telling any of us, not even Conservation or most of the people in Art either . . . something to do with the *Christ* painting, which apparently was an interactive *performance* piece with special effects that no one knew about.'

'But the Tunnel shook from top to bottom, Nikki! It was about to collapse!'

'Yes, here in the Portakabin we thought the same because all our screens vibrated, but it seems it would *never* have fallen. It was all staged. At least, that's what Hoffmann says. He says everything is under control, that there is no damage to any of the paintings, and that he doesn't really understand why there was such a wave of panic. He insists the Tunnel's shaking wasn't that violent, and that it should have been obvious it was an artistic

420

detail because it happened just after the *Christ* "died" on the Cross with a shout . . .'

As she spoke, Bosch remembered that everything had begun when he heard a shout.

'Well,' said Nikki, 'here we didn't understand a thing, of course, but it's modern art, so we're not supposed to try to understand it, are we? . . . Ah, and nobody can find Stein or the Maestro. And Benoit's climbing the walls . . .'

In spite of the double feeling of relief Bosch felt at knowing that not only was Danielle safe and sound but that the apparent catastrophe had been less serious than he had thought, he felt a growing sense of irritation. As the day drew to its end, he looked round at the flashing lights and the crush of policemen on the other side of the barriers. He could hear ambulance sirens wailing. He could sense the confusion on the faces of the paintings, conservation experts, security agents, technicians and guests: the bewilderment and fear in the eyes of all those he had shared those anxious minutes with. A *trick* staged by Art? An *artistic detail*? And there *was no damage to* the paintings? What about the public, Hoffmann? You're forgetting the public. There might well have been people badly hurt . . . He couldn't understand it.

'Lothar?'

'Yes, Nikki, what is it?' replied Bosch, still indignant.

'Lothar, before I forget: Miss Wood has phoned at least a hundred times. She wants to know, and I quote: "Where on earth you've got to, and why you don't answer your phone" . . . We've tried to explain what happened, but you know what the boss is like when she's angry. She started to insult us all. She couldn't have given a damn if the whole world had crumbled with you underneath it, she insisted she had to talk to you, only to you, to nobody else but you. Urgently. Right now. Have you got her number?'

'Yes, I think so.'

'If you press the recall button it's bound to be her. Good luck.'

'Thanks, Nikki.'

As he was phoning April Wood, Bosch looked at his watch: twelve minutes past nine. A sudden breeze that brought with it

421

the smell of oil paint lifted the flaps of his jacket and cooled his sweating back, giving him some thankful relief. He noticed that the Art technicians were taking the paintings out of the central square. They must be intending to get them together in the Portakabins. Almost all of them were wearing their robes. The Angel's wings shone in the crowd.

He wondered what April Wood had to tell him that was so important.

He raised the phone to his ear and waited.

21.12.

Danielle was inside the dark evacuation vehicle. It had stopped somewhere, but she had no idea why. She thought perhaps the driver was waiting for someone to arrive. He did not speak to her or explain anything. He simply sat in silence at the wheel in the darkness, his silhouette only dimly lit by the glow through the windscreen. Strapped into her seat by four safety belts, Danielle was breathing deeply, trying to stay calm. She was still dressed in the long white shift for *Young Girl Leaning on a Windowsill*, and was painted in the four layers of oil paint her figure required. When she felt the earthquake, she was sure one of the layers must have fallen off, but now she could tell it had not. She had started to think of her parents. Once she had got over her fear, she wanted to talk to them, and also to Uncle Lothar, to tell them she was fine. In fact, nothing had happened to her: seconds before the Tunnel had started to tremble, this friendly man had appeared and shown her out, lighting her way with his torch. Then he had strapped her into the back seat of the van and made his way out of the Museumplein. Danielle had no idea what route he had taken. Now he had parked in the darkness and was waiting.

All at once his silhouette moved. He got up and looked round at her. She stared at him anxiously. He was a tall and apparently very strong young man. He came into the back of the van. By the faint light in the van interior, Danielle could see he was smiling.

21.15.

As soon as he had finished talking to April Wood, Lothar Bosch contacted Nikki through his headset. His hands were trembling.

'It's impossible. This time April is wrong.'

Nikki was as surprised as he had been by the first question.

'The evacuated paintings? They're fine, Lothar. I suppose they're a bit frightened, but none of them suffered any damage. They've been taken to the hotel, but not picked up yet. They're all in their vans in the hotel parking lot.'

This was yet another security measure. The paintings could only be taken to their rooms by the corresponding security agent. The evacuation team was simply responsible for getting them away from danger.

'So they're all in the hotel car park?' Bosch insisted.

'Exactly. It was decided at our last meeting, if you remember. We agreed not to take them to the Old Atelier straightaway, because that's empty and locked up tonight, and we didn't want any more security staff . . .'

Bosch did remember. He would have hung up there and then, but April Wood's instructions were clear: he had to make absolutely sure.

'Are all the paintings in the car park now?'

'All of them. What are you worried about?'

'Do the vans' tracking devices all work?'

'Perfectly. We've got their signals on the screen right here.'

'Of them all?'

Nikki spoke with motherly patience.

'All of them, Lothar. Don't worry about Danielle. She's being kept in an armour-plated van and . . .'

'Can you tell me which paintings have been evacuated?'

'Of course.' Nikki paused briefly after she listed each of them, making Bosch think she must be reading them off a screen. *Bethsabe, Young Girl Leaning on a Windowsill, The Jewish Bride, Titus,* and *Susanna Surprised by the Elders.*'

'Only those five?'

'Yes, only those. The others were just being taken out when the evacuation was suspended.'

'Are the signals from all five vehicles appearing correctly on the screen as we speak?'

'Affirmative. Is something wrong, Lothar?'

Bosch was stammering into his microphone.

'Is there anyone with the paintings apart from the emergency personnel?'

'The car park guards. And a security team is on its way. They'll be there any minute.'

Bosch could believe it. The hotel chosen to put the paintings in was the Van Gogh, very close to the Museum quarter. You could reach it walking from Museumplein.

'Martine is confirming it,' Nikki told him. 'We're still receiving all five signals, Lothar. Everything is fine, I tell you. They're in the car park, awaiting instructions.'

What else could he ask? He was beginning to think April Wood's fears were unjustified.

He prayed that, just this once, she might be mistaken.

21.17.

The driver's shadow dipped down next to Danielle. The darkness was even more complete in the back of the van, so that all she could make out were a pair of attractive blue eyes and a fixed smile.

'Are you OK?' the man asked, in fluent Dutch.

'Yes.'

'Some scare, wasn't it?'

Danielle agreed. The man was kneeling next to her seat, still smiling.

'What are we waiting for?' Danielle wanted to know.

'Orders,' said the man.

She had no idea why, but the darkness and silence frightened her a little. Fortunately the smiling man seemed reassuring enough.

21.18.

All of a sudden, Bosch thought of another question.

'Nikki, which was the *first* painting evacuated? Do we know?'

Nikki told him.

'It was in the van in less than a minute,' she added, pleased with herself. 'It must have been a record. The emergency guard was very quick . . . Lothar . . . are you still there . . . ?'

Silence.

A prolonged silence. Nikki thought the communication must have been lost, but then she heard Bosch's voice once more.

'Nikki, listen carefully. Get in touch with Alfred and Thea . . . and with Gert Warfell. This is an emergency . . . No, don't ask me any questions, please . . . I want a security team to surround the hotel in less than ten minutes . . . top priority . . .'

He ended the call and looked around in bewilderment. A loudspeaker was offering calming words. The fire chief was telling the public that what had happened was not due to any problem with the Tunnel and there was no fear it would happen again. The police were appealing for calm as well. That seemed to be the general consensus. Everyone, everywhere, was calling for calm. The people around Bosch were starting to smile again. The tragedy was gently lapsing into the anecdotal.

But inside him, Bosch felt only horror.

His intuition told him April Wood was right yet again.

Nikki had just told him that the first painting evacuated was *Susanna Surprised by the Elders.* And a few minutes earlier, April Wood had told him: 'It's *Susanna Surprised by the Elders.* That's the painting he's chosen this time, Lothar.'

21.19.

After taking them to the Old Atelier and installing them in one of the rehearsal rooms in the first basement, the driver had shown his credentials. It was a turquoise-coloured badge. This allowed him, he said, to make the necessary adjustments to each painting. Clara was not the only one surprised at this: she saw the Elders looking inquiringly at the driver too. Did that mean he was a painter? asked the First Elder, Leo Krupka (he had introduced himself to Clara shortly before), the canvas she had seen at Schiphol airport. The driver said he was not a painter, just one of those in charge of keeping paintings in perfect condition. But wasn't that a job for Conservation? (a question from Frank Rodino, the Second Elder, a tall, heavy man). Yes, but for Art as well. Art carried out 'maintenance' on all its masterpieces, even though it was concerned with its own priorities rather than the well-being of the figures. The driver had instructions to evacuate the painting and store it, but first of all to adjust its stretching. A work such as this could not be simply packed up and sent home.

The young man had been very efficient. At almost the same time as the tremor that had shaken the walls of the Tunnel, he had come up to them and said one word in English: 'Evacuation.' He took them out and put them into his van with remarkable speed. He stopped only to give Clara a robe, because she was still naked, with the oil paint stretching her skin. The two Elders had not even taken off the clothes they were wearing for the painting. Then, as they were changing vans in the hotel parking lot, he had explained to them that the Tunnel had been about to collapse, and he had orders to evacuate the painting and take them to the Old Atelier. He spoke fluent, correct English with an accent Clara could not identify. He was good-looking, although rather too thin, and the most striking thing about him was that pair of light-blue eyes.

In the rehearsal room there was a table with a briefcase and an oilskin bag that apparently belonged to the driver. There were also boxes with labels for the three figures. The driver handed these to them, and asked them to put them on. Rodino's bulk made it difficult for him to bend down and reach his ankle. Then the driver made them sit still in chairs like well-behaved school-children, while he stood by the table.

He told them his name was Matt. He did a bit of everything in the Foundation.

'That's exactly what I'm going to do now. A bit of everything.'

Matt was keen for the figures to understand him. He constantly sought in both Clara and Krupka's faces (the two who were not native English speakers) any indication that they were confused, and if they were, he repeated the phrase, or if there was a difficult word, he gesticulated or changed it for a simpler one. This made them pay close attention, despite being so tired. He had taken off the jacket with the words 'Evacuation Team' on the back, and was wearing only a shirt and trousers. Both were white. So was his face. The whole of Matt was an accumulation of white.

'What are we going to do?' asked Krupka.

'I'll explain straightaway.'

426

He turned his back and opened the briefcase. Took something out of it. Some sheets of paper.

'This is an important part in the stretching of the painting, but don't ask me why. You've all got sufficient experience to know that your duty is to obey the artist's wishes, however absurd they might appear.'

He handed out the pieces of paper. First Krupka, then Rodino, and finally Clara. Buried in a mask of taut skin, his eyes shone expressively.

On the sheet of paper was a short text in English. To Clara the words seemed incomprehensible, a kind of philosophical digression on the meaning of art. Each of them – Matt explained – was to read their text in turn while he recorded their voices. It was important to read well, in a loud and clear voice. If necessary, they would repeat the recording.

'Then we'll go on to the next step,' he said.

21.25.

Bosch's worst fears were confirmed when the security team reached the hotel and found the van for *Susanna* empty. It was then he discovered how carefully everything had been planned. A second van had been waiting in the car park and the Artist had simply switched the painting over. The first van's tracking device was still giving out its signal, but there was no one inside. Fortunately, one of the guards in the parking lot had seen the transfer, so they had a description of the second van. The guard also said that only the driver and the three figures had got into it.

Van Hoore and Spaalze had answered Bosch's call immediately. The evacuation guard in charge of *Susanna* was one Matt Andersen, twenty-seven years old, someone 'efficient, experienced, above all suspicion' according to Spaalze. His fingerprints, voice and measurements were not at all similar to the Artist's morphometric details, but Bosch, who was beginning to realise just how much help the murderer was being given from inside the Foundation, considered this unimportant. It was simple enough for any of the top people in the Foundation to get hold of the morphometric information and change it.

427

'Lothar, I'm not responsible . . .' Van Hoore's voice was qua-vering in Bosch's earpiece. 'If Spaalze tells me Andersen is trustworthy, I *have* to believe him, don't I . . .'

'Don't worry, Alfred. I know you're bewildered: so am I.'

Van Hoore had caved in. He sounded like a tearful little boy spattering the microphone with his saliva.

'For goodness' sake, Lothar! I'll talk to Stein myself, if need be! The evacuation team is made up of highly experienced guards, people we trust! Please, tell Stein that . . .'

'Calm down. No one is responsible for this.'

It was true. Either no one, or all of them. As he listened to Van Hoore's anxious confession in his earpiece, Bosch was busy giving orders and explanations. He could see everyone else reacted with the same incredulity as he had. The unexpected can not happen to the unexpected: lightning never strikes in the same place twice. Warfell for example could not get out a single word when Bosch told him what had happened. That's impossible, his silence seemed to shout. 'The *only* tragedy permitted is what happened in the Tunnel, Lothar: what's this you're telling me now? That one of the paintings *has disappeared*?'

As for Benoit, that was another surprise. Bosch found him in the street, surrounded by riot police, Civil Protection forces, fire-men and what looked like a whole regiment of soldiers, but when he went up to him, Benoit signalled and took him to one side, then showed Bosch the yellow label round his wrist.

'I'm not Mr Benoit,' he said in a guttural voice with a foreign accent, as he gripped Bosch's elbow. 'I'm a copy. Mr Benoit has left me here in his place, but don't tell anyone, please . . .'

Recovering from his initial surprise, Bosch understood that Benoit must feel even more anguished than him, and had put this stand-in in his place. He remembered the joke about the dummy in the window of the lost property office. He wondered if this model was the Ugandan.

'I have to talk to Mr Benoit,' he said.

'Mr Benoit can hear you right now,' the model said. The cerublastyne was amazing: his features were perfect. 'Take my radio, you can talk to him on it.'

Benoit was indeed listening to everything. To judge by the

tone of his voice, he was in some personal nirvana: nothing is happening, I'm not to blame for anything, nothing will go wrong. He refused to tell Bosch where he was hiding. He said he was not retreating, merely undertaking a tactical withdrawal.

'That Mr *Fuschus-Galismus* didn't tell us *a thing*, Lothar!' Benoit moaned. 'I mean about the *Christ* and the "earthquake" in the Tunnel. Hoffmann knew about it, but we didn't . . . !'

The Artist knew about it, too, thought Bosch.

When he succeeded in getting a word in edgeways in Benoit's verbal diarrhoea, he explained what had happened to *Susanna*. Benoit suddenly went quiet.

'Lothar, tell me this isn't the end of the world!'

'It is,' replied Bosch.

Bosch promised to keep him informed, and gave the radio back to his substitute. As he was doing so, he saw a line of vans entering the Museumplein: the evacuated works were returning. They were all there, apart from *Susanna*. He saw Danielle getting out of one of the vans. She was a tiny creature surrounded by immensely tall men in dark suits. Her chestnut hair, shiny ochre body and marble-coloured face made her seem like an optical illusion. The first thing she did as she got out of the van was to lift her foot to check that the radiant signature on her left ankle was still there. Bosch could not prevent a lump forming in his throat at seeing her like this. He understood how *important* this marvellous adventure was for her, and for an instant he almost agreed with her parents' decision. He knew he would not be able to hug her because she was painted and was wearing the clothes for her painting, but he went up to her nevertheless.

Nielle was holding the hand of the evacuation van driver, a tall, well-built man with a pleasant smile. She was very happy. When she saw Lothar, her eyes opened wide in their circle of white oil paint.

'Uncle Lothar!'

It was hard to convince her not to throw her arms round him.

'Are you all right?' he wanted to know. She told him she was. Where were they taking her? To one of Art's Portakabins: they wanted to gather all the works there before returning them to the hotel. No, she hadn't been afraid. The driver had been with her the whole time, and this had helped her not to feel frightened. Her parents had already been informed that she was fine. She wanted to tell Bosch a story, but could not finish it because the guards were in a hurry. Apparently Roland had got very nervous when he was told that his daughter 'had not suffered any damage'. Roland was unaware that this was the expression normally used to refer to the works, and at first had believed they were only talking about the paint covering her. So her father had protested: 'I don't give a damn if the colour has run! I want to know how *my daughter* is!' This made Danielle laugh till she cried. Bosch could understand Roland's fears, but felt no sympathy for him. Put up with it for art's sake, he thought. He said goodbye to his niece and stored her in a safe place in his mind. For the moment, he did not want anything to get in his way.

In Portakabin A everyone was extremely busy. Nikki was in permanent contact with the police and Thea van Droon's people. Even though it was absurd to think they would be in time, the KPLD had set up road blocks on all the exits to Amsterdam. A police inspector wanted Bosch to tell him all the details, but he could not spare a moment. 'I'm not here for anyone,' he said. He sat down with Nikki in front of one of the terminals connected to the Old Atelier.

'No sign of the van as yet, Lothar,' Nikki said. 'Who on earth are we looking for? Is this anything to do with the search for Postumo Baldi?'

This was no time to keep anything hidden, reasoned Bosch. To hell with the crisis cabinet: everything was in crisis now.

'That's right. But it doesn't matter if it's Baldi or not. He's crazy, and if we don't stop him, he'll destroy *Susanna* . . .'

'My God.'

Bosch was looking at the files on *Susanna surprised by the Elders* on the computer. The female canvas was Spanish, twenty-four years old, and was called Clara. The Elders were a Hungarian – Leo Krupka – and a North American – Frank Rodino – who were a little bit younger than Bosch. The North American Rodino was huge, and so would perhaps be some kind of obstacle for the Artist, in the unlikely event that there was a struggle between them.

'Think positively, Lothar.'

For the moment, he just sat there surveying the images on the screen. In particular, he stared at the young woman's face. She stared calmly back at him from the computer.

It's not a woman, it's a canvas. We are what other people pay us to be.

Bosch did not know her, and had never spoken to her. He read her complete name, and tried to pronounce it under his breath. Her family name was quite difficult for him. Rieyes. Reies. Rayes. Miss Rieyes or Reiyes was from Madrid. Hendrickje and he had occasionally spent their summer holidays in Mallorca, and Bosch had been to Madrid, Barcelona, Bilbao and other Spanish cities for various exhibitions. None of that was important now, but details like that helped him think of her as a human being facing danger. Clara Raiyes or Clara Reies had an expressive, sweet look to her, yet deep in her eyes there was a light that not even the computer image could conceal. Bosch surmised that she was a young woman full of life and hopes, someone who wanted to succeed, to push herself to the limit. He thought of Emma Thorderberg and her boisterous cheerfulness. Clara reminded him a little of Emma. How would Miss Wood and he, how would the Foundation and the wretched painter whose works they were meant to be protecting, pay for the destruction of the *hopes* of this young woman? How would 'Grandad Paul' restore the life and happiness that shone from the face in front of him? Would Kurt Sorensen be able to find an insurance company to bring her life back? How much money was it worth to torture her to death? That was something they should ask Saskia Stoffels.

It's not a woman, it's a canvas.

All at once he conjured up the face of Postumo Baldi peering over her. An empty blue gaze like a painted sky in a picture. *His eyes are mirrors.* Then the whirring canvas cutter getting closer and closer to her face . . .

Think positively. Let's think positively. We're all going to think positively about this.

To Hell with it.

He leapt up from the computer.

'Nikki, get me a vehicle and three guards. They don't have to be from the SWAT teams, they just need to be armed.'

She looked at him in surprise.

'What are you going to do, Lothar?'

Precisely. That was the question. What are you going to do, Lothar? *Something*. No matter what, but *something*. I'm not an artist and I don't like modern art, so I have to do something. I'm no good at anything else: I have to do things, I need to do them. That's enough of thinking positively: now it's time to *act positively*, isn't it, Hendri?

'Just remember that the Amsterdam police are on this guy's tail right now,' said Nikki. Bosch saw a different kind of gleam in her eyes. Was she worried about *him*? That was funny.

'I'll remember,' he said.

'You'll have the vehicle and the three men straightaway,' Nikki replied. That was the end of their conversation.

21.30.

Gustavo Onfretti surveyed them one by one. They were all still painted and in costume. The students from *The Anatomy Lesson* were in their dark Puritan clothes and white ruffs, *The Syndics* still had their broad-brimmed hats on. Kirsten, the woman-corpse, had bent double her fantastic, crude anatomy in a chair at the far end of the Portakabin. He himself was sitting with the models from *Ox*, and was still wearing the ochre-painted loincloth. His body, painted in streaks of earth colour and gleaming yellow, was aching from the long hours spent on the cross, from which he had been brought down only half an hour earlier. Conservation had gathered all the canvases together in the Art Portakabin. They probably wanted to make sure the paintings were all in good shape and had not suffered any damage.

Onfretti could not complain, but the astonished expression on his face gave him the look of someone returned from the dead.

How come *nobody* knew *anything* about the special effects for his painting, when everything was supposed to have been planned by the Art Department well in advance? Why had Conservation not been told that the *Christ* was an interactive performance piece, and that at a certain moment he was going to 'die', making the earth tremble and everything go dark?

He recalled how devotedly Van Tysch had planned everything during the weeks they had worked together at Edenburg. 'A nerve-wracking experience,' he had noted in his diary. The moment of his supposed 'death' with his shouts and the Tunnel's mechanically induced shuddering, had been painted and repainted to the point of exhaustion. The Maestro had told him it was very important that all this should happen at exactly the right moment, and he had set up a small warning light at the far end of the Tunnel so that Onfretti would know when he had to start shouting. But the public and Art and Conservation were meant to know about it, and the *quake* was supposed to be a small one. That, at least, was what Van Tysch had told him.

Onfretti wondered why on earth Van Tysch had lied to him.

When he had finished painting him, Van Tysch had kissed him on the cheek. 'I want you to feel betrayed by me,' he had suggested.

Now Onfretti thought the phrase had been more than a suggestion.

21.31.

As Bosch left the Portakabin, he was thinking things over.

If the Artist had taken the painting out of Amsterdam, there was nothing he could do. He would have to let the police or the SWAT team find the whereabouts of the van and pray they got to it in time. But what if he had decided to destroy it *in Amsterdam*? Bosch thought of all the possible places, and immediately dismissed the parks and public places. It wouldn't be a hotel either, because the figures were painted and might arouse suspicion. Then he thought of the man who was helping the Artist from inside the Foundation. Could he have provided him with somewhere quiet so that the destruction could take place without any problem? If that were the case, he must have anticipated that Amsterdam's entire police force would immediately set out in pursuit of the work. The place, wherever it was, had to be *completely safe*. Somewhere with lots of room, somewhere empty . . .

It was then that Bosch remembered what Nikki had told him a few minutes earlier.

At their last meeting, Van Hoore had suggested that the evacuated paintings should *not* be taken to the Old Atelier, because it was 'closed and empty', as Stein himself had told him.

Closed and empty.

It was a chance in a thousand, and Bosch was sure he was getting it wrong, but he had to bet on something. Let's trust our intuition, shouldn't we, Hendri my love?

He saw the three guards coming towards him. He guessed they must have been sent by Nikki. He ran towards them, worried he might slip on the sodden ground. It was raining heavily again.

'Where's the van?' he asked the first man. He recognised Jan Wuyters, who he had been talking to in the Tunnel before everything came tumbling down. It seemed like a good omen that they were together again.

The van was parked in Museumstraat. The four of them ran to it through the rain. The people in the square had dispersed by now, but there were still some police cars and ambulances.

'Where are we headed?' Wuyters asked him as they climbed into the vehicle.

'To the Old Atelier.'

He could well be mistaken, of course, but he had to bet on something.

The girl's face. The whirling blade.

He had to take a chance.

21.37.

'Strange the impression all this makes without furniture or decoration, isn't it? Even the guest rooms have camp beds, neither better nor worse than the one the Maestro sleeps in. It looks more empty or abandoned than monastic, doesn't it . . . but the smell of oil paint adds something different: as if it were brand new, about to be revealed, don't you think . . . ?'

Stein was like a guide commenting on all the noteworthy characteristics of the place for a group of tourists. He waved his hand for Miss Wood to follow him. They chose a door to the left, and entered a shadowy world of echoes.

'It's not that strange after all. We all tend to decorate our homes with things we have found on our journeys. Van Tysch has done the same. But all his journeys have been interior ones. All this is the product of what he has found *inside himself*. The souvenirs of his mind. When I came to the restored castle for the first time, I thought it was all very Dutch. You know, constructivism, Mondrian's clear cool lines, Escher's illusions and geometry . . . but I was wrong: to Van Tysch, nakedness is not decoration, it's emptiness; it's not art, but the lack of it. Come this way.'

Stein's voice sounded weary. His words had the ring of something inevitable about them. He seemed preoccupied by a nebulous idea, as if his thoughts were tiny beings dancing round him.

Miss Wood was clutching the watercolour she had taken from Victor Zericky's house. It showed a naked woman kneeling on the ground, leaning forward with her head turned towards the spectator. Miss Wood had immediately recognised the posture she had seen *Susanna* in during the signing session at the Atelier. She could understand how when he saw the watercolour as a boy, little Bruno's mind would have been set ablaze with dreams. And she could also understand how, as an adult, he could want to recreate it in the defenceless, desirable figure of Rembrandt's *Susanna*. Links between past and present, life and work, were frequent in all painters. What was most troubling in this case were the *implications*. She had decided to visit the castle and confront them. He'll have to let me in and answer my questions, she thought. But the person who received her, standing in the doorway to the inner courtyard, was Jacob Stein.

Now they were walking down a corridor. At the far end she could see another yard with a chequerboard floor. Night was flooding the distant tiles with its lunar tints.

'Who is helping Postumo Baldi?' asked Miss Wood. 'It's obvious he's not working alone. Who has given him all the information? Who has passed him the badges, codes, access numbers, the shifts our guards were working, the paintings' habits? And who told him what was going to happen in the Tunnel today and the exact time?'

A vague smile appeared on Stein's face.

'So you even know that Postumo Baldi is involved . . . Ah, *galismus*, our guard dog, our beloved and faithful guard dog . . . Van Tysch used to tell me: "Be careful with her. She'll pick up the scent and get her jaws on the prey before we're ready." And he was right. You are perfect.'

His praise made her shudder.

'Answer my questions, please.'

'When did you realise it was us?' Stein asked her instead.

Miss Wood's brain raced.

'I never did,' she said, then added: 'Why would Van Tysch want to destroy his own works?'

'Destroy? *Fuschus*, Miss Wood, whoever said that? We are creators, not destroyers. We are artists.'

They crossed the tiled courtyard. Miss Wood had never visited this part of Edenburg castle before. It was very imposing: bare floors and walls. The only architectural detail was the smooth timber columns. The night stretched above them like a sea in the darkness.

'But to be honest, I would not wish to attribute to myself the creation of this work,' Stein said, absent-mindedly once more.

They found themselves in another empty, tiled room. At the far end was another door, but this one seemed different somehow. Miss Wood was still tense. She knew Stein was trying to undermine her defences without facing her openly. Stein was used to manipulating people, not overcoming them. She had to stay on guard.

The door was made of metal and had a lock with a security combination. Stein punched in the numbers, and opened the groaning metal sheet to reveal a completely dark interior. He turned back to Miss Wood with a theatrical gesture.

'The Maestro alone is responsible for the work. But he would be very pleased to know you will be one of the first to see it.'

And he showed her in.

21.40.

The young man called Matt had gone from one to the other of them lifting the portable recorder like a sacred object. The texts were short, so it had not taken long to read them. Krupka and

436

Clara had needed to repeat one phrase because they had stumbled over it. Clara found it hard to concentrate on what she was reading, as well as on what the Elders were saying. This was a shame, because they seemed like very interesting reflections on the true meaning of art. The word 'destruction' cropped up in all three texts. Clara also realised that the fact whether they understood or not what they were reading was of no importance. She was struck in particular by one of the phrases she had to read. 'The art that survives is dead art.' She pronounced this with all due reverence.

Satisfied, Matt switched off the recorder. His next order did not take Clara by surprise – she had been expecting it – but her anxiety increased all the same. She could tell she was trembling as she hurried to carry it out.

Matt had asked them to strip naked.

The Elders took much longer about it than she did. They were not even sure how to get the heavy, oil-painted clothes off without help, whereas all she had to do was take off her robe. She folded it and left it on the chair. Krupka got undressed before Rodino, who was not only struggling with his vast tunic, but also seemed uncertain as to why they had to do all this in the first place. Clara was tempted to give him a hand, but restrained herself. That would have been a hyperdramatic error. The Elders were *detestable*. She was their defenceless victim. That was how things should continue to be. Just thinking about what might happen next made her shudder with disgust, but at the same time she felt a powerful feeling of satisfaction.

'Was it the Maestro who gave all these instructions?' Rodino asked.

'Your clothes, please,' Matt replied with complete calm.

Rodino obeyed without another word. Krupka helped him. Clara, who was standing some distance from them, utterly naked and utterly nervous, had decided not to look at the two men. It was easier for her to imagine them as cruel if she did not look at them. But Rodino's doubts were like cold water thrown in her face. Why couldn't that fat, clumsy canvas just shut up and obey, as Krupka had? Krupka was far more odious than Rodino, more detestable, and therefore the better work of art. By focusing her thoughts on Krupka, Clara managed to feel sick from terror. She suspected that Krupka would not have to pretend to fling himself on her and hurt her: ever since they had seen each other for the first time in Schiphol, he had been constantly devouring her with his sensual, shining eyes. Which meant the Hungarian was a good ally for any 'leap into the void'.

She heard the deep rumble of a curtain coming down. Clara guessed this meant Rodino was finally naked.

She went on staring at the floor between her bare feet. She could see the foreshortened perspective of her painted breasts, with the erect nipples gleaming in rose and ochre. But the silence was so profound she was forced to look up.

Matt had turned his back on them and was searching for something in his case.

'What's next?' asked Krupka.

The young man turned towards them once more. He was holding something in his hand. A pistol.

'This is next,' he said simply.

21.50.

Perhaps it was too late already. 'But don't admit defeat until you have to, Lothar', Hendrickje whispered in his ear. They had crossed the Amstel bridge at top speed and headed towards Plantage through the intense curtain of rain. The windscreen wipers could not cope, so that to Bosch it seemed as if they were driving through an underwater city. All of a sudden the walls of the Old Atelier buildings loomed up in their headlights like tall cliffs. A complicated aerosol graffiti decorated the lower sections. It was signed by a neo-Nazi group.

'Drive into the underground car park, Jan,' Bosch said.

The front door to the Foundation was closed, but that meant nothing. 'If he's brought them to the Atelier, he must have the keys.' One of the men got out and dealt with the electronic keypad that allowed them access. As the van negotiated the descent, the car-park lights came on. Under the blinking fluorescent strips they could see it was empty and silent. But Bosch still thought the other vehicle might be there somewhere.

Then all at once there was the parked van, as if it had been lying in wait for them, beside a block of lifts. To Bosch's surprise this discovery, which apparently confirmed his theory, had the effect of almost totally unnerving him. He swivelled in his seat and hit Wuyters on the arm.

'Here! Stop here!'

The engine was still running when Bosch leapt from the vehicle. He was so nervous he had forgotten he was still wearing the radio headset, and the cable caught in his seat belt, tugging violently at his head as he got up. He threw the headset off, cursing as he did so. His big hands were shaking. He was old: it was a judgment he had no time to reflect on. Leaving the police meant he had got rich, fat and old. He ran towards the other van, sensing that his men were following him. He wanted to shout to them, but could not draw breath. He could not believe how out of shape he was. He was afraid he would have a heart attack before he could even decide what to do.

The van looked empty, but they had to check it out. He opened the front door, looked inside, and breathed in a rasping smell of oil paint. No one there.

Fine, Lothar, fine, you stupid man. You've proved they *might* be here. So now, where are they?

There were five different buildings in the Old Atelier. They could be in any of them. He'll have taken them to the workshops, Bosch reasoned. That's the safest place. But that was not much help either. The workshops were spread over five floors and four basements. For the love of God, which one would they be in?

Think, you old fool, think. A roomy, quiet place. He needs to make recordings. And there are three figures . . .

His men were examining the back of the van. It was empty, but it was obvious that a short time before there had been a painting there.

'The goods lift,' Bosch suddenly muttered.

He was still short of breath, but ran towards the lift shaft.

'If he parked here, it was so he could use the goods lift. That goes down to the basements, so there are four possible floors for us to search. He could be in any of them.'

He stopped to look at his men. They were all young, and all looked as bewildered as him. Their hair was streaming from the

439

rain. Bosch himself was amazed at the assured way he gave orders and deployed his men: two of them were to search the third and fourth floors; Wuyters and he would take the second and first basements. Whichever group found them first would contact the others by radio. First and foremost though they were to protect the art work: if they had to take urgent action, they should.

'I don't know what he looks like, or if he has others with him,' Bosch added, 'but I do know he is a very dangerous individual. Don't give him any chances.'

The goods lift opened. Bosch and his men piled in.

They had all pulled out their weapons. Wuyters had a small Walther PPK as a backup, and Bosch asked him for it. Feeling the familiar weight of the metal 'L' in his hand, Bosch hesitated. He wondered how good his aim was nowadays: he had not used a gun in years. Should he ask for help? Reinforcements? Call April? His mind was a flaming wasps' nest. He decided there was no time to lose. It was up to them. They would have to find the Artist and stop him.

The goods lift moved off agonisingly slowly.

21.51.
The beginning and the end, she thought. The beginning and the end were there, and she was staring at them.

At that moment she would have loved to have been able to count on Oslo's opinion, but she understood that poor Hirum would take a long time to speak, or even to think coherently, after seeing something like this. Faced with this work, Hirum Oslo would hardly have been able to do anything more than stand open-mouthed, eyes wide, for much longer than she did.

'It's almost finished,' murmured Stein, clouds of vapour coming from his mouth. 'What's missing is the destruction of *Susanna*, of course. When Baldi sends it, the painting will be complete.'

What could it be compared to? wondered April Wood, blinking at the sight. What landmark in the history of art was anything like it? *Guernica*? The Sistine Chapel? She walked slowly around it to be able to take it all in: it was spread out on the floor. The

Pietà? The *Demoiselles d'Avignon*? A border, a limit, a point beyond which art changes altogether? The moment when the first man dipped his fingers in paint and drew an animal on the wall of his cave home? The moment when Tanagorsky got up on a platform and shouted to an astonished public 'I am the painting'?

She twisted her mouth, collected some saliva, swallowed. Her heart was beating at a different rhythm to the slow passage of the seconds in the numbingly cold room, a crazy, unhinged rhythm.

Neither she nor Stein dared disobey the silence for several seconds.

They were in a room measuring about eight metres by ten, that was completely sealed, soundproof and at a set temperature. This was controlled from outside, and was several degrees below zero, giving the room the appearance of a mournful butcher's freezer. The ceiling, walls and floor had all been lined with turquoise-blue steel. The dim white light came from a track of small spotlights on the ceiling. They were all pointed at the man on the floor, who seemed to be floating in a frosty lake.

The man was Bruno van Tysch. He lay completely naked flat on his back, arms stretched out above his head, ankles crossed in a pose that immediately recalled the crucifixion. He was painted ochre and blue from head to foot. The veins at his ankles and wrists were slashed; as she peered more closely, the deep cuts were plainly visible. It was easy to see what had happened only a short while before. The coagulated blood around each extremity formed a dense pool of red on the blue of the floor, which made it look as though Van Tysch was nailed to his own blood. Several large rectangular objects, flat as mirrors, were placed around the body. There were three of them: one on the right-hand side, another on the left – arranged so that their bottom edges met close to the painter's ankles – and the third across the top of his head, touching the hands. But they were not mirrors. The rectangle to the right of Van Tysch showed Annek Hollech's body full-size, naked and labelled, placed in almost the same pose as the painter, torn apart in ten places by the ten cuts of a blade. On the left, there was the image of the Walden brothers in a similar pose, and similarly destroyed. These were not simply video images: the burgeoning mound of the twins' stomachs rose above Van Tysch's body like bloody twin peaks. April Wood supposed they must be some kind of virtual image that did not need a visor. The red of the paintings' wounds, and the gleaming, scarlet, real red at Van Tysch's wrists and feet, formed a whole that contrasted with the flesh tones of the four dead bodies. The backgrounds (a lawn for Annek, a hotel room for the Walden brothers) had been cleverly merged in a uniform turquoise that appeared to continue the floor of this strongroom. The tableau had an incredible symmetry and a mysterious but undeniable beauty. Any sensitive observer would immediately think of some kind of all-incorporating idea: the artist and his creation, the artist and his testament, the immolation of the artist together with his works. There was something almost sacred in that naked family with arms and legs outstretched, torn apart and still. Something eternal. The horizontal panel, much larger than the others and still dark, broke up the harmony. That must be where – thought April – the images from the destruction of *Susanna* are to go.

'Don't ask me to explain it to you,' said Stein, seeing her expression. 'It's art, Miss Wood. I don't think you'd understand it. And it's not for the artist to try to explain it either—'

At that moment another unexpected voice interrupted his. April Wood almost jumped in terror at this unforeseen outpouring of underground words amplified to an inhuman degree. It was Annek Hollech. Gentle harmonies by Purcell underscored her trembling words.

'ART IS ALSO DESTRUCTION.'

A brief pause. Then the solemn strains of a baroque funeral march.

'IN THE BEGINNING, IT WAS NOTHING ELSE, IN THE CAVES THEY ONLY PAINTED WHAT THEY WANTED TO SACRIFICE.'

Another pause.

April Wood's hair was standing on end. She was shivering as though an unending line of ants was crawling over her.

In the mirror, Annek's image seemed to have changed. Still naked and hacked to pieces, her face appeared to be moving. That was where the voice was coming from.

Stein and Miss Wood listened to the rest of the recording in respectful silence.

When Annek had finished, her face turned back into the hollow mask that was part of her corpse. Immediately afterwards, a chorus of angels seemed to transform the tearful, floating features of the Walden brothers: they came to life and spoke into the air as if saying a prayer or a sacred incantation. Again, neither Stein nor Miss Wood felt they could interrupt them.

When at last the twins subsided into a blood-filled silence, Stein said:

'Van Tysch insisted on having the canvases' original voices, although we improved the quality in our studio. They're programmed to start up every so often, twenty-four hours a day, every day.'

The art that survives is the art that has died, April Wood thought. If the figures die, the works survive. Now she understood. In this posthumous work, Van Tysch had found a way to convert a body into eternity. Nothing and nobody could destroy what had already been destroyed. Nothing and nobody could put an end to what had already been ended. The inhospitable electrically controlled cold would ensure this work lasted forever.

His work. His last work.

'Van Tysch prepared Baldi . . .' she murmured. In that room, where every sound was an unwelcome guest, her voice was almost a scream.

Stein agreed.

'Step by step, ever since 2004, in secret. When in 2001 he painted him in an unimportant painting, *Figure XIII*, he realised at once that Baldi would be the perfect material for his last great work. He used to call him his "paper". "I write and draw on Postumo, Jacob", he told me, "I make notes and develop my plan for my life's last work."'

Stein glanced at Miss Wood through the blue-tinged darkness of the room. They were both enveloped in vapour, as though their spirits had decided to leave their bodies but not to stray too far.

443

'*Fuschus,* there's no need to look like that. We couldn't tell you *anything,* could we? If you had known something, you would have collaborated with us of course. But then the work would have been *yours* to some extent as well. And you're not an artist, April. Not an artist, nor a canvas,' he added. April Wood could detect the cruel way he insisted on these words. 'We had to do everything without involving you, because this was our work, not yours.'

'I understand,' she said.

'No one else knows about it: not Hoffmann or anyone else in the Foundation. I myself only learnt of it a few months ago. Bruno brought me here and explained it all. He showed me this room, and the shape the work would take when it was complete. This won't be the first time, he told me, that a work demands such a sacrifice from artists. Nor will it be the first time that a painter wants to destroy his best works before he dies. He had planned everything perfectly, down to the *Christ's* momentary distraction in the "Rembrandt" exhibition. He knew the police and his own security department would have taken a lot of pre-cautions. But he had faith in Baldi: he'd trained him carefully to turn him into the perfect tool, into the paper on which he could draw his greatest work. I told him I agreed with him, but I was upset that *Deflowering* and *Monsters* had to be destroyed. "They're your best paintings, Bruno," I said, "the ones you love most, the ones that represent the most for you." "That's precisely why I'm doing it, Jacob," he replied. "They're my beloved creations. I'm doing this out of love." He asked me to help him with the final brushstrokes. Everything was meant to finish today, 15 July 2006, the four hundredth anniversary of Rembrandt's birth. As you know, artists like to close circles. Rembrandt was born on this day, Van Tysch died on this day. I told him yes, I would help him. *Fuschus,* of course I did . . .'

All at once, to April Wood's utter amazement – she was expecting anything but that – Stein burst into tears. It was an unpleasant snivelling sound, as if he had caught a sudden cold.

'I said I would, and I would have said the same a thousand and one times over . . . a thousand and one times . . . "Here's your poor Jacob," I told him. "You can trust him, he's like your own reflection" . . . Today everything was to be finished. That's what he said "everything is to be finished" . . . I helped him paint his own body and . . . and all the rest. I won't deny it was the most difficult order to obey of all the ones I've received from him . . .'

He dried tears April Wood could not see with the back of his hand. She thought that Stein might be telling the truth, but not the *whole* truth. There was a screenplay, and he was following it. Van Tysch was about to be substituted, and his desire to die with his last work suited you fine, Jacob. I bet you've already chosen the artist who will take his place . . . I wonder who the lucky person is . . .

A small stand was placed on the floor next to the work of art. While Stein was still sobbing, April Wood went over to it. The card on it, illuminated by a small lamp, had one word on it in Dutch, English and French.

'*Shade*?'

Stein nodded.

'I took the liberty of naming it . . . Van Tysch did not want to give it a name, but untitled works do not pass into eternity . . . Do you know how it occurred to me? Van Tysch insisted there had to be only a little light. And his last words were: "Jacob, remember the light. The most important thing in this work is the shade." And he repeated it several times, each time more faintly: "the shade, the shade, the shade . . ." When he died, the word dissolved in his mouth. So I thought it would make a good title . . .'

'What about her?' asked Miss Wood.

She pointed to Murnika de Verne's body. Van Tysch's secretary was lying in a distant, even darker corner of the room. Perhaps she had merely fainted, but Miss Wood surmised she would not be alive for much longer, because the thin black dress with slits up the sides could not protect her from the extreme temperature in this ghastly cold storage. Her legs were bent under her, her face entirely covered by a dishevelled mass of hair. She looked like a doll tossed away by a careless child.

'That's where she'll stay,' said Stein. 'In fact, Murnika is part of the painting, too. *Shade* is a work bringing everything together, the greatest ever created, because Van Tysch wanted *us all* to be part of it. Not just Murnika, but you and I as well, Baldi and the

445

destroyed canvases, their families, the police who are searching for Baldi, the meetings of Rip van Winkle, all the ornaments present at those meetings, the entire "Rembrandt" exhibition including the *Christ*, of course, as well as all the works in "Flowers" and "Monsters", and the other Van Tysch canvases which had to be withdrawn . . . and beyond those, the artists and models, all the art works in the world that considered themselves part of this, as well as any member of the public who had ever looked at a hyperdramatic painting. The whole of humanity. That was the reason for leaving a copy of the recordings beside the destroyed bodies: Van Tysch wanted us all to be involved as amazed, unwilling figures in the work. *Shade* is the only example of *stained art* that Van Tysch has produced, Miss Wood and *each of us* is its material. We'll have to keep it concealed for a while, of course, but the day will come when we make it known to the world . . . and then people will react . . . Just imagine the horrified or astonished faces, the surprised looks, the ears terrified by the voices of the paintings speaking from their corpses, the painter immortalised by his own death . . . This is the centre of the work, of course, but *every one of us* is part of it. Can't you see how the room is getting bigger? Can't you see how infinitely large it is becoming . . . ?'

Then, following a short silence in which neither of them did anything other than stare into each other's eyes like two chess players, or a single person looking into a mirror, Stein went on:

'There may even be a book written about it. Then it would no longer be necessary actually to see the work to become part of it: all you would have to do is read it and react.'

Yes, react, thought April Wood, acknowledging that in this respect at least, Stein was right. She herself had already reacted. She stared at *Shade* knowing it to be Van Tysch's greatest work, perhaps the greatest, most sincere work of all time. Her artistic awareness told her so, her *passion* told her so. To give up on *Shade* signified not only giving up on art but on the obscure meaning of life as well. A part of April Wood's soul, an unexplored territory that had nothing to do with her coldly calculating brain, *understood* the Maestro's intentions, his way of 'crossing out' his 'beloved creations' in the same way his father crossed out his drawings, his way of cancelling the debt he owed to his past and

446

seizing every last nuance of his own creative suffering . . . *Shade* was a liberating work. Through it and his death Van Tysch was showing her how to break free of her bonds and escape all her memories. *All* her memories. I understand. I understand you, she wanted to say to the Maestro. I understand what you mean. Seen in this way, the destruction of *Deflowering, Monsters* and *Susanna* was not only comprehensible, but *necessary*. The world, as Stein suggested, might never understand it: but then the world never understands the miracle of a terrible genius.

For the first time in many years, April Wood felt happy. Her eyes shone, and her breathing, in the freezing atmosphere of the room, came ever more quickly.

She suddenly felt a vague sense of concern.

'Where is Baldi now?'

She looked down at her watch as Stein did the same.

'It's almost ten. If everything has gone according to plan, Baldi will be in the Old Atelier, carrying out his instructions. As you can imagine, he has to avoid falling into the hands of the police. No policeman could understand this. They're all paid employees, just as you are, but they are much less open than you are. They would start talking about crimes and guilty people, justice and prison, and all the art that a work like this encapsulates would mean nothing to them. They would be capable of . . . they would be capable of ruining it. Of leaving it unfinished.'

Miss Wood felt increasingly concerned. Stein raised his eyebrows.

'I have to tell Bosch,' said Miss Wood.

'Bosch is no problem,' Stein replied. 'He has no idea where Baldi has taken the painting. At ten o'clock sharp *everything will be finished* . . .'

'I prefer to make sure.'

She opened her bag and took out her mobile. Her hands were like frozen claws.

It could not be. She had to stop it. This at least she had to put a stop to. It was his great work, the transforming work. And she wanted to protect his art because she worshipped it with the same terrible passion as the Maestro did. April Wood had not the slightest doubt about what she had to do.

At all costs, she had to prevent *Shade* from remaining unfinished.

21.58.

Lothar Bosch was observing Postumo Baldi through the two-way mirror in the rehearsal room. Dressed all in white, the figure hypnotised him. It was as if Baldi was a cartoon character, a computer game moving according to mysterious instructions.

Wuyters and he had just discovered Baldi at the far end of the corridor in the first basement. The room was soundproofed, and the glass allowed them both to study Baldi without him realising they were there. Just as Bosch had suspected from the outset in spite of the cerublastyne mask he recognised him immediately when he saw his eyes. They really are mirrors, he thought.

They came upon Baldi as he had finished placing the woman in position. The three naked canvases were properly labelled, and were lying on their backs on the floor. They did not appear to have suffered any damage. Baldi must have finished making the recordings and was about to cut them up. Bosch shuddered.

'Shall we go in now?' asked Wuyters, raising his weapon.

'Call the others first,' said Bosch.

They had placed themselves by the door, at the ready. They grasped their guns firmly in both hands. Wuyters switched on his headset and warned the other two. Bosch could see the young man was as nervous as he was, perhaps more so. When Wuyters finished speaking, he looked towards Bosch for further instructions. Bosch signalled to him to be ready to throw open the door to the room.

At that very moment, his mobile phone rang. Still keeping his eyes on Baldi, and despite being aware that he could not hear them, Bosch answered as quickly as he could. He was so pleased to hear April Wood's voice he answered at once in an anguished whisper, before she had the chance to speak.

'April! Thank God, we've got him! He was in the Old Atelier! He was in one of the rehearsal rooms, and he's about to . . .'

That was when April Wood silenced him with her urgent appeal.

*

448

21.59.

It had all happened very quickly. First, the surprise shot. Rodino and Krupka were so defenceless they did not even have time to react. Matt shot Rodino first. He lifted a hand to his throat and opened his eyes wide. Neither Krupka nor Clara could see the dart stuck in his neck. Then, just as quickly, Matt cocked the gun, aimed at Krupka, and fired a second time. Then he turned towards her. Instinctively, Clara protected herself with her hands.

'Stay calm,' Matt told her.

He came over and pushed her hands away from her neck as gently as a lover.

A glass bee stung her throat. Then the dimensions of the room began to fade.

The first thing she saw when she came round was Krupka. He was staring at her from the floor, a horrified expression on his face. She understood she must also be on the floor, like him and like Rodino, who was flat on his back breathing heavily.

Her head hurt. And either the floor was extremely cold, or she was completely naked. The hard layers of her skin told her she was still painted. But she could not recall what she was doing there, under this surgery lamp, laid out like a patient awaiting the knife. Krupka and Rodino were also naked.

A pair of white shoes moved around her head. The shoes came and went, as if they had no fixed destination. At times, she could see a shadow looming over her. Krupka was staring upwards, his eyes dilated with terror. Rodino was groaning. Clara also tried looking up towards the ceiling, but the fluorescent lights blinded her.

'What are you doing?' she heard Krupka say. Or perhaps he had said: 'How are you?' Krupka's English (especially in circumstances like these) was hard to grasp.

Footsteps again. Clara lifted her head and saw the man coming over wielding that strange instrument. He bent over her, and grabbed a handful of her painted hair to force her head down. It hurt as it jerked back. She wanted to raise her arms or move, but felt too weak and dizzy. All at once she remembered who this young man was, with his plastic face staring down at her as blank as a white wall. His name was Matt, and he had told them he was going to repair them according to Van Tysch's instructions.

Matt brought the instrument close to her eyes. What was it? It looked like something typical of a dentist or barber.

Matt's fingers came to within two centimetres of her face, and the instrument started up. Clara could not help shrinking back. It was a kind of spinning disc that made a deafening whine. It set her teeth on edge, as though someone were dragging a metal table across a tiled floor towards her head.

She was scared. She should not have been, because all this was art, but she was. She screamed.

22.00.

Bosch listened to April Wood as he watched Postumo Baldi bending over the girl, canvas cutter in hand.

'Shouldn't we go in?' Wuyters shouted desperately.

A sober traffic policeman, Bosch held up all movement with an imperious wave of the hand, while he listened intently through his earpiece.

He was listening to April Wood. To the woman he most loved and respected in all the world. When she paused, he managed to get out a faint plea.

'April, I don't understand . . .'

'I didn't understand either,' said April Wood, 'but now I do. You ought to see it, Lothar. You ought to be here to see it . . . It's called *Shade* and it's . . . it's a *very* beautiful painting . . . Van Tysch's *most beautiful and personal* work . . . It's a biographical self-portrait. Even the crossings out his father made on his drawings are here . . . You ought to see it, Lothar . . . My God, but you should see this!'

April, you should see this, thought Bosch. My God, April, but you should see this!

Jan Wuyters' face, scarlet with rage, fear and sweat, loomed in front of him.

'Mr Bosch, he's *cutting up* the girl! . . . What should we do?'

The room was soundproofed. Even so, Bosch could have sworn that the girl's screams, as sharp as the finest needles, were piercing the walls like ghosts and lodging themselves in his hearing. Her silent protest deafened him far more than Wuyters' horrified shouts or April Wood's frenzied commands.

'You're not a policeman any more, Lothar!' she had said before she hung up. 'You work for Art and for the Maestro. Tell your men to protect Baldi when he's finished, and to bring him to Edenburg safe and sound!'

After that, Bosch's headpiece gave off only an intermittent buzz.

What's there in that room are not cursed works of art, they're human beings . . . and that guy is slaughtering them! He's cutting them to pieces like cattle in an abattoir! . . . They're not works of art, they're not works of art! They never were! . . .

That was what he wanted to tell her, but she had already rung off. April Wood's silence was terrible, cruel. But what did that matter now? His whole life had been a miserable failure. He felt sick, overcome with nausea. He had never had what it takes. As if that were not enough, it was Van Tysch who had given him the only really important job he had ever had. His brother had done much better than him: Roland had known how to carve out a future for himself. Having a decent salary was one thing, but what about convictions . . . what had happened to his convictions?

Baldi had finished with the girl and stood up again (oh, pure virginal flame!). Now he was busy doing something on the table. Perhaps he was playing with money, because he seemed to be throwing away some coins and picking up others. No: he was changing the blade to cut up the next figure. There was no blood to be seen. What a pure, luminous creature. What perfection in every one of his features. What beauty. Beauty can be terrible. A German poet used to say so: Hendrickje liked to read him. Bosch did not read German poets or understand modern art, but nor did he blush when asked his opinion of a Ferrucioli, a Rayback or a Mavalaki. Shit, he might not be as cultured as Hendrickje, or as much as his father had wanted him to be. But he knew what beauty was.

Baldi was as beautiful as a snowy dawn in the outskirts.

Bosch stared at Baldi. The painter was no longer looking at the girl. He did not want to see the work until it was finished.

451

They are not works of art. No human being is art. Art isn't human. Or perhaps it is. It doesn't matter what it is. What matters, what really matters is . . .

He pulled off the phone headpiece and peered at it as if he had no idea what such a strange thing was doing there in the palm of his hand.

What really matters are people.

In the end, what else could he do? Stein had been the one who had made the mistake when he put his trust in such a mediocre individual as him. Van Tysch would never have taken him on. Bosch felt himself to be grotesque and vulgar, an overgrown child examining glass filigree with burlap gloves. He loathed his own vulgarity. Hendrickje had seen how vulgar he was. Maybe that was why he had always thought she detested him. Now April Wood detested him, too. It was strange how all these superior spirits could suddenly come to detest you. Contempt was a bolt the gods struck you with. How pityingly they smiled at you, how patiently they looked on you! Hendrickje and April Wood, Van Tysch, Stein and Baldi, Roland, even Danielle: they all belonged to the superior race, the chosen ones, the race of those who *did* understand life and art and could decide the meaning of both. He was born to protect this race, them and their works, and he was not even any good at that.

He sighed deeply and gazed sadly at young Wuyters' despairing face.

'Put your weapon away, Jan. We're not going to intervene. That guy is working for Van Tysch. He's creating a work of art.'

'I don't understand,' Wuyters murmured, his white, drained face turned towards the interior of the room.

'I know, I don't either,' said Bosch. 'It's modern art.'

22.01.

Postumo Baldi, the Artist, was not a creator but a tool of creation, like the beings he was destroying. Some day it would be his turn, and he was ready for it. He was an empty bag which needed to be filled with things. It had always been like that. He tried to be better each day, to develop his perfection to fit in with the artist's desires. A blank sheet of paper, as the Maestro called him.

It had taken him a long time to reach this stage. Now all he had to do was to go on. Van Tysch's preparation had been exquisite: not a single mistake, everything perfect, everything gliding along gently. This was thanks to the painter, but also thanks to him. Van Tysch had laid his hand on him, and he (an extraordinary glove) had adapted to his ways. His mother had also been an extraordinary, if undervalued, canvas. Now he was reaching a summit she could never have dreamed of. In twenty-four thousand years, people would still be talking of Postumo Baldi and the absolutely perfect way he carried out the Maestro's instructions, of how he had become the Artist without really being him. For centuries they would speak of how he had carried out the obscure aims of the most important painter of all time. Because there is a moment when *work and painter become as one*.

Jan van Obber had once told him he was very ambitious. Baldi was happy to admit it. Of course he was. An empty bag fills up with air, after all.

He had brought the whirling blade close to the girl's face neatly and precisely. She had screamed. They all screamed at this point. Postumo suffered with them, he was horrified, carried away by the brutal tidal wave of horror he himself was producing. Postumo was as smooth as the skin he cut to perfection in straight strips ('Don't forget,' Van Tysch had told him, 'four crosses and two parallel cuts. You must do it the same always'). He could understand the canvas' pain as it was cleaved to the core. The Maestro wanted the canvas to understand it, too, so Postumo tried to make sure the paintings were alive, and almost aware of what was going to happen to them, what was happening to them. This was not cruelty, it was art. And he was not a killer, but simply a sharpened pencil. He had killed and tortured according to very precise drawing instructions. He had suffered and wept together with the canvases. And if necessary, when the time came he too would submit to the terrible test of steel.

The girl with red-painted hair squinted desperately as Postumo brought the blade up to her face.

It was then he realised his mistake.

He had not chosen the right blade. He had decided to destroy the largest of the figures, the Second Elder, first of all, but then he had changed his mind and chosen to start with the female figure. But the canvas cutter he had was for the biggest body. If he cut the smaller one up with it, the face would be reduced to a mass of splinters. He did not want to crush it: he had been told the crosses had to stand out.

He let go of her hair, switched the blade off, and stood up. He went back to the table and chose the finest blade. He used different kinds, sometimes for each part of the body, depending on the bone structure. For the twins he had scarcely needed to change blades at all, but the young girl had been a nightmare, because she had such a tiny, almost ethereal, anatomy. He tried not to remember all the different changes of blade he had needed to cut up *Deflowering*, all the interruptions with the girl's body half destroyed, the blood gleaming as it spouted from a still-beating heart. His task might have been simpler if he had used several different canvas cutters, but he could not risk carrying so many objects on him. His work was meticulous; he was forced to go slowly.

He found the blade he needed. It was next to the digital video camera he had taken out of his oilskin bag to use to film the results of his work. Behind his back, the canvases seemed finally to have gone to sleep. That was no problem: they would wake up with the first cut.

He unscrewed the thick blade from the metal handle and threw it on the table. He snapped in the fine one. He switched the cutter on to test it.

Then he turned round and walked towards the girl once more.

22.02.

She was about to cross it.

The looking glass. At last.

She had approached its smooth, chill surface and discovered this iceberg world fascinated her. She was frightened, of course, frightened to open the door into a closed room, to penetrate the darkness. The fear of a small girl: a feeling that was unpleasant but tempting, the sweet hidden in the witch's gingerbread house. Come and get it, Clara. And she would walk in and take the sweet, whatever happened. She would do anything to get the deserved, the terrible reward.

'Look at yourself in the mirror,' the painter ordered her. His eyes were colourless, the rest of him endless white. 'Look at yourself in the mirror,' he repeated.

A moment earlier, Matt had let her go, but now he grasped her hair again and brought that strange whirling, deafening object up close to her face.

She knew that *the thing* she was about to see, that she was on the verge of seeing, was *the horrible*. The finishing touch to her body in the art work that was her life. Let's do it, she told herself. Let's do it. Be brave. What else was *real* art, what else was a masterpiece, if not the profound result of passion and courage?

She took a deep breath and lifted her head, presenting it to the sacrifice as if she was running towards the outstretched arms of a loving father.

The horrible. At last.

At that moment there was a thunderous crash and everything was over for her.

22.05.

Bosch had fired straight through the mirror. A living cylinder thrashed around the floor of the room. The canvas cutter was still switched on, its blade furiously sawing the air.

Wuyters, who had obeyed his order and put away his gun, was staring at him dumbfounded. Bosch had not wanted to get him mixed up in what he had decided to do. He needed to be the only guilty one. An old policeman's scruples had led him to ensure that Wuyters did his duty right to the end.

Everything was over, but Bosch stood there motionless. He did not lower his gun even when they told him Baldi was dead. Nor when they assured him that the canvases were out of danger, and that Baldi had not succeeded in cutting the girl in his second attempt, when he changed blades after Wuyters and he had thought he had already started the destruction. The echo of the shot had already faded and the crash of the broken glass as well, but Bosch still held the gun in his outstretched arms.

It was strange – he thought – what had happened with Baldi. He had seen how the bullet had struck his head, and the blood spurting like paint, but he had not noticed any spattered organs, nothing really terrible: just a red stain spreading everywhere across the smooth white surface of his skull. Bosch remembered that once as a boy he had spilt an inkwell, which had produced the same effect on his drawing pad. He guessed it must be the cerublastyne that kept everything so neat and tidy looking. Then through the shattered mirror he saw one of his men strip off bits of the mask to reveal the destruction beneath. Baldi's face was gone. His brain was like chewed-up paper. I'm sorry, thought Bosch, staring at this unaesthetic mass, this scrawl of bones and white strands; I'm sorry. I've killed the canvas. He knew that Baldi was not the guilty one. Nor was Van Tysch: Van Tysch was merely a genius.

He, Lothar Bosch, was the only guilty one. A vulgar little man.

He finally managed to lower his arms. He could see Wuyters next to him, still staring.

'Do you know what, Jan?' Bosch said, immensely weary, by way of explanation. 'The thing is, I've never liked modern art.'

22.19.

April Wood listened in silence. Then she hung up and spoke to Stein:

'My colleague Lothar Bosch has prevented Bruno van Tysch from completing his posthumous work. He takes full responsibility and will accept whatever consequences may arise from his actions. He also told me he has decided to resign.' She paused. 'I beg you to add my resignation to Mr Bosch's, but also to *put all the responsibility* for this on to me. I did not succeed in informing Mr Bosch properly about what was happening, and therefore he acted on a misapprehension. I am the only one responsible for what happened. Thank you.'

Stein burst out laughing. It was a silent, disagreeable laugh. It was like a continuation of the sobs he had produced moments before. Then he stopped. His face betrayed a certain annoyance, as though he were ashamed of the way he had behaved.

Miss Wood did not wait for any further reply, but turned and walked down the tiled corridor.

The half moon shining in the night of Edenburg had risen in the sky.

Who if I cried would hear me from the hierarchies of angels?

RILKE

Epilogue

For a while there were sounds. Then silence reigned.

As he was folding his socks and putting them in his suitcase, Lothar Bosch thought that perhaps this was the only peace and happiness people like him could hope for in this world. Nothing better, he thought, than to smooth a pair of socks and carefully place them in a suitcase. He surveyed his half-completed packing, the case yawning open on the bed. The sun outside his bedroom window brought a cool, watery Holland to his nostrils. His bed, like a mysterious soft chessboard, was covered in pieces: columns of underwear, socks, books and shirts. Bosch had begun the ritual unwillingly, but by the end was thankful for it. It no longer seemed to him such a bad idea to spend the rest of the summer with Roland and his family in Scheveningen. In fact, he was beginning to look forward to it. He had no job, so it was time for him, as his brother said, 'to start to live the life of a pensioner'.

It would also give him the chance to see Danielle. He had bought something special for her in a shop on Rozengracht.

The presents for Hannah and Roland had been easy to choose. They were expensive, as befitted his position as a widower with no children and substantial savings: a diamond brooch from Coster's, and a new digital camera. But Nielle's present was more difficult. At first he had considered a Japanese computer program which had an almost human creature on it that had to be cared for, brought up, taken to school and protected from the dangers of adolescence until the moment she left home, something which almost never happened unless the program had errors or a virus. Then in a toy shop on Rokin he found something much better: a mechanical dalmatian that could move, bark and whine if left alone for too long. He was about to buy it when in the same shop he spotted an enormous felt dog. It was a majestic, soft animal, a Saint Bernard as big as a double pillow. The

Saint Bernard did not do anything, it did not move, or bark, but Bosch thought it looked much more alive than the mechanical toy. He gave the necessary instructions for it to be sent to Roland's house in The Hague.

But then, on his way home from the toy shop, he passed by a shop in Rozengracht, and saw it.

He thought for a moment, and retraced his steps. He did not want to cancel his order for the Saint Bernard: he simply requested it be sent to his own house. He would decide later on what to do with that fluffy brown monster. Then he went back to Rozengracht and finally bought the perfect present for Danielle.

The gift would probably arrive before he did. It would bark and whine like a mechanical dalmatian, but it would also do poohs and pee on the carpet and scratch the wood on doors with its claws. It would not be as well behaved as a computer or as sweet as a fluffy Saint Bernard. And – as Bosch knew – when it broke down, nothing and nobody in the world would be able to repair it, and nothing and nobody in the world would be able to restore or substitute it. When that present broke down, it would be completely and forever, and the infinite loss would tear the heart out of more than one person.

From this point of view it was undoubtedly the worst possible gift he could give a ten-year-old girl.

But perhaps Nielle would see its advantages.

Bosch was hopeful she would.

As the plane began its descent, April Wood glanced at her watch, took a small looking glass from her bag, and studied her face. She found it acceptable. The traces of sadness had disappeared. If they had ever existed, she thought.

She had got the news the day before, just as she was preparing to move to London after having dismantled her office in Amsterdam. She recognised the doctor's voice across the kilometres that separated her from the private clinic. The voice assured her it had all been very rapid. Miss Wood could not agree to that. In fact, it had all been very, very slow. 'Your father had already lost consciousness,' the voice told her. That she could believe. Where was her father's consciousness? Where had it been all these years? Where had it been when she had known him? She had no idea.

She gave all the relevant instructions. Death does not end with death: it has to be concluded with economic and bureacratic instructions. Her father had always wanted to lie under the ruins of classical Rome. All his life he had felt more Roman than British. Exactly that: Roman, because he did not care for Italy and had not even bothered to learn to speak Italian properly. It was Rome that he cared for: the grandeur of having an empire beneath his feet. Now you'll have it above your feet. Enjoy it, Poppy, she had thought. Transferring his body was going to cost her almost as much as the transfer of her paintings.

Her father would travel in a box to Rome. The paintings from her Amsterdam office would travel in private flights to London. 'A good summing-up of my life,' she decided.

She put the looking glass back in her bag, closed it and put it down by her feet.

She had not yet decided what she would do when she got to London. She was thirty years old, and supposed she had about the same number of years of professional activity left. There would be no lack of opportunity, of course: she had already received several offers from art security firms who wanted to be able to count on her. But for the first time in her life she had decided to take a break. She was on her own, and had all the time in the world. Perhaps more than she imagined. Up in the empty sky above the London clouds, with her only family and her only job both dead and gone, April Wood thought that perhaps she had all eternity on front of her.

Holidays. She had not had a real holiday in a long time. Perhaps she would go to Devon. In summer, Devon was ideal. You could have quiet or things to do, as you chose. That was it then: she would go to Devon.

No sooner had she decided that than she remembered Hirum Oslo lived in Devon. She had not given him a thought until now. Of course, she did not rule out calling on him and asking him all the questions that remained unspoken (why he had paid a woman artist to make a portrait from a photo of her, for example). She was not thinking of going to see Hirum again though.

461

She did not see what going to Devon had to do with paying him a visit.

Nothing at all.

Anyway, if she got bored, she could always consider it.

Money is art, thought Jacob Stein. This new phrase seemed a response to Van Tysch's famous dictum, but in fact it changed things completely. Yet the facts bore it out. In the past few days he had carried out several masterstrokes. He had held private meetings with Paul Benoit, Franz Hoffmann and Saskia Stoffels, and told them the whole truth. Together they had taken some quick decisions. Two days later, he informed the investors. To do so, he gathered their representatives on the Ionian island of Kefalonia, ten kilometres north of Agios Spyridion, and decorated the place with artefacts by Van der Graar, Safira and Mordaieff. He also acquired, especially for the occasion, five brand-new and well-trained adolescent Tongues by Mark Rodgers.

'We've not only controlled the situation, we've succeeded in profiting from it,' he told them. 'We've let it be known that Van Tysch committed suicide, which strictly speaking is true. We've said that what happened with the *Christ* was an accident that nobody is completely responsible for, although we have half-suggested that Van Tysch knew what was going to happen and had planned it. The public is quick to forgive madmen and the dead. And we've revealed part of what Postumo Baldi was up to. We've said he was crazy and was intending to destroy *Susanna Surprised by the Elders*. All this has caused a great commotion. It's too soon to speak of definitive figures, but since last week the "Rembrandt" works have increased spectacularly in value. In the case of the *Christ* for example, the price has gone sky high. The same with *Susanna*. That's why we've dismantled the "Rembrandt" collection and decided to send the original models home after removing their priming and rubbing out the signatures. We'll soon be able to use substitutes. Now the Maestro has disappeared and can no longer authorise any substitutes, it's vital to play down the importance of the originals, and use substitutes straightaway so that the collectors can get used to the idea. Otherwise we'll

462

be running a risk that the paintings fall in price almost to the level of unofficial copies.'

With the Ionian sun tanning his face, Stein uncrossed his legs and moved his feet. The Tongue lying on the ground in front of him, completely naked and painted rose and white, blind and deaf due to the protectors it was wearing, groped forward with its straw-coloured head until it bumped into his other shoe, and went on licking.

'We've decided not to make public the destruction of the originals of *Deflowering* and *Monsters*,' he went on. 'All the interested parties will keep quiet about it, and we'll secretly substitute both works. As far as the transfer is concerned . . .'

Stein paused while he settled back in his chair. As he did so, he noticed that the back supporting his own yielded a little. This was not a design fault: it was simply making an adjustment to please him. He was slender enough for the two athletic bodies which made up this Mordaieff Armchair to be able to bear his weight easily. From time to time the slight tremors in the youthful backside where he was resting his own made him sway gently, but they were calculated, controlled and delicate movements. Mordaieff made excellent pieces of furniture. One could write with neat lettering sitting on these fleshy seats, or illustrate a book of miniatures without one's hand shaking. And best of all: it was so pleasant to slide one's hand down and touch them while one was talking business.

'*Fuschus*, the transfer was quite simple, believe me,' he said.

It had not been so straightforward, in fact, but he was trying to convey the idea that money can resolve everything. This was false, but it could become true in the future on one condition: if there were more money.

It was a couple of years earlier that he had first seen a work by Vicky Lledó. It was *Body Lines*. It was on show in London as part of an exhibition by artists living in the city. He had not much liked the canvas, who was British and was called Shelley, but Stein knew how to recognise a good work of art painted on a mediocre canvas. Of course, he said nothing to anybody. A few months later, when the canvas was substituted, Stein parcelled Shelley up and took her to Amsterdam on the pretext of doing some tests on her, although he never spoke to her personally. Shelley enthusiastically answered all the questions. The list included some enquiries into the character and private life of Miss Lledó. Stein stored away the information for future use. The Foundation had to hand over power – the 'transfer' as the investors called it – because Van Tysch was in decline, and although Stein knew the Maestro had not said his last word, it was essential to be prepared. He spent months collecting information on unknown painters. Everyone was in a panic over the transfer. Stein was in a panic over everyone's panic. He set himself to teach them all that the miracle of creating a genius is much easier than the effort of keeping one alive.

By the start of 2006 he had already decided that the successor would be Vicky Lledó. That the balance of posterity should tilt towards Lledó had several advantages: she was a woman, which would be useful to counteract the macho idea certain sectors had of HD art; she was not Dutch, which helped show that the Van Tysch Foundation was happy to welcome any European artist; and lastly, choosing her would put a brake on the worrying rise to power of people like Rayback. The first step had been to give Vicky that small Max Kalima Foundation prize. 'I can assure you that the Maestro has seen Lledó's work, and is fascinated by it', he told the investors. That was not true. The Maestro saw nothing beyond himself. Stein was sure he was not even aware of the existence of a young Spanish artist called Vicky Lledó. Van Tysch only cared about preparing his swan song, his farewell to the world, his last, most risky work. Stein had taken all the decisions.

The end was near, and he had to invent a new beginning.

Shade would remain untouchable and unfinished in Edenburg. And so it would be until the world was ready to look on it, and its appearance would be profitable. The former might happen at any time, or perhaps had *already* happened (the world was almost always ready for anything). As for the latter, a committee of investors headed by himself and Paul Benoit would take care well in advance of all the steps necessary to reveal the work to the world. There would be talk of 'the Maestro's testament', of his 'swan song', of his 'terrible secret'. 'A miracle requires a revelation and a secret, Jacob,' Benoit had rightly concluded. 'We already have the revelation. What we need is a secret.'

'Let's allow the idea to mature,' Stein told the investors, pensively stroking the long thighs of his chair.

For a while there were sounds. Then silence reigned.

She had received an avalanche of phone calls: above all from Jorge, desperate at first but calmer when he could talk to her. When was she thinking of coming back? I don't know, Jorge, we'll see. I want to see you. We'll see. All of a sudden she realised she did not miss him. To her, Jorge was like the voice of the past: undeniable, but finished with. She also got calls from Yoli Ribó, Alexandra Jiménez, Adolfo Bermejo, Xavi Gonfrell and Ernesto Salvatierra. Calls from painters and canvases. One of the most affectionate was from Alex Bassan. They were all delighted she was fine and had been signed by Van Tysch. One night she heard her brother's voice. So even her brother was interested in the painting's welfare! Without completely abandoning his natural reserve of a lawyer outside court, José Manuel talked of their mother, of how much they missed her, of how she had told them nothing. 'We didn't know anything about all this,' he said. 'We only heard about it thanks to Jorge Atienza.' How was she? Fine. Would she be back soon? Yes. They wanted to see her. She wanted to see them, too. When it came down to it, it occurred to her, life and art are based on the same thing: going and seeing.

And Vicky? Vicky did not call her.

She suspected she would have to be the one to take the first step, now that the painter had become so important.

Vicky was going to hold a retrospective for the Foundation: Stein had announced it at a press conference. Among the twelve works on show were two for which Clara had been the original: *Instant* and *The Strawberry*. Stein had also said that Vicky Lledó was one of the great exponents of orthodox modern hyper-dramatism, and that the Van Tysch Foundation, 'now that the Maestro was missing', would strongly support the work of this young artist.

The news had made a great impact on her, to the extent that

for some time she did not know what to feel. Eventually she decided she was pleased for Vicky, but then concluded that she felt this way because she did not love her enough to feel sorry for her.

'Both of us immortal, as we wanted. Good.'

After the calls dried up, she switched off the television, too. The news was always the same, and she knew it by heart. Nor did she allow herself the consolation of the many jazz records that Conservation had given her to help pass the time. She felt fine as she was, submerged in her own silence. Or her own noise.

Because life had a noise of its own, she suddenly realised. She could feel life returning to her just as one hears a different wave travelling to shore. They had decided to remove her priming, rub out the signature, and send her home. They would let her rest for a while and then, if necessary, would call on her to show *Susanna* again. She would, of course, keep the money, that would not change. They stopped her F&W tablets, and soon afterwards she realised that a human being is something that wants things. Art stays still and content with itself, but life demands continuous satisfaction. After that they stripped off her priming. When she got back to her hospital bed and looked at herself in the mirror, there could be no doubt about it: she was Clara Reyes again. Her blonde hair, her skin with its open pores, old scars, the graphism of her life, her smells, the shapes from her past. She still had no body hair, of course, but this was an image she had come to accept. Her unprimed face recovered its old expressions, so different from the yellow monster that had so astonished Jorge. She was no longer painted, had no labels. It was not easy living without labels or paint, but she would have to get used to it.

And on the Friday afternoon, after having lunch and sleeping a lengthy siesta, she heard a gentle knocking at her door.

Gerardo smiled as he came in.

'So this is what you look like without any paint on, sweetheart. The truth is I prefer you this way. The natural look, you might say.'

She smiled back at him. She was sitting on her bed in pyjamas, her hair a mess, her eyes still full of sleep. She let herself be wrapped in Gerardo's arms, and discovered his presence made her very happy.

'I heard you were getting out today, and I wanted to come and see you,' Gerardo explained. 'Justus would have liked to come, too, but he suggested I come as an "advance party".' He laughed and his eyes shone, but he quickly became serious again. He had heard about the madman's attack and had been trying to see her ever since, even though he been told many times that she was fine. 'How are you really?' he asked.

'I don't know,' she replied frankly. 'I suppose I'm fine.'

She felt as though she had been asleep and had woken up in hospital. She felt empty. I've been dreaming, she thought. But what happens when everything you are and have been forms part of the same dream?

They had time before they had to go to the airport. Did she want to say goodbye to anywhere in particular? he wanted to know. Clara looked at the newspapers crumpled on her bed. She had read that this Friday 21 July, 2006, they would finish dismantling the Tunnel.

'I'd like to go to the Museumplein to see how they're demolishing the Tunnel,' she said.

'No problem.'

Night had fallen, and stars were beginning to appear above the quiet waters of the canals. It was a splendid summer night. The moon shone brightly, trying to reach its own perfection. Gerardo drove with Clara towards the Museumplein.

'I was thinking,' said Gerardo, breaking the intense silence, 'that I might travel to Madrid soon. I'd like to finish a painting I've left half completed,' he added with a smile.

Later on, she came to think of this as the exact moment when she realised *Susanna* had left her body completely. There in the dark seat of Gerardo's car, she touched her legs, her arms, her face, and was sure of it. *Susanna* had been rubbed out. From underneath, for good or ill, had emerged Clara Reyes. The event – she thought – had something of a frustrated attempt at divorce about it.

Gerardo was talking to her.

'I'd like . . .'

467

He was making a series of sincere confessions which she could scarcely hear. But she understood that now she was Clara once more, she would have to get used to hearing sincere confessions again. Because *Susanna* was drifting off into the starry night sky. *Susanna* was floating through the immense tunnel of night, further and further away, increasingly indifferent. Welcome to the world, Clara. Welcome to reality.

The work in the Museumplein was being carried out calmly and skilfully. Several workmen undid each curtain panel: first one wall, then the other, finally the roof. They were advancing along the whole length of the horseshoe. They were not even stopping for the night: Amsterdam had to greet the new day without the Tunnel, dawn had to rise over the naked square, dotted with its usual statues and gardens.

Gerardo parked nearby, and they walked along looking upwards, like freshly arrived tourists.

'What do you feel?' he asked her. She was staring at the huge dismantling effort.

'I don't know. Hold me tight.'

As they renewed their walk, she thought of a reply.

'It's as if I'm breathing for the first time,' she said.

They walked on. Clara looked back over her shoulder.

At that moment they were undoing one of the roof panels. The immense square fell with the sound of distant waves, dragging its darkness with it. The clear moonlight effortlessly glided into the empty shade.

Author's Note

Everything has been done in art. A novelist's imagination could never compete with the infinite ways and kinds of experimentation the reader can discover as soon as they enter the fantastic universe that is contemporary art. In spite of this, hyperdramatism does not exist, although various tendencies, such as *body art*, use the human body as the basis for their works. Art-shocks, 'stained' art, *animarts* and human artefacts are also fictional creations, although *performances* and *events* are terms known to all followers of modern art. The business of buying and selling painted human beings is not, as yet, a common phenomenon. I have no idea whether that situation will change in the future, but I tend to think that if someone discovers how to make money out of it, it will not be moral considerations that prevent this human market from flourishing in the same or even more spectacular fashion as in my novel.

Many other things are fictitious in this work, in addition to the characters. Some of the public buildings such as the Obberlund in Munich or the Ateliers in Amsterdam, private galleries like the GS or the Max Ernst, and the Wunderbar and Vermeer hotels, are all imaginary. Any coincidence between these names and places existing in real life is purely accidental. The museums mentioned are real, although the cultural centre in Vienna's MuseumsQuartier is I believe still under construction. Perhaps it will have been completed by the time this novel comes out. Of course, the hyperdramatic works exhibited in these galleries are fictitious and absolutely no connection of any kind should be made between the characteristics of the works and the real institutions mentioned in the novel.

Certain works in the bibliography I consulted are too important not to mention. The classic *Story of Art* by Ernest Gombrich (Phaidon, 1995) and the no less classic *Art Materials and Techniques* by Ralph Mayer (Tursen-Hermann Blume, 1993) became my bedside reading. Among the infinite number of books on Rembrandt, good choices were *Rembrandt's Eyes* by Simon Schama (Allen Lane, The Penguin Press, 1999) and *Rembrandt* by Emmanuel Starcky (Portland House, 1990). On contemporary art, I found *XXth Century Art* by Ruhrberg, Schneckenburger et al. (Taschen, 1999) and *Art at the Turn of the Millennium* by Riemschneider and Grosenick, eds (Taschen, 1999) unbeatable. The two verses by Rilke quoted at the beginning and end are from the first elegy in his *Duino Elegies*. All the Carroll extracts are from his *Through the Looking Glass and What Alice Found There*. The ellipses indicate words left out.

There are gaps no books can fill. Among the persons who helped me improve the novel with their advice or information, two merit special mention. Antonio Escudero Nafs, a good friend and an extraordinary painter, explained some of the most basic aspects of his art to me, and the equally talented painter 'Scipona' stoically put up with my questions about openings, gallery owners and dealers, and gave me invaluable help. In the end, however, my novel was not about inanimate canvases as they thought, but about human paintings, which obliged me to take great liberties with the information they gave me. All the errors my work may contain about the complex world of art are therefore due entirely to my own negligence or to the liberties I have taken.

J.C.S.
Madrid, 2001